The Keys of the City

Michael Pearson is the author of several non-fiction books and
the best-selling novel, *The Store*, which has sold more than one
million copies in fifteen different editions and has been trans-
lated into five different languages. He is married with three
children, enjoys riding and skiing, and is currently working on
his third novel.

Michael Pearson

The Keys of
the City

Pan Books
London and Sydney

First published in Great Britain 1985 by Pan Books Ltd,
Cavaye Place, London SW10 9PG
987654321
©Michael Pearson 1985
ISBN 0 330 28970 5
Printed and bound in Great Britain by
Hazell Watson & Viney Limited,
Member of the BPCC Group,
Aylesbury, Bucks

For Tess Sacco

'When the daie of apoinctment came ... the bur-
gesses of the toune (Roan*) in good ordre came to the
Kynges lodgyng and there delivered to hym the keyes
of the citee ... beseeching hym of fauor and copas-
sion.'

Hall's Chronicle (1548):
'The Victorious Actes of Kyng
Henry the Fifth'.

Keys: 'In pregnant sense, with reference to the power
of custody, control, admission of others, etc., implied
by the possession of the keys of any place; hence as a
symbol of office and (fig.) the office itself.'

(Oxford Dictionary)

* Rouen.

Acknowledgements

In a novel of this nature, ranging as it does over various subject areas, an author needs much help beyond what he can obtain from books and in this respect I have been most fortunate. In particular, I would like to express my gratitude to Richard Mansell-Jones of the long-established merchant bankers, Brown Shipley & Co. — as well as to Tim Bacon of the same organization — for his guidance on the financial world and, especially, for the many hours he has devoted to the checking of the manuscript for technical errors.

With regard to other specialist scenes, I would like to record my appreciation of the assistance received from Peter Brockes of the National Motor Museum at Beaulieu in respect of detail of the days of early motoring; from Alan Jacobs of the Shell International Petroleum Company for arranging the review of the oil drilling episodes; and from Tony Weir, of the University of Liverpool, where the Cunard Archives are housed, for Atlantic shipping material.

I have, of course, had recourse to hundreds of books and the search for suitable material has, as always, been much eased by Joan Bailey, of the London Library, and the helpful staff of the British Library.

At a personal level, I am in great debt to my wife Susan who has endured seemingly endless discussions and made many suggestions for plot and characters; to my agents, Julian Bach and Leslie Gardner for their ever strong support; and to Lynda Davidson and Janet Brunning who have typed and re-typed the manuscript in its many versions without revealing any of the impatience they must have felt.

Part 1

June 1902

Chapter 1

[1]

For a few seconds, on that warm night in June, the low blast of the SS *Lucania*'s siren drowned the noise of the crowd on the jetty. The tugboats eased the liner from the pier into the mainstream of the Hudson. From the rails of the boat deck I waved to the small bunch of people who had been the main figures of my past.

That afternoon, in St John's Old Presbyterian Church in Brooklyn, I had transformed my life. I had married Richard Alexander and become the envy of every girl I knew – which was ironic in a way, because I did not seek what they did.

I did not want a husband, not even a rich one. Not yet, anyway. I wanted power, and wives, though they may exercise influence, do not have power. I wanted to make changes in the world, like the men who had built the railroads. I wanted to be part of our new age of invention, like the promoters of the turbine and telegraphy. I wanted my own hand on the lever of the engine.

And I wanted Richard Alexander, with a longing that until then I had never known.

In short, I wanted both, as men had both. And I was aiming to get both – which might seem overly ambitious, even acquisitive, considering the facts. For I was a girl from a very modest home and, by marrying me as he had, Richard had challenged the whole might of the Alexanders.

I have never doubted we were right in what we did that day, nor wished I was fashioned in a different cast, but I can still feel the shock of sudden sorrow that pierced me as I watched that forlorn little group of family and friends on the pier. I was conscious that, although I had changed my life, I had not altered theirs. No matter what I did to aid them, that little ceremony in Brooklyn had forged a division between us that nothing would truly alter. And they knew it. Illuminated by the quayside lights, they stood out, almost as though they were in uniform, in bleak contrast to the mass of people around them who were cheering, calling out last-minute exhortations across the widening gap of water between the streamer-bedecked ship and the wharf – all the old clichés, in hoarse drunken voices: 'Don't take any wooden nickels! Write if you get work!'

I looked at each in turn: my father, white-haired, his arm half-raised in a farewell gesture that imparted all the defeat that marked him now; my mother, smiling, unable to wave because she needed both hands for her walking sticks; my two sisters, so different in their response – Laura, coldly envious, like the bitter husband beside her ('Well, some people certainly fall on their feet, don't they?') and Mary, radiant with her generous spirit, blowing me a sudden kiss. And, at the side of them all, like a recruiting sergeant, stood Great-Aunt Abigail, holding herself rigid, all bust and posterior.

Aunt Abigail had come to live with us when I was sixteen. My father's business had just collapsed and my mother had become a permanent invalid. By then Aunt Abbie was already seventy and something of a legend since, according to family lore, she had once killed a hostile Indian.

She was a formidable lady who had a great influence on us three girls, with her clear strong views that were totally unsentimental but rooted in solid values. 'Marriage,' she would say, 'is a contract that should be judged like any other contract: does it suit the parties?' – which, since she discounted passion as transient and unreliable, we knew was her way of saying why marry a poor man if you can marry a rich one. But there was always a proviso: a wife must honour the bargain – be an honest, loyal partner, observe the marriage vows and raise the children to have integrity and faith. 'You can be sure of one thing,' she would say. 'You reap what you sow.'

'Well, Aunt Abbie,' I had said to her with a smile during the little farewell gathering in our state cabin on the liner before sailing, 'the contract's executed, isn't it?'

She fixed me with her dark eyes, revealing only a glint of humour. 'Yes, Quincey,' she answered, 'now you must make sure it's a contract that suits the other party . . . Isn't that right, Mr Alexander?' She turned to Richard, who had just come up to us, a glass of champagne in his hand. He was thirty-seven, very tall and rangy, with an easy manner. He had a face already craggy, moustached but not bearded, and grey eyes of a strange softness that could change when he got angry, to seem as hard as rock.

'It's the best contract I've ever negotiated, Miss Brown,' he answered, in his lazy voice. 'I've got myself a bargain.'

Aunt Abigail gave me one of her sharp looks. 'Yes, Mr Alexander,' she said, 'I think you probably have . . . ' which I found moving, for Aunt Abigail and I were a team.

Just then the bell rang to warn those not travelling to go ashore and Mr Etherington, head of the Wall Street office of Alexander & Co., approached Richard and slipped a telegram into his hands. 'This came in from London about noon,' I overheard. 'I've replied, of course . . . '

Richard studied the wire for a second. 'What did you say?' he asked.

'That it was too late for further action,' Etherington answered.

Richard glanced at him, serious for a moment. Then he burst out laughing. 'I couldn't have phrased it better myself, Mr Etherington.'

'Good luck to you both,' said Etherington. 'With your permission, I'll kiss the bride.' He embraced me and I was close to tears, for I owed much to him. A gracious man, with a large paunch decorated by a gold watch chain across his waistcoat, he had been my employer since, at eighteen, I had joined Alexander & Co. as one of ten women 'typewriters' on the staff of the bank. A few months later he had found me alone in the office during the luncheon period, eating sandwiches, and asked me to undertake some urgent work for him.

This, in fact, was why I remained in the building every day at this time. 'You should be there when no one else is,' Aunt Abigail had advised, 'when all the other girls are out in drugstores or looking in shop windows. Then . . . Well, you never know, do you . . . ?' It was the opportunity she had predicted. When I had finished the work, Mr Etherington complimented me on my speed and competence.

After this he had entrusted me with other tasks, guiding me eventually to the post I had just relinquished as assistant to Mr Hanley, head of the bank's dealing department.

The family followed Mr Etherington out of the cabin. 'For all their wealth,' Papa whispered as he kissed me, 'Richard's lucky to have got you . . . You're rare, Quincey . . . ' Mama, leaning over her sticks, her body gross from the inactivity of a cripple's life, pressed a jowled cheek against my face. 'Write often, won't you?' she said. Aunt Abigail just gripped my shoulders without words.

At last we were alone and Richard loomed over me, giant-like, and bent down to kiss me. For a second, I clung to him. 'Now, may I see the telegram?' I asked.

'Later,' he answered. 'We'd better get up on deck or they'll casting off . . . '

'Now, please,' I insisted. 'It can't be very long . . . '

He shrugged, took it from his pocket and unfolded it before me. 'Insist you return London immediately for discussion,' I read, 'before you take irrevocable step that could greatly damage family interests – Caesar.' The codename, taken from the days of Ancient Rome as they all were, told me it was from his uncle, Julius Alexander, head of both the bank and the family. I had seen many of his telegrams, witnessed managers dismissed, companies bought and sold, prices in the markets driven up or forced down, conflict conducted with men of power. But it was the first time that I had read a wire from Caesar of which I had been the subject. My immediate reaction was anxiety, but it was replaced at once by anger. How dare he, I thought? How dare he form such a view before he has even met me?

'And have you greatly damaged the family interests?' I challenged Richard, half-serious.

He laughed. 'I've enhanced them,' he said, 'with a priceless new asset . . . Come on now, we're going up-top to wave goodbye . . . ' And he had pulled me out of the cabin after him so firmly that I almost tripped over my skirts.

From the upper deck, as the distance grew between us, we could not make them out for long among the crowd; I went on waving, though, for a few seconds. Then the tugboats slipped the towing lines and took up their customary station behind the liner as she proceeded under her own power down that great wide river towards the sea. From where we stood we could see most of

Manhattan spread out before us, a long island of lights, stretching north and south.

There was a bright moon and the skyline of the city, with its sharp corners, was clearly delineated. Familiar features stood out: the high silhouette of the Flat Iron building, New York's tallest monument to man's ingenuity with its twenty-one storeys, which was soon behind us; the clock tower and dome of City Hall, the slim spire of Trinity Church on Broadway.

The warm night air was tangy now with the smell of the ocean. I breathed in deeply and tightened my fingers within those of the husband I had met for the first time only four weeks before.

That day had started in a fashion that was unremarkable. My father and I left home together and, as we always did, took the horse-car across Brooklyn Bridge. We alighted at the corner of Broadway and Pine and walked together the two blocks to Wall Street where he left me, with that pained smile I hated, to continue on his way to Exchange Street, where he was a clerk with a stockbroking firm named Stephenson & Gray. He had developed a slight stoop which I suspected was deliberate – a kind of bearing of his wounds.

I went on up Wall Street to Number 6, where Alexander & Co. occupied four floors, and was just unpinning my hat at my desk when one of the girls entered the office and said: 'Mr Alexander's just asked to see Mr Hanley at once . . .'

'Mr Alexander?'

'Mr Richard Alexander . . . Didn't you know? He arrived last night . . . .'

'I thought he wasn't due until next week,' I answered, with a calmness I did not feel. For this was another of those rare opportunities for which Aunt Abigail had always urged I should stay prepared. The London directors – the members of the family – seldom came to New York and, when they did, they met only the senior staff. But Mr Hanley was ill and Mr James, his deputy in the Dealing Department, was in Albany. So it was I who would have to respond to the summons of Mr Alexander.

I took up from my desk the list of closing prices of the stocks of special interest that was drawn up every evening – stocks for which

17

the bank had standing buying or selling orders. I had guessed the purpose of Mr Alexander's visit. The bank, as part of a syndicate, was at war with another powerful group that included the Rockefellers, who had founded Standard Oil – each of us vying to win control of certain companies. The field of battle was base metals – lead, zinc, copper, tin – for which there was then a surging demand, mainly because most of them were essential to the electrification that was spreading throughout the world.

I studied the mining shares on the list – noting one in particular, a medium-sized company with big prospects, that had dropped sharply towards the end of the day. This was odd in view of the strength of mining stocks. So I asked our switchboard girl to connect me with one of our brokers. 'Mr Evans,' I said, 'It looks like someone's selling United . . . Could you see if you can find out who it is?' Then I walked over to the Cable Room and asked the clerk to wire London, where the market had been open for some hours, and inquire the trading pattern of the stock.

I went into the Ladies' closet and, standing in front of the mirror, I combed up my hair to the top of my head, containing the strands that had become loosened on the journey from home. For a moment I studied the girl who was about to be exposed to one of the Alexander family. I was no beauty but I had a lively face, which became animated when I grew enthusiastic. And I had good eyes – quite large, and a high blue in colour that would not have been all that striking if I had been fair. But my hair was as black as ebony for which, Aunt Abigail said, I should be grateful, because the contrast was unusual. It was better, she said, to be unusual than a Helen of Troy.

I touched the collar of my blouse into position and went upstairs to the room next to Mr Etherington's, which was used by important visitors.

I knocked on the door and entered, to find the occupant of the desk totally concealed by the *Wall Street Journal*.

'I . . . won't . . . keep . . . you . . . a . . . second,' he said from behind the newspaper, speaking slowly, his attention clearly fixed on what he was reading. Then, after a few seconds, he laid it down and stared at me with amazement. 'Good Lord,' he said, obviously surprised to see a woman in the entrance when he had sent for a manager.

'I fear Mr Hanley's indisposed today, Mr Alexander,' I said, 'but I work for him . . . I'm Miss Brown . . . Perhaps I can be of some assistance . . .'

He looked at me dubiously. 'Well, I don't know,' he said in an easy drawl that sounded odd with an English accent. 'I really don't know . . . I'm interested in the mining sector. We've certain plans. . . I've been out of touch crossing the Atlantic.'

'Well, possibly I could help,' I said. 'It's my duty to execute Mr Hanley's orders to brokers. If you would be a little more precise . . .'

The doubt in him was still obvious. 'Well, for example, there are a couple of stocks in particular – Associated Smelting and United Mining. I see United closed last night at three and a half . . .'

'Three fifty-two offered,' I volunteered. 'It was three eighty earlier in the day, despite our own buying. Someone's obviously selling fairly heavily. I've asked brokers to report – and wired London for today's price movement. As for Associated, we were buying at four eighty-two by last evening, which was twenty points up on the opening levels . . .'

For a few seconds he was speechless, frank amazement in his soft eyes. 'How in the world did you know all that?' he asked, incredulously, 'Without . . . well, without checking?'

I smiled for the first time. 'But I *have* checked, Mr Alexander . . .'

He laughed. 'You must forgive me,' he said. 'I'm not used to finding ladies in an office. It's rare in London. Mr Etherington tells me the custom here dates back to the Civil War, when there were so many men away fighting. I wonder why United's off so sharply. . .' He was not actually asking me so much as thinking aloud. 'Is it profit-taking,' he mused, 'or something adverse, like that new mine of theirs in the Chugash Mountains? Perhaps it's not as good as it seemed.'

'Or perhaps they just want us to think so,' I suggested. 'News that they're selling might convince us . . .'

He leaned back heavily in his chair, long legs stretched out. 'Now that's a sneaky thought,' he said. 'If you're right, I suppose there'll be rumours being spread here on the floor of the exchange . . .'

'If that's the intention,' I agreed.

'So one or two speculators'll fall for it and start selling short,

19

which'll push the price down further. We'll stop buying pending inquiry, and all the time our friends of the opposition'll be carefully taking in the stock under different names in small orders through several brokers. That's the picture, isn't it?'

'Well, possibly . . . ' I conceded reluctantly. Really, I had no solid reason for thinking this yet.

'Mmm . . . sneaky,' he repeated, then asked suddenly, 'Why are you so sure nothing's gone wrong with the company?'

'I didn't say I was sure, Mr Alexander.'

'But you suspect it, don't you?'

'Well,' I answered carefully, 'United have an exceptional Chief Engineer, as I'm sure you're aware in view of your interest in the company . . . ' I broke off.

'Please go on,' he said. He was holding his hands, palms flat together, fingertips just touching his chin, watching me closely.

'Four years ago he joined them from Amalgamated Metals,' I said, feeling foolish, sure that he knew. 'He had options on a couple of mines in Colorado which he traded to United for a share of the capital. They were spectacular, of course. He could have made a mistake now in the Chugash. You need hunch in mining, and he's human, but . . . ' I ran out of words.

For a moment there was silence. 'You know all that, Miss . . . Miss Brown, was it?' I nodded. 'How do you know all that?'

'Naturally, we've investigated the management of the company.' I answered.

'Naturally,' he repeated. 'Will Mr Hanley be back tomorrow?' he asked suddenly.

'I rather doubt it,' I answered, 'but Mr James'll be here on Thursday . . . '

He was silent for a moment. Then he said: 'Well, Miss Brown, I wouldn't have said you were doing so badly without the help of either, so perhaps I should explain exactly what we're aiming to do – and then you can tell me how we should set about doing it.' And a broad grin of wonder spread slowly across his face, making me feel like a performer in a circus.

The moment I got home I could tell that Aunt Abbie sensed something different had happened, but she did not ask about it at once. I was later than usual and they had already finished supper. Papa was sitting in an armchair by the stove, intent as usual on the evening paper. 'Jesus,' he was saying, 'United Steel's selling at 54 . . . How come I never saw that in the tape in the office today? Mark my words, it'll double. Just give it a couple of months . . . '

Aunt Abbie did not interrupt him in what was an evening routine, his way of cushioning the reality of his life, of regaining a little of his self-respect. 'Lord,' he went on, 'look at the price of rubber. It's hedge-buying, of course, against a fall in gold. Won't hold – too much rubber about . . . My God, if only I had 50,000 dollars at this moment, I could make it into a million.' It was all talk now, of course, but it had not always been. We had not always lived in three rooms in a 'dumb-bell' tenement block near the dockyard. He saw me then. 'Hallo, Quincey, you're late back. Been keeping you busy, have they?'

Aunt Abbie was eyeing me shrewdly. 'You look like a kitten that's got at the butter. Something interesting go on today?'

'A bit out of the ordinary, you might say,' I answered casually as I took off my coat. 'I've been working with Mr Richard Alexander . . . Planning strategy.' I gave a self-mocking grin. 'Getting grand, you see. From now on it's "Miss Quincey", please . . . .'

'Mr Alexander!' my mother echoed, deeply impressed. She had become obese from her life in a wheelchair, but her face still bore the traces of the pretty woman that she had once been. 'My, if that isn't a great honour, surely, Quincey. I thought the Alexanders all stayed in London.'

'He's only just arrived . . . wants me to be his personal adviser. I'm not kidding, honestly,' I added, with a smile. 'Aunt Abbie,' I said, flopping down on my heels beside her, 'it was just like you've always hoped – that chance in a million you've said'd come some-time so long as I was ready for it . . . Well, it came. I can't recall another day in the past two years when Mr Hanley and Mr James've *both* been absent at the same time.'

'Lady Luck, eh?' Papa put in, with a wry smile. He often spoke of

Lady Luck — too often, in fact.

'Could be,' I agreed. 'There's a big operation in hand — and Mr Alexander actually listened to what I suggested — I mean *really* listened. Mining stocks . . . of course we've been buying in for months, but now they're seriously going for a big position.'

'Scope there,' said Papa. 'Mines are bouncing up and down like hot beans. Maybe I can help, Quincey? Why, I was buying and selling mines before you were even thought of.'

'Would you, Papa?' I responded eagerly. 'I'd be so glad if you would. You know the sector so well. You'd be an enormous help.'

For a second there was a sad expression on his face, and I wondered if he suspected that the warmth of my enthusiasm was aimed to please him. Perhaps, too, I had been thoughtless in being quite so buoyant with my news which, when examined coolly, had a fragile foundation. Still, I could hardly have kept it from him — and he would not have wanted me to. All the same, I knew it turned the knife in the wound.

Papa was a broker's clerk — and had been most of his life — but the time had come when opportunity had beckoned and, as he repeated so endlessly, 'when Lady Luck bends the finger, girl, you run . . . You really run.'

For the clerks on Wall Street in those halcyon days there was often opportunity since, under the system whereby stocks could be bought 'on margin', they needed to pay only a fraction of the price in cash. They could deal on the market, therefore, with little in the way of savings — so long as the price went up. If it went down, even a couple of points, then because so much was borrowed they lost their investment very fast. Still, some managed to do well. A few even became millionaires, and there was a brief period when my father had seemed destined for this happy state — mainly because of Thomas Ryan, the railroad Titan.

Ryan was a client of my father's firm and took a liking to him, slipping him useful inside information and often shrewd advice. As a result Papa had blossomed into a speculator, resigned from the brokers, and our life had changed. With his success he had become a different man, developing a jaunty confidence. For two wonderful years, his instinct had seemed infallible. We moved to a big house in Monroe Place on Brooklyn Heights and he smoked fat cigars and had a usual table at Delmonico's and joined the Seacliffe Yacht Club. He urged my mother, who was not cut out for that kind of life at all, to buy gowns at Lord & Taylor and ride about in a carriage and pair and give lavish entertainment — until she fell ill, that is, when he had to switch his flamboyant socializing to restaurants or the Waldorf-Astoria or the Yacht Club.

And always he had talked a lot, with that confident expression on his face and the cigar smoke hanging in the air around him. 'Don't let anyone confuse you with the jargon,' he would say. 'Supply and demand, that's all it is, though sometimes we try to anticipate it.' He would expand on the effect on stocks of wars; of grain surpluses; of disasters such as typhoons or floods; and of the impact of confidence, of the way men like Diamond Jim Brady or James R. Keene, who was known as 'The Silver Fox', only had to express a view of a company in the Waldorf-Astoria's Mahogany Bar, where the important men would meet after the market closed, for the price to move next day. He would speak with airy amusement of the battles between the giants of finance, and report their tactics as they fought their ruthless, bitter struggles-to-the-death for the control of an industry — all of which had a certain awful irony, because he himself was ruined in such a contest between Thomas Ryan, his patron, and James R. Keene, 'The Silver Fox'.

Those few days when our fortunes changed remain with me in vivid detail. I can still hear the horses on the evening when George Smith, one of Ryan's top men, had approached the house. Goodness knows, horses were a common enough sound, but instinct warned me that this time they brought danger.

I sat on the stairs above my father's study and, because the door was slightly ajar, I heard Mr Smith say: 'Rumour has it that you're short on Consolidated Sugar in quite a way.'

'Are you asking me or telling me, George?' my father answered in that provocative, self-confident tone. He would, I knew, be standing, with a smile on his face, in front of the fireplace, rocking backways and forwards on his heels, his hands clasped behind his back. He had sensed nothing of what I knew for certain, even though I was barely sixteen. Important men did not usually arrive uninvited in the evening, as Smith had come.

'I'm not asking,' Smith had answered. 'I'm telling you: get out while you can.'

'That price can't possibly hold, George,' my father insisted confidently. 'There's massive overproduction . . .'

'It's nothing to do with production,' his visitor retorted. 'it's to do with a fight between two men who hate each other's entrails. Ryan's going for Keene. He's going to twist his tail right off, Franklin, even if it costs him half a million. He heard you were short and thought I should warn you. Cut your losses, pal.'

'I appreciate it, George,' my father answered. 'You'll tell him for me, won't you? I'm grateful for the tip.'

But he did not take the tip. He just closed his ears. We were living in the path of an avalanche and Papa blithely ignored its warning rumbles. Mama and my sisters did, too, convinced that nothing could ruffle the tranquil surface of our affluent life. Their attitude was more understandable than Papa's, for none of them had ever listened to his endless talk. To them, the market was a bore – as it had been to me until one day when he had been dealing in a corporation that, four years earlier, had built the first power plant on Niagara Falls. 'Made a clear two bucks a unit today in less than three hours,' he declare jauntily. 'No doubt about it, you girls've got a clever papa.'

'But what's the plant do?' I asked, thinking that a Falls was strange site on which to build it.

'Do?' he queried, puzzled. 'Why, it makes electricity, I guess – from the falling water.'

'From the water?' I echoed. 'Isn't that a marvellous thing, Papa?'

'Sure it's marvellous . . . ' he agreed uncertainly. 'It's creating power for all those other plants up there in the North – which means more business, more companies, more profits, more chances for your wily old Pa.'

He was a market man, excited only by his deals, by outwitting his opponents, by clever manuoeuvres – and he was good at it. He could sniff a change in sentiment like a tracker dog could find a new line of scent. He knew by instinct if the market was due for a rise or a fall; if a stock was cheap or overpriced.

But he had caught my imagination with the Niagara power plant. I asked more questions about other corporations and realized that the stocks and shares he traded were not as dull as I had thought. They reflected most of man's endeavour on the earth. He had entered into the game with me and, though hurt at my bland response to the wealth he was amassing, he elaborated at length about the companies he dealt in. Avidly, I would follow his finger as he showed me on the map those areas of the globe in which he happened to be interested at the time. I *cared* if it was the season of the rains in India. Small wonder I became his favourite daughter, for he did not have a son.

In passing, of course, I learned a bit about the market – and in time this, too, with its colourful operators who raided stocks like pirates, began to grip me. So, young as I was, I knew exactly what Mr Smith had called on him that night to say.

Papa had been speculating. Instead of buying shares in the hope that they would rise, he had reversed the process and sold stock he did not own, planning to buy it back when the price dropped – as 'bears' operate in the Stock Market. But in a 'bear squeeze', which is what Mr Ryan was levering on Mr Keene, there comes a time when there is no stock left to buy.

Mr Smith had given Papa fair warning, and the next day he could have bought enough Consolidated Sugar stock to cover his sales, albeit at a huge loss. But delay meant that he would be 'caught short', unable to deliver what he had sold, which would be disastrous. For he would then face ruinous suits for breach of contract.

It was with alarm, therefore, that when he returned that night, I discovered that he had taken no action. 'The sqeeze won't work,' he asserted confidently, with an impish grin. 'Conditions don't suit it.'

'It'd seem that Mr Ryan thinks they do,' I said.

He shook his head firmly. 'The market'll force the price down no matter what he does.'

'Surely, Papa,' I pleaded, 'You should at least buy in some stock while you can . . . Just in case he's right.'

He put his arm round my shoulder. 'That's my little girl,' he said. 'Don't you worry . . . Just trust your old Papa.'

I *did* trust him. At least I did until I realized with horror that he was merely relying on Lady Luck to extricate him from a painful situation that he just refused to countenance – which oddly, I was to discover, was a common fault among clever, even cunning men.

By the next evening, Papa knew he was locked in. It was the only time I had ever seen him in tears, and it was an awesome sight. He was like a deflating balloon, seeming half his normal size. It created in me confused emotions. I loved him and I knew his faults. In an odd fashion I enjoyed these faults, expressed as they were in the extravagant personality he had developed with success – in the perfect cut of his clothes, in the hint of swagger in his walk, in the attentive charm he displayed to lower mortals such as brokers' clerks; and women, of course, including my friends at school, who would enthuse about the wonderful handsome father I had. And I did have a wonderful handsome father, though I knew it was all superficial. 'You know Papa,' my sisters and I would say to each other with a fond smile. 'We all know Papa.' He was our own Yankee dandy.

That evening I grew up. He became maudlin with the bourbon, slopping it over the table as he kept filling his glass. 'I've let you down,' he kept repeating, 'let you down . . . We'll have to sell the house. You'll have to leave the academy, Quincey, and you, Mary.' He was referring to the De Witt-Clinton Academy for Young Ladies, which we both attended. It was a prospect that left me unmoved, a sign of the change in me. I had cried for Papa at first, but now my tears had gone. That night he was not a very dandy Yankee.

'I'll do something about Mama,' he said. 'I'll find a way.' One of Mama's lungs was badly infected and she was due to go into Mount Ephraim Hospital for an operation. 'My God,' he exclaimed, 'if I can't find five hundred dollars, it's a poor state of affairs.'

But already I suspected it was a poor state of affairs, and I was right. Both Mama's lungs were doomed to deteriorate, and this in turn was to affect her circulation, which would make it hard for her to walk.

Suddenly there was no security any longer, and that night I knew panic. I remember forcing myself quite consciously to control my fear. With Papa collapsed and drinking, I was the only one in the family who even began to understand our position. Was there not something, I asked myself, even at this late stage, that could be done to alleviate the full impact of the catastrophe? Tautly I asked Papa:

'Does Mr Ryan hold all the Consolidated Sugar stock?'

He looked up at me, the tears wet on his gnarled cheeks. 'And his friends,' he croaked.

'Wouldn't Mr Ryan help?'

He shook his head in desolation. 'Not now. You were right, Quincey, I should have acted.' And he began to sob, his shoulders heaving.

I knew I must retain my nerve. 'Well, how about his friends?' I persisted. 'Would they include Mr Johnson?' Mr Johnson was one of the regular visitors to our home and had always been especially attentive to me. I was convinced that he would help us if I asked him. But Father reacted most violently. 'That lecher!' he exclaimed angrily. 'Don't you think of going near that man, do you hear, Quincey?'

Later, I asked my sister Laura what a lecher was and she told me. 'Do you think it hurts terribly?' I said, as though it was like a visit to the dentist. 'Isn't it over quite quickly?'

'Quincey!' Laura had exclaimed in horror. 'Mr Johnson's an old man — and an ugly one.' Which, as I saw it, was surely not the point. We were speaking of a sacrifice. I was confused, of course, and innocent, but a visit to Mr Johnson as a last bid to extricate Papa seemed my duty to undertake. In truth, I did not believe there was any risk. Whatever Papa might say, I knew Mr Johnson to be a gentleman.

Even so, I felt a certain sense of drama when I lied to Mama that I was going to visit my schoolfriend Lucy, who lived in Lower Manhattan, and set off to the offices of Mr Johnson's firm on Wall Street.

I was received by a friendly young clerk with a severe rash of acne. He told me with a smile that he would inquire if Mr Johnson was engaged, and returned to say that he would see me at once.

Mr Johnson stood up behind his large desk as I was shown into his room, and came forward to greet me. 'Why, Quincey,' he said with a big smile, 'what a delightful surprise . . . You'll take something to drink? Coffee? Lemonade?'

He was not really ugly, as Laura had said. A robust man with a leonine head of strong grey hair, he had a red complexion and a full moustache over lips that were strangely delicate in line, like a woman's. His smile was warm and embracing; his voice, considering his bulk, surprisingly gentle.

He invited me to sit down on a large leather sofa. 'Now,' he said, 'to what do I owe this honour?'

'I hope you'll forgive me calling on you like this,' I began, 'but. . . well, I wondered if you'd heard of my father's difficulties.'

His bonhomie was replaced by concern, and he nodded gravely. 'You thought I might be able to help?'

The young clerk reappeared with a jug of lemonade and placed it on a long low table beside me. Mr Johnson took a cigar from a humidor, cut the end and lit it. 'Tell me,' he said, 'does your father know you've come to see me?'

I shook my head. 'He'd have forbidden it.'

'He wouldn't want you to ask a favour – as a pretty girl?'

I was disconcerted, and he laughed. 'I'm making you uncomfortable. You must forgive me. I just wondered if you understood your position. After all, you're very young.'

'My position?' I repeated. It seemed an odd remark to make.

He inhaled deeply on his cigar. 'Let's assume for a moment,' he said, 'that I was able to help . . . Have you considered that there might be implications for you – a quid pro quo, as it were?'

It was a forthright question. I looked down at my hands, fingers tautly entwined. 'I find your question surprising, Mr Johnson,' I said quietly.

He came towards me and lifted my chin with one finger. 'I think the cards should be on the table, Quincey. How old are you?'

'Sixteen, Mr Johnson.' My heart was quickening.

'Delightful,' he said. I felt the colour flood to my face and he smiled gently. 'You're blushing . . . quivering like a fawn.'

He returned to the fireplace. 'Well, let's be practical,' he went on. 'I could perhaps persuade some of the buyers of your father's stock to waive their rights. It wouldn't be easy, but possible, I'd say. The question is, Quincey, what'd you do for me in return?'

Suddenly, I was shocked. 'I don't think I understand you, Mr Johnson,' I said in cold reproach.

He met my gaze coolly. 'You understand, Quincey,' he declared. 'You're here to trade with me. You've come as a girl, and you have what a girl has to offer.'

28

'Surely, Mr Johnson, you don't think . . . ' I began, but he cut in with a weary tone: 'Do you think I'm unaware of my reputation, Quincey? You knew you were walking into a lion's den, didn't you? But you thought you could get away without a scratch . . . Well, you *can*. You can just finish your lemonade and walk through that door.'

'And Papa?'

'Ah,' said Mr Johnson, 'well, there's the rub, isn't it? That's where you have to make your choice.'

I sat up very straight, glaring at him. 'I'm amazed at you, Mr Johnson, I truly am.'

My words made no impact. 'Well,' he asked, 'do you want to leave – or stay?'

I did not know what I wanted. I wanted him to help my father, to save the family from the disaster that threatened us; but I was unprepared for such a blunt analysis of the options. I was frightened, too, but also curious, even perversely a little stimulated by Mr Johnson's frankness.

'I'll lock the door,' he said, 'because I don't want us to be disturbed, but you only have to say if you wish to go.' And the click, as he turned the key in the latch, echoed like a rifle shot.

'You know,' he went on conversationally, 'I've known a lot of young girls like you. At first they've trembled and blushed, and then as we've explored together they've come to enjoy the potential of their bodies without shame. In fact, sometimes I've been hard put to comply with their demands. Would you credit that, now?' And the big open smile came to his face, making his words seem oddly commonplace.

'And if I do what you ask,' I blurted out, 'will you save my father?'

'Let's explore a little,' he suggested. He held out his hand. 'Stand up, Quincey.' He began to caress my face gently with the back of his fingers, running them lightly over my cheeks, my forehead, my mouth. 'There's nothing to fear,' he whispered. Then he leaned forward and, without hurry, lightly kissed my lips several times from corner to corner. 'There – is that so objectionable?' he asked with a soft smile, adding, when I hesitated: 'Well, is it?'

He put his hands to the sides of my neck, stroking me, fingering

29

my ears with the softest touch.

'You have a lovely young face,' he said. I felt his hold on the back of my neck and I was shocked to find myself arching to it like a cat. Deftly, he unpinned my hat. Then he took out my combs, catching my hair in his cupped hands before spilling it through his fingers down my back.

He kissed me again, and tried to part my lips with his tongue, but I resisted this in disgust. 'Don't fight it,' he said gently.

I turned my head from him. 'How do I know you'll help my father?' I said sharply. He feigned an expression of pain, 'Surely, I've made myself clear, Quincey. I'll do my best to help, provided you and I become . . . well, friends, shall we say?'

'How can I be certain?' I asked, surprising myself with my cold persistence.

'What do you want,' he returned with a smile, 'a written contract? Who'd you show it to if I reneged?'

'A judge, perhaps?' I demanded in challenge. 'I'm under age, aren't I? It's against the laws of New York.'

He clapped his hands, excited by my spirited response. 'Boy, what a little tigress you are! A contract, indeed. The door's there, Quincey, you can walk out.' He saw me hesitate. 'Otherwise you'll just have to trust me won't you?'

Again he began to kiss me, his hands ranging lightly over my body, touching my breasts, my hips, my stomach. I stood unyielding, though my breath quickened. He started to undo my jacket, but I stopped him. 'I need more time, Mr Johnson.'

'Time's short, Quincey. You know that.' I made no effort to check him then as, with skilful fingers, he slipped off my jacket. He began to undo the buttons of my blouse. 'You're trembling, little fawn.'

'Does it surprise you?' I demanded, thinking suddenly that he must be the Devil. The Devil did not have a forked tail. He looked like Mr Johnson. He divined my thoughts. 'I'm not as bad as all that,' he said, 'as you'll see.'

He slid my blouse from my shoulders. 'Your skin is as soft as a rose's petals,' he whispered, releasing my skirt so that it fell to the floor.

'Please don't go on, Mr Johnson,' I said. I was wearing two

petticoats but no man, not even Papa, had ever seen me without a skirt.

He stood back, smiling. 'You want to go?' he asked softly. 'Shall I help you put on your skirt?' He made as if to bend down but he was watching me and realized that I was not resolved, that I was still trying to balance the issues. If I allowed him to continue, my father might survive.

He gave me a little time then, just holding me in his arms, kissing me gently. 'Just relax,' he said gently. Skilfully he unhooked my corset, released my petticoats so that I stood before him in my chemise, with nothing beneath it above my waist.

'Now the chemise, little one,' he said. I did not move. 'Think of your father,' he whispered. 'I'm going to help your father. Just lift your arms . . . ' And slowly I did as he instructed. 'Don't look so sad,' he chided with a smile, lifting the chemise carefully over my hair. I had never known a moment of such embarrassment. My whole body felt as flushed as if it was burning. I cowered, covering my breasts with my arms but, grasping my wrists, he drew them apart so that nothing was concealed. 'Exquisite,' he whispered as he surveyed me. 'Quite exquisite.'

Suddenly, I was a child. Tears began to stream down my cheeks. 'Little one,' he reproached softly, 'why are you weeping?' He leaned forward and kissed a nipple – a child's nipple that hardened like a woman's. He took the breast in his mouth, brushing the tip with his tongue.

Shame surged in me like the sudden heat of hot Manhattan streets. My father's face, creased with the sobbing of the previous night, appeared before me. What would he think if he saw me now? He would be appalled, even though I was acting in his cause. My cold, clear plan for noble sacrifice collapsed. Deep emotions, rooted in instinct, were suddenly touched, exposed – privacy, self-respect, even guilt. There was no doubt now that I must leave.

'Please stop, Mr Johnson,' I said. He did not seem to have heard me. 'You said I could go, Mr Johnson.' Sweat was pouring down my face. I was shaking, panting, gasping for breath. The office was stifling. Great sobs began to rack my body. I was overwhelmed by a need to escape those insistent lips and fingers.

My action then was instinctive; I put both my hands against his shoulders and thrust him away as hard as I could. With a cry he staggered back, tripped on the low table and fell with a crash on the floor, striking his head on the corner of his desk as he went down.

For seconds I stood still, appalled at what I had done. He lay on his back without moving. Blood oozed from a gash in his head. His eyes were open, staring sightless. He was unconscious, I thought. Then I wondered if he was dead. For the second time in twenty-four hours I experienced panic and again forced myself to control it, desperately trying to think clearly what I should do.

There was a knock on the door and I stared at it helplessly, standing half-naked as I was, my heart thumping. The handle turned but the door was locked, of course, and I heard retreating footsteps.

I tried to gather my thoughts. Obviously I must attempt to leave the building without being seen. Strangely, my first fear was that my father would discover where I had been. It was only as I tried to dress with trembling fingers that it dawned on me that the police, too, might be interested by my presence in that room.

The thought induced another wave of panic. Calm yourself, I whispered aloud, or you are doomed. I forced myself to stand quite still for a few seconds, taking several deep breaths. I scanned the walls for a mirror but could not see one, so I gathered my hair by feel and secured it as best I could under my hat.

With a care that surprised me later, I looked round the room. I straightened the table that had been knocked askew as Mr Johnson fell. I checked that I had left nothing on the floor or the chaise longue, bending to peer beneath it – no hairpins or combs. Then I went to the door and listened. There was no sound, so I turned the key in the latch and stepped quickly into the corridor. I walked along the passage to the stairs, only to see Mr Johnson's clerk approaching from the floor below. 'So you're leaving now, Miss,' he said with a grin. 'I hope the interview was satisfactory.'

'Thank you,' I answered. 'Good day to you.'

The following week my father's failure became formal, since he was unable, as they put it, to meet his commitments. He did not cry again but retreated into himself, still drinking heavily, saying little, looking more haggard every day. Mama's condition declined fast, as though she felt that the fight for health was no longer worth the effort.

I lived with constant fear, expecting every knock to herald the arrival of the police. I knew that Mr Johnson was indeed dead, because it had been reported in the *Wall Street Journal* and Papa had read it out at breakfast. Foul play had been suspected at first, but there was no sign of a struggle, no bruising.

A few weeks later, I encountered Mr Johnson's clerk in the street. 'Hallo, Miss Brown,' he said, and I was startled that he recalled my name.

'I was sorry to hear about Mr Johnson,' I said.

'Bit of a mystery,' he said, 'but I didn't tell the police about you. No point. There'd been trouble before, stupid old man . . . '

'I'm obliged to you,' I said.

I was relieved by what he had told me, for the dread had still been with me, lying in the back of my mind. Strangely, apart from the fear of detection I had felt no emotion about the experience, not even guilt or distaste. Then it had faded in my memory, becoming a detail of the whole devastating calamity that had overtaken us.

Occasionally, I would see the clerk in the street or a store and the picture of Mr Johnson would emerge from the recesses of consciousness. Always, I would avoid speaking to the boy if I could.

Our house on the heights was sold and we moved to the tenement building on Plymouth Street where there was always noise and the smell of cooking cabbage on the stairs. Mary, being still young, attended PS Brooklyn II, to finish her schooling. Laura and I went out to work in Manhattan stores, for now the money we could earn was badly needed.

That year was one of the bad ones that enveloped Wall Street with such relentless regularity, so Papa was fortunate to get a position once more as a clerk – and, what is more with his old firm of Stephenson & Gray. 'They know a good man when they see him,' he declared, with the faintest glimmer of his old bravura. It was not often evident. Just occasionally, when he was on his fifth bourbon.

Aunt Abigail came to live with us since, with Mama's decline, someone had to run the home. She became the focus of our lives. I recall thinking once that she would not have made much impact at the Yacht Club Ball, where Father had cut so effective a figure, but she would have known exactly what to do if there had been a fire.

Her wise counsel had a value to me that was incalculable; for the ambition, sown in me two years before by the revelation of the Niagara power plant, had found deep roots. Since then, I had been exposed by Papa to many other marvels – to the tapping of the earth's resources, to the amazing new products of science, to the skill of engineers who, throughout the globe, were constructing dams and canals and bridges, building new kinds of ships, new sorts of buildings, new types of railroads. I yearned to share the vision, the planning, the execution that had made such things possible.

From Papa, too, I had acquired something of his animal sense of the market – and I had learned the bitter lesson of his devastating error. Speculation required more than judgement and reliance on Lady Luck. It needed caution, the covering of flanks, the closing of exposed positions.

I found I was being drawn to his world in the same way as aspiring young actresses were drawn to the theatre. While they dreamed of playing Juliet or Ophelia, I dreamed of damming the Nile or funding the development of a new vaccine. Also, I had a need – vague and undefined as it was – to pick up the standard that Papa had dropped and to challenge the dragons. 'It's more than a need,' I said to Aunt Abigail when at last I could bring myself to speak of it. 'It's a compulsion. Do you think I've gone a little crazy?'

She smiled, then nodded. 'Most people who achieve things are a little crazy. The cost'll be high, you realize. Battles leave wounds.'

'I'll keep a medicine chest.'

'You may need it more than you expect.' She paused, eyeing me. 'All right, if you're sure that's what you want, I'll tell you what to do. First, you learn typewriting and stenography. The YWCA in Manhattan've just started classes – you can go there in the evenings after you're through at Stewarts. Once you're qualified, then maybe you can get yourself a position in an office on Wall Street. There, you'll be able to observe what the men do, become so good you're indispensable, stand out among the other girls. Read the market pages so that you understand. Listen to your father. Study all the books you can get your hands on. Then be ready for your chance when it comes . . . *if* it comes. Deserve it, and it probably will.'

I deserved it. The tuition was costly. So I had to save the fees from what was left of my wages after paying my share of the family budget. To save money I walked to work, bought only those clothes that were essential. A young girl did not need much. For eighteen months, in the store and the YWCA, I laboured seventeen hours a day.

Neither of my sisters could understand my single-minded purpose. 'You're only young once,' Laura would say with a laugh. 'You should enjoy yourself while you can.'

'What's a year,' I answered, 'out of a whole lifetime?'

Laura had callers. She was twenty by then. Time she was married, Aunt Abigail would say, and for Laura it was. I had no callers, of course. I had no spare hours in the day.

At last the moment for action came. I was eighteen and I had finished my course. One lesson I had learned from Papa was that it was the big fish who ruled the pond, who could buy time when it was needed, who had the power. Aunt Abigail firmly concurred. 'Swim with the big fish,' she said.

'Do you know anyone of importance in any of the investment banks, Papa?' I asked.

'Yes,' he said, 'as a matter of fact I do – Etherington at Alexander's. Once I did him a bit of a good turn.'

Papa was pleased when I was taken on. 'Still got a bit of influence, you see,' he said. 'Something's left.' A lot was left, in fact – enough knowledge to fill fifty volumes, the instinct of a mongrel, an understanding of the men in the Waldorf's Mahogany Bar. I listened and learned. I matched what I saw at the bank, where big money was deployed, with Papa's daily assessment of the market's changing pattern, of the tactics the speculators would be planning. In five years, I had become fairly skilled myself – able to converse with Papa on almost equal terms.

That evening, after Mr Alexander had arrived, a knowing smile came to Papa's face. 'Well, girl,' he said, 'Lady Luck bending the finger, eh?'

'I wouldn't trust Lady Luck, Papa' I said, 'if I saw her across the

35

street.'

One of those sad smiles came to his face. 'You don't understand, Quincey. Lady Luck's another way of saying God.'

I shocked him then. 'Does that alter anything?' I asked.

'You mean you wouldn't trust God?' he inquired incredulously.

'I guess not – not if I saw him across the street dressed like Lady Luck.'

[3]

'Caesar?' repeated Mr Alexander. 'What's Caesar like? What you'd expect, I suppose – a man of power, but with feet of clay . . . He can't be with us much longer now.' It was late and the market had closed. We were sitting in his office, as we often did at that time of day, reviewing trading, assessing our latest position. 'Even my uncle's mortal,' he added.

'You mean he's dying?' I asked. I did not understand. There had been fifteen telegrams from him during the past few hours. They took only three minutes to cross the Atlantic and we had direct lines into Western Union both in London and New York, so it had been an active dialogue – peremptory instructions, questions that were often caustic, angry ripostes, changed orders to meet new situations on the trading floors, just once a message of approval. He had seemed very alive and kicking to me.

'He's had two strokes,' Mr Alexander explained. 'The last in January was a bad one, leaving him paralysed for days. He's still lame. The doctors said he must retire, give up the crown . . . He just laughed. "This bank's my life", he said. "I'll direct its fortunes till the day I'm boxed." The third attack's usually fatal, so the sands are running out.'

'What'll happen then?' I asked.

'Oh, then there'll be a bit of a duel, I suppose . . . me and my cousin Howard.' He spoke in his usual lazy tone, with an easy smile on his face. 'It's started already, of course. In fact, it's been going on since we were boys. Not in theory . . . We'll both have equal shares, but in practice one of us'll have to take over Uncle's chair. That's why this operation of ours here in New York could be important. I had to weigh up whether it was better to come out to direct it in person, or stay in London to guard my rear. I opted for this, so we've got to win, Miss Brown.'

'We'll win, Mr Alexander,' I answered. Strangely, I was confident – even though we *were* up against Standard.

'A bit splendidly, I mean. A proper win, not a skirmish, so people'll hear about it back in London; for God knows what Howard'll be doing to exploit my absence.'

He talked often of his cousin, changing the wording sometimes of the wires I took him before coding for dispatch to 'Tiberio', as he was addressed in secret cables. 'That'll annoy Howard,' he would say. 'I rather like annoying Howard.' And he would grin like a schoolboy. 'But it'll impress the mighty Caesar.' And he made a mocking gesture of obeisance.

Always, when speaking of the tensions at Old Broad Court, the home office in London, he would make the Alexander family and the bank it encompassed sound like an ancient monarchy. He spoke of politics, of tactics, of managers who were in or out of favour, of his uncle's whims and the means needed to gain approval for an unconventional course of action.

Though he often called him 'Caesar', or spoke with light sarcasm of 'the royal presence', he was clearly fond of 'Uncle'. 'We get on, which is odd. He loathed my father, who was his brother, of course. His son and I have always had the daggers out. He plays on it too, mischievous old man that he is.'

That first week in the office with him was an experience that was completely novel for me – as indeed, he was to say, it was for him. We were together often during the day but it was later, when trading had stopped and we could relax a little and talk of the next day's plans, that we forged a partnership which we both considered unique.

He would lean back in his chair, hands clasped behind his head, long legs stretched out beneath his desk, and watch me with a kind of continuing astonishment as I tried to assess for him the situation in a company or analyse the planning tactics of the men who were dealing in its shares. 'Where in the world did you learn of such artful and convoluted manoeuvring?' he asked. 'As a woman, I mean?'

I grinned. 'I'm a street dog, I guess.' It was Papa's game, but I had come to enjoy it. Mr Alexander found it funny, the idea of my being a street dog.

As for me, I had never before met a man with the education and sheer mental breadth of Richard Alexander. I was well versed in the ways of Wall Street but he thought in global terms, in which Wall Street was only a part. He had invested millions in markets throughout the world – especially in the 'City' of London, which was then undisputed as its financial centre – doubtless with that same sense of unhurried ease which I found so unusual. It was the first time I had worked with anyone who, for all the telegrams, had authority of immediate decision on such a scale.

We came to know each other very quickly, for in our long reviews in the late afternoon we spoke about our lives that were so different. I told him about Papa and Mama and, of course, Aunt Abigail – and how we once lived and how we lived now. And he would speak of his parents, both of whom were dead – especially of his father, whom he had greatly admired – and of Shere, the family's big country estate in the New Forest, and of the Alexanders' life in London. He talked of his sister Stella, who sounded severe, being a staunch pillar of the church always urging him to mend his ways; and of James, his ebullient favourite cousin who, at only twenty-five, worked as his personal assistant at Old Broad Court.

I would watch him, as he talked, with a deep fascination, deriving pleasure from every expression that came to his face, every lanky movement he made. I was highly conscious of him physically – if our hands touched by chance, in particular, or if I had to stand near him to make some point in a report I had brought him – but I took no account of it, not even once when I began to tremble. That morning, I had noted, was still cold for May. There was no real problem. He was impressive and attractive, of course, but he came from a world that was remote – like a man from Mars, I told myself once with a giggle. Far more important was his position in the bank, the chance he represented to display what talents I might have.

One evening, as we were reviewing trading, we spotted the potential for the 'splendid' coup he needed. He was studying the latest list of stockholders in the two companies he had spoken of the day we met: United Mining and Associated Smelting. They were our prime targets, though we 'feinted' sometimes to confuse the opposition by selling before buying back under different names through other brokers, even covering our tracks by dealing in other stocks to conceal our real intentions. By now we owned quite a portion of each company. 'I noticed something interesting just now,' I said. 'There are two London trusts who've *both* got holdings in *both* United and Associated.'

'That's true,' he said, his eyes on the list. 'Blackwell Jones and Higgins & Smith. We often deal with them in London.'

'Are they on good terms?' I asked. 'On their own, their parcels are quite big but not significant, but if they were to join forces . . .'

At once, he saw what I meant. 'Great Scott, Miss Brown, you're right. Together, they'd be partners to be reckoned with. Would they agree to a trade, is what you're *thinking*? *We'd* take their shares in United . . .'

I nodded eagerly, excited by his quick response. 'And *they'd* take our stock in Associated . . .'

'Now, what'd that do for us in United?'

'It'd leave us needing to gain only another 7 per cent of the shares in the Market to take us over the 50 per cent we need for control of the most progressive company in American mining. That shouldn't take us too long if we're careful. . .'

'And what'd it do for Blackwell Jones and Higgins & Smith?' He was playing with me, a half smile on his face, for he knew the answer.

'Give them such a big holding in Associated that its value to them'd soar.'

He laughed and shook his head. 'You've got quite an eye for the ball, haven't you, Miss Brown? Well, I suppose someone in London should sound out our two friends – in confidence, of course . . .'

'Shouldn't we get that 7 per cent in United first?' I urged. 'They might feel out the opposition before we were ready. Then the cat'd be running down the alley.'

'What, break a confidence?' His expression was close to shock. 'These are English gentlemen, Miss Brown.'

'Forgive me, Mr Alexander,' I apologized. 'I'd overlooked the fact.'

His face was serious, as was mine. 'As you say,' he rebuked lightly, 'you're a street dog.' His eyes lightened. 'Still, it can hardly hurt to wait, can it?' Then he invited me to dinner.

He collected me in the carriage that had been put at his disposal by the office although I had suggested that, since equipages of such quality were rare in Plymouth Street, we should meet at the restaurant. Then he insisted on climbing the stairs to be introduced to my parents and Aunt Abigail with whom, he said, since he had heard so much about them, he already felt well acquainted.

I had hoped we would not be dining anywhere too grand because I had only one evening frock and that was pretty old. He had foreseen my concern. We went to the Café Savarin, which was amusing but not in the class of Sherrys or the Waldorf.

On the third night we dined together, we went to the big restaurant of the Grand Hotel on Broadway and 31st Street, where there was a pleasant string orchestra, and he asked me to marry him, using tactics that . . . well, in anyone else he would have condemned them as 'sneaky'. He loved Cherrystone clams, which you could not get in England, and he had just finished his last with obvious satisfaction. He lifted his glass and sipped the cold Mountain Chablis studying me intently. He gave a little weary sigh, and said: 'I ought to tell you more about my battle with my cousin Howard.' I suppose I should have realized then what he was about to say, that he was describing problems I would have to share, but it did not occur to me. We had known each other only two weeks. The Man from Mars would soon go home – and I would have had my chance to show what I could do.

So when he spoke about his cousin, I thought he was just rambling on idly about his life, as we did so often. 'The roots are deep,' he went on. 'Uncle and my father were always opposed, too. Uncle, you see, was always traditional, concerned with prestige loans to governments or the biggest corporations – never speculation. But Father was fascinated by the flood of invention that was changing the world out of all recognition. He believed that banks should finance and even invest in it, both as a duty and for gain. The risk was huge but, if it succeeded, so were the profits.'

He was playing with a salt cellar as he talked, turning it with his fingers. 'The crisis came with oil. We were still just traders then, and we were shipping oil in barrels from Baku on the Black Sea. Father guessed that the real scope lay with tankers, which were then just converted merchant ships, so liable to explode that they were banned from many ports and canals, including Suez, which was the new short route to the east.

'One day, he said to my grandfather, old George Alexander: "Why don't we have a tanker specially designed to carry oil – one that Lloyds'll insure, that meets all the Suez safety standards?" Uncle was horrified at the gigantic risk, but the old man fancied it and Father won the day. Before the first keel was laid, we'd plunged for a fleet. We caught Standard, the Goliath of world oil, napping, – and for two glorious years only Alexander tankers could pass through the Canal, while Standard's ships had to go all the way round the Cape. By then the family was already quite rich, but oil took us into a different class.'

A smile, marked a little by sadness, came to his face. 'So you see, we've long been divided. Howard's cast in *his* father's mould – a sound conventional banker. I'm like mine, I suppose. What oil was to him, motor cars are to me. I'm going to make Alexanders the biggest producers of automobiles in the world.'

I was amazed. 'Surely your uncle'd never agree to that.'

'He wasn't keen,' he said with a grin, 'but it's a family business ... not even a partnership like most merchant banks lent a company with shares owned by the family trust ... So for all his power, he's got moral obligations ... And this didn't demand much of him after all ... He saw motors as a sport, a passing fad, so he humoured me – agreed to our buying a major stake in a small company. Howard knew better, of course, and fought it as hard as Uncle himself'd fought against oil, but he was overruled. "Don't be a spoilsport," Uncle chided. "We must let Richard have his little toy."

'It's a bicycle firm called Masons that's branched out into

41

motors. Mason himself's as mad about them as I am, but it's taken time to get going. We've done it, though – got a machine that's revolutionary. We've called it The Leopard and it's racing for the first time in a couple of weeks – Paris to Biarritz . . . If she wins that, there'll be no stopping us.'

I enjoyed hearing him talk like this, with his eyes alight. I had, of course, been in love with him from the morning we met but that moment, as he spoke of his motorcar, was the first time I had faced it without reservation. Our ideas were so completely in harmony. His vision, enthusiasm and, at times, his sheer, cool daring had totally captured me.

He gestured to the waiter, who refilled our glasses, and started for the first time to speak of his racehorses that I did not even know he owned. There had been so much ground for us to cover. 'Did you realize,' he said, 'that all thoroughbreds in both Europe and America stem from three Arab stallions imported into Britain in the seventeenth century? But the Arab blood's been weakened in the breeding, so I'm experimenting with a new infusion. Last year, I bought a stallion from the Bedouin in the desert. He's white – the most beautiful animal you've ever seen. To ride him is a new experience. You must ride him, Miss Brown. You do ride, don't you?'

'You're thinking of bringing him to America, then?'

'No,' he answered, 'I'm planning to take you to England . . . ' I had stepped right into the hole. He paused, watching me, the glimmer of a smile on his face. 'That is if you'll do me the honour of becoming Mrs Alexander.'

It was my turn then and even now, years later, I still smile as I recall his look of shocked surprise. For I turned him down flat.

The colour came to his cheeks. 'I'm sorry,' he apologized. 'I've misunderstood. Taken too much for granted . . . you must think me very conceited.'

'You misunderstand nothing,' I said. 'I've loved you from the instant I saw you peering at me over the Wall Street Journal.'

He hesitated, perplexed but controlled. 'Then I'm baffled,' he said.

'It's simple enough,' I explained. 'I don't want marriage. I'll come to England with you, because I'd find our parting very hard, but not as your wife.'

'You mean . . . ?' he began in disbelief. 'Surely you don't mean . . . ' He broke off again, perplexed. 'But why, Quincey?' he asked. His proposal, it seemed, had put us on first-name terms.

'Think what marriage'd demand,' I answered. 'You'd expect me to entertain your rich friends, gossip with their wives, drive in the park, give balls, spend hours at the dressmaker's, attend the events of the Season . . . Just like wealthy wives do here in New York, only it'll be more so in London because you've got a king and queen at the top of it all. No, Richard, not for me.'

He looked at me, puzzled. 'Don't you want children?' he asked.

'In time, when I've achieved something.'

He shook his head in disbelief. 'Quincey,' he said, 'I'm thirty-seven and you're the first woman I've ever proposed to. You've become completely vital to me. Change your mind, please.'

'Don't press me, Richard,' I pleaded softly. Oh Lord, it was tempting. To have a man speak words like that when you've been aching for him to touch you, when you've been so obsessed by thoughts of him at night that you could not get to sleep. I knew I had to cling to my resolve, or everything I had worked so long for would be lost. 'No, Richard,' I insisted firmly, 'No . . . . What's happened between us is quite magical. Don't let's spoil it, please.'

'Spoil it?' he echoed. 'I'm offering you my life.'

'And I'm offering you mine,' I retorted, 'but if I marry you, I'll be forced into a mould, and I'm not ready for that mould.'

'You're teasing me, aren't you?' he said anxiously. I had never seen him so serious. But there was no teasing in my eyes. 'It's quite impractical,' he went on. 'We won't be living in the artistic circles of Paris; I'm a banker from the most conservative place on earth. The old 'City' of London – they call it the Square Mile – it's a state within a state, enclosed and feudal. Even the King asks permission of the Lord Mayor before passing Temple Bar. You'd lose your reputation and gain nothing in return.'

'There must be a way,' I insisted. 'Goodness, I'm not the only woman there's ever been who's rejected a domestic life and loved a man as well. Great Saints, Richard, I adore you but I must have an identity . . . '

'An identity?' he repeated. 'I'm not going to lock you in a tower.

You'll have an identity. Why, as Mrs Alexander you'll . . .'

'I don't want to be Mrs Alexander,' I cut in. 'I want to build bridges and mine for copper and,' I added softly, 'love you as well.'

He shook his head. 'This is an absurd argument . . . You *must* marry me.'

'No.' I snapped, a note of panic in my voice. 'Thank you. I'm much flattered, but quite definitely no.'

He glared at me in frustration. 'Is that decision,' he asked tautly, 'in any way negotiable?'

'Yes,' I answered.

He heaved a visible weary sigh. 'And what terms would you consider?'

'Just one — a full-time position in the bank in London, at Manager level. I'd have a chance then.'

He signed as though I was a stubborn child. 'You're impossible,' he said. 'Uncle'd never agree to it for one moment. Even after he's dead *I* won't be able to. We're up against customs that are centuries old.'

Suddenly, I was furious with him. It was not his fault, but he was there across the table, representing all I was against. 'Then that's that, isn't it?' I said.

'No,' he answered calmly, 'That's not that. Quincey, what's happened to you? When you're dealing on the market you're as cunning as the street dog you often speak of, yet the moment I mention marriage you're charging at the fortress walls with all the subtlety of Don Quixote. Why?'

'Because I'm scared,' I snapped.

'What are you scared of?' he asked. 'As my wife, you can build bridges if only you deploy a little tact. How many bridges do you think you'll build on your own?' He reached across the table and took my hand in his. 'Look, in London you can live what life you like. There'll be duties sometimes, but you don't have to drive in the park or gossip or give balls. You can share much of my own work. You can advise me, just as you have done here. You can help me run the motor business. In time, perhaps, we can chip away at the bigger barriers, but just for the present . . . ' He paused. ' . . . Well, that's all I can offer, I'm afraid. You've got me up to my highest price.'

I had been watching him with mixed emotions, fascinated by the different expressions that ranged across his face, so moved suddenly that it was all I could do to stop myself throwing my arms round his neck.

'You're a most generous man,' I said quietly, 'but . . . ' But I still feared a trap.

He saw my doubts. 'Don't you see, Quincey,' he urged, 'we'd be a team — perhaps like Pierre and Marie Curie in medicine. Together, we can achieve so much. Please join the team.'

Suddenly I wanted to cry, but I fought the tears. 'You truly mean that?' I asked, suspicion still lingering in me.

'I truly mean it.' He spoke in the tone of a witness on oath.

'Would you be prepared to write it down?'

He shrugged with a smile 'If you wish.'

'And sign it?' He nodded.

'And write down those other things you said, about advising you and helping you with the motor company . . . and not driving in the park?'

'Every single point.' He was watching me, amused.

'All right, Richard Alexander,' I said. 'On those terms I'll marry you. Now please ask the waiter to bring a sheet of paper.' Which he did, at the same time ordering a bottle of champagne. Solemnly, he wrote out the list and signed it. I recorded my agreement to be his wife and signed that, too. Then we drank to our life together.

In the carriage on our way home, he kissed me for the first time. And as I clung to him, the need for him — which I had held in check so desperately during our negotiations over dinner — surged in me with such force that there was a singing in my head and I thought I was going to faint. I did not care. I wanted to faint.

After he had left me in Plymouth Street I stood for what must have been ten minutes before the door to our apartment, pondering the events of that dramatic evening. I suppose I was in a state of mild shock — confused, slightly breathless, dazed, suddenly exhausted, unsure exactly of what was real. For a few seconds, I questioned whether the power I had sought for so long — the building of the bridges, of the ships — was as important as I had believed. I felt a certain shame at the thought, as though there was within it a betrayal of some kind. I stood up straighter — literally.

Had Richard's kissing, overwhelming though I had found it, affected my resolve? Why should it? There was no conflict, for he had generously agreed to the type of marriage, the shared life, that I had sought.

All the same I was perplexed, alarmed by the strength of my response to him. For it had revealed a depth of emotion in me that I had never glimpsed before. It had brought home to me with a new poignancy that, contract or no contract, I would do anything for him – possibly, under conditions of extremity, even die. And that scared me.

Three days later, I walked into his office and said: 'We've got that 7 percent we need in United Mining.'

He looked up, surprised. 'Quicker than we expected?'

'Sudden sale . . . I was warned early, so I don't think the other side'll have noticed.'

'Then I take it, Miss Brown,' he said formally, 'that now there's no objection to our opening dealings with Blackwell Jones and Higgins & Smith?'

I shook my head with a grin. 'The time'd seem appropriate, Mr Alexander.'

'Then perhaps you'd draft a telegram to Caesar,' he instructed.

I moved to leave the room, but at the door I turned back to him. 'I hope it's not untoward of me, Mr Alexander, but I do have a small favour to ask.' He looked at me with a smile of query. 'Would you please, please kiss me,' I said, 'before I take utter leave of my senses.' And, locking the door, I ran to him and knew again that singing in my head.

'You're like a drug,' I said. 'Did you know that? You just have to touch me and I go on to a different plane.'

'It's an addiction we share,' he countered softly.

'I'm worried,' I said. 'I think I'm an immoral woman. Should you marry an immoral woman?'

'I'm absolutely positive,' he said, holding my face in both hands and kissing me gently to start with until the passion gripped him and his mouth was on my neck, my eyes, my ears. Then he moved me away from him, holding me by the shoulders, out of breath. 'I thought, Miss Brown,' he said with a smile, 'you were supposed to be drafting a telegram to London.'

'Forgive me, Mr Alexander,' I answered. 'Just for a moment, it quite slipped my mind.'

The following week, he was recalled to London. When I took the wire to him, he was reading a letter from his young cousin James. He glanced at the telegram. 'We'll be home just too late to attend the Paris-to-Biarritz. We'll be at sea, not even in touch by wire . . . Still, James writes that The Leopard's done better in the latest test runs than Mason hoped. He's even more confident we're going to win. It's all a big secret, you realize. Mason's kept her out of the public trials and hill-climbs, which is how new cars usually show their paces. That way, he reckons, the impact of her success'll be much bigger. I think you'll like Mason.'

Deliberately, Richard had delayed his telegram to London about our marriage until the day before we sailed – which, in fact, was the eve of the wedding. By then, it was after midnight in London. He knew that his uncle would be violently opposed to the very idea of me as his bride – a member of their own staff, an American, what is more, with a background as limited as mine? Why, he would think Richard had gone out of his mind.

'Should you not go home and prepare him first?' I asked.

He smiled lazily and slowly shook his head. 'When he meets you,' he answered, 'You'll be Mrs Alexander, and no amount of talk will alter that.'

For a moment, I was silent. 'He'll hardly receive me with open arms, will he?' I remarked – which I had always known, of course, but only then squarely faced.

'He may need a bit of time to get used to the idea,' he conceded.

'Won't it give Howard material that he can exploit to damage you?' Oddly, I had not considered before that I might be an adverse factor in his feud with his cousin.

'Possibly,' he agreed.

'Then won't that negate the United Mining coup? You wanted that for the impact it'd make, didn't you?'

'It was a tactical moment to wag my tail,' he confirmed. 'Give those old men in the Square Mile something to talk about over lunch.'

'Then surely you shouldn't have been swept off your feet by a hussy in the office? They'll talk about that, too, won't they – even snigger about it?'

He laughed. 'You're no hussy. What's more, I'm positive that Uncle will approve my choice – as the others will. Know why I'm positive? Because you'll convince him. Because if there's one man in London who can help you advance those grand plans of yours, it's Uncle.' He paused. 'While he's there.'

'While he's there,' I repeated, feeling suddenly sad. For though I had never met him, he had long been a part of my life – like a kind of angry god.

'You'll win Uncle,' he said.

Chapter 2

It is hard for me to describe those few days as we crossed the Atlantic. I do not think I have ever known such sheer conscious happiness, such lightness of spirit. The weather was gloriously fine throughout the journey except for the last few hours, which was as it should be, for we needed them to prepare ourselves for our ordeal.

We behaved like children — my respectable banker husband, with all the maturity of his thirty-seven years and even I who, at twenty-three, was not exactly in the first flush of youth. We laughed at the silliest of jokes; we played juvenile tricks on each other; we found excitement just striding up the deck with the wind in our faces. Sometimes, to the astonishment of our fellow-passengers, we even ran — races, I mean, like who would be the first to reach the end lifeboat. Once he chased me all the way to our state-room, almost knocking over the purser and colliding with a steward who was carrying a tray, piled high with food, which he dropped with the most enormous crash. Richard, slamming the door of our cabin behind him, did not even stop to apologise. 'Now be careful,' I said, 'or you'll tear my blouse.' But he was not careful, and he did. 'I'll buy you a hundred blouses,' he declared.

Much later, I was to wonder that my searing experience with Mr Johnson did not cast a dark shadow over this aspect of my life with Richard. But that terrible afternoon was locked away in my mind. It never occurred to me to link it to the sublime enjoyment I knew with my husband. Laura had said she hated this part of marriage, but I wondered if she was just voicing the ruling view of the wife's burden or whether she truly did find it so distasteful, as I had heard other wives complain. 'Do you think there's something wrong with me?' I said to Richard at one point. 'I want to do this all day . . .'

'It's very simple,' he whispered. 'God made you for love.'

'He made me for love with you, then,' I answered softly in his ear, then asked: 'Why are we whispering? No one can hear. I want to shout for sheer joy.' And shout I did, though Richard called it

49

screaming and nearly stifled me with his lips, for fear that this, at least, would penetrate beyond our cabin walls.

'We were whispering,' he said, when he could speak, 'because we seemed, for a few swift fleeting minutes, to be beyond mortality. We were whispering from awe – perhaps as we might if we were looking at the most magnificent painting that had ever been created. Leonardo, perhaps . . . '

I was most lucky with my lover, as perhaps Laura was unlucky with hers, but everything has its price, even gifts from heaven; and the flame that Richard ignited, the potential for passion he revealed in me, was to have another aspect – like the dark side of the moon.

Strangely, no one seemed to object to our behaviour, selfish and indulgent as it was. Even the elderly passengers would grace us with friendly smiles as if we were both eighteen though even that age would have demanded more decorum. Perhaps, though, we were not so obtrusive as in retrospect it seemed. Certainly, the purser readily forgave Richard. The steward appeared delighted with his reward for the mishap with the tray.

This tolerance spoiled us a little – the fact, as Richard said, that mankind really did seem to love a lover. We began to think we were blessed by some special ordinance.

I recall, at one heady moment of elation, flouncing up to the Captain, who from the start had treated us as important passengers, since Alexanders were bankers to Cunard, and Richard's uncle was on the company board. 'Captain,' I said, 'would you please do me the greatest favour?'

His bearded face creased into a broad and willing smile. 'Anything in my power, Mrs Alexander,' he asserted.

'Reduce your speed . . . Make the journey last a little longer.'

He laughed, his eyes shining. 'We're not halfway yet, Mrs Alexander,' he said. 'Come with me and I'll prove it to you.'

With a wink at Richard, he had taken me to the chartroom behind the bridge. 'There,' he said, pointing to our course across the Atlantic, depicted on the parchment map. 'That's where we are now . . . it's a long way from land.' And I looked at the land he was speaking of – Cape Clear, on the South Western tip of Ireland. 'Shall we be able to see it?' I asked.

He nodded. 'The Fastnet Rock is the first lighthouse.' He pointed

50

to it on the chart, just south of Cape Clear. 'Then Old Head of Kinsale . . . and Roche . . . and Ballycotton . . . and Connigbeg . . . and Tuskar . . . '

I felt a shiver as his finger indicated each in turn. 'They sound like a Celtic lament, don't they?' I said. My attention focused on Tuskar. 'That's the closest point to Wales, I see. It's like a gateway, isn't it?'

'That's right,' he agreed. 'Tuskar Island . . . No question about it. Then you'll be within British shores.'

I did not meet Millicent Russell, who was to make such an impact on my life, until we had been at sea for three days – which, even though she was travelling with her uncle, whom Richard knew well, was not so surprising, considering there were 526 first-class passengers on the *Lucania*.

Stewart Russell was a prominent London broker, associated with a New York firm that had been opposing us. He was a portly man of about fifty, with a superior but not unfriendly manner. 'Going home already, Alexander,' he inquired as we encountered the couple on the promenade deck, 'while the troops are still engaged?' He did not know, of course, that by now we would have control of United Mining.

'Ordered from the field,' Richard answered easily, 'by the Commander-in-Chief.'

'And here, I presume,' Russell said, beaming at me, 'is the new Mrs Alexander. My heartiest congratulations. May I introduce my niece, Miss Millicent Russell.' She was blonde, about twenty-five, wearing a blue and white striped linen dress. She surveyed me boldly with brown eyes that were bright but mocking. 'Of *course*,' she exclaimed. 'This is the lady you were telling me about, Uncle . . . Wall Street's agog, I gather,' she added to me. 'There you were, typewriting away in the bank, when in walked the Prince himself, tarara! Even touched the hearts of those hard men of money . . . '

I stared at her coolly. 'You're not a romantic, I gather, Miss Russell,' I remarked. 'I trust you've not been crossed in love.'

She giggled. 'Romantic? No, I'm a realist, aren't I, Uncle?'

'Embarrassingly so,' he said with a shudder – though clearly he was fond of her – adding gloomily: 'A doctor, a socialist . . . Ever met a woman doctor, Alexander? Or a socialist? And then there's something in the slums I try never to think about.'

'Oh, you do talk nonsense, Uncle,' she rebuked. 'He's speaking of my clinic,' she explained to me. 'I give advice on motherhood – and how to avoid it. It shocks some people, but, as I keep telling my uncle, these huge starving families just don't make economic sense, quite apart from the human suffering they cause, though I know that's not important. Shouldn't worry my pretty little head about that, should I, Uncle?'

'I'm not going to be needled, Millie,' he said. 'Some brisk walking in the sea breeze is what you need. Why can't you be a nice young lady, as Mrs Alexander so obviously is?' He tipped his hat to me as he made to move away. But she held on to his arm, looking at me shrewdly. 'I'm not positive she's so nice,' she said – then winked.

That evening, I found myself sitting next to her at dinner. The tables stretched the length of the *Lucania*'s luxurious saloon, and we sat on little wooden armchairs on pedestals fixed to the deck. 'What are you doing travelling first-class?' I inquired mischievously, 'as a socialist?'

She smiled. 'I had to go to New York for my work. Only way I could get there. My uncle always travels first-class; he'll go to hell first-class . . . ' She glanced at me: 'Aren't you throwing stones from a glass-house? Marrying a rich banker . . . you should be ashamed – and frightened, too.'

'Why frightened?'

'We'll be hanging you at Tyburn, come the revolution. Wives of rich bankers'll be the first to go.'

'Are you safe yourself, as a niece of a rich stockbroker?'

'I'll be holding the rope. Anyway, I'm not rich, though my uncle is.'

Our dialogue was tart, but touched with fun. I liked the sharpness of her. 'Why are you so against bankers?' I asked.

'Parasites. Leeches living off the talents and efforts of other men, and growing fat on it.'

'Whoops!' I responded. 'You don't hold back with the whip, do you? What'd we do without them? Traders couldn't operate. Governments'd be starved of funds. Great ventures could never get started.'

'Oh dear,' she said, 'I knew you were a romantic, but about

52

bankers? Oh, I see now, the penny's dropped . . . The pioneers of progress, that's it? Rubbish, Mrs Alexander. Profit is the only God, the one cause. If you talk with eloquence of any great venture – the railways, for example, that could hardly help but benefit the world – then I'll speak of the web of crooked operations that'll entwine it.'

'Crooked?'

'Not legally crooked, perhaps. Doesn't have to be when the power's there, when the deals can be made to corner markets, to create cartels and monopolies so there's no competition, to raid stocks in public corporations so that the prices are artificial – and all with one result: the fleecing of the people.'

I was silent for a moment. There was much truth in what she said. The Niagara plant was a brilliant enterprise, but behind it lay the marketplace where men like Papa's patron, Thomas Ryan, could make thousands by devious means in the course of one afternoon. It was the two sides of the coin. 'Where would the service come from if there were no merchant bankers?' I asked.

'From the state, of course, for the benefit of the people. We'll seize their wealth, destroy the markets . . . '

'Do you really think the system'd work without incentive?'

'Without greed,' she corrected.

'That's a rude name for the same thing,' I countered. 'All the world's major trading empires, its marvels of engineering, have been built on incentive – and duty.'

'Duty?' she mocked. She eyed me shrewdly for a moment. 'You know, I detect a difference. You're not just a girl who's landed a rich husband, as I thought. You're going to go out there and have a try, aren't you? You're going to use Alexander money for achievement if they'll let you, like Cecil Rhodes in Africa. A woman pioneer – am I right?'

'You make it sound naïve,' I said.

'It is, but commendable. Lofty ideas of vision are always commendable, but the process will warp you, like it warped Cecil Rhodes, and then you'll become like the others – and humanity'll go on suffering . . . ' A sudden friendly smile came to her face. 'Still, I wish you luck. Don't delay, though. There's not much time left.'

There was another meeting on the voyage that in time was to be of note. One morning I was on my way alone to join Richard on the boat deck, passing by the second-class section of the ship, when I was greeted by an old man with a face that was deeply furrowed beneath a ragged grey beard.

'You're Mrs Alexander ain't you?' he said, speaking with an accent that was an odd mixture of Irish and cockney. 'Mr O'Sullivan Smith, that's me. I may well call on that husband of yours,' he continued. 'I come from Paulina, Oklahoma, and I know there's oil there. They tell me there's not. They say there's never oil in marshy land, but I know there is. You Alexanders'd do well to have an oil-field. You've got plenty of tankers, but you ain't got much oil. You need oil.'

'Well,' I responded with surprise, 'thank you, Mr Smith.'

'O'Sullivan Smith.'

'I'll tell my husband what you say . . . '

When I joined Richard, I told him of my encounter. He laughed. 'There are a lot of them about, these old men who can 'smell' oil. Like the ones who can 'smell' gold. But he's right – supply is our weak point.'

By the morning we awoke to find Ireland in sight, the weather had changed. It rained until after tea, when I suggested we should go on deck. I put on the blue serge bolero jacket and skirt that I had bought specially for cooler days on the trip, and pinned a straw hat to my hair, securing it with a chiffon scarf.

I saw the flash from Tuskar a few minutes after five, and knew that at last we were in hostile waters. The thought induced in me a surge of excitement – the kind of excitement, touched with apprehension, that a fighter must feel as he steps into the ring. We were standing at the forward end of the boat deck, bracing our bodies against the wind which was chill even then in June.

I found myself waiting, almost mesmerized, for the flash from Tuskar to come again; felt the subtle change in the direction of the breeze as the ship altered course, edging a few points north towards the Irish Sea. I turned and stared at the opposite horizon that concealed the coast of Pembrokeshire – a faint line, dividing the grey white-tipped ocean from the clouded sky, unbroken except for a sole vessel.

The sea was getting rougher, short from the northwest, as we had been told by a passing officer. Sometimes the waves washed over the bows, sending up clouds of spray and foaming round the capstan and the anchor cable on the foredeck as it drained away.

We had not said much to each other, the bubbling high spirits of the earlier days of the voyage having lessened as we approached the shores of Britain.

'You've got that determined expression on your face,' Richard commented at one moment.

'We're embarked on serious business,' I answered.

'The journey isn't over yet,' he said. 'We've still got a day before we even get to Liverpool.'

But he was wrong, as he discovered almost at once. He bent towards me, intending to kiss me on the cheek, but it was then, over my shoulder, that he saw the vessel that had previously been too far off to recognize. I felt his whole body tauten, heard the muted clang of the engine telegraphs before the *Lucania* lost speed. I turned round slowly and saw the big black steam yacht still two or three miles off, ploughing through the sea towards us.

The purser hurried up, a broad smile on his face, expecting his news to be welcome. 'Mr and Mrs Alexander,' he declared. 'They're sending a launch from the yacht. We'll be heaving to soon.'

As the purser left us, striding off importantly, there was the first real silence there had ever been between us.

'Your uncle can stop an ocean liner?' I asked in surprise, my eyes fixed on the yacht, still travelling at speed, thrusting its bows through white sea, smoke gushing from the funnels. 'So he really *is* a Caesar' I said, and suddenly I was filled with a surging fury.

Then I looked at Richard and saw he was as angry as I was. I leaned forward and kissed him. 'We'd better get below,' I said, 'or we'll keep them waiting.'

Chapter 3

[1]

'That's my cousin Howard,' Richard said as the launch wallowed through the choppy sea towards the yacht. 'There at the head of the gangway . . .'

He was a tall, broad-shouldered man, wearing a peaked naval cap and a dark double-breasted jacket. He stood without movement, like a sentinel, while sailors moved around him, attending to their duties.

I was willing him to wave to us, or at least to make some kind of gesture of acknowledgement, but he just continued to watch us, standing quite still. Even as I clambered up the gangway steps his face was devoid of expression as he looked down from the rails above.

However, when I reached the deck he greeted me with formal courtesy, welcoming me aboard the yacht, though still he did not smile. He was a black-haired man in his late thirties, with a saturnine appearance made more sombre by thick straight eyebrows.

His greeting of Richard was hardly warm, but there was no sign of the hostility between them. He shook hands with him and said he hoped we had enjoyed the crossing. 'As you'll have expected,' he said, 'the family were surprised – and disturbed, of course. You'll grant it was unusual.' His serious eyes rested on me for a moment in appraisal. 'My father thought you'd like a little time in your cabin before being exposed to us all,' he said to me, 'so I'll conduct you there, if I may. We'll be meeting in the drawing-room at seven. You'll find a maid waiting to attend you.' He turned back to Richard. 'My father would like to see you alone at once . . .' he said.

The yacht was my first real exposure to the Alexander wealth. In New York I had seen the impact of their money and resources, but the family owned no mansions there, displayed no panoply of personal possession.

At 1,600 tons, however, the SS *Kilena* was one of the largest and

56

most luxurious private yachts to leave a British shipyard. She had walls panelled in walnut and satinwood, ceilings corniced with exquisite patterns of seashells, bathrooms of black marble with running hot and cold water that issued from gold taps in the form of dolphins, furniture fashioned after the style of Louis XVI. There was a crew of more than a hundred and thick-carpeted state suites that made the first-class cabins on the *Lucania* seem like steerage.

Even after Maisie, the young maid who had been allocated to me, had helped me out of my outer garments – which was a new experience in itself – I just stood shoeless in my chemise and petticoats, turning round slowly in wonder as I tried to absorb the magnificence of my surroundings.

'Almost as vulgar as you'd expect, isn't it?' remarked a young man as he stepped out of the wardrobe. 'As you'd expect, I mean, from the *nouveaux riches* – but it has a certain style, I think, don't you?'

For a second, I was so astonished by this intrusion that I could say nothing. Instinctively I clutched my arms across my breasts – though the chemise was hardly immodest – at which moment Maisie entered from our bathroom. 'Mr Stratton,' she exclaimed in horror, 'what on earth are you thinking of!'

'Oh, do shut up, Maisie,' he said. 'Just put something round Mrs Alexander, and then disappear. I want to speak to her alone.'

He looked away tactfully as she hurriedly draped a peignoir round me, and then turned back to me. He was in his early twenties, with long fine fair hair that tended to escape across his forehead and a friendly, impudent smile.

'Do you often hide in ladies' cupboards?' I inquired, a little acidly.

'Good Lord, no,' he said with a grin. 'I do apologize . . . but it was the only way I could get to meet you before the others. The orders from on high, you see, are to receive you in the drawing-room *en famille* – or *en phalanx*, I should say. I wanted to have a first . . . ' He broke off, surveying me openly.

'A quick peek?' I suggested coldly. 'A private view?'

He nodded, still appearing to be assessing me. 'Nice,' he said, 'quick, too, and not far off-target . . . I must say,' he went on approvingly, 'I can well see why you captured him.'

'I didn't capture him!' I retorted sharply.

'That's it!' he exclaimed with delight, slapping his knee as he sat down on the bed. 'Marvellous! Bit of that and you'll have the old man down in no time . . . I meant, of course, Mrs Alexander, that I could see why Richard had captured *you* – and a lucky fellow he obviously is.'

I had recovered something of my poise by now. 'Would you think it astonishing,' I said, 'if I were to ask . . . .well, who in the world you are?'

'I'm Richard's cousin, James Stratton – the black sheep of the family – or, rather, the son of the black ewe. My mother eloped with a horse-dealer and my grandfather cut her off without a penny, which I can't help feeling was a bit of a pity. Perhaps Richard mentioned me in passing.'

'He's talked of you a lot,' I said.

'We're great friends as well as cousins. The news about you has sent the whole family sprawling, of course, which is why I thought I'd canter up and offer a bit of guidance. You see, I know my uncle very well. I've studied him . . . been forced to . . . My cousins have rights under the family trust, but I've had to get by on my wits, so you might find me useful. For example, this restriction to your cabin until dinner . . . '

'Restriction?' I repeated. 'I didn't realize I was under lock and key.'

'Well, not exactly,' he said. 'But look at the trouble I've had just for a quick word. Uncle, you see, has a sense of occasion. He wants to think of your preparing yourself – bathing, arranging your hair, putting on a fine gown as though for a ritual . . . Another thing – the old man can fool you. Suddenly, he starts being very very friendly, then, with a flick of the wrist, he's in there with his rapier under your guard. So we'll have a signal, you and I. If you see me put my hand idly to my ear like this . . . ' he touched his lobe . . . 'then it means you're relaxing too much. Don't be alarmed. He'll like you, but he expects to be consulted before major events like marriages, and he'll demand some penance.'

'You make it hard to believe he's not well . . . his telegrams did, too.'

'Oh, he's with us still, no doubt about that. An old campaigner,

58

tough as rawhide, but it's bound to come soon. When he goes, I doubt he'll linger: it'll be like that!' He flicked his fingers. 'Of course, it's intensified things between Howard and Richard – the battle for the throne . . . With equal shareholdings, it'll all depend on status, on the Board of Directors. They'll be influenced by various things, not least by what the old patriarchs of the City think of it all. Richard's ahead, of course, but Howard's putting in a fast run, and he's not too bothered by the rules of racing. You've met him, of course.'

'He received us as we arrived on board. He was very polite.'

James burst out laughing. 'Oh, he's polite. Gentlemen are always polite, and a gentleman's what he'd like to be . . . More – a statesman. He has a vision, which is to make Alexanders rank with the Rothschilds instead of being about twenty-eighth down the line . . . '

'Twenty-eighth?' I echoed, astonished.

'Rich but not yet accepted. The irony is that it's Richard who's the statesman. Always been the same. At Eton Richard was captain of cricket, stroked the first eight, classical scholar, head of school – all without seeming to try. Everyone liked him. Have you seen him on a horse?'

'Not yet, though I've heard much about his stallion.'

'He's poetry . . . becames part of the animal. See Howard on a horse and he's like a sack of coal . . . symbolic. The same at school. No good at games, not much regarded, ragged about the Alexander money by the sons of aristocrats . . . They pointed at Uncle's sumptuous carriage, with its elegant four-in-hand, and mocked that he was *arriviste*, a 'Johnny-come-lately'. Typical, they sneered . . . ostentatious . . . vulgar . . . No one ever called Richard vulgar, though it was the same money. Worst of all, even Uncle's admired him from an early age. Beginning to understand now?'

'You mean Howard's jealous?'

'Oh, more than that. He needed a base to face a world that was not exactly welcoming, and he found it in the bank. It was there that he gained his confidence, his purpose. It became a natural home. He worked day and night to master its operations, to excel at the skills that were needed, to learn every nuance of an arena where the gladiators were giants. If there's one thing that Howard understands it's power, and if there's one thing he'd sacrifice his life for, it's to take his father's place at the head of Alexanders. Add those together and you've got a deadly ruthless animal . . . Why, Richard, my dear fellow!'

He leapt from the bed to greet his cousin as he came into the cabin from his audience with his uncle. 'What's the sentence? A flogging round the fleet? A keelhauling? Worth every agonized scream, I can see, now I've met her . . .'

Richard gave his cousin a friendly punch. 'Just as awful as ever, I see.'

'I've fallen madly for your wife. What should I do? Shoot myself or jump overboard?'

'Neither. I need you. So does she. Now,' he said with eager impatience, 'how did The Leopard fare in the Paris–Biarritz?'

For a second there was anxiety on James's face. 'Sorry, Dickie. She went lame and had to be pulled up – clutch trouble, but the car was running a close second for a good hundred miles. Behind a Benz, too. About to overtake when it happened . . . Rotten shame, eh?'

'What a disappointment!' said Richard. 'Mason must be terribly upset. Is he still as confident?'

'More so. He just can't wait till next time.'

'Mason's a good man. What about United Mining? Have we got Blackwells and Higgins holdings?'

James shook his head. 'Uncle was away, and Howard delayed. Right people weren't in London, he said. Climate was wrong . . . Now both are being difficult. Got wind, possibly, of our intentions, though I can only hazard a guess as to how.'

Richard wandered to a porthole and glared at the sea, hands deep in his pockets. 'You mean he sabotaged it?' he said.

'The race is getting hotter,' James admitted.

'But surely,' I put in, 'he wouldn't act against the Alexander interests?'

James shrugged. 'We've still got big holdings in United and Associated – plenty of influence – Howard weighed it up. Perhaps he could exploit it later himself. Either way, he'd strip the credit from Richard at this critical time. No long-term damage . . .'

Richard turned suddenly. 'It's disgraceful – even for Howard.'

'It's not all, Dickie. Firstly, I don't think The Leopard failed by chance.'

'Good God! What are you suggesting? That he paid someone to tamper with the clutch?'

'I don't know, but Mathew went to Paris for the start of the race, which suggests a surprising interest in the motor business.' Mathew, I knew, was Howard's younger brother. 'Also, I saw him at lunch the other day in the White Swan in Cannon Street with that director of Panhard you had some dealings with.'

'Monsieur Lanardine . . . Surely you're not saying Panhard nobbled the car, for heaven's sake?'

'I don't know, Dickie . . . All I know is that she *was* nobbled. At least, I'm pretty sure she was. And now they're selling the motor company to Panhard.'

'They're *what*?' Richard exclaimed in angry astonishment. 'They can't!'

'They *are* . . . When your wire came in about your marriage Uncle was like a wild bull for a few hours. Aunt Elizabeth was petrified it'd bring on the fatal stroke. Then The Leopard failed and Howard grabbed his chance. By noon, Mathew was on his way back to Paris to negotiate a sale with Panhard.'

For a few seconds Richard stood in the middle of the cabin, body taut, fists clenched. Then he strode out through the doorway.

James and I were silent. 'He shouldn't have gone to America, should he?' I said at last. 'He made the wrong choice.'

He shook his head. 'He didn't. This is just a setback. He'll win the war – especially with you to help.'

'That's kind of you,' I said gratefully, 'but all I can see is damage.'

'Nobody's met you yet. After tonight they'll know you're someone to be reckoned with – especially Uncle.'

'If I survive the ordeal,' I said with a grin.

He winked at me. 'You're a survivor all right. We're both survivors. That's how I know.'

'You're being a tremendous help. Tell me, have they got a good price for Masons from Panhard?'

'What – after The Leopard failed? Heavens no. They're making them a present of it, all wrapped up with ribbons and pretty paper. Still one or two details to be settled, but they're minor.'

61

'You mean,' I said, 'that contracts aren't signed? Is there a chance of saving it, then?'

He shrugged. 'I suppose there's a slim chance. Not that Richard'll be getting far with Uncle at the moment. The old man will smile in his bland way. "We'll review it," he'll say. "The Board'll decide . . . " '

'When?' I asked. 'When'll the Board decide?'

'At the next meeting. That's two weeks Friday.'

[2]

'Well?' I asked, as I stood before my husband in the gown we had chosen together in New York, 'am I suitably attired for the role I have to play?' It had come from Paris – deep blue silk, so that it went with my eyes, as he had urged, cut in the close-fitting Princess line, with a white lace bodice.

He did not speak at once, just stood there in his dinner jacket and studied me with wonder in his eyes. 'You look enchanting,' he said.

He leaned forward and kissed me lightly on the lips. 'Just remember,' he said. 'We're on strong ground. He can't change anything. Now we'd better go.'

As we walked together along the passage, I was nervous, of course. I was about to face a challenge of a stature I had never known before. From the start, I had planned to be bold, but I knew I was not dealing with a simple bully. Caesar was a man of power, tuned to all the tonal variations that went with it. My boldness would have to be displayed with subtlety.

'Remember what I've just said,' Richard reminded me as he gripped the handle of the door to the main saloon. I nodded with a smile – and he opened it.

The drawing-room, as they called it, occupied the whole width of the yacht. In the far wall, overlooking the bows, was a line of windows, and Richard's uncle was seated with his back to these. On either side of him, standing in the form of a wide semi-circle, were the seven members of the Alexander family – as though posed for a photograph. He was an enormous man, his body bulging over the sides of the chair. Aged about seventy he had a large square-shaped head, close-cut grey hair and dark spectacles that were unusual, having large lenses that slanted back from the bridge of his nose.

For a moment I stood in the doorway with Richard, taken aback, despite James's warning, by the sight of the family arrayed, as it were, in formation. Even Richard, though he held my arm, seemed uncertain.

It was his uncle who broke that tense silence, speaking in a deep resonant voice that was strangely soft. 'Mrs Alexander, I presume,' he said. 'The newest Mrs Alexander . . . The youngest Mrs Alexander . . . Certainly the most unexpected Mrs Alexander.' Suddenly he smiled.'You must forgive me if I don't rise to greet you,' he continued, 'but I have some difficulty . . . ' He touched a big stick, hooked beside him to the arm of the chair. 'So perhaps you'd consent to come to me.' And he held out his hand with a movement that was commanding, but not ungracious.

I crossed the silent saloon unhurriedly and stopped before him. 'Welcome, Mrs Alexander,' he growled quietly. 'The unexpected Mrs Alexander . . . but inform me, pray: Why *are* you unex-pected?'

'Uncle . . . ' Richard began beside me, to be checked by an upraised hand. 'I put the question to your wife, Richard.'

I smiled at him. 'We found it unexpected, too,' I said.

'This passion?' he demanded in his muffled tone. 'This passion that swept up like a desert wind and overwhelmed you both . . . ?'

'You put it well, Mr Alexander,' I said. 'You clearly have a gift for words.'

He eyed me carefully, not caring for my response. 'That's cordial,' he said, 'but no answer to my question.'

'Surely, with respect, Mr Alexander,' I countered, 'you've just answered it yourself.'

'Passion?' he said. 'Passion's not a reason for haste, but for delay. Passion blinds, destroys judgement, as it clearly did to you. Why, you'd only met a month before . . . '

'A rare month, Uncle,' Richard interposed, 'as I told you. We worked together much of every day. Quincey's highly skilled. The United Mining deal was *her* idea. It'd have been a great success if it hadn't been mismanaged here. We've no man on our London staff, I can assure you, who's got half her sense of tactics.'

'Tactics?' his uncle inquired, and began to chuckle. 'Tactics,' he repeated, savouring the word. 'Tell me, Mrs Alexander . . . Your parents . . . did they not question so rushed a marriage?'

'They accepted my decision,' I answered. 'I'm twenty-three, after all . . . ' As an answer, it was banal.

He nodded. 'So they considered that infatuation was a sound basis for a lifetime as man and wife?'

'It was not infatuation, Mr Alexander.'

'This gift of the angels, then,' he mocked in his low voice. 'This visitation from heaven . . . This satisfied them? Or did they think it time you were a wife, no matter how fast the courtship? Or did they think . . . ' he was purring now. 'Did they think that Richard was a CATCH?' The word was rapped out suddenly but not loudly, the consonants emphasized.

'Uncle!' Richard broke in. 'That's a scandalous thing to say!'

'I wish you'd stop interrupting, Richard,' his uncle rebuked sharply. I sensed the energy within him as he watched me through his dark glasses. After two strokes? But I had guessed his purpose now – and I knew how to block it. This was a time for tactics if ever there was one; for feinting as a fighter did, for leading him stumbling on to even greater rudeness. '*Well*, Mrs Alexander?' he demanded.

'My parents liked Richard very much,' I ventured uncertainly.

'Well, he *is* likeable, isn't he?' His voice was touched with sarcasm. 'But would they have found him quite so likeable if he'd been a clerk in our office earning fifteen dollars a week?'

I knew then that I had him trapped, for all his power. I allowed a big wide-eyed smile to spread slowly across my face. 'Why, Mr Alexander,' I said, 'isn't that a bit ungenerous?'

'Ungenerous?' he echoed, seeming genuinely astonished.

'My parents like my sisters' husbands,' I went on, 'and they're *both* clerks. If Richard was a clerk, I'm sure they'd like him, too . . . and now, perhaps, I may have the pleasure of meeting your family – *my* family, I should say, shouldn't I?'

I had won — the first round at least. For a second, he surveyed me, then conceded the bout. 'I stand corrected,' he said. 'You've met Howard, of course . . . and there, on your right is my wife, Richard's Aunt Elizabeth . . . and next to her is Howard's wife, Nina . . . and Richard's sister, Stella . . . '

Aunt Elizabeth, a large comfortable lady in her sixties, gave me a warm smile. 'It's a pleasure to have you with us, my dear,' she said. Nina was a thin, angular woman in her late thirties. Stella was plumper but quite handsome, though with a hard face. Both nodded to me as though uncertain how to greet me.

'Then on your left,' he went on, 'is my nephew Mathew and his wife Frances.' Mathew was lean, pinched and, unlike his brother, very short in stature; Frances was a pretty woman, all curls and buttons and bows ' . . . and finally my nephew, James Stratton.'

James moved forward with a welcoming smile and extended his hand. 'Let me be the first, Mrs Alexander, to commend my cousin's choice.' Then he winked at me.

'He was a rogue, my father,' he was saying, 'a buccaneer . . . My God, I couldn't do what he did — not on that scale. The market'd sense it was me in a moment and send the price soaring.' He broke off for a second to taste the wine, and nodded to the butler.

'He made a million pounds in months buying rice in Shanghai. He was a trader. Only twenty-two . . . There was a huge glut and they were almost giving it away, so he borrowed what he could, pledged everything he had — including his soul, I'd guess, for the Devil was clearly with him. The next year saw the worst drought in memory and rice prices soared beyond his wildest dreams. But Richard'll have told you,' he went on, 'and I mustn't bore our newest Mrs Alexander.'

'Oh, you're not boring me,' I assured him.

'Perhaps there wasn't time. The hours race by, do they not, under the force of passion?'

'Now Uncle,' Richard rebuked idly, 'you're being unjust again. We were in a stock battle, exchanging telegrams with you several times a day.'

'Doubtless,' the old autocrat persisted, 'such mundane matters as how our company was founded ranked low in the scale of conversational priorities.'

I guessed he was just playing, flicking the tail a bit. Throughout the meal he had been most genial to me, the quiet words in his deep voice coming from him smoothly, so even in pitch that with the slightest change in tone, he could indicate sarcasm, humour, pain, concern.

He had placed me on his right hand and inquired if I liked the dishes, explaining his chef's intentions in the blending of the flavours. He had discussed the wines, declaring that good wine was like great music: repeated acquaintance increased the understanding.

I saw James, who was sitting opposite, put his hand to his ear in signal to me. I was relaxing too much, for Julius Alexander, with his mellifluous voice, had a seductive charm that was unusual for so gross a man.

At that moment, Uncle — as I already called him in my mind — was regarding me with open admiration, sitting slightly askew in his chair. 'You know, Richard,' he said, 'She's a prize, this wife of yours, with her sense of market tactics. So I ask again: why no warning? Could you doubt I'd approve of such a prize?'

'Oh, Uncle,' Richard responded with a light sigh, 'I've told you that we . . .' but the old man broke in: 'Didn't your bride consider we should be informed?'

'She urged me to come home,' Richard said.

'But you were able to resist her urging. Did that surprise you?' he asked me, 'or did you ensure it? Did you argue that he should come home, but take care that he did not?' And suddenly his face, with its fat cheeks, folded into a broad, winning smile.

I found the challenge confusing, clothed as it was in apparent cordiality. I controlled the urge to reply sharply. Richard was thirty-seven, after all, years older than me. 'You speak as if Richard's a child,' I said, 'as if I had . . . well, some kind of extraordinary powers over him.'

He studied me. Then slowly he began to laugh, his belly shaking. 'Now I never considered that,' he declared. 'Extraordinary power . . . It's a thought, isn't it, by jingo. Perhaps you're a witch. Why, I do believe I can smell the smoke.'

He beamed, expecting me to melt to his beneficent humour, but he had gone too far. 'In New York, Mr Alexander,' I responded coldly, 'It'd be considered impolite to call a lady a witch.'

Out of the corner of my eye, I saw James suppress a smile. 'Now see what you've done, Julius,' Uncle's wife rebuked him from her place at the other end of the table. 'She's upset – and with good reason. He doesn't mean it, my dear,' she said to me.

He leaned towards me, resting his hand on my arm. 'Witch,' he pleaded softly, 'I apologize. No offence intended. Let us be friends, please. Tell me I'm forgiven.'

I conceded with a smile and he leaned back in his chair. 'Good,' he said expansively, as the stewards cleared the plates after the trout. 'Of course,' he went on, 'you must understand our situation. We've awaited your arrival with concern, with apprehension. Until an hour ago, you weren't much more than a name to us – a lady wrapped in mystery . . . Isn't that correct, Howard?'

'Indeed, Father,' Howard answered, 'she was a potential danger.' He was on the far side of the table, slightly to my left, sitting up very straight, his body still. 'Any lady whom Richard married,' he added, 'was a potential danger to the family – especially one he'd only just met.'

'You see?' Uncle said, as though he had required confirmation. 'Perhaps, Howard,' he mocked lightly, his eyes still on me, 'we should still take care.'

'Perhaps, Father.' Howard was not jesting. His hands were on the table in front of him and I noticed that all the time he was turning a large gold signet ring on one finger.

'Mathew'll agree,' said Uncle. 'Mathew thinks everyone's a danger – even pretty ladies.'

'Pretty ladies are the most dangerous of all,' said Mathew sourly. He had sly grey eyes set in a thin, almost skeletal face.

'Please, Uncle,' James put in, 'Mrs Alexander'll think you're serious . . . My uncle's just being playful,' he added to me.

'Playful?' Uncle inquired, clearly tolerant of his youngest nephew. 'Well, let's ask her. *Are* you a danger?' he challenged softly.

'To whom?' I demanded. 'Surely any wife should be a danger at times, like any mother.'

He laughed. 'I can see why you haven't rushed to your wife's defence, Richard.'

I experienced a feeling of unreality, as though we were in a game – as in a sense we were. At present, Uncle had control of the bank as sole trustee of the family trust that owned most of its stock. But when he died the trust would break, as required by law, and its stock would be divided between the male heirs of Uncle himself and of his late brother – between Richard, in short, on the one hand, and Howard and Mathew on the other.

The next head of Alexanders, the man who would assume Uncle's chair, was sitting at that table, and this knowledge hung over it like a cloud.

For me, it made a potential enemy of almost everyone there – as it made me for them. During all the exchanges with Uncle, I had been conscious of Howard studying me with his dark eyes, assessing the woman I was, analysing the influence I might exercise on Richard. Mathew, too, had been watching me with the detached care of a biologist examining an insect. He served his brother, Richard had said, like a devoted satellite. One of his duties was to gain the secret information so vital to a merchant bank. In this cause he performed delicate missions, meeting at times people with whom no one else of his rank in Alexanders would consider shaking hands.

I glanced at Nina, Howard's wife, who was eyeing me with cool scrutiny until she looked away under my answering gaze. She had a skinny body that made her look frail, but shrewd determined eyes belied the impression. I switched my attention to Stella – finer-looking than Nina, with a well-formed figure, but just as severe. The two women had been friends since school, and I wondered where Stella stood in the feud between her brother and the husband of her friend. However, her hostility towards me was unconcealed.

I was aware that Frances, Mathew's wife, was scanning me, as the others were, but her expression was warmer. She appeared amused by my arrival among them, which was romantic, after all. Frances, Richard had said, was shallow – 'a feather-brain', as he had put it.

The wives began to question me, intrigued in particular by the concept of women working in the bank. Were there many lady typewriters in the New York office? Nina inquired. Was it not embarrassing to work with men? asked Stella. How in fact had I met Richard, Aunt Elizabeth wanted to know, and where had he proposed?

What fascinated them most, though, was why Richard, at the late age of thirty-seven, had chosen me as a wife – and they searched for the answer like terriers.

'We'd began to think that Richard'd end as a crusty old bachelor,' said Nina. 'Had an eye for the ladies – and it was mutual. Queuing up, they were. Why, once he rejected the daughter of a duke.'

'Couldn't blame him for that,' Frances put in idly. 'She had spots.'

'Quite a few romances, but nothing permanent,' Nina continued. 'Then suddenly *you're* there – in four weeks flat . . . well, we wouldn't be human, would we, if we weren't at least *un petit peu curieuses?*'

'What's your secret?' inquired Stella disdainfully. 'I suspect I can guess . . . Men are so weak, aren't they? But, as our dear Saint Paul warned them so often, "They that are after the flesh . . . " '

I could hardly believe what I had heard, with its insulting inference. 'I don't think I understand you,' I said as coolly as I could.

She shrugged. 'Nothing to understand . . . I'm sure you'll make my brother a most desirable wife.' Her smile was mirthless.

I had known this would be an ordeal, but I had not expected to have to parry thrusts from so many different directions. The supreme test, however, still lay ahead.

To the women, it was clear, I was in the class of a showgirl from Hammersteins. This they could understand. Men were always making idiots of themselves over actresses. In short, as Stella had virtually said, I was a scheming little minx.

However, I was *their* minx – an Alexander minx – and Nina, it seemed, saw it as her duty to make me as acceptable a minx as possible. 'You'll find England very different,' she declared, 'both in our ways and the society to which you've been accustomed. Still, we'll do all we can to help you, *n'est ce pas*, Stella?'

'Of course,' Richard's sister replied, with another tepid smile.

'There'll be problems,' Nina went on. 'Servants, for example . . . Servants can be trying. And entertainment . . . I don't suppose you've done much entertaining. And clothes, too . . . No doubt our fashions'll differ from those of the New World, but we'll advise you, won't we, Stella? *Laissez tout à nous.*'

'If the gown she's wearing now is any guide,' growled Uncle, taking command once more, 'she'll not need much advice.'

I welcomed his intervention, but I should have stayed on my guard. He was still Howard's father – and the man whom Richard had defied. 'You look like a princess, Quincey,' Uncle went on softly, a slight smile hovering round his lips, 'in that fine blue dress . . . I have your permission to call you Quincey, I hope?'

Permission? I was seduced, enticed into the parlour, flattered by the naïve belief that I had won him. I assured him I would much prefer it if he did. The challenges seemed over, the tests survived.

'Quincey,' he repeated, 'unusual name . . . John Quincy Adams, President of the United States . . . Two presidents . . . Related to the Adams, are you?' He inquired. And when I laughed at the notion, he remarked: 'I must say you've no side. I like that. Take me as I am – that's what you're telling me, isn't it? Well, I've got no choice, have I? You're bargaining from a strong position, are you not?' He was smiling at me broadly, and my response was instinctive, born of all the family talk at home of marriage. 'Bargaining, Mr Alexander?' I echoed with a laugh. 'Surely not bargaining. My Aunt Abigail'd say I had a contract.'

I knew what I had done at once – even without the involuntary wince I saw cross James's face. I had been too bold, too informally 'American' for so early a stage in my relations with this capricious English autocrat.

For a few slow seconds, he was silent, and when he spoke his voice was frigid. 'Yes,' he said. 'You have a contract, but what's a contract? Contracts are material for argument. Contracts are the food on which lawyers gorge.'

'It was just a light-hearted jest, Uncle,' said Richard, in an attempt to appease him.

His uncle regarded him without expression. 'How can you be so sure, Richard, when you've known your wife only five weeks? Perhaps it was a jest, and perhaps it wasn't' He turned to me. 'One million pounds,' he said.

'I beg your pardon, Mr Alexander?' I asked.

'I'm offering to buy your contract for one million pounds.' He took from his pocket a pen and a small notebook, flipped open the cover and began to write. 'It was you who mentioned the contract, not me.'

I could not believe I had understood him correctly. 'You mean the marriage contract?' I asked incredulously.

Even Richard, who had known him all his life, was astonished. 'Now Uncle,' he cut in, 'I can't allow this . . . I really can't.'

'Think what she could buy with a million pounds, Richard,' he responded, his eyes on the page as he wrote ' . . . a huge mansion. . . a yacht as big as this . . . A string of racehorses like yours . . . '

'She can enjoy those anyway as my wife.'

'Only through you,' his uncle answered, still writing. 'I'm offering her independent wealth . . . freedom . . . the right to do what she likes.'

'It's outrageous,' Richard said, his voice taut. 'Even for you, Uncle, it's outrageous.'

'You *are* going a little far, Julius,' Aunt Elizabeth put in. 'It's only a game, my dear,' she said to me.

'Game?' he echoed, looking up, 'I'm serious. Now listen . . . ' He began to read from what he had written ' . . . I, Julius Alexander, hereby agree to pay Mrs Quincey Alexander the sum of one million pounds on condition she renounces her rights under the marriage contract to Richard Gilbert Alexander.' He signed his name with flamboyant style, tore the page out of the notebook and placed it on the table in front of me. 'There,' he declared, 'the offer's documented. If you agree, I'll call in one of the secretaries to draw up a formal deed.'

'Quincey,' Richard said, 'We'll leave the table.' He stood up, but instinct warned me not to go. I tried to fathom his uncle's purpose. Was he serious, as he said? And, if so, why? Could a break in the marriage be worth a million pounds to him? Was there some alternative bride he had in mind? Whatever it was, I knew I must face him out.

'Quincey . . . ' urged Richard, when I remained seated.

'I think your Uncle's issued a challenge,' I said to him. 'So I must answer it, mustn't I?'

71

'It doesn't merit an answer,' Richard insisted.

'Please . . . sit down,' I appealed quietly, 'just for one moment.' Then I picked up the slip of paper his uncle had placed before me and read the words he had written. 'It's a colossal sum,' I said.

'It's often a mistake to make too low a bid,' his uncle answered, watching me carefully.

'And it's not a game?' I inquired. 'Your wife said it was a game.'

'It's not a game,' he answered.

'You're offering to buy me out?'

'You could put it that way.'

'You'd require me to return to America?'

'No doubt you'd wish to.'

'And the divorce?' I asked.

'That'd need arranging carefully to avoid scandal. Somewhere in the north of New York State, I'd think, where no one knew any of us . . . Buffalo, perhaps . . . '

I pursed my lips, considering what else I needed to know. '*Why*, Mr Alexander?' I asked, unable to resist my curiosity. 'Why are you making this strange offer?'

'You ask that?' he responded. 'With your sense of tactics? Do *you* tell people your purpose when you're negotiating?'

I studied his paper once more. 'Do I take it you accept?' he asked, when I did not speak.

I looked up at him and smiled. 'Gracious no, Mr Alexander,' I said. 'It's not nearly enough.'

He gave a short laugh. 'So you're bargaining . . . well, it's negotiable to a point. What would you say to . . ? '

'Uncle,' Richard interjected firmly, 'I insist you cease this farce at once.'

Uncle ignored him. 'One million, one hundred,' he said to me.

I shook my head. 'One million, two fifty,' he offered. I shook my head again. 'Three fifty?' I rejected it once more. 'One million four?' And on seeing my negative shrug, he added: 'Four fifty? Seventy-five?'

I waited to see if he would go higher. 'The extra twenty-five, surely, Mr Alexander?' I said, when he hesitated.

'Twenty-five thousand pounds is a great deal of money,' he answered.

72

'Not out of one million four seventy-five,' I countered. 'Why, it's only one point four per cent.' I guessed that would impress him.

'Quincey,' said Richard, 'please . . . this is demeaning.'

I put one silencing finger to my lips in a request for patience. His uncle was leaning back in his chair, studying me. I wondered for a moment if the percentage I had quoted had been even remotely correct. Speed, rather than accuracy, was what had been important.

'*Would* you take one million five then?' he asked.

I was slow to reply – deliberately. He was eager for my answer, like a poker player before an important card is revealed. The silence was heavy, broken by no sound, no movement at the table. No knife touched a plate. No one lifted a glass. 'Well, would you accept one million five?' he repeated, with a sharpness in his voice.

'Pounds, not dollars?'

'Of course.'

'Cash, not stock?'

'Cash.'

'To be paid within two days?'

'If you wish . . . My God, you've got a passion for detail, haven't you? Do we have an agreement then?' he pressed. 'Well, do we?' he demanded, growing angry as I paused.

I gave a wry smile. 'For a gift of angels, Mr Alexander, as you called it? What price'd seem enough for that?'

And with slow, deliberate movements, holding my hands well above the table, I tore his sheet of paper in half, and in quarters, and in eighths – then released the pieces so that they fluttered, spreading wide as they fell among the plates and the glasses and the cutlery.

There was no expression on his face as he watched me do this. Then suddenly he started to laugh. 'I'd hate to play your wife at chess, Richard,' he said. 'She'd have my queen before I'd made a dozen moves.'

'And now,' I said, 'perhaps you'd forgive me . . . and you, Mrs Alexander. It's been a long day.' I stood up. 'Good night to you all.' And I walked out of the dining saloon with Richard, as he had asked – but with credit now.

A few minutes later, I sat before my dressing-table mirror. Maisie had helped me disrobe and left me, as I had asked. I was wearing a pleated nightdress of white chiffon which buttoned to a ruffled collar and my hair was down, brushed so that it lay on the front of my shoulder. I was completely exhausted, drained of all energy.

Richard had not said much to me as we walked to our suite, just affectionately held my arm. While Maisie was with me, he had gone into our day cabin. Now he returned and stood for a moment at the doorway. 'You were quite magnificent,' he said.

He came behind me and we looked at each other in the mirror. He put his hands to the sides of my neck, slipping his fingers beneath my hair. As always, his touch sent a tremor through me, despite my fatigue. He began to undo the top buttons of my nightdress until he exposed my breasts in mirrored reflection. On impulse, I turned to him and clutched his body tightly with both my arms. 'I want you to make love to me slowly,' I said, 'Very, very slowly . . .'

Part 2

July 1902

Chapter 4

[1]

Uncle paused in the doorway of the big drawing-room, with its chandeliers and great balconied windows overlooking the square, and surveyed us all for a moment as we waited for him as usual. 'I've astounded them,' he declared, 'those men of medicine who've examined me today. Couldn't believe it, they said. Constitution of a buffalo, if I'd forgive the expression.'

He limped towards us, leaning heavily on his stick, and I wondered if the doctors had been telling the truth. He gave an impression of strength and power, as always, but his colour was high, even tinged with blue.

'Fitter than a lot of men half my age,' he went on. 'That's what they said. Even after two attacks.' He stopped at the fireplace and turned. 'There now . . . It seems you've still got me with you for a time.'

'Of course we have, my dear,' said Aunt Elizabeth. 'We only have to look at you to see you'll be with us for years.'

'No "of course" about it,' he said. 'Encouraging, though. I enjoy this world. Not quite ready for the next.' He looked at me admiringly for a second. 'You're looking very fetching this evening, Quincey.'

'Thank you, Uncle,' I answered, as it had been decreed I should address him.

'We've a guest for dinner tonight who'll interest you,' he went on. 'Sir Ronald Blackwell . . . Think she'll know who Sir Ronald Blackwell is, Howard?'

He was being provocative again, putting the question to his son. Not much missed the old man, as James had said. Howard was unperturbed. 'I should imagine so, Father,' he answered in his deep voice.

'And is Howard correct?' he asked me. '*Do* you know?'

'The president of Blackwell Jones, I presume,' I said carefully, unlikely to forget either of the big London stockholders in United Mining.

Uncle grinned, turned to Richard. 'Thought it might amuse her to meet him,' he said airily.

Life in Number 7, Grosvenor Square had stately echoes. We were expected to observe a daily ritual, one part being to gather in the drawing-room at seven in the evening to await the arrival of Uncle, who would appear last, like a king. Indeed, the mansion was a kind of court – an alternative headquarters of the bank. Wherever Uncle went – his home, the yacht, the family estate in Shere in Hampshire – his staff of secretaries, supported when needed by clerks and telegraphists, would be on hand. It was a rare dinner that was not interrupted by the duty secretary with a telegram.

Both Howard and Mathew had houses in the Square and dined with him regularly, accompanied by their wives, as one large family – as James did, too, though his home was only a couple of modest rooms in Kensington. Sometimes the men came to breakfast, joined often by visitors, before travelling to the City with Uncle in a procession of carriages. Number 7 was always full of people.

We had accepted his invitation to stay there until arrangements had been made for our own home, though Richard had been reluctant. He deeply resented the negotiations to sell the motor company over his head, which Uncle had personally sanctioned, and also the ordeal to which I had been submitted on the yacht; but his bachelor apartment – his 'set' in Albany, Piccadilly – was unsuited to a wife, and to move into a hotel would seem like pique. Most important of all, though, was that, living in Uncle's home, he would be well placed to monitor events.

For me it had a special value, since it enabled me to get to know the family, especially Uncle, whom I intrigued, as at first I had intrigued Richard, because he had never before met a woman who could discuss with him the bank's affairs. I used the fact quite shamelessly. 'And how does the newest Mrs Alexander view the markets today?' Uncle would ask every night as we sat down to dinner – teasing, of course, even patronizing, though he would listen to what I suggested. 'You may have a point there,' he would sometimes respond. 'We'll have to see what Smith in the Stock Department has to say about that . . .'

I recall that one evening I had answered his regular question by saying: 'If I was Mr Smith, I'd be selling Rand Goldmine stocks. They're far too high.'

He glanced at me quizzically. 'We're buying,' he responded. 'The South African war's over. The mines'll be in full production soon.'

'Not soon, with respect,' I corrected, knowing I was on firm ground, since we had conducted a special study of them in New York. 'The war's left them with big problems. The price must drop. Would you care for a wager?' He chuckled without replying. 'I wish I could work for your bank, Mr Alexander,' I said.

He always said no, of course. 'This isn't New York,' he declared. It was part of the sparring that had developed between us. 'Keep the idea in his mind,' Richard had advised.

Despite Uncle's mercurial temperament, I found him easier to deal with than the other members of the family. He liked to maintain an appearance as an Olympian figure, reigning high above us bickering mortals, and – although I knew this to be a delusion – it reduced the restraint between us.

'Well, Howard?' Uncle had asked that evening. 'Do you think Smith's wrong on golds?'

'No, Father,' answered Howard, his eyes settling on me for a moment, probing in a way I found discomforting, always questioning.

'There,' Uncle said to me. 'Perhaps I should take your wager after all.'

'You speak of golds,' I responded. 'Do you think in a year or two we'll speak of motors?'

The silence then was like that of an empty church. I had uttered a forbidden word. Of all the conflicts that racked my new family, Masons was in a special category, touching basic, primeval elements. It was small, but its importance was enormous; it symbolized the difference between Richard and his dead father on the one hand, and Uncle and Howard on the other, about the future, about the very soul of the bank. It lay under the shadow of oil, the most daring speculation the Alexanders had ever undertaken, which now produced so large a part of their revenues.

This was why the proposed sale, due to be ratified at the next Board meeting, had caused a family crisis. But it was not discussed. Monsieur Lanardine of Panhard had arrived from France to confer with Howard. Richard was meeting lawyers every day. But the family meals were cordial. Even the two rivals, who between them would control the bank when Uncle died, avoided contention at table. So how could there be a crisis?

Later, Nina said it was a *'Faux pas'*, but I had acted deliberately. I could not 'do as Rome does' all the time. There was much I missed of home – the bustle of New York, the elevated trains, even popovers and maple syrup – but worst was the constraint I found in London: the smooth good manners that could clothe some waspish comment, the servility of the servants. Heavens, have they no pride, I would wonder, when I heard the staff discussed disparagingly in their presence. In New York, no servant would have stood it, as I declared at one moment to Maisie as she was doing my hair. 'Maybe in England, Ma'am,' she chided with a smile, 'we know our place.' She was a country girl about my age, with glowing red cheeks and wisps of hair that were always escaping from her cap.

'Aren't you ever tempted to say something?' I asked.

'Sometimes, Ma'am,' she admitted, 'but I know better'n to do so.' They all knew better – clerks, shopgirls, cab drivers, even police. Often I was tempted to disturb that tranquil surface. That evening, with my question about motors, I had yielded to the urge, and failed. Uncle just chuckled and shook his head as if I was a wayward child. 'Where did you say we were dining tomorrow, Elizabeth?' he asked.

United Mining did not touch the sensitive note that motors did in the Alexander family, for it was conventional. But it was crucial in the duel between the two cousins because it was both big and spectacular. So the sudden invitation of Sir Roland Blackwell at that particular time was curious, to say the least.

At dinner, I was seated next to Uncle with James on my other side. Sir Roland was opposite me – an amiable red-faced old man, with thick grey whiskers. 'What's Uncle up to?' I whispered to James. But he was as lost as I was.

The two rivals had fought out the question of United Mining, but the quarrel had left Richard uneasy. The failure to approach Black-wells and Higgins Smith was strange and unexplained. Howard had been at his most bland, not even trying to justify it. 'From our position in London,' he had said, 'it seemed inadvisable.'

Uncle had declined to rule on the matter. 'I think, my boy, that this fiery young bride of yours has overheated you a little.'

We had just finished the *Côtelettes de cailles au clamart* ('Quails,' James had whispered) and the footmen were preparing to serve the *selles de presale à la niçoise* (Saddle of Lamb,' guided James) when Uncle inquired: 'Well, Blackwell, how did the meeting go today? I've not had a chance yet to talk to Howard.'

'What meeting?' James asked me softly, with concern. I looked at Richard and saw the same question on his face.

'I ask now,' Uncle went on, 'while the ladies are with us, because our young Mrs Alexander here is acquainted with the matter.'

'Would you believe it?' said Nina. 'She worked in our New York office.'

'She was my personal assistant,' Richard added, clearly feeling that Nina had not given due credit.

'I'd advise you not to underestimate her, Blackwell,' Uncle warned, 'Or she'll have the shirt off your back.'

Blackwell glanced at me with a tolerant smile. 'Well, it's all been very satisfactory,' he told Uncle. 'At first, old Higgins couldn't see the huge benefits to our two companies, but your son handled the matter with his usual skill. It was a clever proposal, I have to concede.'

'*His* proposal?' I whispered to James. '*Howard*'s proposal?' I felt his hand on my arm, checking me, as Howard said: 'You do me too much credit, Sir Roland. The concept emanated from New York. My cousin was there, as you know, and I gather, too, that Mrs Alexander had much to do with it.'

'I'm sure she did,' Blackwell condescended. 'You're a modest fellow, Howard,' he said. 'I've always admired that side of you, but who was it that swayed old Mr Higgins?'

'Mr Higgins?' I echoed, unable to control my anger any longer. 'Sir Roland, if you'll permit me . . . '

'Quincey,' Richard curbed me gently. The Alexanders did not quarrel in public, of course. I had forgotten. 'The idea was my wife's', he explained with a smile. 'So she feels a little possessive.' He could have saved his breath, for Blackwell knew that wives did not have ideas of that sort.

'Tell me, Howard,' Richard went on idly, 'why didn't you mention to me that the matter was being negotiated? I might have been some help.'

'Didn't I?' Howard answered. 'I thought I had . . . In passing, of course, for I knew you were greatly pressed so soon after your return. There wasn't much left to be settled, just final details. We've announced it today in New York.'

And I knew how it would have been announced. 'Mr Howard Alexander reported today in London that an Alexander consortium had acquired a controlling interest in the United Mining Corporation Inc.' There would have been no mention of Mr *Richard* Alexander. When Howard went into his club tomorrow, or strolled on to the floor of the Stock Exchange, he would be told he was a dark horse, congratulated on his surprise Alexander coup – which was the kind of picture that made men seem suited to become heads of merchant banks.

For all his appearance – often heavy, sometimes ungainly – he had stolen Richard's success with an ease that was deft. And he had given him full credit, as well as me, but in such a way that it would be discounted.

'He may look like a sack of coals on a horse,' I whispered fiercely to James, 'but he's won that race well enough.'

'By about five lengths, I'd say,' James agreed, with a self-deprecating grin. James prided himself on knowing the most secret affairs of the bank, but he had learned nothing of this. 'Have to talk to the jockey,' he said.

When the men joined us later in the drawing-room, Howard stopped by my chair. We did not often have cause to speak to each other, but I was often conscious of him looking at me. His face was strangely immobile so that his eyes, with their intense quality, seemed at times like those of a man who was masked. 'You do realize, don't you,' James had said to me, 'how much you attract him? You would anyway, I'm sure, but there's an extra reason: you're Richard's.'

Whatever the reason might be, I had already realized that the attraction was strong.

Howard paused now, smoke from the cigar he held swirling a

faint cloud before his face. 'Your idea for United was ingenious,' he said. 'You're clearly a most remarkable young lady.'

I glared at him. After what I had witnessed, his praise appeared arrogant. He seemed about to elaborate, to explain perhaps, but he could not find the words and wandered off in his awkward way to join some of the others.

James sat on the arm of my chair. 'I think you've got to be very careful after tonight,' he said. 'Howard's never acted as openly as this before. Perhaps he's learned something from Uncle's doctors. If any kind of contact is made with you, tell me at once, won't you. It'll come from Mathew, probably.'

'What kind of contact?' I asked, surprised.

'I don't know . . . just a feeling I've got. Remember – I've known them all my life.'

That night, as I was brushing my hair at the dressing-table, Richard sat on the end of our bed, as he often did at this time, and watched with obvious pleasure. It was a sensual movement and it excited him. 'I love your long hair,' he would say.

He took the brush from me and draped the tresses over his hand as he stroked the bristles through them.

'You haven't talked of what Howard did to you today,' I said. 'James says he's never seen him act so openly. He says I've got to be very careful.'

'James always makes too much of Howard's devious ways.'

'He didn't make too much of it tonight. Howard was outrageous. That was James's point. He wondered if there was something we hadn't discovered.'

For a few seconds, Richard did not respond, just divided my hair, draping it forward on either side of my neck so that it lay against both shoulders. Then he moved in front of me, half sitting on the dressing-table. 'You know what?' he said, idly taking the two bunches of hair in his hands as though they were pigtails. 'The best man'll win.' He smiled at the doubt in my eyes. 'Do you love me?' he asked.

'Hopelessly . . . It worries me sometimes how much I love you.'

'Then how can Howard win? With you loving me, I'm invincible.'

'The team?' I suggested laughing. 'Like the Curies?'

'The team,' he agreed. He drew me towards him gently by my hair and began to brush my lips lightly from side to side with his own.

'Take me to bed,' I whispered, 'Please.'

He picked me up as though I was a child and held me over the bedclothes that Maisie had turned down. 'You believe I'm invincible, don't you?' he said.

'I believe you're a god,' I teased. 'With a power to please me that's not of this world.'

'You say some pretty things,' he said, with a soft, serious expression in his eyes. He laid me on the bed and began to kiss my face. 'May the rites proceed,' he said and, lying down beside me, he began to unbutton my nightdress.

[2]

For over a week, James's warning seemed groundless. Howard was courteous, if a little remote, on the few occasions he found himself near me at Number 7. Then one afternoon, Mathew approached me, and there was no doubt any longer that I was part of my husband's struggle. He chose a strange venue – the Coronation Bazaar in Regent's Park. For it was July 1902, and the new King was soon to be crowned.

The band was playing selections from *Die Fledermaus* as I strolled with Nina and Frances along the broad walk between the tented stalls, fronted by trellis that was threaded with crimson rambler roses. Progress was slow because of the crowd. 'You've arrived in London at an ideal time, Quincey,' remarked Nina. 'I've never seen so many women of fashion in one place. Look at the ladies serving in the stalls. Scarcely one who's not a countess. It's an honour to have got tickets, shows how well the family's coming to be regarded.'

'It shows we've given thousands to charity,' corrected Frances, with a flicker of a wink at me.

I thought how much it would have amused Aunt Abigail. I was a lady in society. I had never seen such dresses, such hairstyles, such jewels.

My purpose, expressed so strongly to Richard at the Grand Hotel, my resistance to being a wife, had not weakened. Faced, though, with a new city where I was '*une étrangère*', as Nina kept describing me, it seemed wise at least to learn the customs. She was a willing tutor, escorting me to dressmakers, milliners, stores and even to Madame Pomeroy, who was a wonder at removing freckles, as well as suntan, with such remedies as Pelleta, Icilma Water or Ivory Massage. In a few days, I had spent enough money on clothes to keep the family at home for a couple of years – as I was crude enough to remark, to Nina's distaste.

Nine had advised me on my behaviour, my table manners and how to manage the servants. Driving with her in the carriage in Hyde Park, I had been told the gossip of every lady of title we had passed.

'Nina,' James had explained, 'helped to create the Howard we see today. She was a daughter of our local vicar at Shere, not high up the social scale. Parsons are invited only to tea in the great houses, never lunch. Her father was invited to lunch at Shere, though, for Grandfather liked him. So did Uncle, and anyway what do you expect of Johnny-come-latelys? Nina saw Howard's potential which, at twenty, no one else did, and came to share his passion for the bank, for making the Alexanders a family to be reckoned with like the Rothschilds or the Barings. Until now, she's seemed unchallenged as the future Queen – not even a runner-up in sight until you came streaking up from the back of the field.'

I was impressed by Nina, not least when walking beside her at the bazaar. Her pride in the family was evident in every aspect of her appearance – the way she held her head under the wide-brimmed hat, trimmed with silk; the self-possession on her narrow bespectacled face. She walked with small smooth steps, so that she seemed to glide, as doubtless she had learnt young by watching the ladies of quality at the tea parties to which parsons and their daughters could be invited.

If I had given her any personal fears as a rival, she did not show them. 'You look delightful,' she said. 'In perfect taste.' She had been anxious lest my choice in fashion might lean towards excess, as might be expected in an American showgirl, and I had allowed her to select my gown for the Bazaar. There would be time enough to take my own line when I had, as it were, assessed the market.

'I'm sure Mrs 'Oward knows best,' Maisie had assured me as she helped me dress. 'It's most dignified, Ma'am.'

'Dignified? I'm only twenty-three, Maisie.'

She gave a wide grin, revealing all her front teeth. 'Can't be too careful, can we, Ma'am.'

But I had been, I realized the moment I saw Frances's response to the dress of soft ecru voile and the black crinoline hat. 'Charming,' she said, 'if a touch restrained.' I rather liked Frances. She was irreverent and smart with her dressing. She had even made passing reference to the crisis that was ignored by everyone else. 'Don't worry, old thing,' she had said. 'It'll be better after the Board meeting.' I had to remind myself she was Mathew's wife. Later, I wondered if she knew what her husband intended that day.

James joined me. 'I've got to take care today, Quincey,' he said with a grin. 'Leone's here. She can be a terror when she's jealous – and I only have to talk to another girl! Literally! It's all that red hair!'

'Your one great weakness?' I mocked, since this was how he spoke of the women in his life. Couldn't resist a good filly, he would say, try as he might – though I doubted he tried too hard. 'I'm glad I'm married if Leone's that formidable,' I said.

He did not hear me. His eyes were fixed on a young blonde girl in a dress of yellow silk. 'Phew!' he exclaimed softly, 'They've brought her along well since I last saw her run . . . That exquisite creation, Quincey, is Miss Daisy Burroughs. Her aunt's one of the richest women in England.'

Richard appeared on my other side. 'Enjoying it?' he asked, with a smile. 'They're all very proud of you . . . Why,' he greeted a friend, 'hallo, Arthur. You haven't met my wife . . . Lord Blandford, my dear.'

I was surveyed by an elegant man with an appreciative smile. 'What a fortunate man you are, Alexander,' he said. 'A real winner, if you'll forgive me, Ma'am. Talking of which, how's that Arab stallion of yours?'

'First foals this year. They look good, but we can't tell yet, of course.'

We found Uncle near the Royal Pavilion, where Queen Alexandra, in a fashionable blue toque, was entertaining several Indian princes. He reminded me a little of a wounded lion as he stood there, supported by his strong stick, with Howard and Nina, speaking, as I could tell from Nina's expression, to a man of importance. Howard saw me first and introduced me to Lord Cromer, whom I knew to be senior partner in Baring Brothers, bankers in London for more than a century. He was an old man with a broad shaggy beard. As he removed his top hat to me, Nina put in: 'Richard Alexander found her in our office in New York. Isn't she charming?'

It was an error, I suspected. She had to tread a difficult line. I needed to be presented as an asset to the family, but not so big an asset as to be a suitable wife to the next head of Alexanders — a delightful young filly, perhaps, though with good potential.

Uncle did not approve, as he had indicated at dinner with Sir Roland Blackwell. 'I'll wager you've never met a young lady like this, my lord,' he said. 'She's an expert on golds. Would you believe that? Insists that Rands are riding for a fall.'

His lordship studied me with amusement. 'Is that so?' he asked. 'Madam, some people'd say that was an absurd proposition.'

'Alexanders are among them, Lord Cromer,' I returned.

He raised his eyebrows. 'Personally, though,' he said, 'I agree with you. At Barings, most of our clients are out of Rands. It's a pleasure to have met you, Mrs Alexander.' With a bow he left us. I gave Nina a friendly shrug.

Not far away, I saw James talking to Miss Daisy Burroughs. She was giggling. Archly, she reprimanded him, slapping him with her fan in an obvious response to some outspoken compliment. Then I saw Leone, about twenty yards from them, divided by the crowd. She had red hair, but that was not how I knew it was Leone. She, too, had seen them and her anger was manifest.

James took his hat off to Miss Burroughs with a gallant flourish of farewell. She dipped to him in the mocking start of a curtsey, then departed with a flirtatious backward glance. At that moment, James saw Leone glaring at him.

I reached him a second before she did. 'James,' I gushed with a wink as she approached, 'did Miss Burroughs agree to speak to her aunt?'

He understood fast enough. 'Unhappily, she said her aunt only gives to her own charities . . . Why, Leone!' he declared with a delighted smile, as though he had only just seen her. 'You haven't met Richard's bride.'

'At last,' I said as he introduced her. 'He never stops talking about you – and now I can see why. He's been doing sterling work for me with Miss Burroughs.'

I doubted if she believed me, but it blunted the attack. 'You were a real sport,' James said later. 'I'd have come down at the fence there if it hadn't been for you.'

I never saw Mathew approach, but I felt his presence. Suddenly, there he was walking beside me. 'The British at play,' he said sardonically, with a gesture that encompassed the band and the Royal Pavilion and the fine clothes. 'Do you have this sort of function in New York?'

'Oh yes,' I said, 'but of course I never attended any.'

'I suppose not,' he said, understanding that I was not then in that kind of social circle. A thin smile came to his gaunt face. 'How does your father get on with Mr Stephenson? I hear he can be an awkward customer.'

I was surprised he knew of my father's employer. 'I don't think there's any difficulty,' I answered.

'It was good of them to take him back after the débâcle.' He was looking ahead, walking in his awkward way, as though he had no flesh on his bones under his clothes. 'You need big resources to play the market as a bear.'

'You appear to be well informed,' I said coldly.

'We made a few inquiries,' he responded, 'as you'd expect, surely . . . ' He eyed me, a glint of a smile in his small grey eyes. 'You'd become important to us – very suddenly. We needed to know *something* about you.'

'I hope I passed muster,' I said sharply.

'Without question,' he agreed. 'Of course, inquiries about anyone tend to reveal curiosities from the past.'

'I can't think that my past was very curious,' I said.

He paused. 'It was a Mr Johnson I had in mind.'

The shock rendered me breathless for a moment with the dread I had not felt for seven years. 'Mr Johnson?' I forced myself to repeat. 'I don't think I recall a Mr Johnson . . .'

I was not looking at Mathew, but I knew he was noting my reaction.

'He was an associate of your father's, involved in his misfortune. He came often to your home, Quincey.'

'There were so many,' I answered, my face rigid. I was swinging my parasol – rather too much.

'It's not of moment,' he said, 'I was just interested. He had an accident, a fatal one, during your father's crisis. You must have heard of that, surely.'

My heart was racing and I hoped that the colour was not high in my face. 'The whole period was a nightmare,' I said. 'So many things were happening . . . our life was collapsing . . .' I made myself look at him. 'I don't recall the event,' I said. 'I was only sixteen.'

He did not believe me. 'It must have been a bad business,' he sympathized. 'I'm told you called on Mr Johnson in his office, which is an odd thing for a schoolgirl to do, wouldn't you say? But perhaps I'm misinformed.'

'You are indeed,' I insisted.

'Our informant was present,' he went on gently. 'Worked there as a clerk . . . Recognized your photograph.'

We walked on, and he allowed the silence to hang between us like a cloud. 'This dispute between Howard and Richard's distressing. An accommodation between them'd seem desirable, don't you think?'

'Accommodation?' I inquired. 'After what Howard's done with Mason Motors and Sir Roland Blackwell?'

'A fight'll be damaging to everyone, especially after poor Father goes. A truce'd be better, surely?' He took his hat off to a lady we were passing. 'If Richard would only concede a little.'

'You mean withdraw from the match?'

He gave a shrug. 'There are many ways to kill a cat, to balance minuses against pluses . . . much scope for negotiation.'

'Providing Richard concedes over which of them takes Uncle's chair? And agrees the Mason's sale?'

'Oh, the motor company's a lost cause, if only Richard'd face it. The sealing of it by the Board's a technicality. You could help, Quincey – and do a service to the bank, to the family and Richard, of course – if only you could persuade him to be a little more flexible.'

I shook my head. 'I haven't seen Howard being very flexible.'

He sighed. 'Quincey,' he went on, 'if you *had* visited Mr Johnson to plead for your father, and if the door of his room *had* been locked, just before his death . . . Then I wonder what view Richard would take of the whole bizarre affair. Or, for that matter, the police.'

I stopped walking. 'Just what are you trying to say to me, Mathew?'

'See what you can do, Quincey . . . ' he said. And left me.

I felt oddly defiled. Mr Johnson had always occupied a special tainted compartment in my mind that I could usually blank off from my conscious thoughts. The fact that Mathew had penetrated it was a brutal exposure, an assault on my privacy, that had left me shocked and numb.

I told James, as he had urged, but not for a few days. He was astonished, but sympathetic and even admiring of my courage at a tender age. 'They won't use it,' he said. 'They can't. They're just trying to force you to put pressure on Richard in a way that only a woman can.'

'Do you think it'd shock him terribly?'

'I doubt it,' James said, 'but you can never be sure how a man'll react about his wife. But it won't come to that. Just assume it never happened.'

This was not easy, though there was much diversion. London was at its most brilliant. In any year at the height of the Season there would have been a profusion of balls, receptions and garden parties. But the capital was also *'en fête'* for the Coronation. The streets were illuminated with electric lights. Flags fluttered. Buildings were adorned with bunting and great banners portraying Edward and Alexandra and the words: 'God bless their majesties'. In the streets, the mood of the people was high-spirited. Coronations, like weddings, inspire optimism. Everywhere, people were laughing.

As a family, we attended a number of functions. Sometimes our hosts were City acquaintances of Uncle. He would show me off, as he had to Lord Cromer, like a precocious child with a talent for the piano. 'Ask her about the war,' he would say. 'She believes that all our problems are due to the 200 million sterling it's cost us.' They would think he was jesting, and he would chuckle as I showed I could maintain the point. I would pay him back in kind, though it was harder now to make jokes with Mathew's father. 'I'll be working for the bank soon, won't I, Uncle?'

He would always shake his head. 'Next, she'll want to join the Guards.'

Always, on these occasions, James was vital to me. If ever I got into difficulties, he seemed to be on hand with whispered guidance or the odd deft remark that would divert the conversation.

Once I asked him about his loyalty to Richard. 'Dickie?' he replied. 'Without Dickie, I'd have been at the knacker's – wouldn't have stood a chance in a two-year-old sprint, not if Howard had got his way. One day I'll repay him. I'll come romping home at a hundred to one.'

Despite his assurance that Mathew had been bluffing, however, I could not rid myself of my anxiety. Several times, while lying in bed in Richard's arms, I thought of telling him, warning him – but even James had not been certain what his reponse might be. Once, in a moment of boldness, I started to speak of it. 'Richard darling,' I ventured carefully, and lost my nerve at once. 'Hold me,' I went on, 'very tightly.' Sensitive as he was, he guessed there was more to it, but by then we were making love and his curiosity was blunted.

As for Mathew himself, he did not speak of the subject again for some days but, with the odd secret look, he ensured that I did not forget it. Then, while sitting next to me at dinner one evening, he remarked: 'It doesn't seem as though you're being very persuasive.'

'I'm not trying to be,' I snapped.

'Now that's a pity,' he said.

[3]

Meanwhile, my relations with Stella reached a climax. I wondered if she knew what Mathew had discovered, for it would have confirmed her suspicions of me. Certainly her dislike had seemed to grow more intense after the bazaar, but that might not have been the cause. For I found her totally unpredictable.

Sometimes she was quite warm; at others openly hostile. The change would often be sharp. Her eyes would harden and she would grip the gold cross she wore round her neck so tightly I thought it might break.

Religion was an overwhelming force in her life. She spent much time in church, often hours alone in a single day, but she had none of the spareness that frequently marks the excessively devout. Her ample figure might possibly have suggested a generous, even a jolly nature if it had not been for her severe, drawn face.

At the bazaar itself, though, she had been pleasant, walking with me at moments, introducing me to acquaintances. The occasion had clearly offended her. Apart from the excessive opulence, it was marked by a mood of sensuality, heightened perhaps by the fashion for close-fitting gowns in fine materials that clung to the lower body. The day had been fine and sunny and there had been much elegant flirting, possibly plans for assignations. 'You can actually feel the sin here,' she had whispered angrily at one moment. 'The King's got much to answer for. He's always been a libertine.'

'Everything's been much more relaxed since the old Queen died,' James commented later. 'More colour, more gaiety, more mischief – like a horse that's been held in, then given its head.'

'Has there ever been a man in Stella's life?' I asked.

'Only one, and she couldn't have him . . . Richard.'

'Richard?' I echoed. 'You're not being serious?'

'I only suspected it for the first time three years ago,' he said. 'I was with her when he was knocked unconscious in a bad fall. He was steeplechasing. She was in a terrible state.'

'Well, she is his sister.'

'I've never seen a woman cry like that, not even a widow. She was quite hysterical. But I've probably got it all wrong.' He gave me a smile and put his arm round my shoulder.

James's theory had left me perplexed – and a little scared. But it gave reason to her dislike of me.

It was at breakfast one morning, after the men had left for the City, that she asked me suddenly: 'Has Richard shown you over our old house yet?' She was speaking of their family home on the other side of the Square which had been closed since their father had died seven years before. Richard had thought we might live there, unless we opted first for somewhere smaller.

'Not yet,' I answered. 'He's been so occupied.'

'Would you like to see it? Why don't we go today?' I was astonished. This was where they had spent much of their childhood together. It was sure to be rich with memories.

'Thank you,' I said, uncertainly. 'I'd like that very much.' Why had she offered? If James was correct in his suspicions, it could surely only open wounds.

It was an eerie experience to stand in that house where no one had lived for so long. The huge ground-floor rooms, with carpets rolled and furniture covered by dust sheets, were thick with the grime of years. Cobwebs entwined the banister rails beside the big staircase as we ascended tentatively as though fearing the building was haunted – which, in a sense, was true.

From the moment we had entered, Stella had not spoken. It was only after we had peered into the bedrooms they had occupied as children and gone on into the nursery that she said: 'He was a lovable, pretty child. We were very close.'

'He speaks of you a lot,' I said.

'He does?' she queried in cold disbelief. 'I think not.' We went downstairs to her parents' bedroom. Here too sheets, heavy with dust, covered the furniture. I moved to the window and looked through a dirty pane into Grosvenor Square. I could just make out Number 7 across the central gardens. I felt her eyes on me and turned. 'I suppose this is where you'll sleep with Richard,' she said. She was standing, her hands clasped in front of her. Her tone was friendly, but it seemed an odd thing to say.

'I suppose so,' I agreed.

'There in that bed.' Still there was no hostility. She could have been discussing plans for the furnishings. What colour curtains did I have in mind? 'Does he kiss your breasts?' she asked, in the same politely curious tone.

I could not believe I had heard her correctly. But the expression in her eyes had changed and I knew there was no doubt, which made me question if she was quite sane. '*Does* he kiss your breasts?' she persisted with cool conversational interest.

'Stella, *please*,' I rebuked quietly. 'I really can't allow you to speak like this.'

'Why? Are you ashamed of it?'

'Of course I'm not ashamed . . . I'm his wife.'

'Of course,' she agreed. 'With my body I thee endow . . . I suspect you find it easy, Quincey.'

'Easy?'

'For a man,' she went on, 'some carnal need may be natural – a necessary imperfection for the race to continue. But not for a woman, Quincey, not for a woman of sensibility or morality. For a woman it's a duty. For most women, that is.'

'It's a sharing,' I said carefully, for she was voicing what many believed, including Laura. 'It's the ultimate union of man and woman.'

'The ultimate is a child,' she snapped.

'Of course, but you can't divide it. A child comes from loving, the essence of marriage, and surely what God intended.'

'What God intended?' she echoed, incredulous that I should believe such a thing. 'It's the Devil you fool! That's how he works, how he worked in you, as you've just admitted when you said you felt no shame.'

'Shame for what?' I challenged.

A hint of a cold smile came to her face. 'The pleasure, Quincey,' she answered. 'Can you deny there's pleasure?'

For a moment, I was speechless and a bit confused. For the anger in her, no longer concealed, was so muted, her words still soft, the only sign of tension being her tight grip on the cross that hung from her neck. 'Be on guard, Quincey,' she warned. 'Recognize the real source of your ecstasy, and then, if you value your soul, you'll fight it with all the energy you can muster. You'll cauterize it as the evil it is.'

I realized her purpose then. Virgin though she was, she understood that love was delicate, especially when the bloom was young; that it was open to suggestion. It was a desperate move by a jealous sister to taint the joy I knew with Richard – and it shook me to my roots.

'Well?' she demanded, when I did not answer at once.

'Coming here's upset you, Stella,' I said as calmly as I could. 'I think we should go back now. You're clearly quite distraught.'

'Distraught!' she echoed, her poise suddenly gone, replaced by such shocked fury at the word I had used that I thought she was going to strike me. Then, to my astonishment, her eyes filled with tears, which began to course slowly down her cheeks. She sat on the bed, covered as it was with a filthy dust sheet, seeming oddly smaller.

The sobs came slowly at first, increasing to great convulsions that shook her whole body.

I felt sad for her, despite her awful words. She looked so forlorn and unhappy. 'Stella,' I said, and went to put my arm round her shoulders. 'Don't you *touch* me!' she said, flinching from me as though my hands might contaminate her – then allowed herself to fall sideways on to the bed, her tears smearing the dirt from the cover across her cheeks.

For a few seconds, until the spasms that were racking her slowly eased, she kept her eyes tightly closed. Then she opened them, staring at me silently from her prone position with such dislike that I knew there was nothing further I could do.

I left the bedroom, descended the great staircase beside the cobwebbed banisters and stood for a moment in the musty hall. I looked around me. 'So this,' I said aloud, 'is to be my home.'

I did not return to Number 7. Just for an hour or two, I wanted to be apart from the Alexanders. I walked – a long way, through Piccadilly, with its Coronation buntings, down Haymarket, into Trafalgar Square. I stood at the foot of the Nelson column, taller even than the rooftops of the big surrounding buildings.

'Why do you think they put him so high?' I turned at the question and saw Millicent Russell's impish face. 'Perhaps he doesn't look good close-to,' she went on, 'The price of heroism.'

I was pleased to see her. 'What are you doing here?' I asked.

'Just been to Charing Cross Hospital. It's over there across the Square. Patient in a ward. Felt like a breather. Admiral Nelson was a great patriot . . . Sad really when you think of all the suffering that patriotism's caused. Soon it'll be as dated as the horse and carriage. Won't exist. Never used to . . . quite new in history really. No, it'll be class then – or no class. The working man hath no country, to quote the Communist Manifesto.

'You're always giving me lectures,' I complained.

'Perhaps I think you need them. You've got potential – and ideals, even if they're the wrong ones. You care a bit.' She flashed me a grin. 'Time I was off or I'll be late.' And she hurried away through the pigeons, strutting the middle of the Square.

It was about four in the afternoon when I returned to Number 7 to hear Richard's voice in the library, which was just off the hall. It was early for him to have returned from the bank, so I peered round the door. The mood in the room was tense. Richard was on his feet and, at first, I thought he was just with Mathew, who was half sitting on the nearest edge of the table. Then, beyond him, I saw that Howard was seated at the far end, both hands before him on the leather surface, slowly rotating the big gold signet ring on his finger. His head was slightly bowed. He seemed remote from what the others were discussing.

As I entered, Richard turned, and one look at his face told me what had happened. 'Do you know what Mathew's just been telling me?' he asked, in a voice that had no anger.

'I can guess,' I answered quietly.

'You gave me no option, Quincey,' Mathew put in.

'Do you want to speak of it?' said Richard.

I looked at the others. 'Is there any point?' I asked.

'There could be. Judging by the course of our discussion . . . '

Howard spoke for the first time. 'I want peace between us,' he said, his eyes fixed on the moving ring on his finger.

Richard was leaning idly against one of the bookstacks, his hands in his pockets. 'Peace on terms,' he corrected. 'Howard's negotiating. He wants me to agree now to his having control of the bank when Uncle dies.'

'You mean sell him your stock?' I asked incredulously.

'Just a few shares'd be adequate for the purpose. It follows, of course, that he'd be Managing Director and Chairman.'

'Is that all?' I responded lightly, matching my tone to his. 'Just Uncle's chair?'

Mathew seemed angered by the banter. 'He's willing to pay a high price,' he said. 'And it's logical. They've completely different views about the future of the bank. There'll be boardroom friction, and that's bound to leak out.'

He broke off, watching me. 'Go on, please,' I said.

'Well, this way they could run their enterprises how they liked, couldn't they? Howard's willing to concede the oil interests, the biggest earner we've got by far . . . '

'And the most vulnerable,' Richard put in.

'Can I believe my ears?' Mathew mocked. 'High profits go with high risks. Isn't that your philosophy, Richard, as it was your father's?'

'Within a balance of bank investment, with the risks properly hedged – as you well know.'

Mathew shrugged off the comment. 'You see, Quincey,' he said, 'Richard could then concentrate his energies on motors and the other novelties that interest you, like oil. Masons, perhaps – Richard's dream.'

'You mean Howard would no longer force the sale issue?' I pressed. 'We could keep the company? Poor Panhard . . . '

'Oh, there'll be some way to soothe Panhard's wounds,' said Mathew.

'You see,' Richard put in, the sarcasm barely evident in his voice, '*if* I concede Howard future control, I can have anything I want in the world. Well, you can't say he's unreasonable, can you? I can name my price — providing, that is, I forgo the right to direct the bank my grandfather founded.'

'You'd still be a director of the bank,' Mathew reminded him. 'And a big stockholder.'

'Just as *you're* a director,' Richard retorted, 'but Howard could overrule me on every issue.'

I eyed Mathew uneasily, only too aware from Richard's words as I had entered that Mr Johnson was somehow involved. 'Mathew,' I said, 'you knew Richard would never agree to any of this. Not in a million years.'

'Those are strong words, Quincey,' he answered, 'and hasty ones . . . As I said, Howard's willing to pay. Not just oil and Mason Motors, the price is much higher.'

'There's no price that's acceptable, Mathew,' I said, turning to my husband. 'Is there, Richard?'

'None,' he agreed, 'But there *is* a complication — and it concerns you.'

I looked back at Mathew. 'What complication?' I asked.

A pained expression came to Mathews's face. 'It's just possible, Quincey,' he said, 'That the New York Police might discover the truth about your Mr Johnson.' It was still a shock. I could not hear of Mr Johnson without a shock. But in a way it was a relief. The blade was out, its point revealed. 'We wouldn't tell them, of course,' Mathew went on. 'The source'd be anonymous — and local to the scene of the crime. Not murder, since you were under age at the time, but a penal offence of no mean stature . . . Just one short wire is all that's needed.'

'What he means,' Richard explained, 'is that if the matter comes to public knowledge, I might have to resign.' So that was it. That was how they would try to use that error of my innocence.

Slowly, I wandered past Mathew and stood before Howard. He did not appear to be aware that I was there — sitting hunched forward over the table, making no movement except that of his fingers with the ring. 'Is that what you wish Mathew to do?' I asked.

He nodded without looking up.

'You'd never countenance a scandal, Howard, you know that.'

From behind me Mathew laughed. 'It wouldn't be much of a scandal, Quincey. Men make fools of themselves over girls sometimes, everyone knows that. But it'd be politic for Richard to resign, as he says. His judgement could be questioned, couldn't it? By severing his connection with the bank, he would focus the criticism on himself.'

I had not turned when Mathew spoke. It was between Howard and me now. My hands were on my hips, which tightened the front of my dress so that my stomach and thighs were more clearly delineated. He was still leaning forward on the table, eyes averted, hands clasped; but I was close to him and I could see that his fingers were tightly clenched.

'Why are you so fearful,' I asked quietly, 'that you're going to lose?'

For the first time he looked up at me, with a movement that was slow. 'I'm going to win,' he answered.

'Then why all these underhand, desperate tactics?'

'You don't understand what you're involved in,' he said. There was pain, almost a pleading, in his eyes. 'The issues are so vital that . . .'

'That they merit anything?' I continued softly. 'Then send your wire to New York.'

He leaned back in his chair, as the chairman of the Board might do, a new confidence in him. 'You haven't properly considered the matter,' he said, 'so I'll give you time.'

'I need no time,' I said. 'Do you, Richard?'

'Only to regain my patience,' he said coolly.

'You have until noon tomorrow,' declared Howard. Unhurriedly, he got to his feet and, without another word, walked from the room. Mathew followed him to the door and then looked back, with a thin smile. 'That was good, Quincey,' he said. 'Convincing. . . Are you sure she wasn't an actress, Richard?'

He left us then and I moved to the window, my back towards Richard. 'Will you have to resign if they do what they've threatened?' I asked without turning.

'Depends how much of a stir it makes. It's not the sort of thing the City likes, but I might be able to sweat it out.'

'So there's a risk for Howard. There could be a scandal without achieving the object.'

'There's often risk. The question is always: Is it worth it? If there's a fuss in the press, Uncle may ask me to go. I'd have to decide then whether or not to refuse. The Board could dismiss me, of course.'

'Which'd make a greater scandal.' I turned suddenly and looked at him. 'I'm so sorry to have done this to you,' I said.

He smiled softly. 'It's hardly your fault, is it? But why in the world didn't you tell me?'

'I was ashamed.'

'Good heavens, why?' he asked. 'At sixteen, for Lord's sake? Surely you knew I'd understand . . . '

'I've tried not to think of it. Thank you so much, darling,' I said softly. And I ran into his arms. I cried, though I am not sure why. All the years I had kept it hidden, I suppose.

Mathew never sent that wire, as James knew. With the aid of a clerk in the bank's cable office, he had monitored all the coded telegrams to New York. One evening, I found myself alone with Howard before dinner in the drawing-room before the others had appeared, and I deployed my secret knowledge. 'Well,' I asked, 'has Mathew telegraphed New York?'

He fixed me with a dark stare. 'There are times when it's better to reflect,' he said.

'I'm glad,' I said. 'If you'd approved the action, I'd have found it hard to credit.'

'You think I couldn't have brought myself to do it?' he demanded sharply.

'Oh, I knew you had the stomach, it's the wisdom I'd have questioned – the tactics, if you like.'

He gave a heavy sigh. 'I knew you didn't understand. The only thing that matters is the bank, Quincey. We'll all die in time – Richard, me, you – but Alexanders'll still be there in Old Broad Court. It'll be more important then, it'll be in the front rank with a reputation that is unsurpassed – if we do what is required of us, if it is directed in the way a great bank should be. No motors or other frivolities, not even advanced ventures, as oil tankers were . . . '

'But even Rothschilds went into oil,' I broke in.

'Rothschilds could afford to . . . ' he paused. 'That's the true cause of our dispute. That's what'll lie behind the issue of Mason Motors when the Board meets tomorrow. Now that Richard's rejected my proposal, it's as vital as it ever was that the Masons is divorced from the bank.'

'You mean that if you'd gained control, it would have been different.'

'If I could have been certain of my father's chair, then there would have been no problem . . . Masons could have existed as part of a separate organization – Richard's empire. I'd have commanded all the bank's business; I could have protected the House of Alexander, maintained the course that'd bring long-term progress and dignity and the respect of the world.' He paused, his eyes on me for a second. 'But that wasn't to be, was it, Quincey? Not yet.'

'No,' I agreed. 'It wasn't to be.'

[5]

It was about ten minutes after noon on the morning of the Board meeting that the carriage came to a halt in the strange peace of Old Broad Court. For a few seconds, I sat and looked up at the mansion that was the fortress of the Alexander wealth. It had a discreet, Georgian façade, suggesting the home of a personage of great importance rather than a place of business. The Gothic letter 'A', inscribed in the stonework above the entrance, was the only indication of its owner.

James conducted me up the marble entrance steps and, as we reached the head of them, the great front door was opened noiselessly before us by an attendant in a morning suit adorned with gold buttons.

I was led through a lobby into the general office. This was an enormous pillared hall, lit by overhead skylights, in which more clerks than I had ever seen in one place – over a hundred, I was to learn – sat on high stools at tall sloping desks, terraced in rows of four and lit by identical lights with green china shades.

Around the sides were doors that opened into the various subsidiary departments of the bank, as James pointed out. 'Bills of Exchange', which arranged overseas payment for clients; 'Foreign', which handled currency; 'Dividends', which distributed interest for companies to stockholders and raised the capital they needed; 'Stock', which organized market dealings; 'Shipping', which controlled the tanker fleet; 'The Cable Room', where clerks were stationed twenty-four hours a day, among the litter of codebooks, reading out their messages letter by letter on direct telephone lines to the telegraph companies.

'And that's where Uncle and my cousins work, over there on the left,' said James, indicating a half-glazed door that seemed unimpressive in contrast to the surroundings. 'It's known as 'The Room'. If the blind is drawn over the glass, no one is permitted to enter if he hasn't been summoned.'

As I looked around me, trying to absorb the detail of that massive building, I became excited. This was a base of power, all right. From here, without question, the world was changed with the aid of Alexander money. Canals were constructed. Rivers were diverted by dams. Minerals were mined. Ships were designed and launched. Roads were hewn through forests. Parts of the globe previously peopled only by primitive natives were transformed into prosperous townships. All from where I was standing.

For a second, Millicent Russell's grinning face came into my mind. 'Profit's the only god,' she had mocked. 'Look for the web of crooked operations, of deals to corner markets, to create cartels, to fleece the public.' But the canals were still built. Plants were still powered from Niagara, no matter who was raiding the stock in the market. The thought of her did nothing to blunt the heady surge I felt in my resolve. This was what I had been seeking from the age of sixteen. Nothing would stop me playing a part in the direction of this great business.

It was then, as I stood in that huge hall, that I became conscious of the sound of tinkling – at first muted, but then gradually growing in volume. For a few seconds, I was disconcerted. Then I realized what was happening: the clerks were tapping their green china lampshades with rulers and, throughout the hall, they were looking at me, big grins on their faces.

'They're welcoming you,' said James.

I did not know really what I was expected to do. Some kind of acknowledgement was clearly needed; so I gave a little bow, as actresses do when they take a curtain call, which caused the noise to swell.

The office manager stepped down from his desk, on a high dais from which he could view his army of employees, and came forward to greet me. 'It's an honour to receive you here, Mrs Alexander. I hope you'll forgive my clerks. It's a tradition we've found it wise to tolerate.'

'I look forward to meeting some of them,' I answered.

'This afternoon, perhaps,' he said, 'for at this minute, Mr Julius is waiting for you upstairs for luncheon.'

James held open the door to the dining-room. For once, I had ignored Nina's advice and dressed to be striking – in a jacket and skirt of dark green satin, with Frances's quilled tricorn to match – and as I entered I was glad.

The tension was almost tangible, as I had expected, of course. Because of Uncle's disability, the men were already seated at a large round table of polished mahogany. It was laid for lunch with lace mats, Venetian goblets and silver cutlery. Richard and Howard were facing each other like tomcats before they spring – with apparent leisure as they manoeuvre for position, but with bodies taut.

They all stood as I entered, except Uncle, who beamed at me like an amiable Buddha. 'Goodness, Quincey,' he declared, 'you're looking especially comely today.' He introduced me to three directors I had not met and suggested I should sit beside him.

'We've been having a Board meeting this morning,' he went on. 'Apart from minor matters like lending millions to the government of Chile, we've been considering this little motorcar enterprise of Richard's. Feelings, I fear, have been high. Your husband can be stubborn, just like his father. Reminded me of the day we decided to invest in tankers. I was strongly against it but, my father overruled me. Mind you, that wasn't a pittance, as this is . . . '

'At present,' Howard put in darkly. 'Soon it'd have been soaking up money like a sponge.'

'Would have been?' I inquired.

'One day you'll thank me,' Uncle said. 'Perhaps fortunes'll be made. If they are, then fortunes'll be lost too. And why should we take such risks?'

'I'll buy it!' Richard said suddenly. 'I'll buy the bank's shares in the motor company.' Even I was surprised, since he had not mentioned this possibility to me – but it delighted me.

Uncle shook his head in mock rebuke. 'What am I going to do with you Richard? When will you realize you're a banker, that with Howard and Mathew you're going to own this great enterprise . . . ' He gestured with both hands to indicate the entire building '. . . yet you yearn to be a pioneer.'

'Surely,' I put in, 'pioneers are to be admired.'

'Of course,' he agreed, 'But most of them fail. You only hear of the few that succeed.'

'I'll take the risk, Uncle,' said Richard. 'Since you've decided to dispose of our interest, permit me to acquire it.'

'You can't,' said Howard sharply. 'Not under our Articles of Association. No director of the bank can take part in any other business.'

'We're permitted to own investments,' answered Richard.

'In public stocks, that's implied. Masons are not a public stock. Father, don't you agree with me?'

Uncle gave a nod. 'The direction of the bank requires your full energies, Richard. I'm sure we should let Panhard have the company, as the Board's decided.'

Richard was cornered. It was not obvious, for he still managed to appear relaxed, but I could feel the frustration within him. Then a notion occurred to me. 'Tell me,' I inquired, 'do the Articles say anything about directors' wives?'

For a few seconds there was silence. I realized I had found a loophole. Of course, the Articles said nothing about wives. 'Could I not buy the company,' I asked, 'without breaking the rules of the bank?'

Just to see Richard's reaction was ample reward. The smile

104

spread slowly across his face as he, too, searched for the flaw. 'She's right,' he remarked idly, 'there's nothing about wives.'

'She'd be acting on your behalf,' Howard insisted, but he was uncertain of this line of argument. 'It'd be the same as you doing it yourself. A technicality . . . '

'You don't know Quincey,' Richard responded lazily. 'I'd be a lucky man if she even asked my advice. Uncle, you can hardly object to Quincey's proposal.'

Uncle wanted to, I could see, but he liked to regard himself as fair and impartial.

'Father, it's just a ploy,' Howard insisted. Now that his desperate attempt to force Richard to concede future control had failed, it was vital to him that Mason Motors should be stripped totally from the family. Otherwise it was sure in time to be back within the orbit of the bank, and his whole grand concept for Alexanders would be endangered. 'It's a façade,' he added.

'Perhaps,' said his father, 'but I can see no grounds on which to refuse it.' I suspected then that Howard had made his dramatic approach to Richard without his father's knowledge, and this surprised me.

Howard had no chance to argue further, for Mathew hurried into the dining-room. 'Henry Thomson of Morgans has arrived in London,' he announced.

'Thomson?' echoed Uncle sharply. 'I wasn't aware he was expected.'

'He came on the *Americana*, which docked at Liverpool last Friday,' Mathew added.

Anger clouded Uncle's face. 'You mean,' he declared, 'that he's been here a week and we didn't know?'

He was deeply disturbed – with reason, as I was aware from my years in the New York office. Motors and Alexanders' future policy were forgotten. The feud between Howard and Richard was put aside, the ranks of the family closed. Mathew's news meant we were about to join battle with Morgan.

John Pierpoint Morgan was not a contestant that Alexanders would have chosen. He was the giant of Wall Street bankers, the man who had organized the world's largest steel merger and rationalized much of the American railroad system. It was as bankers and advisers to the Cunard company that Alexanders found themselves facing this formidable antagonist. For Morgan had conceived a mammoth plan to create a consortium of all the Atlantic shipping lines – and Cunard, as the most famous of them all, was vital to it. He had tried to buy Cunard, and been rejected. The alternative was war.

War in the ocean was not new to the firm. It had been waging it for sixty years, since Samuel Cunard had first won an Admiralty contract to run the mails to America. With his early paddle steamers he had struggled tenaciously against the Black Ball liners, whose crews would jeer at his captains when their vessels' engines failed, as they swept past under full sail. He had battled with New York's Edward Collins, who had used luxury on his steamships to capture his customers. And as paddles had been replaced by screw propulsion, his firm had held its own against a whole range of new competitors – especially from Germany, with ports that were closer than Britain's to millions of emigrants and with a kaiser determined that his nation's flag should be borne by the biggest and fastest liners in the world.

But the Cunard company had never before faced an antagonist like Morgan; nor had the Alexanders who, as its bankers, manned the guns beside them. Already, Morgan controlled the main United States companies, six British firms, and had as partners the two principal German operators. He was well positioned for attack, which was why the sudden secret arrival of one of his most senior colleagues was disquieting. Why had Thomson come?

For about half a minute, Uncle sat saying nothing, just staring in front of him through his dark spectacles. 'Howard?' he rapped out at last.

'I don't understand it, Father,' his son answered. 'Unless Thomson's initiating some new approach – to Furness, perhaps.'

'Any indications to support that?' Uncle asked Mathew.

'None that has been reported to me.'

'I suppose you didn't hear anything in New York, Richard?' he asked.

'There weren't even any rumours,' Richard replied.

The old man nodded, then turned to me. 'We're not being courteous, are we?' he apologized. 'I should explain to you who Mr

Thomson is . . . '

It was one of those moments I would dearly have loved to share with Aunt Abigail. I gave a cool smile, trying not to appear smug. 'Oh, I know who Mr Thomson is, Uncle,' I said. 'In fact, I'm well acquainted with him.'

He was astonished. 'You're acquainted with Mr Thomson?'

'He was a friend of my father once. Used to visit our home quite often, though I was only about fifteen at the time . . . ' I paused. 'Would it help, do you think, if I paid him a social call?'

Uncle folded his arms and surveyed me thoughtfully. 'I wonder,' he said. 'Mr Morgan needs Cunard badly. With it, he could gain every other line in Europe. Without it, his plan'll fail. If he can't buy it, his only option is to drive Cunard out of business by cutting prices below cost.

'Cunard are going to fight but, they'll need big financial help. The obvious source is the government. We're an island that depends on its ships; Cunard liners are a national asset. The Admiralty are dragging their feet, but in the end they'll be forced to intervene. So what we need at present is time to convince them. Time's crucial . . . could you gain us time, Quincey? Could you even discover something of what Mr Thomson's up to? He'll suspect you, of course, now that you're an Alexander, but you'll intrigue him. Could you tempt him from his lair, do you think?'

'I'm willing to try,' I said.

Uncle studied me for a moment, still pondering the issue. 'I think something could be said for a social call,' he remarked at last, 'to talk over old times . . . ' And that familiar smile appeared upon his face.

Chapter 5

[1]

I was early for my appointment with Mr Thomson, so I waited for him at a table in the lounge of the St James Hotel. He had responded warmly to my note, sending his reply by messenger suggesting a meeting the following day, since he was about to depart for France.

I had dressed carefully, in an afternoon gown that was fairly simple, but with a rather elegant hat from Paris.

It was eight years since I had last seen him, but I recalled him clearly among the many people who had visited us during my father's period of success – a rather fine-looking man with very blue eyes and protruding ears. He had often spent weekends with us in the summer, when he would go sailing with Papa.

After the collapse, their ways had parted, as happened with most of the friends Father had made during the good years, but I remember him being especially hurt when he was dropped by Mr Thomson because he felt their friendship went beyond the business connection. There was, therefore, I reflected idly, a certain irony in my situation that day. The schoolgirl had grown up to become a rival.

In fact, I still found it hard in those early days to regard myself as an Alexander. Certainly, the events of the Board meeting had sharpened attitudes within the family. To Howard, I had won back vital ground that he thought he had taken. 'You were skilful today,' he had said to me the same evening, 'but you did the family a great disservice.'

The fact that I owned a company was disturbing for the women, except for Frances, who just thought it-funny. 'You're a strange one, for sure,' she said with a laugh. Nina found it incomprehensible. 'It lacks dignity in a woman,' she insisted.

My thoughts were interrupted as Mr Thomson walked across the hotel lounge towards me. Now in his late fifties he was still handsome – though his hair was now white – and more assured. As he approached me, dressed in a morning suit and carrying a dispatch case, no one could have doubted his importance.

He beamed at me. 'Mrs Alexander,' he declared. 'What a great pleasure this is. I see you've more than fulfilled the promise you offered as a young girl, if you'll forgive the personal comment.'

'Personal comments of that nature will always be welcome, Mr Thomson,' I responded with a smile.

He ordered tea – with muffins and cucumber sandwiches – and inquired after my father as though their friendship had never ended. 'That was a sad business,' he said. 'The financial world can be very hard . . . ' He paused. 'And here you are now as Mrs Alexander. That was a surprise, I must confess. They're a fine family, the Alexanders.' He gave the smile of a veteran campaigner. 'We've had some skirmishes in our times. In fact, we're in the throes of one at present, as no doubt you know . . . '

'I really don't have much to do with the bank,' I answered.

His smile was sceptical. 'I've only met your husband once,' he went on, 'but I know Julius Alexander quite well. He's a cunning fellow, all right . . . ' He hesitated. 'Indeed, the thought had crossed my mind that it could have been at his suggestion that you'd written to me.'

'Gracious,' I replied with surprise, 'whatever made you think that, Mr Thomson?'

'Well,' he said, 'it could have been a clever way to approach us, because he could always have pretended that he hadn't, couldn't he? That there was nothing more to our meeting than a chance to talk of the past – which, of course, I welcome.'

'You make me sound like a spy, Mr Thomson,' I objected.

He laughed. 'You know,' he said, as the waitress arrived with a loaded tray, 'I rather wish he had sent you with the devious intention I've mentioned.'

'Good heavens, why?' I asked, my eyes wide.

'Then I could employ you in the same manner, couldn't I?' he answered. 'And pretend I hadn't should this prove advantageous.'

I inquired how he liked his tea, and after pouring it, passed it to him. 'I'm intrigued, Mr Thomson,' I said, 'to know for what purpose you could employ me?'

'Well, I know of course that you worked for Alexanders in New York.'

'Only as a typewriter. I was a bit of a noodle, I'm afraid, so far as high finance was concerned.'

'I'm sure you're just being modest, Mrs Alexander.'

'Well, put me to the test. What would you have me do? A muffin, Mr Thomson?'

He accepted and leaned back in his chair stirring his tea, a slight smile on his lined ruddy face. 'I take it,' he said, 'that you're aware that the Cunard company is a matter of issue between us.'

I thought for a moment. 'At dinner the other night, I heard some talk of Cunard. Mr Morgan wants to buy the company, doesn't he?'

He nodded. 'So far, Mr Alexander's advised his clients against this, but suppose he was to change his mind . . . Do you get my meaning now, Mrs Alexander?'

'Your meaning, Mr Thomson?' I inquired, looking perlexed.

'You and I could explore without commitment, couldn't we? I could speak of a sum at which we'd consider dealing . . . say £22 a share . . . Then we could meet again, to reminisce about the past, of course, and you could give me the response. And it'd all have been kept . . . how shall I put it . . . ?'

'Secret?' I suggested.

'Between us, shall we say,' he corrected. 'I must say, these cucumber sandwiches are excellent, aren't they?'

A pageboy approached the table. 'Mr Thomson, Sir,' he said, 'There's a telephone call for you.'

Asking me to excuse him, Mr Thomson followed the boy, leaving the dispatch case that he had brought with him, together with his hat, on the seat beside me.

I am sure that he would not have thought for one second that a lady such as myself would examine its contents in his absence. However, I had nothing to occupy me and, placed where it was, it was extremely accessible, which, I suppose, is why I found myself testing the latch, which flew open at my touch. Temptation overcame me. I lifted the lid of the case a few inches and caught a glimpse of a document that I realized at once to be of great value. It was a list of the larger Cunard stockholders with a note of the latest sales and, in particular, the identity of the real owners of the shares bracketed beside the names of nominees – nominees being the method people employed to keep their holdings secret. Morgans, it was obvious, had an information service of exceptional skill.

One recent purchase of shares was of special interest. It had been made for a lady living in Berlin, a Frau Helen Schuller, who already owned a large block of stock, held for her in smaller parcels by several banks as nominees and, therefore, probably unknown at Old Broad Court.

I did not linger over this information, but closed the case and clicked home the catch.

As Mr Thomson returned to the lounge, he took his watch from his waistcoat pocket. 'Good heavens,' he said, 'I'd no idea that time had passed so fast. I'm already late for an appointment. I must ask you to forgive me, Mrs Alexander . . . . but think on what I've said, and we must meet again soon, and really talk this time of those happy days, of your charming mother and those sisters of yours . . . '

Alone in the carriage, I considered what my father would have thought of what I had done. Hurt though he had been by Mr Thomson, he would have been shocked. I had broken the rules. But I knew I had struck diamonds.

'Henry,' I called out to the coachman, 'Old Broad Court, please.'

Uncle listened intently. 'That's interesting, Quincey,' he said. 'Frau Helen Schuller, eh? If you're right, she owns far more stock than we thought to be in the hands of any single shareholder, apart, of course, from the ones we know of. She could be extremely important – to Morgan or to us.'

That night one of Mathew's corps of messengers, who doubled as investigators, crossed the Channel on his way to Berlin.

[2]

'Will the meeting please come to order,' I said with mock formality. Five of us were sitting round a table at the Mason Bicycle and Motor Company Limited, mugs of tea before us. Apart from

111

Richard and myself, there was Mason and his two sons, who were in overalls, having been summoned from their duties in the factory – Steven, twenty-one, fair and bearded; Martin, some three years younger, dark and moustached.

Richard had invited me to take the chair, since I now owned the bank's majority shareholding in the company. He was joking, of course, since it was not a proper meeting, more a family discussion. But the joking was a little forced, since the problems we faced were stark enough. For no one there now doubted that The Leopard had been 'nobbled' in the Paris-to-Biarritz race, nor that she would otherwise have won. Despite everything that had occurred since our return, Richard still found it hard to believe that Howard had been involved – or that Panhard had. For even though the French motor industry was well established by 1902 – way ahead of that of any other country – motoring was still a sport of gentlemen.

The facts, though, were hard to deny, and the facts centred on an engineer named Stanley Reitson.

Mason had been waiting for us on the platform at Winchester Station, a tall broad-shouldered man in his fifties, with a rugged deeply lined face and an iron-grey moustache. 'Have you been tempted by the monsters, Mrs Alexander?' he asked as Richard introduced us. 'If not, you soon will be, I promise. They become irresistible, like sirens, don't they, Alexander?' He led us to the station yard, where his 'monster' was waiting – a Lanchester tourer, he explained, since The Leopard had only two seats. 'I hear you're our governor now,' he said to me as he drove us out of the town, 'so we'll have to watch our p's and q's won't we?'

From the back seat, Richard began asking questions and I could soon see why the two men had formed so great a rapport. Despite the grave setback, the excitement as they talked of their joint venture was obvious in their voices. Together, they were conquering a new world.

Mason had built his thriving bicycle firm from very small beginnings. It was a sound base for a motor venture, as Richard had explained in America. 'The business is booming, the sport being so popular, so the profits've cushioned the teething mistakes. Also it's ideal for making cars – some of the same machinery, same skills, same shops for selling them.'

But Richard would have wanted Mason, I knew, even without his company. For he was obsessed by motoring, as were his two sons, who worked in the business with him.

The first requirement for the venture had been a designer, preferably of genius and, a few weeks after they had formed their partnership, Mason arrived at Old Broad Court. 'He walked straight into "The Room",' Richard had told me, 'ignoring all the Front Hall men, gripped me by the lapels and literally shook me. "Alexander," he declared, "I've found our man . . . odd cove named Reitson. Working for a firm making coin-weighing machines at present. Built a car in a shed at his home. Useless as a car, but you should just see the engine, Alexander . . . It's got four gears constantly in mesh. There's no other vehicle in the road with four gears in mesh!" '

Reitson had exceeded even Mason's hopes as gradually, over months, he had assembled the car in the bicycle works near Winchester, buying some components from other makers, as was the custom. When at last The Leopard was ready to perform, Mason had decreed it should be kept secret, no competing in public until the race from Paris-to-Biarritz. For if it won this as an unknown contestant, the victory would be dramatic and orders for it would pour in from all over the world.

And that is exactly how it would have been, but for others who ensured that it would fail. 'I really can't believe it,' Richard had insisted to me when he had returned to Number 7 from his first meeting with Mason after our arrival in England. 'Mason himself was driving. Reitson was riding as mechanic. For a hundred miles she went like a dream. Mason didn't press her, just stayed within easy distance of the leader, which was a Benz. At Vendôme they stopped to fill up with petrol and Reitson checked the engine, as he always did, of course, whenever they stopped. It was shortly afterwards that the clutch went, burnt up — just as they were overtaking. Mason's positive that at Vendôme Reitson sprayed the clutch plate linings with oil, but he can't prove it.'

'Then why's he so positive?'

'The linings are leather, have to be treated with a little oil anyway, it's a question of how much. But the main point is that soon after that Reitson resigned, and I'll give you three guesses who he went to work for.'

'Panhard?' I suggested.

'Panhard, whom Mathew was in touch with . . . No proof, of course, but it's obvious, isn't it?'

'You mean they bought Reitson?'

Richard nodded sadly. 'They say that everyone's got his price. So Howard got the failure he wanted and Panhard would have got the company cheap because the car hadn't won — except for my clever young wife.' He leaned forward and kissed me. '*And* The Leopard patents,' he whispered in my ear. 'That's what they were really after, but we've still got them, my darling, and by God we'll show those Frogs, won't we?'

I saw the contained excitement in his eyes, with its boyish quality, and thought again how much I loved him. 'We'll show them,' I said with a smile. On impulse, I flung my arms round his neck, aching for him suddenly, with a desperation that made me find his mouth, kissing him with the urgent surging passion that always scared me. I tore my lips from his. 'Are you *sure* there's nothing wrong with me?' I asked. 'I can't be near you for seconds without hungering for you . . . Do you think other wives respond like this?'

'Only the ones whom God has smiled on,' he answered.

'Stella says it's the Devil in me, that he helped me trap you, which is why we're doomed.'

'Stella sees the Devil everywhere,' he said, preventing me from speaking further with his mouth. Then, after a moment, he asked: 'Did Stella really say that to you?'

I nodded. 'She was a bit upset one day,' I replied, adding quickly: 'When do I get my first outing in The Leopard?'

'About Reitson's replacement,' Mason had said as he drove us from the station along the narrow Hampshire road towards the works. 'I'm giving my son Steven a try in his place, if that's acceptable. He's trained in engineering and he's good, despite his youth. Got some novel ideas . . . just spent six months in France with Peugeot. Of course, you haven't seen our beautiful monster yet, have you, Mrs Alexander?'

114

On our arrival I had been conducted round the works, which were bigger than I had expected, and 'the monster' was displayed to me in all her shining, spotless glory by Mason's two boys, who spoke of motoring in hushed tones as though it was a religion. 'The engine's quite novel,' Steven explained, opening the bonnet. 'As you can see, it's vertical.'

'And it's got a half-compression device that's absolutely amazing,' added his brother Martin.

'And the exhaust camshaft's so ingenious that . . . ' Steven broke off as he saw my confused smile. 'We're getting too technical?'

'You could be talking Chinese,' I answered, 'but if enthusiasm can bring success, then Masons' will be dominating the motor car industry in no time.'

'Tyres, boys,' Mason interjected. 'You haven't even mentioned the tyres . . . You see, Mrs Alexander, speed's not the only way to win a race, as I keep trying to bang into the heads of my lads here. As long as two years ago, Napier had a car that could do eighty-five miles an hour, but it weighed three and a half tons and there were no tyres up to it. So our policy is to sacrifice speed for reliability. The Leopard may not always win the races, but it'll finish by God – at least, she will so long as no one interferes with her – which means she'll sell. The boys want to start with speed and work backwards, but I doubt if that's the way to make profits, at least not yet . . . '

He smiled at them, but they both looked glum. 'You speak of profits all the time, Father.' said Steven quietly.

'Of course I do,' Mason answered. 'That's how we'll get the capital to really make our mark on the industry.'

'We want to make the finest motorcar in the world, Father,' Martin added.

'And we will, we will,' Mason responded. 'First, though it's money we've got to make to impress Mr Alex . . . ' he broke off. 'Forgive me,' he said to me with a smile, 'to impress *Mrs* Alexander . . . We've got to show we merit the investment.'

Our informal meeting round that bare works table did not last long, but decisions were taken. Already, orders for The Leopard were coming in from customers, impressed by her performance in last month's race, despite the mishap. Mason was planning to start production for sale to customers in September. Meanwhile, his longer-term aim was to win the next big gruelling race, scheduled for 1903. It would be longer than any that had yet been held – the 800 miles from Paris to Madrid. 'We've got a fine chance,' declared Mason, 'but we must work to correct our weaknesses, Steve, show that the car's reliable over that kind of distance.'

'Yes, Father,' Steve said quietly, his disagreement obvious.

I listened intently as the discussion continued. Then I made a suggestion which I had not spoken of to Richard, for I had not until that morning seen the open space around Mason's factory buildings. 'The bicycle business is making good profits,' I said, 'but these are being swallowed up by the start-costs of the motor venture, so the company as a whole is making a heavy loss . . . '

'That's correct,' Mason agreed.

'But if you were to buy, say, another two good bicycle firms, one in the Midlands and one in the North, you could extend your works and transfer their production here, so that you could dispose of their factories, thus cutting costs. Would this not increase your profits very considerably?'

'Of course,' he answered with enthusiasm, 'we could well become one of the biggest bicycle manufacturers in Britain.'

'Oh no, Father, please!' Steve's exclamation was almost involuntary. 'Surely we should be concentrating all our effort on making cars.'

'Mrs Alexander doesn't want us to limit our car production,' said his father.

'What she's proposing will help it,' Richard put in.

'How can making more bicycles increase our motor prospects?' asked Martin.

'Because if her theory's right, it'll help to check the losses . . . In fact, I was about to suggest that your father should try to gain some agencies for selling foreign cars in England to increase our revenue.'

'We'll need more capital, of course,' said Mason.

'That'll be much easier to raise,' answered Richard, 'if the company's making good progress than if it's seen to be replying on hope.'

'Hope?' echoed Steve indignantly.

'Steven,' Richard said, 'Times have changed. You're no longer funded by the bank as a concession to me. You've got to make your living.'

The colour rose in Steven's cheeks. For a moment he was silent. Then he turned to me. 'I was wondering, Mrs Alexander, if you'd care to take a drive in The Leopard . . . Perhaps we can convince you that our faith in her is based on more than hope.'

As we drove out of the works yard, I understood his pride. The long gleaming yellow bonnet reached ahead of us, the thirty-horsepower engine throbbing loudly beneath it.

At first we proceeded at a stately pace, within the twelve-mile-an-hour limit imposed on English highways. Then, after we had been going some five minutes, Steven began to drive faster along the twisting country road. Soon I was forced to bend my head against the wind, supporting with my hand the veil and scarf that held my hat. I realized he was trying to scare me. 'How fast are we going?' I shouted.

'About thirty-five,' he called back with a grin.

'You're mad,' I responded. 'That's faster than a horse at full gallop . . . on *this* road!'

'Nervous, Mrs Alexander?' he taunted.

I laughed. 'Trying to prove you're brave?' I mocked. 'What happens if we meet a wagon?'

'Who knows?' he answered. 'We'll have to see . . . '

All the time, he was increasing his speed and I realized that he wanted me to beg him to go slower.

'We're going at over forty now!' he taunted.

'More fool you!' I shouted.

We approached the brow of a hill and I felt my body stiffen with apprehension, for anything could be on the other side. There was — but fortunately not close. A small farm cart was approaching us about a hundred yards ahead. Steven slowed down to pass it, 'Got to think of the horse,' he explained. 'Motors still scare horses.'

'How thoughtful of you,' I said with light sarcasm.

'It was the only way I could demonstrate how she performed at speed,' he explained. 'Now I'm going to show you how she can climb like a goat.'

A minute later, he turned off on to a side road. 'We're going up Stamford Hill,' he said. 'Famous around here, since it is quite

117

something. One in four mostly, that's why they use it for motor rallies.'

The road began to steepen sharply and soon we were navigating a series of hairpin bends — in one case so slowly that I asked if we were going to stop. 'No,' he said confidently. 'As long as the rear wheels can gain a grip, she can get up anything.' We emerged from the corner, gaining speed laboriously as we progressed up a straight section of the hill.

He slowed to take the steepest bend we had yet encountered. We were ascending through varied country. Quite a lot of trees and bushes, a stream, a little pasture, mainly for sheep. A small lane reached off the bend through an open gateway towards a cluster of farm buildings. The noise of the engine seemed to me to be loud with high-pitched complaint. 'Aren't you straining the engine?' I asked.

'No', he answered. 'She won't stall . . . She's a beauty . . . Look, I can give her more still.' The whine of the engine increased as we managed to surmount the last part of the corner, which seemed almost sheer, and began climbing a long stretch of road that appeared no less demanding.

'What happens if she does stall?' I asked.

'The engine'll cut and you'll have to jump for it.'

'Jump for it?' I echoed in alarm.

'No brakes going backwards,' he said with a smile. 'None of the monsters have . . . Didn't I tell you?' He knew he had not told me. 'Don't you worry, Mrs Alexander.'

I glanced down at the valley below. There was a wagon moving slowly across a field. It looked as small as a toy. Anxiety began to rise in me, for this part of the road was carved out of the rockface and the hillside beneath was almost vertical.

He saw my fear. 'I haven't convinced you, have I?' he said. The engine noise approached the level of a scream.

'Are you *sure* she's all right?'

'Positive,' he answered. He directed at me a confident, masculine grin — which suddenly froze. For the engine stopped. 'Jump, Mrs Alexander!' he yelled. 'Go on — jump now!'

I do not know why I hesitated. Perhaps I sensed that Steven himself was not going to, and instinct bade me stay with him.

Within a second it was academic, for The Leopard was careering backwards down the road too fast for any jumping and Steven, steering with one hand, was looking behind him grimly, his body twisted in his seat.

Gaining speed all the time, we raced in reverse towards the steep corner we had surmounted so slowly a minute before. Through my terror, I realized that he was planning to attempt the seemingly impossible manoeuvre, at high speed, of steering the car backwards round that hairpin bend. As we hurtled into it he hauled the steering wheel hard over, using both hands, throwing the whole weight of the vehicle on to my side. Pressed against the door by centrifugal force, I felt the right-hand tyres lift and I was certain the car was going to overturn. 'Down on the floor!' yelled Steven, 'now!' But before I could obey, he heaved the wheel in the opposite direction so that I was flung against him as he swung The Leopard into the second loop of an S-turn, aiming it at the lane which led from the bend to the farm. The car scraped the gate-post as she went past, running on towards the house and barns, losing speed now, for the track, following the hillside, was no longer steep.

At last we came to a halt. For a second neither of us could say anything, both of us gasping for breath. Even then, angry as I was, I recognized that it had been a brilliant display of driving.

'At least' he said coolly, 'you've seen what she can do on a hill.'

I did not reply, just looked at him with cold anger. He turned the car and we drove back in silence to the works — within the limit of twelve miles an hour. I knew that one reason for his behaviour was that I was a woman. The other was my age, for he was only two years my junior.

He pulled up in front of the office buildings and grinned. 'Enjoy it, Mrs Alexander?'

I gazed at him. 'You certainly believe in taking risks, don't you, Steven . . .'

'We're all in the hands of the Lord, Mrs Alexander,' he answered. 'As you saw.'

'I'm not against risks,' I said, 'not risks that are properly planned, but you've just been plain damned stupid. You've endangered my car and my life, as well as your own. If there was any good purpose to this, I'd accept it. Can you suggest one?'

119

He was silent and avoided my eyes. '*I* could,' I retorted. 'Do it again – and you'll be sacked.'

I stepped out of the car and walked towards the office entrance, where I turned. 'You've got a fine machine there, I'm sure,' I said. 'See you take good care of it.' And I went into the building.

Chapter 6

[1]

Those two months of high summer and early autumn will always be vivid in my mind. Spanning as they did so wide a range of emotions, I can recall in detail almost every single day. At the end of July, as was his annual custom, Uncle moved his base of operations to Shere, the Alexanders' thousand-acre estate bordering the New Forest in Hampshire, where wild ponies and deer roamed free for miles. He himself resided at Shere Manor, together with his secretaries, clerks and telegraphists. Howard and Mathew had large country homes nearby. The yacht was moored not far away at Lymington. One of the family directors was expected to spend the week at Old Broad Court and they took it in turns, returning to Shere at weekends.

Richard, too, had a house at Shere, but it was no mansion like his cousins'. It was a large cottage really, but the moment I saw it, I fell hopelessly in love with it.

I remember sitting on the terrace the morning after he first took me there and trying to write home about how I felt. I was in the shade of a cherry tree, wearing a large straw hat. I gazed at the Isle of Wight three miles away across the waters of the Solent that separated it from the mainland and felt a sense of peace and freedom that I had never known before, which possibly was why I did not entirely trust it. 'It's so remote,' I wrote in my letter, 'that we could be in another world. James says the place is graced by pagan deities — benign ones who are festive, even sensual, a bit shocking . . . And at dusk, when the mist is lying, the notion doesn't seem so silly. If he's right, I just hope they're not too fickle like that lady you're always speaking of, Papa.

'The cottage itself is pretty enough, but you should just see the position! To the north, dividing us from reality, as James puts it, are thick woods. Beside them curls the Beaulieu River, which borders our lawn before flowing into the Solent. To the west, there are the huge paddocks with their great oaks, where some of Richard's brood mares graze together with their foals. Oh, and his stallion

. . . I almost forgot Tamburlaine . . . Have you ever heard such a pretentious name for a horse? Well, it didn't seem quite so pretentious when I first saw him, nor when Richard rode him . . . .' I broke off, the end of my pen in my mouth, recalling those tense few minutes.

Two grooms had held the horse at the bit, as Richard mounted. Then they let go and the stallion bounded forward, twisting immediately into a series of corkscrew bucks. Richard heeled him to keep him moving forward, for bucking is easier to ride if a horse is in forward motion, holding his head in with a rein that did not seem especially tight. He wore no spurs, carried no whip.

James and I were watching from the paddock fence. 'It's a fight they have every time Richard's been away for a while,' he explained. 'The horse has to make his point.'

The stallion reared up, his front legs pawing. Gently, Richard pressed him down, in total control, then urged him into an easy canter. He rode superbly, moving with the animal, but with complete economy of effort. 'Don't think it's over,' said James.

Suddenly, the horse stopped dead, bracing his forefeet – and again, arching his back, leaped into a high twisting buck, following it with another that curved his body the opposite way. Insistently, he tried to dip his head between his knees to give full thrust to the sharp movements of his hindquarters, but Richard curbed him.

Once more, the stallion reared – so high this time that it seemed he must fall over on his back, crushing the man under a backbone carrying half a ton of equine flesh. Again, though, under his rider's pressure, his front legs came down. Immediately, without any warning, he dropped to his knees, dipped one shoulder and lay rolling on the saddle. Richard stepped off him as he went down, standing waiting, still holding the reins, just out of reach of the flailing hooves. Then, as the horse got up, he moved forward quickly so that the animal rose with him on his back. The stallion stood and, it seemed, conceded victory.

Quietly, Richard urged him into an easy canter on a light rein round the edge of the paddock. He turned him so that he was riding towards the middle of the field. He turned him again, this time to the other side, checked him back to the trot, then galloped towards us at the fence and stopped abruptly. He slid from the saddle and stroked his nose. The horse nuzzled him. 'I don't think you've met Tamburlaine, have you, Quincey?' he said to me with a smile.

I went on writing: 'We don't have staff living in. Richard's requirements have always been met by servants who came over during the daytime from the manor. In the evenings we just have a simple supper which the cook leaves prepared, so I can manage easily enough, and James is adept in the kitchen.'

Again I paused. During the three weeks we had spent here, James had joined us often, especially at weekends. At first, fond though I had become of him, I was suprised by Richard's invitations, since we had enjoyed so little time alone – but I soon realized his reason. James provided a catalyst. Somehow we were always laughing when he was there. The three of us became close, sharing a kind of private life that was very free and easy. In the evenings, we did not wear formal clothes. The two men were usually in smoking jackets and shirts that were open at the collar, adorned, when they felt dashing, by a cravat. For my part, I would wear simple skirts and blouses with my hair down.

It was all a bit Byronic. In fact, often one of us would read Byron aloud, along with other poets, as we drank wine and lounged in that long living-room with its wonderful view across the Solent. Richard and I were strangely uninhibited by James's presence. He was part of our life. Often I would sit on the floor at Richard's feet or lie on the sofa with my head on his lap and he would run his fingers through my curls. Sometimes, he would even lean down and kiss me.

When we were in the mood, we would play backgammon and Richard would let out great yells of triumph when a move was successful and groan with disappointment when he was out-manoeuvred. 'Nobbled you there, by George!' James would shout.

On occasions Richard and I would sit together at the piano. I was not accomplished, but he played well and sometimes he would tease me, subtly striking the wrong keys to produce the kind of discords that characterized my own performance. I would attack him, pounding his chest with my fists in simulated tearful anger until, laughing, he would beg forgiveness. 'Why,' I demanded repeatedly of James, 'did I marry such a conceited prig? You'll play us a waltz as penance,' I insisted to Richard, 'and James and I will dance . . . ' James would join the game and we would go swirling round that room, with him trying to make me dizzy, until we both collapsed laughing on the sofa.

It was a wonderful period — so wonderful that it frightened me sometimes. James, of course, on his visits, kept us in touch with a degree of reality. The builders, he reported, were making good progress with our house in Grosvenor Square, where we had now decided we would live. The Cunard battle was intensifying. Howard had gone to Berlin to negotiate with the mysterious Frau Helen Schuller for the purchase of her stock in the company; but representatives of the Morgan organization were there, too, with the same purpose. My discovery of the lady was conceded to have been a coup, though no one inquired too closely about my methods. Even Howard had agreed reluctantly that it was an achievement.

One morning, too, Mason had driven over to Shere in The Leopard with the news that he had been offered a good bicycle firm in Manchester. On studying the figures together, we readily agreed to the purchase. Meanwhile, he had obtained a couple of agencies of continental motor firms. We shared a bottle of champagne and gave a toast to the Mason Company, whose prospects were starting to seem rosy.

Mason gave me a lesson in driving The Leopard which, after a few failures with the gears, when I stalled the car, I succeeded in mastering. Feeling the power under that long yellow bonnet, I felt exhilarated, driving faster and faster along the straight road that crossed the Forest. 'Hey, Mrs Alexander,' he shouted in caution. 'You're not in a Gordon Bennett Race . . . '

'Too soon?' I called back.

'Better be sure you can walk before you run,' he responded, a tolerant smile on his strong face. Obediently, I slowed down, 'Wonderful stuff, champagne,' he said.

The magic of those carefree days of high summer came to a fitting, haunting climax on a Saturday night. It was the end of a windless day that had been especially warm, and a full moon shone from a cloudless sky. Suddenly, after supper I said: 'Let's take a walk in the woods. We've never seen them in the dark. Let's go this very minute.'

Both men looked at me as though I was insane. Then Richard's imagination was caught. 'Why, that's a fine idea,' he said.

So we went out on to the lawn, the three of us, arm in arm, the moonlight striking shadows on the grass ahead of us. We walked down to the bank of the river, which was running as fast as it always did at half tide on the full ebb. We watched a log swirling by and the splash as a fish leapt from the water.

'Come on,' I urged, running into the woods along a path that followed the line of the stream. It was a strange experience. There was constant movement in the undergrowth — foxes, hares, birds. At times we were in eerie darkness, when the foliage of the trees was close above us, and then suddenly, when there was a gap, the rays from the moon would illuminate every detail of our surroundings and even of ourselves against the blackness of the wood. 'I feel like a nymph,' I declared, 'and you're a couple of satyrs.' And, with careful ritual, I kissed them both gently on the lips. 'I wager I can beat you back to the house,' I exclaimed suddenly, and ran back along the twisting path that we had followed, with them both chasing behind.

Emerging from the trees, I raced up the lawn, not towards the house, but drawn by some odd impulse towards the paddock where Tamburlaine was turned out, looking silver in the moonlight. I had no fear of the stallion. In a way, I was possessed that night. I could have ridden any animal, achieved any purpose. 'No, Quincey!' I heard Richard call out behind me. But I was in the grip of a strange elation. I clambered over the fence and ran towards the horse. He did not react adversely, just looked at me with his ears pricked, and then stood while I mounted him by pitching myself across his back far enough to get my right leg over his hindquarters. He even waited, gentleman that he was, until I was firmly astride him, as though he understood what had drawn me to him. I took hold of his mane, and he began to canter slowly round the field. I sat up very straight on him, my skirts forced above my knees, my head held back so that I could look at the sky, knowing a complete affinity with the horse and the night.

After a couple of circuits, he stopped at the fence by James and Richard, who stroked his nostrils. It was as though the horse was saying: 'Well, I've humoured her, haven't I, but enough's enough for a chap at this time of night.'

I slid from his back. 'He's a satyr, too,' I said.

The three of us walked back to the cottage, as we had left it, arm in arm. While Richard got a bottle of hock from the cooler, I stood at the big window looking out at the glorious night. 'There's a ship passing,' I observed. 'I wonder if she's bound for New York.'

When Richard had poured the wine into the glasses, I sat on the floor beside him. 'It's a happy time, isn't it?' I said.

We retired soon afterwards to our respective bedrooms and Richard and I made love. It was good, but unreal like the night.

Later, though, when we had slept for several hours, I found myself awaking very slowly, hot with longing, for he was stroking me, though still asleep himself. I could see him clearly, for we had thrown back the sheets for coolness and our bodies were whitened by the moon.

I eased myself on to my back and luxuriated in the desire that was escalating under the slow and gentle movements of his fingers. I watched his face as still he breathed with the deep, even regularity of sleep. His features were relaxed, reflecting nothing of his dream.

I touched his body lightly with my hand, caressing the bones of his hips, the soft skin of his stomach, the haired firmness of his thighs.

He stirred, awakened like me by the demand of passion. He saw me looking at him, our faces close on the pillows and, smiling sleepily, he kissed me several times – lightly, then deeply. His lips grew urgent, sweeping to my neck and to my breast.

I had never known a union with him of such intensity, or even glimpsed the level of ecstasy to which we rose in the early hours of that strange morning. The experience was totally basic, of the earth; yet at times I lost touch with my body, knowing a duality of self like some Eastern *sannyasi* in the heights of spiritual elevation. Time lost its meaning. Hours could have passed, or mere minutes. Much I cannot recall for, like some extremes of pain, it went beyond the range of human memory. Some stays with me still as an aura that I could never adequately describe. I do remember one clear moment of an overwhelming need to consume him, to take all of him into my body, like a returning child.

I cried; I screamed; I scratched – and I conceived. Of that, though

126

it is said you can never be sure, there was no doubt. And as we lay there, out of breath, with Richard still hard within me and the tears wet on my face and my body shaking, I whispered to him: 'You know what happened then?'

'I know what happened then,' he answered.

The next morning, a trap from the Manor arrived with a message from Uncle, asking us both to visit him as soon as possible, and we drove back with the groom. As we crossed the wild, open country that lay between us and Uncle's big home on that fine, cloudless day, I breathed deeply of the scents of the gorse and the heather and thought what a beautiful place the Forest was. We crossed a small bridge, with some trees and bushes screening the road that bent slightly beyond it, and came suddenly on a small group of wild ponies, grazing at the roadside. With an oath the groom hauled on the reins, but they scattered before we drove into them.

I knew Stella would be at the Manor, and wondered, just a little smugly, what she would have thought about the happenings of last night. No Devil there. That much was sure. She had never referred to our scene together. Even at dinner, on the day I had left her crying so helplessly in the dirt of the dust sheet on the bed, there had been nothing unusual in her behaviour.

Uncle was waiting for us in the library. 'Ah . . . come in . . . come in,' he greeted us genially from behind a large desk. 'You must forgive me for disturbing your holiday, but we have an urgent problem which you, Quincey, might be able to assist us with. At least, that's what Howard thinks. He's in Berlin, as you may have heard, to meet your Frau Schuller.'

He leaned back heavily, clasping his hands in front of him. 'We know something about her now. She is indeed a large stockholder, as you reported Quincey, even a crucial one. She's been buying into Cunard skilfully for three years now, in secret. She's not German, though, she's American – and intriguing. Lived most of her life in New York – a bit *demi-monde* it would appear – the sort of lady who entertained powerful men, but never met their wives. Then, in her forties, she married and became respectable. Husband owned the Schuller Line at Bremerhaven until he died five years ago. He left her rich . . . I fear poor Howard isn't making much progress.

This wire came in overnight . . . '

He handed me a decoded telegram. 'Lady refuses to sell to us,' I read, 'but says undecided yet to negotiate Morgan stop doubt I can change her mind but just possible our own lady might be more successful stop both are women both from New York both personalities that might be compatible stop urge she comes Berlin soonest if practical stop I will meet Potsdammer Bahnhof – Tiberio.' I could hardly credit that the wire had come from Howard, of all people, though I knew Tiberio was his codename.

When I handed it to Richard, he said: 'You must go, of course.'

'We need Frau Schuller's shares, Quincey,' Uncle went on. 'If Morgan gets them, they would immensely strengthen his position when added to the other stock that's open to him. If *we* get them, with the Cunard families' holdings, we'll retain control. That'll buy the time we want until the Admiralty steps in to help – as they'll have to, or watch the company go under. It's all come at the wrong moment in history for us. The Germans are well ahead. The *Kaiser Wilhelm der Grosse* outclasses any liner we've got. Cunard has some good vessels, but her future really rests in two ships still in blueprint – the *Mauretania* and the *Lusitania*. They'll be superb, Quincey.' A proud smile came to his face. 'So you'll do it, won't you? You'll cajole the lady to sell to us . . . '

'You mean, Uncle,' I challenged lightly, 'that you're asking me to work for the bank?'

I caught the glint in his eyes behind his dark glasses. 'It's a favour I'm asking,' he said cautiously, 'that's what you could say – a service. Now, can you leave from Victoria Station tomorrow morning on the ten o'clock train? It's not much notice, I realize, but the urgency is great. You'll pick up the Express du Nord from Paris at Liège. Tickets and a sleeper reservation'll be waiting for you in London . . . ' He leaned back in his chair and smiled broadly at me. 'I've great confidence in you, Quincey,' he declared. He looked in particularly good health.

On the way back to the cottage, I said to Richard: 'You didn't seem surprised that Howard should summon me to Berlin – *your* wife, of all people?'

He laughed at me. 'You still don't understand Howard, do you, my love? Why, he'd summon Satan if the need was there.'

128

'And what'd Satan do when he appeared?'

'Bargain for his soul, I should think.'

'We don't want his soul, do we? What *do* we want?'

He glanced at me. 'You're still a street dog, aren't you? No bargains, Quincey – not on a matter as important as this. You ask what we want? We want Mrs Schuller's stock.'

'And if we get it, Howard'll have won again, won't he – by using *your* wife . . . '

'Alexanders'll have won. We'll have held Morgan. They'll all know that.'

'*Howard*'ll have held Morgan, that's what they'll know.'

'My love,' he said, 'you fear Howard too much. He can play all his tricks, but the fact is that I'll be at the head of Alexanders when Uncles goes. I never really doubted it, but I've been assured now by enough members of the Board . . . '

'Why didn't you tell me?' I demanded in hurt anger.

He winked at me. 'Can't tell you every little detail. Just serve the bank, darling. Leave the City streets behind. You've got a pedigree now.'

When we got back to the cottage, I told James what he had said. He looked dubious. 'He's probably right, but I hope he's not counting the chickens. Nothing's written down, is it – or even verbally bonded, like a stock deal. He's always tended to underrate Howard, even now, when he's broken cover.'

[2]

The morning, as I arrived with Maisie at the Potsdammer Bahnhof, was cold and damp. For a few seconds, after I had clambered down from my coach in the Express du Nord on to that busy platform, part-clouded by steam, I could not see Howard. Then, as the crowd thinned at one point, I detected him some fifty yards away, standing motionless – a dark figure, exceptionally tall, shoulders slightly stooped, in a long overcoat and a top hat. He caught sight of me and walked firmly towards me through the moving throng of people. His gaunt, immobile face, with its thick black moustache and deep brown eyes, was serious as always. He shook my hand formally, as though we were unrelated, and ordered a porter to take charge of our luggage.

'It was good of you to come at short notice,' he said, with such serious courtesy that I had an odd feeling that I might have imagined all his tactics of those past weeks.

We walked with the crowd of passengers towards the head of the platform. 'I've reserved a suite for you in the Hotel du Rome in the Unter den Linden,' he went on. 'I myself am staying at the Central in the Friedrich-Strasse . . . They're quite close.'

As we travelled in a droshky along the Königstratzer-Strasse, which bordered the Tiergarten, he told me about Frau Schuller. 'She's a formidable lady. Holds court in a huge apartment in Voss-Strasse which is usually full of people – ministers sometimes, ambassadors, leading performers from the opera or the theatre, officers of the horseguards . . . perhaps even a member of the Kaiser's entourage.

'She's played cat-and-mouse with me, inviting offers, then pleading difficulties . . . You must realize that we're not just up against Morgan. The Kaiser himself supervised his agreement with the German lines, so he wants Morgan's plan for the Atlantic cartel to succeed. The German companies would greatly benefit. There's great pressure, therefore, on Frau Schuller from the Königliches Schloss – that's the imperial palace – so the opposition, you see, is formidable.'

The droshky passed under the huge arch of the Brandenburg Gate, with its massive Doric columns, and progressed into the Under den Linden. 'Impressive, isn't it?' Howard said. 'One of the world's great streets . . . ' He paused for a moment, allowing me to enjoy that elegant tree-lined avenue bordered at first by mansions – like Piccadilly or Fifth Avenue – before becoming a thoroughfare of shops and cafes and crowded pavements. 'The negotiations,' he went on, 'are nearing their climax now. Our chances are slim, but she's a volatile lady of sudden enthusiasms. You might just snatch victory if she takes to you . . . ' He broke off, his eyes resting on me, as though assessing my marketable qualities.

I found the silence oppressive. 'I'll do my best,' I said.

'You've much in common,' he went on, 'and, if you'll permit it, I shall introduce you not only as Richard's wife, but as a colleague of mine in the bank without being specific. She's a lady of independence, of spirit, so this may intrigue her and explain your presence in Berlin. You know how tongues can wag, and fortunately you've the experience to support the . . . ' He broke off, trying to think of an appropriate word.

'The lie,' I suggested, with a straight face.

He glanced at me, embarrassed. 'She's holding an "at home" this evening,' he went on quickly, 'and I thought we might go, if you've not been too fatigued by the journey . . . '

The droshky came to a halt outside the Grand Hotel du Rome. It was not yet ten o'clock in the morning. 'I don't know how you'd like to spend the day,' he said. 'An hour or two now to settle in, perhaps. If you would like it, we could take luncheon together. Then I expect you'd like to sleep this afternoon, before we enter the arena.'

This was a different Howard from the man I had known in England. There was concern for me, though I realized that it was practical, like a general resting his troops before a battle.

At lunch I asked the question straight out. 'Was it hard for you? The decision to send for me?'

He raised an eyebrow in query. 'No – why should it be?'

'I'm Richard's wife. Had you forgotten?'

His gaze was steady. 'Another glass of wine?' he asked.

I recognized the look in Frau Schuller's eyes the moment she saw me. I was unexpected, and all her instincts were alerted. Immediately, she concealed it with a smile, but I knew then that Howard had not warned her – which seemed unfortunate.

The occasion itself was glittering, almost literally. There were about thirty guests in a large reception room. The women were expensively jewelled in well-made gowns of fine materials; most of the men exuded a relaxed sense of established position.

Helen Schuller was a vivacious, still handsome woman in her late fifties, with dark brown hair, a figure that was becoming ample, and an obvious obsession with diamonds – for they featured in her necklace, in her head combs, in a large brooch attached to her bodice, and in rings on her fingers. She came forward to greet us, laughing, with her arms extended in warm welcome, but shaking her head at Howard in rebuke. 'Mr Alexander,' she demanded, 'may I please ask who is this attractive young lady?'

'I'd like to present Mrs Alexander,' Howard answered, 'my cousin's wife.'

'Your cousin's wife?' she echoed. 'But you said you were bringing a colleague from your bank in London.'

'Mrs Alexander *is* a colleague, Frau Schuller. She worked for years in our New York office, which is where my cousin met her.'

'But you didn't say your colleague was a woman,' Frau Schuller persisted, 'and from my own country, at that.'

'Well, naturally, had you asked . . . ' Howard began, his expression as impassive as ever.

'How could I expect such a thing?' she scolded. 'It has the feel of deception, of a card up your sleeve, Mr Alexander – but a delightful one, I must admit . . . A queen . . . ' She smiled at me. 'I'm delighted to welcome you, Mrs Alexander. You must forgive my surprise. I look forward to your joining our discussions, my dear, that is, if anything remains to be discussed . . . '

'You've made a decision, then?' Howard probed.

'Oh, this is no occasion to talk about such matters,' she answered. 'Come,' she said, taking me by the arm, 'I must introduce you to some interesting people, and you and I must have a long talk about New York. I'd enjoy that. Tomorrow morning, perhaps? Will you call on me?'

We approached a group of three men. 'Now, Mrs Alexander,' she said, 'may I please introduce Captain von Grumme, aide-de-camp to His Majesty, the Emperor . . . Mr Edward Hide, the correspondent here in Berlin of the London *Times* . . . and Mr John Hollis, of the Morgan organization . . . You'll all be astonished to learn,' she told the three men, 'that Mrs Alexander is a banker.'

They reacted with surprise. The captain asked a few probing questions, which I deflected carefully. I noticed Mr Hollis studying me, trying to assess my merit as a potential and unusual rival, while Mr Hide inquired if he might interview me for his newspaper, as he was unaware that there was a lady banker in London. At which hotel was I staying, he asked?

'I couldn't agree to an interview, Mr Hide,' I answered him, 'but certainly you may call on me.'

In the droshky on the way back to my hotel, Howard remarked: 'I think that was a good start . . . '

'You did?' I asked sharply. 'Now may I ask why you didn't warn Frau Schuller to expect me . . . ?'

In the light of the street lamps, I saw him look at me blandly. 'Because then it would not have been so good a start. Both of you were irked by my omission. Now you and Frau Schuller are comrades.'

Certainly, we *became* comrades. The next morning, I called on her as she had suggested. We talked about New York, about Berlin, about London and about our respective lives. She had a bubbling sense of humour and, under the smallest provocation, would start to giggle. She saw life as one huge joke, much as a cartoonist might, even though her early years had been extremely hard. Evidently she enjoyed the meeting, for she insisted I stay to lunch. The subject of her stock in Cunard did not arise.

We lunched again the following day, this time at Borchardts, the best restaurant, she said, in the city. We went on to tea together at a society gathering and she demanded that I should join her party that evening at the Deutsches Theatre.

After that, we met every day. She was an entertaining companion, with an endless repertory of stories – true stories, garnished with indiscreet, wide-eyed descriptions of the men she had known in America before her marriage. They included senators, well-known actors, Titans of the commercial world, and even a president. For Frau Schuller – or *Mrs* Schuller, which she said was more suitable – men were the source of enormous enjoyment. She was fascinated by their motivations, their weaknesses and their strengths. She spoke of them almost as if they were another species, or at least came from some far-off nation like China, where the customs differed. She had studied them like an anthropologist, informing herself of their world, as few women did, so that she could talk intelligently of the matters that occupied them.

We spoke of our childhoods, though her early life as the daughter of a stevedore in Hoboken, New Jersey had been harder than mine. She found it amusing that our homes were so close, separated only by the Hudson River. 'And here we are in Germany,' she declared, 'participants, even antagonists, in an international battle.'

'Hardly antagonists,' I said.

The whole concept that I was a banker appealed to her immensely, and I elaborated on the fiction. I spoke of going to Old Broad Court every day, of my desk in 'The Room'. After my years in New York, the deception was easy to sustain.

Only five days after we had met, Mrs Schuller cemented our friendship in public by giving a large dinner party that, though informal, was for all practical purposes in my honour.

The occasion was stimulating. Even the lady guests treated me much as they would a celebrated actress, and questioned me admiringly about the difficulties I encountered with men when negotiating international deals.

'I have become an expert liar,' I wrote to Richard in my daily letter, 'and am considering adopting fraud as a profession. Oh, I wish so many times a day that you were here, and at night, of course, the longing's worse . . . At times in those dawn hours I question my resolve . . . I wonder if I should not just live to serve you, as most wives would, to raise your children . . . I lie there and re-experience that strange wonderful last night at Shere . . . In the morning, I regain my faculties, my individuality . . . I talk to Howard, which brings me back to cold reality, but for once at least we're on the same side . . . We seek the same end . . . '

My relations with Howard had changed in Berlin. We would meet every evening in the hotel's winter garden to consider progress, and he would question me carefully about my conversations with Mrs Schuller. We had come to understand each other better. To me, he was still my husband's rival who, as he had shown, would deploy almost any means to achieve the end he believed to be vital to the bank. After my one question that first day over lunch, I did not again refer to the irony of my position, but it was in my tone at times – as he noted.

On the second evening he said: 'Quincey, there must be truce between us, though I know there's much you resent— a genuine truce, I mean. Just while you're here . . .' His plea revealed a glimpse of him behind the mask, and in an odd way, to my surprise, it touched me.

He was obviously right. There must be no reservations. 'Of course, Howard,' I agreed. 'I'm here for a purpose we share in common.' And because my words had sounded pompous, I added with a grin: '*Pax*, Howard.'

It cleared the air a little. The distant formality he wore like a shell grew thinner. As I answered his questions and responded to his orders, communication between us became easier. At times, we were almost intimate. He talked of his youth with Richard, of holidays at Shere, of his life with Nina. 'It was fast for you with Richard, wasn't it?' he said. 'Was it at first sight, as they write in those stories women read?'

'Not quite,' I said, 'but it got off to a strong start, as James'd say.'

He gave a little nod. 'I didn't know it could happen.'

'Nor did I.'

There was a sudden sadness in his eyes. In Berlin, because we had to meet so often, the physical need for me that I had recognized in London became more pronounced. It hung round him like an aura of magnetic force – an adverse aspect of our *Pax*, so vital to our mission, because this pierced a degree of light through his reserve. I became more conscious of his feelings in ways that were subtle. I would register his exact proximity to me to an extent I would never have done before. I knew how near his knee might be to mine beneath a table, though, of course, they would never touch. The way he would look at me sometimes – as he had done from our first meeting on the yacht – no longer perplexed me. I knew just how much I disturbed him, understood, too, that now we were thrown together as partners this was growing harder for him.

He spoke much of his daughters, especially the elder, Emmeline, who was thirteen and, so he told me, a bit of a handful. 'I suppose *you* were a handful,' he said. It was the nearest to a joke I had heard him utter, but it touched delicate ground. His dossier reported incidents in my own mid-teens, not too far in age from Emmeline. Suddenly the shadow of Mr Johnson lay between us. His mood changed sharply. 'You must have a son,' he said. 'As you know, we only have daughters . . . so's Frances.'

'There's time still,' I said.

He shook his big head. 'Not for Nina, it's impossible . . .Dubious for Frances . . . ' He looked at me in his direct, dark way. 'So *you* must have a boy.'

Suddenly I saw him as a tragic figure. Here he was, engaged in a duel with Richard, so ruthless that there were no means he would not deploy – yet even if he won, he would be forced to concede in time. For the only boy who could follow him as head of Alexander's would be Richard's son. *If* Richard had a son.

He perceived my thoughts in his disturbing way. 'Someone must direct the bank,' he said, 'in the future . . . An Alexander . . . ' There was a second of silence between us, then he returned quickly to the reason for our evening meetings. He was concerned that Mrs Schuller, usually such a chatterer, had not once mentioned to me the matter of her stock in Cunard. 'Morgans could be making progress without us knowing,' he said. 'Speed's becoming vital.'

I shook my head. 'She knows why I'm in Berlin . . . We grow closer every day. I'm sure we should keep our nerve, leave her to make the first move.'

Howard relapsed into a pensive, almost glowering silence that was broken by a pageboy with a telegram. He read it and passed it to me without comment – which surprised me because it reported that Uncle was ill, though not seriously. It also alerted us that Mr Thomson was on his way from Paris to Berlin.

'I hope Uncle's all right,' I said.

'There don't seem to be grounds for concern,' he said. 'No more than usual, at least . . .' He left the subject quickly. 'Morgans are deploying their big guns with Thomson. It means they're worried. I think tomorrow you should start to press Mrs Schuller.'

The telegram was not the only sign of anxiety among the opposition. The next morning Captain von Grumme, whom I had met at Mrs Schuller's, called on me soon after breakfast. He was about thirty-two, correct in manner, with a high red complexion, a waxed moustache and black hair, brushed tight to his head.

The Captain spoke of the Emperor's great interest in the Morgan scheme for the Atlantic. He talked, too, about a large programme that was being considered at Kiel – no fewer than four dry docks. The cost, he said, had been estimated at six million sterling. 'Usually,' he explained, 'Messrs Rothschilds handle such loans for us, but it's occurred to His Majesty that we might invite Alexanders to undertake this issue.' His round, red cheeks expanded into a smile.

'That would be most welcome,' I responded. There was a snag, of course – as I knew.

'It might then,' the captain went on carefully, 'be some consolation to you in the event of Morgans acquiring Frau Schuller's stock in Cunard.' He stood up. 'You know where to find me . . . in the Königliches Schloss.' He bowed with a click of his heels and departed – just as Henry Thomson walked into the room.

'Well, Mrs Alexander,' he said, approaching. 'I hear there's been a miraculous change in you. Only a few weeks ago you were a noodle, and now here you are representing the bank on a most important transaction – and doing well, I'm told.'

'Oh, the matter's such a simple one,' I said.

A sceptical smile came to his face. 'We're dealing with a strange but clever lady,' he said, 'and I have to admit it: there are gloomy faces among our men here. I'm just going to have to see what I can do myself to pull a plum out of the pie.'

Well, Mr Thomson did pull a plum out of the pie – and a great big juicy one at that. In fact, he had already issued the necessary orders before leaving Paris.

However, when later that morning I rode in the carriage in the Tiergarten with Mrs Schuller, she said suddenly: 'Aren't you supposed to be negotiating with me, Quincey?'

'I've been enjoying myself,' I answered. 'Putting off the business . . . '

'There's been much concern at Morgans, you know. I'd almost reached agreement with Mr Hollis by the evening we met, so you were only in the nick of time. It was clever of Uncle, as you call him, to send you out here – set a thief to catch a thief, eh?'

She ordered the coachman to stop the carriage. 'Let's stroll for a few minutes.'

We walked idly towards the fishpond in the middle of the Tiergarten and, realizing that the time had come, I probed cautiously: 'You know, Mrs Schuller,' I said, 'I sense a contradiction. You're in a very strong position. Powerful men are entreating you to negotiate. The great J.P. Morgan . . . Uncle . . . even the Emperor . . . Yet I get the feeling that the price, the big profit you could take, is not really important to you.'

'I knew it!' she cried, clapping her hands with delight. 'You've seen through the smoke! None of the men can understand anything but price. For me it's like playing poker . . . you didn't know I could play poker, did you? This is poker. As soon as I heard about Morgan's great shipping plan, I knew he'd need Cunard. That'd be the hard one for him. So I thought it all through, and now I hold the cards, don't I?'

She looked at me with a conspiratorial twisted grin. 'So what do I do? I can take my winnings in the poker game, of course . . . I'd more or less decided to sell to Morgan before you came because it was logical – the end of the game, to lay down the cards – a Royal Flush. So why am I not content with it? Tell me that, Quincey.'

'That's hard to answer,' I said. 'It's so personal . . . '

'It's what you're here for, isn't it,' she challenged with that strange giggle of hers, 'to persuade me . . . ?'

I hesitated. 'I can see what concerns you,' I said. 'The idea of a poker game surely is to outwit your opponent, to win . . . That's your Royal Flush, isn't it? Winning?'

'Of course, Quincey,' she agreed.

'But if you sell your stock to Mr Morgan, then *he'll* win, won't he? He'll have got the stock, which is all he wanted from the start. But if you deny it to him, then he'll have lost the game to you, won't he?'

Mrs Schuller stopped walking abruptly. 'You're absolutely right,' she declared, a pleased smile on her face. 'I'm glad you thought of that. You see, I want *you* to have the stock. I want you to be able to show that uncle of yours just how good a woman can be . . . but I needed you to prove it to me. You understand? Mind you, I'm not promising yet, but in your shoes, I think I'd feel optimistic . . . Now tell me, when am I going to meet this Richard of yours? You've spoken of him so much.

'Why doesn't he come to Berlin? Isn't that a good idea? Why not telegraph him to join you here for a few days?'

138

I was tempted — and a bit ashamed. Uncle's illness added logic to her request. I could argue that we should humour her. Howard would leave and Richard would replace him to share in the success that would impress the Cunard Board. We would be the team of which he had spoken so glowingly in New York. But he would not approve, I knew. Too much lingering in me of the street dog.

Howard was pleased when I reported to him, in the winter garden that evening, what Mrs Schuller had said about her stock. He nodded his head several times in pensive approval. 'Good,' he said, 'but we must take nothing for granted.'

Our meeting was brief, for I was due to dine with her, but I returned to the hotel before midnight. I was about to retire to bed when there was a knock on the door of my sitting-room. I was astonished to find Howard in the passage. He looked haggard. 'Forgive me for disturbing you so late,' he apologized, 'but I've had news from London. My father's had another stroke . . . '

'Oh Howard, I'm so sorry,' I said softly. 'Come in, do.'

He sat down on my sofa while I poured a glass of brandy for him. 'It's a bad one,' he went on, 'as expected . . . The doctors doubt he'll survive.'

'You must leave, then, mustn't you?'

'I'll take the morning train. They've asked for an urgent report on the situation here by private cipher. The question is whether you, too, should return.'

'That's impossible!' My exclamation was involuntary and seemed insensitive. I handed him the glass. 'I mean we're so close to success,' I added.

'Or whether someone else should come out to support you,' he said. 'Richard wouldn't come at this time,' he mused, as though he had read my thoughts. 'He'd feel he should be in London. Mathew couldn't . . .' He looked up at me, the pain evident in him. 'He was a remarkable man, you know. Liked you a great deal, said you'd got spirit . . . approved of women with spirit.'

'Not *was*,' I corrected softly.

'It will be soon,' he said. '*You* know that. The urgency's obvious in the wire. I'll be fortunate to get home in time. He's always had such hopes for the bank, you know . . . '

'And they've been achieved, surely, haven't they?' I said.

He shook his head with a look that was distraught. 'Not to the extent he hoped. He should have been honoured by now with a title. The position we've won should have been recognized.' I stayed silent, watching him as he sipped from his glass. 'I recall the first time he took me into the bank,' he went on. 'It was my eighth birthday, and the family had made a special occasion of it. My grandfather received me in 'The Room', sat me on his knee and gave me as a present this ring, which he took from his own finger.' He held up his hand. 'It had been given to him by a Siamese princess, though I was not told why. Being so young, I wasn't allowed to keep it, but I was allowed to view it under supervision until I was old enough to wear it. always just to look at it, to touch the soft smoothness of the gold, was a great treat for me.

'Father was deeply touched, seeing it as an accolade for him as well. When we left my grandfather that day, we stood together in the great hall of Old Broad Court. "One day," he said, "this will rest on your shoulders as it rests on mine." It seemed an awesome prospect to a small boy – as he realized. "I'll help you prepare for it," he said. He didn't count Richard. It was before the tanker speculation, before oil . . . Father was far stronger as a personality than his brother. He assumed I'd be the strongest, too . . . ' He drained his glass and stood up. It saddened me to watch him. Being so big a man, he seemed like a wounded animal. In only a few hours, he appeared to have put years on his age. 'You must stay in Berlin, of course,' he said, 'Until matters crystallize. I see no point in anyone else coming out. You've done well. I'll prepare a telegram.' He hesitated, his grief manifest. 'The train leaves at ten. Perhaps we could meet at the station.'

What happened then is confusing to recall. I was greatly disturbed by his distress. Instinctively, I moved to give him comfort. For a second he held me tightly by the shoulders. 'Good night,' he said, and I thought he was going to kiss me on the cheek, which would have been proper enough under the circumstances, but his lips found my mouth – needed my mouth in the emotion of the moment. He drew back mortified, as though I had struck him. 'I must beg you to forgive me,' he said, in horror, 'I don't know what came over me . . . '

'There's nothing to forgive,' I said, but he had left me, striding

140

away along the passage, moving his broad shoulders in an odd kind of roll.

I saw him off the next day at the station and he handed me the coded telegram to dispatch. 'Give my love to your father,' I said, 'if he's . . . Well, I trust his condition is better than you fear . . . *and* to my husband, please.'

'Of course.' He stood in silence at the carriage window, his face gaunt. The train began to move, and he raised a hand. I smiled encouragement and waited as the coaches passed me. My feelings were mixed. I felt for him, yet I knew his measure as an enemy. Almost certainly, by the time I next saw him, the final battle would have started.

Later that day, I lunched with Mrs Schuller in the apartment. I explained the reason for Howard's sudden departure. 'So you're alone now,' she said. 'Well, you'll be glad to hear I've decided. You'll have my stock. I've given instructions for the transfers to be prepared – at the price agreed with Morgans. The Emperor will be put out, of course, I'll not be received for a week or two. But I think it's important that we women should stick together, don't you, Quincey?'

On the way back to my hotel, I stopped at the telegraph office and wired the news to Old Broad Court. I was not as elated as I might have been, I reflected in the droshky. I had achieved a remarkable success, won my spurs as a woman and made a big stride towards the place of power I had always wanted. But the shadow of Uncle, fighting for life in England, had spoiled the pleasure. I would have liked him to have known. I was going to miss Uncle.

The droshky came to a halt before the Grand Hotel du Rome. I walked into the entrance hall only to stop at once in total amazement. For there, sitting in an armchair waiting, was my father.

At first, I could not believe it. Then he smiled and stood up. 'Papa!' I exclaimed, and ran forward to embrace him. 'What in the world are you doing here?'

'Surprise, eh?' he said. 'You're looking wonderful, Quincey. I'll explain why I'm in Berlin. Is there somewhere we can talk?'

I conducted him up the stairs to my suite, questioning him excitedly about my mother and my sisters and Aunt Abigail. I invited him to take refreshment but he declined, sitting awkwardly on the sofa. He looked better than he had when I had last seen him on the day we had left New York, his face seeming less drawn. There was something of his old 'dandy' bravura.

'I've come to ask a big favour of you, Quincey,' he said, 'and you won't want to grant it.'

'I can think of no favour I wouldn't willingly give you, Papa,' I said impulsively.

He looked up at me. 'I'm here to act for Mr Morgan in the matter of the Schuller stock . . .'

For a few moments I could not speak. I got up and, in my agitation, began to pace the floor. 'Oh, it's brilliant,' I said. 'It's quite, quite brilliant. This really is a plum from the pie . . . Papa!' I said, trying to keep the desperation from my voice, 'the negoti-ations are complete.'

'How complete?' he asked. 'Are the transfers signed?'

I shook my head. 'So there's still time,' he said.

'Time for what?' I cried.

'Quincey,' he said quietly, 'if I'm successful, Mr Morgan has promised to set me up in business again. I can hardly believe it really; I thought I was doomed to be a clerk for the rest of my life. He's agreed to lend me funds at low interest, introduce business even, not that I'll need that once it's known that Morgan's behind me. It's a chance to get back, Quincey . . .'

'A home on the heights?' I asked wanly. 'The usual table at Delmonicos? The Mahogany Bar at the Waldorf-Astoria?'

He gave a laugh that had no humour. 'I'll be a man again, Quincey . . . I'll be using the talents it pleased God to give me.'

I sat down beside him and took his hand in mine. 'Papa,' I said, 'I've wired home the acceptance. Is there not some other way we can achieve the same object? I'm sure Alexanders'd put up the capital for you to start again – and introduce business . . .'

A half smile came to his face. 'You're my daughter all right,' he said. 'The instinct for finding common ground . . . but it's no good, Quincey. I've got to show them I can still do it. That's the only way I'll regain their confidence. Don't you see?'

For a moment I was silent. 'What do you want me to do, Papa?' I asked. 'Tell Mrs Schuller we're no longer in the market? Gracious,

142

what do I say to the Alexanders? The issues are so important. Why, we're talking about national interests, huge corporations, the future of Atlantic shipping . . . '

'Quincey, I'm nearly sixty,' he said gently, 'I'll never get another chance. You're young, married to a rich man, you'll get chances galore. And don't exaggerate the issues. I can assure you that when national interests are crucial, ways are always found to protect them.'

I looked down at my hands. 'I don't know, Papa, it's very difficult . . .' How could I refuse him? I had learned at his knee – profited, even, from the experience of his ruin. Yet if I agreed, I would betray the mission on which I had been dispatched, let down the bank – worse, possibly concede Cunard to Morgan. At Old Broad Court I would never be trusted again. How would a man respond, I agonized? I knew the answer.

'You asked me what I wanted you to do . . .' His voice was soft. 'Go home, Quincey. That's all. Just leave it in the competent hands of Howard Alexander.'

'Howard's left,' I said. 'His father's dying.'

He smiled in a way that I remembered so well when a deal had been successful. 'Then it's simple, isn't it? I hear she's a lady of mercurial temperament . . . ' It was pure Mr Thomson, of course. Get me out of the city. That was the plan. And it was a good one, too, I suspected. In my absence, Mrs Schuller's enthusiasm for women standing together might well start waning.

I stood up. 'Papa,' I said, 'You'll have to give me time to think it over. We'll meet later.' And as he looked up at me, the lines deep on that anxious face, I was suddenly back in childhood and wanted to cry. I bent down and kissed him.

Later that afternoon, I received a telegraph from Richard. Uncle had died. I had already made my decision by then, but the news enforced it. From the start, my father's logic had been undeniable. I could argue about my duty but I was rich, a member of a powerful family.

For my father, by contrast, this was a rare chance to repair a shattered career and benefit everyone at home without the challenge to their pride that had made them reject every suggestion I had made.

Even so, back to the wall as I was, I questioned whether there was not some other course open to me. Papa had always said that every position could be turned to profit by means that, later, were often obvious. The trick was to predict them. Was there a trick that I had not seen?

Thus occupied, I took a walk in the fading light, strolling past the shops and cafés of the Unter den Linden, my hands deep in my fur muff. I heard my name called and, turning, I saw Edward Hide, correspondent of the London *Times*. 'Mrs Alexander,' he said, 'I was sitting in the Café Bauer and saw you pass . . . Won't you please join me for a few minutes?'

I liked Edward Hide, who was a short, pug-nosed man of about forty, with a lively mind. He had called on me, as I had agreed, and we had enjoyed some stimulating discussions. 'I'm glad I saw you,' he said as we sat down, 'for I'm leaving for London on the night train. I hear you've won the Schuller stock in Cunard . . . Congratulations!'

I shook my head sadly. 'I think you'll find that Morgans have been successful, Mr Hide. It's a pity, isn't it? Cunard's a great national institution. I don't really like to think of it being swallowed up by that gigantic trust, do you?' I was never sure whether my remark was deliberate or subconscious. Mr Hide worked for the most influential newspaper in the world, but I had not until then considered invoking the power of the press.

'It is indeed sad,' he agreed. 'Cunard liners have been crossing the Atlantic for over sixty years.'

'I mean,' I went on, 'these great cartels are greatly condemned in my own country. It makes one wonder where Mr Morgan will stop. Do you think English railways'll be safe, for example?'

'Good heavens, Mrs Alexander, why not?'

'Mr Morgan's a railroad mogul, isn't he? That's why he's gone into shipping. His trains had to stop at the ocean . . . '

Hide laughed. 'It's a thought,' he said.

'Then ships and railroads need steel, don't they?' I mused. 'Would he want the British Steel Mills? After all, he's the biggest steelmaster in the world.'

'And steel furnaces?' he mocked, 'need coal, don't they, Mrs Alexander?'

'You're ahead of me, Mr Hide,' I said, 'I hadn't thought of that . . .'

He smiled. 'I don't believe you,' he said. 'I think you're leading me on – delightfully, I'd add. You're drawing a picture of a rapacious giant grasping everying in Britain, perhaps even aspiring to the throne . . . his Majesty, King Morgan . . . '

'Now that really is fanciful,' I responded, 'though I suppose it has some logic.'

'But no evidence.'

'Except the ships . . . '

He looked at me intently for a moment. 'I think I detect what's in your mind,' he said with a smile, 'but, if you want my aid, I need to be told everything . . . every little detail . . . '

'In confidence?'

He nodded. So I told him – about Morgan's campaign to buy control of Cunard or to break it, most of which he knew, of course; about my dispatch to Berlin because I was a woman from New York, like Mrs Schuller; about my father; about the plan to buy time until the Admiralty acted, as Uncle had always predicted that, sooner or later, it must.

When I finished, he did not speak for a moment. The he smiled. 'So we must make it sooner, mustn't we? We must make the Admiralty act at once, give Cunard the funds it needs to square up to Mr Morgan, to ensure the company retains its independence . . . '

'And how can we do that?' I asked.

'You don't fool me, you know, Mrs Alexander,' he answered gently. 'You know as well as I do it's a good story . . . Why, here's Morgan, the wicked foreign baron . . . Here's the government allowing our island heritage to slip through its fingers . . . It won't, of course – and never intended to – but just one article in the *Times*'d have it rushing into action before an angry British people. It's got all the elements to appeal to a patriotic nation – and to an editor. The duty of the press . . . dilatory bureaucrats . . . Plus a lady banker and her poor father in his last chance to redeem his fortunes . . . '

'That was in confidence.'

'Well now,' he said, 'let's get down to how much was in confidence . . . let us open negotiations, Mrs Alexander . . . '

From the upper deck of the ferry boat, I braced myself against the autumn wind that tore at my veil, numbing my cheeks. I could see the port of Dover clearly, nestling under its great chalk cliffs, and I watched it with apprehension, uncertain of what awaited me in England. I had telegraphed the bare fact that we had lost Mrs Schuller's shares in Cunard, but its impact on a family already reeling under Uncle's passing would have been somewhat muted. A whole era had come to an abrupt end. He had literally been the bank, symbolizing its power in his strong dynamic personality. Business would continue at Old Broad Court, but a few weeks would be needed before the vacuum was properly filled.

The bows of the ferry dipped, sending back a shower of spray, and I thought of my last hours in Berlin. I had done exactly what Papa asked: departed from Berlin. I had sent Mrs Schuller a note, saying I had been urgently recalled for the funeral. 'If you wish,' I wrote, 'the stock transfers can be sent to London for execution, but a strange thing has happened. My father is in Berlin – for the other side! *There*'s an irony for us all. I've enjoyed our meetings so much. Please visit us in England.' To remove any doubts of my intention, I had added a postscript: 'It'll be a pity if Mr Morgan wins the game – but with your royal flush, I suppose *you* win as well. Can there be a dead heat in poker?'

There had been one big benefit to my retreat. I had called on Captain von Grumme at the Königliches Schloss. 'When we last met, Captain,' I said, 'you made me an offer. You said we'd be invited to issue your Kiel dockyard loan. That is, if Mr Morgan should acquire Frau Schuller's Cunard stock . . . I take it the offer's still open?'

'Of course, Mrs Alexander,' he said.

'We look forward to receiving your instructions,' I said.

Richard was waiting for me on the quay at Dover. He waved with a grin, looming above the others on the wharf. 'Oh, I'm glad to have you back,' he said as he embraced me. 'It's seemed like a hundred years . . . Let me look at you properly . . . ' He held me by the shoulders, studying me for a moment, and I looked back happily at his craggy face, his moustache that needed trimming,

146

and the grey eyes, soft with emotion. 'I think you're even more beautiful than you were before you left,' he said. 'Come on – let's get ashore.' As we walked down the gangway I inquired about poor Aunt Elizabeth and the family, saying I presumed the funeral would be at the church at Shere.

As we reached the quay, I asked about Cunard. 'Is it a disaster? Have we lost our client?'

'Lost?' he echoed. 'We've won! The Admiralty are putting up one and a half million . . . '

'What – just like that?' I queried.

'Well, there *was* a little pressure . . . *The Times* threatened to charge their lordships with letting Morgan steal a national asset under their very noses. That was enough – the danger of bad publicity frightens admirals more than the biggest broadside. There are conditions, of course. Further sales of the company's stock to foreigners is to be banned . . . all directors, managers and captains are to be British . . . '

'What'll happen to Mrs Schuller's shares?' I asked.

'I don't exactly know,' he answered, 'but Morgan won't want them now. They'll still be a sound investment for her – in the long term, anyway.' He was looking ahead of him as we walked along the quay. 'Did you, by chance, meet a Mr Edward Hide in Berlin?' he inquired idly.

'Occasionally,' I answered. 'In fact, we took coffee together in a café the other day.'

'I thought you might have done,' he said. 'I suppose it's a case of once a street dog always a street dog, eh?'

'Perhaps,' I agreed, 'a bit of one, at least.' He stopped and faced me and there, in front of everyone, he kissed me.

Chapter 7

It was two weeks after we had buried Uncle, one of those crisp autumn mornings when the sun shone on the water and the paddock grass was white with dew and the brown leaves on the oaks were starting to fall.

I awoke suddenly with a feeling of elation. I remember rushing to the windows and throwing back the curtains. 'I'm so utterly happy,' I thought. I turned and saw Richard watching me from our bed with a tolerant expression on his face that would have seemed supercilious if his sheer enjoyment of me had not been so evident. I wallowed in his pleasure, as sensual as a cat, stretching my arms slowly so that my breasts protruded under my flimsy nightdress. 'Why am I so lucky?' I asked.

'Because you deserve it,' he answered, 'but touch wood all the same. We must appease the Furies.'

Impulsively, I ran to the bed like a child and flung myself on him, my lips on his, my tongue seeking his. 'Oh, I love you,' I said breathlessly. 'No woman's ever loved a man as I love you.' I slipped under the sheets. 'Gently,' I said. 'I thought I felt him kicking in the night. Hallucinations, of course, for it's far too soon . . . but gently, all the same.'

We had spent much time at the cottage since my return, mainly because the rest of the family had stayed with Aunt Elizabeth at Shere. They were all dazed, as people often are by death.

Richard spent part of every week at Old Broad Court, when we would stay at Number 7, directing the bank the rest of the time with Howard from the Manor, where there was a nucleus of staff. Howard had been deeply affected by his father's death, but he was prepared for battle. No shots had yet been fired, the two men being too occupied so far with formalities and hours of consultation with the family lawyers.

James had joined us at the cottage at weekends and we had walked miles with him through the woods beside the river. We had ridden, too, with Richard on Tamburlaine and James and I on horses that were less demanding. All of us had spent much time at the Manor.

On this beautiful morning, we were due to go over there again for Richard and Howard to have another of their long discussions in the library. In fact, the three of us were just about to depart by trap when a motorcar emerged from the lane that led through the woods. We could see from its long distinctive yellow bonnet that it was The Leopard, but a different model — a four-seater tourer which I had heard was planned. Steven Mason was at the wheel, with his brother Martin beside him.

'Good morning, Mrs Alexander,' he greeted, with the usual touch of mockery in his tone. 'We've brought you a present from my father. What do you think of her?'

'A present?' I queried. 'You don't mean of the car, surely?'

'He thought you'd advertise it well. Did you know we've had orders for more than twenty?'

'It's extremely kind of him.'

'He thought it was fitting, too — since you're our chief now. Do you fancy a spin? There've been one or two changes in the control design which I could show you . . . '

'We're just about to go to the Manor.' I said. 'My husband has an appointment.'

'Why not drive over in the car?' Richard put in — then realizing that, with James, there were too many of us for the vehicle, he added: 'I'll go on Tamburlaine. I feel like a ride anyway.'

He called to one of the grooms to saddle the horse and I went indoors for a scarf and veil. We watched him mount. 'I wager I'll be there before you,' he said, and rode through the paddock gateway before cantering across the big field. As he neared the far fence, he checked the stallion and turned to wave. Then he jumped the timber and disappeared out of our sight behind some trees.

Steven held the offside door open for me. 'I expect you'd like to take the wheel, Mrs Alexander. I hear you can drive now. Father said you terrified the life out of him. Naturally, I didn't believe him — not after the scolding you gave me. I told him he must be mistaken . . . '

'If he truly said I can drive,' I responded, 'then he was exaggerating.'

'We'll hold on tight,' Steven said with a grin, and swung the starting handle.

We set off down the lane, with Martin and James in the back. Feeling the throb in that big engine, I felt the same excitement I had known with his father that day in the summer. 'She's going well,' I said to Steve.

'Oh, she's golden,' he answered with a fond smile.

'Did you know, Mrs Alexander,' Martin said over my shoulder, 'we've touched fifty-five in her?'

'What did your father think of that?' I called back, recalling his differences with them about tyres.

'It was with his blessing. We were experimenting with a new kind of tyre . . . Had carbon in the rubber. . . '

'They're on the car now,' Steve put in beside me, 'so you can go as fast as you like. Well, fingers crossed . . . We could still get a puncture, but they're an immense improvement.'

'What about the law?' I asked. 'Twelve miles an hour . . . '

'The forest road is straight,' he answered. 'You'll be able to see the police.'

'You're talking like a criminal,' I mocked – and stalled the car. 'I told you I wasn't very good,' I said as he got out.

He laughed. 'Are you out of gear?' he asked before he swung the handle.

As we came to the end of the lane and I turned on to the main route to the Manor, Steve turned to his brother: 'I reckon we're in for it now, Martin . . . The open road . . . Father *did* warn us . . . '

'No doubt about it,' his brother agreed. 'Speed intoxicates some people, like alcohol . . . '

'I think you're both being rather impertinent,' I rebuked.

'Sorry, Mrs Alexander,' said Steven, with a hurt look on his face that made me feel I had reacted too sharply. We were close in age, even if I was married. However, it made me drive faster.

I applied the brake as we approached a slight bend. I found the pedal high and remarked on it. 'Can it be adjusted?'

'A bit,' he answered. The road reached straight ahead of us for about five miles. 'Nothing to stop you now,' urged Steven.

I increased speed, enjoying the feeling of the wind. I began to gain confidence. 'Am I doing all right?' I inquired tentatively.

'Anyone'd think you'd been driving for years,' Steven answered.

'How fast are we going?' I asked.

'About thirty-five . . . Pretty slow really . . .'

I opened the throttle and felt the forward thrust of the car, my hat tugging at its securings of scarf and veil.

I saw Richard when he was about two miles distant, riding through the forest bracken towards a point on the road ahead of us. I honked the horn while the others waved, and shouted. He responded with a raised hand.

He reached the road about half a mile ahead of us and, instead of turning away towards the Manor, as I expected, he cantered slowly towards us along the verge. I presumed he planned to ride the rest of the way alongside the car, as horsemen often accompanied carriages.

He was hatless that day and with his hair flying in the wind and mounted on that superb grey horse, he made a fine figure. Instinctively, eager to reach him, I increased our speed. 'Over forty now, I reckon,' Steven said. I smiled back at him.

Richard was approaching us from the other side of a small bridge over a stream – the same bridge where, when Uncle had summoned us for the Berlin discussion, we had surprised a group of ponies because a cluster of small trees and bushes screened a slight twist in the road.

We were a good hundred yards from the bridge when I began to slow down. I could see Richard still cantering easily towards us, the stallion collected under his complete control. I moved the throttle lever to slow the car further. As we got closer, I realized that we might meet on the bridge, which was narrow, so I planned to stop before we reached it. Still, though, Richard had not reined in the horse.

Suddenly, as the trees screened the road, the engine surged in a noisy whine without my touching the throttle, giving the car a sudden impetus I had not intended. 'My God!' Steven exclaimed. 'The governor arm's broken on the carburettor!' He leaned across me and turned off the ignition switch on the dashboard to cut the motor. But the car was still moving forward faster than planned. I stamped on the brake but, awkwardly high as it was, my boot slipped off it. From behind me, Martin reached forward and hauled on the handbrake.

It was all too late. We met Richard and the horse on the bridge. There was no collision and we had come to a halt, but it made no difference. We had appeared before the stallion suddenly from the blind of the trees, with a loud noise he had never heard before. He snorted and reared.

There is no doubt, that day, the gods were against us. Had it happened a few yards away in either direction, it would not have mattered. Richard could have controlled the stallion easily and soothed his fears. But there was limited room on the little bridge. One of the horse's hocks touched the low protective wall at the side, and he sprang from it. Then a foot slipped and he came down, rolling, hooves flailing, as he tried to get up.

What happened then remains indistinct. I remember letting out a scream as I jumped from the car; I can still see Richard sprawled on the bridge, unconscious, his skin white, his hair thick with blood. I can hear myself saying: 'Oh my God!' as I knelt beside him – and James's caution: 'Don't move him, Quincey. His back may be broken . . .'

I recall disconnected images – the car going off, accelerating fast as Steven went for a doctor; James's hand on my shoulder; the blood on my dress; the grey pallor of Martin's shocked young face; the horse reaching down with his head at one moment towards Richard's still body until I checked him gently, holding his nose. I knew Richard was dead but my mind would not accept it. I did not cry. I did not even feel. His eyes were open, with nothing behind them. It was not Richard, I thought. It cannot be Richard.

I remember them coming with both a trap and a carriage – a lot of people. Howard, Nina, a doctor, grooms. I declined the carriage, preferring to travel with Richard in the trap in which they laid him on the floor. Odd the little things that come to mind. I can precisely recall the horse that drew the trap – a chestnut with a short mane and a scar in his left rump – and the weather. I remember the weather, for the sun had gone and by the time we reached the Manor gates the sky had clouded and it began to rain. The trap entered the Manor drive and I thought of what I had said that morning – 'Why am I so lucky?' – and touching wood to appease the Furies. And still I felt no pain. I knew it would come, though, and already I feared it, for I knew there was no balm for that kind of pain, no choloroform that would blank it out. That was an agony that would have to be borne unless I chose to die, but I needed the agony. I needed to be consumed by the agony like flames at the stake.

'Come, Quincey.' James, who had accompanied me in the trap, was holding his hand outstretched to help me step down. His voice was gentle. There were grooms standing around wanly with their hats doffed. Aunt Elizabeth, clad in black, was in the doorway, horror and compassion on her face. 'Quincey,' James urged quietly. I knew it was all a dream, of course. I would wake up soon and everything would be as it was.

And then my illusion ended. I was still in the trap when Stella stood there on the gravel in front of the house. I can still see the hate in her eyes, already wet with tears, as she said in a strangely muted voice: 'I hear you've killed my brother!'

Chapter 8

Already it was dusk on the bleak winter day when Howard's carriage emerged from the lane that led through the woods and stopped in front of the cottage. I was waiting for him, knowing he would be punctual to the hour he had suggested in his note, and I watched his arrival from the window of my bedroom, standing in semi-darkness with the candles still unlit.

As he climbed out of the brougham, I saw that he was wearing an old-fashioned frock coat and a high shirt collar, assuming presumably that this attire was suited to the occasion. When we met I was sure he would speak in a muted tone. I heard his knock, followed by the sound of movement below as one of the maids went from the kitchen to admit him. I prepared to go downstairs. I knew what he wanted from me – and how I would respond.

Grief affects people in unexpected ways, and the weeks that had passed since Richard's death had been for me a bewildering period. At moments, I felt as though I had been transformed into a different woman who was completely unfamiliar to me – even into two women, one being an observer of the other. The funeral was never distinct in my mind. It was like an old faded photograph that had always been blurred by movement of the camera. I could recall the figures in the picture. I knew who they were, but their faces were unclear.

I was an unusual widow, with no close family to share my distress. I had stood at the graveside with people who at worst were enemies and at best were strangers – except James.

James had loved him, too, and me in his way. After the wake he had gone back with me to the cottage. The restraint I had displayed, despite my widow's veil, was required no longer. The numbness since the day he died had gone. The agony was naked, and I broke down, weeping unashamedly. James held me tight in his arms, his own cheeks wet with tears. 'If only there was something I could say, Quincey,' he kept whispering.

'If only there was something anyone could say,' I had answered.

James became vital to me. My marriage had been brief. I had been denied a whole lifetime with my husband and I ached for compensation. I developed a voracious appetite for knowledge that I could no longer gain directly, a hunger to know every tiny detail of his life. It was a desire that James was eager to feed, finding consolation in it too. We would talk for hours with me questioning him about Richard, like an interrogator, demanding description of every minor thing he could recall, taking him through his life in sequence from the first day he had encountered him as a child.

I had declined Aunt Elizabeth's invitation to stay at the Manor, preferring to remain at the cottage, the only place I had shared with Richard, though now staff lived in. Often, though, I was drawn to that big house for there, too, were people who had been a part of Richard's life. Nobody who had known him was spared from my obsession. Once, I found Emmeline, Howard's thirteen-year-old daughter, sitting on her pony among the trees at the edge of the wood, staring at the cottage which, because of its remoteness, had always been regarded uneasily by the family. She must, I knew, have had some contact with her uncle. 'Why not come in for a moment?' I suggested. 'A glass of milk or lemonade?'

She looked at me warily, perhaps guessing my purpose. 'No thank you, Aunt Quincey,' she said 'I'd better get back or they'll be cross with me.' And she cantered away through the trees.

I even sought to establish relations with Stella, despite her hostility and appalling accusation on the day of Richard's death. There was no pride in me. Stella had known Richard better than anyone. 'We're mourning the same man,' I pleaded. 'Can't we try to be friends?'

She looked at me with astonishment. 'How can we ever be friends?' she challenged, her face twisted in shocked anger, and hurried from the room.

By the following day Stella had reconsidered my approach to her. Without warning, she arrived at the cottage, looking hollow-eyed as though she had not slept all night. 'I'm sorry,' she apologized. 'You were right . . . We've much in common . . .' I did not trust her change of heart, but trust was not a vital element.

She had perceived the full dimension of my craving. After that first visit, she came over quite often and talked of her childhood with him, of their homes and parents, of valued servants and close friends. Understanding my need as she did, she would exploit it – satisfying me at times with vivid accounts of occasions that came to her, describing the actual clothes he had worn and what he had said, complete with family nicknames and words that as a child he had mispronounced; and at other moments she would play with me cruelly, holding back incidents she knew I yearned to hear. She would break off at a gripping point in the middle of an anecdote, saying, 'I can't recall what happened then' or declare with a shrug, 'Oh, that's not very interesting . . . ' When I pleaded with her to continue, she would insist: 'No . . . it's not interesting . . . ' She would study me then, watching the effect she was having on me, and I knew that the malice was still there.

Sometimes, we went out in the two-horse phaeton she drove herself. On one afternoon, we passed the grooms exercising some of the horses kept at the cottage stables. 'That's Richard's Arab stallion, isn't it?' Stella asked and, when I confirmed it, she looked at me with surprised horror. 'I don't know how you can bear to have him there still,' she said.

'It wasn't the horse's fault,' I responded. 'He was Richard's favourite . . . Vital to his breeding theory . . . I'm positive he'd want that to continue.'

'How can *you* judge what Richard'd want?' she demanded, glaring at me, her face contorted in contempt. 'You didn't know him . . .'

'Oh, I knew him,' I said. 'I loved him very deeply.'

'You trapped him – then you destroyed him,' she insisted. 'One of these days, God will even the balance . . . ' I did not feel much pain at her outburst because I lived with permanent pain. I was protected.

'I couldn't keep that horse,' she went on, her voice calmer. 'Really, Quincey, I find you impossible to understand . . . ' She said it in a way that was almost matter-of-fact – as though she had never spoken the harsh words of seconds before.

Some days during those early weeks, I saw no one but the servants. I enjoyed the isolation, going for long lone walks in the woods, with trees now bare of leaves, conscious of the child I was carrying. I would wonder often what he would be like — whether his hair or his eyes would be the same as Richard's — and I would think much about a name for him. Always this induced a sharp pang in my general state of longing. I needed to talk to Richard about the name. Names were vital. People grew into names. I wanted him desperately just to have seen him, if only once. I questioned why God, even our pagan gods, did not save him at least for that, which made me fear during the bad times whether other tragedies lay ahead in the divine plan. Would the child be whole? Would he be insane, blind, deformed? I would fight for faith as I strode along the woodland paths, scolding myself sharply for such morbid thoughts, forcing myself to regard the child as a reward, as a prize of God, the bright purpose of our union. There was logic there, for what otherwise could be his aim in placing us together from different continents, for so short a period? A great destiny must be planned, I told myself.

So the weeks passed, with sharply changing moods in a woman who was strange to me. With the winter drawing in, the weather worsened, but I would still go out, taking a perverse pleasure in cold rain on my face or a wind that thrust its chill through any clothing. I drifted in this fashion with the passing days in a kind of keening, while the wounds dried a little. By the afternoon of Howard's visit, the scabs had begun to form.

Howard was standing with his back to me as I entered the room, looking through the window at the light evening mist that lay over the Solent water. The fire was casting moving shadows on the wall, for the lamps were low. He turned as he heard the door latch, and faced me, seeming too big for the dimensions of the cottage, his stoop emphasized by the low ceiling. ' It's good of you to receive me,' he said in his formal way.

'You're most welcome, I can assure you,' I replied.'Berlin seems an age ago, doesn't it?'

I indicated a chair and took one opposite. 'I've come to speak of mundane matters,' he said, breaking off as a maid brought in a tea tray. For a second his eyes met mine, marked by the intense expression I recognized but could never quite interpret. It hinted at a restless spirit, controlled, always seeking release. I think, too, that dressed in mourning, I affected him, touching some emotional string. He glanced away, commented on the room and its exceptional view. 'You know, of course, of Richard's will,' he continued when the maid departed. There had been no formal reading of it but the lawyer had called on me to explain that, except for a legacy for James, I had inherited everything he possessed.

'I expect you know, too,' Howard went on, 'that the family trust was broken at my father's death. Richard's stock has now passed to you, Quincey, which places me in a situation that's . . . well, delicate, at least.'

'Delicate?' I echoed, passing him a cup of tea. 'You're unchallenged now, aren't you? You're Chairman and Managing Director of Alexanders. No dissension . . . No boardroom rift . . .'

'That's true,' he said carefully, 'but without your support, I don't control the bank.'

I smiled at his concern. 'Oh, you'll have my support, Howard . . . usually, anyway. I'll want Richard's ideas to be reflected in bank policy, as if he'd still been here. But that gives room for compromise, surely, doesn't it?'

'To a degree,' he said. He shifted in his chair. 'This isn't easy for me, Quincey,' he went on, 'but . . . well, I've been wondering if you'd thought yet of the future. Your family are in America — your roots, one might say . . .'

'So you were thinking,' I said, 'that I might prefer to live there?'

He made a slight movement of his big head in assent.

'And dispose of my stock?' I asked lightly. 'That's the mundane matter you had in mind, I presume . . .'

My words had a sharpness that I had not intended and they offended him. He looked down. 'I thought it might suit you,' he said. 'Your shares are worth a great deal . . . millions . . . You're a rich woman, Quincey, and since there'd seem to be no reason for you to stay in Britain . . .' He gave a little shrug.

I stared into the fire for a few seconds. 'There *are* reasons to stay, Howard,' I said. 'I'm going to have a child. I think Richard would have wanted him raised in England, don't you?'

He was astonished, rendered speechless for a second. 'It's something I hadn't considered,' he said, 'though I don't know why. It's important for all of us.'

'You told me I must have a boy,' I added with a smile, 'so I'm going to.'

'Let's hope so,' he said dubiously.

'Anyway,' I went on, 'I'd have chosen to remain . . . I expect you've guessed that I'd wish a closer link with the bank.'

Caution came into his expression. 'I don't think I understand,' he said.

'I want to take Richard's place,' I said, 'at his desk at Old Broad Court.'

He stared at me as though he had not heard correctly. 'That's quite impossible,' he declared.

'Why, Howard?' I asked. 'In Berlin you introduced me as your colleague . . . '

'That was tactical.'

'You were good enough to compliment me . . . '

The frustration in him was evident. He stood up suddenly and, striding to the window, stared into the darkness, hands clasped tight behind his back. 'Quincey, we can't afford yet to fly in the face of custom . . . What you're proposing would affront a lot of people – our staff, our clients, other bankers – our associates.'

'What exactly do you think'd happen?' I asked.

'We'd be a laughing stock,' he answered, 'we'd lose clients. Worse, we'd lose trust . . . '

'For goodness' sake why, Howard?' I responded. 'I realize it'd need tact and discretion, but Captain von Grumme seemed content to deal with me. I gained you the German government. How many clients do you have of such prestige?'

'You still don't understand, do you, Quincey?' He moved suddenly in anger, almost striking his head on a ceiling beam. 'The City consists of a web of understanding in which a woman could find no place. There are daily meetings, discussions, tacit unspoken agreements, nuances I couldn't begin to define – all between men. The result'd be most adverse . . . '

'How do you know,' I asked simply, 'if it hasn't been tested?'

'God give me strength!' he exclaimed – not loudly, but he apologized at once. 'Quincey, I'll agree to anything you want . . . anything reasonable. But not this . . . In your own interests . . . ' He paused ' . . . *and* your child's . . . '

The last point seemed vicious and angered me. 'You said you needed my support to control the bank.' I reminded him.

His eyes became darker than I had ever seen them. 'That's blackmail,' he said.

'*You* dare speak of blackmail?' I demanded, recalling Mr Thomson. 'It's negotiation.'

'You're giving me no choice?'

'None, Howard.' The argument had changed me, shaken me from my state of self-pity. I would mourn for long, but the time had stopped for lonely walks in woods. 'I will arrive at the bank on Wednesday,' I said. 'At ten o'clock.'

'In mourning?' he inquired in a tone of shock.

'What better place for me to mourn,' I asked, 'than my husband's desk?'

He stood up to leave with a sigh, his face drawn, and I rose to conduct him to the door. 'Give it a fair trial, Howard,' I appealed quietly, 'and you'll find me a loyal partner.'

His eyes were on mine, still perplexed. 'I'd always known I'd have to fight Richard,' he said. 'I never dreamed I'd be fighting you.'

'Not fighting, Howard,' I said. 'Oh, I hope not fighting . . . Working together . . . Partners with an aim in common . . . *You* see – I'll surprise you.' And on impulse, I leaned forward to kiss him – as the wife of his late cousin, as family, as reassurance, even as a pleading. But, as on the occasion in Berlin that had been marked by emotion, too, our lips met without intention. They lingered, in contact for barely seconds but it was longer than before and he did not recoil in shock as he had then. He stared at me, not understanding. Then he turned without another word and left the house.

From the porch I watched him climb into his carriage. I do not think he looked at me from within it, or even raised a hand as it departed, but I could not see clearly from the darkness. As for me, I was bewildered, and troubled, and strangely drained.

On Wednesday morning the sky was overcast and light rain was marking the windows of the brougham as I travelled to the bank. I wished the day had been finer. It was as though the City was receiving me with a somewhat sour expression.

I had come up from Shere the previous afternoon, spending the night at Number 7 – which, without Uncle's big personality, now seemed a strangely colourless house, as the Manor did.

My own establishment in Grosvenor Square was ready for occupation, but no staff had yet been employed. I had asked James to dine with me. Our mood was marked by an eve-of-battle colour. 'I feel like Joan of Arc,' I said, 'about to attack the British at Orléans.'

For all my apprehension, at the bank I was well received. The very moment the carriage came to a halt in Old Broad Court the front door opened and Mr Wells, the major-domo in charge of 'the Front Hall men', stood at the head of the marble steps with a broad beam on his face. 'Welcome, Mrs Alexander,' he declared.

I entered the huge general office where, a few months before, I had received so unique a reception. This time the clerks pretended to ignore me, hunched over their tall desks, observing me furtively. I must have seemed a dramatic figure, standing there on that vast expanse of marble, dressed in mourning, though I had reduced this to the minimum – a plain linen skirt and mantle and a simple hat, all black of course, but I wore no veil. I had come to work. Suddenly, I felt very young.

James was at my elbow, and walked with me toward the half-glazed door of 'The Room'. 'Something's happening,' he said, 'though I'm not sure what . . . Richard's desk has been prepared for you with great care. There's even smelling salts and a needle and cotton in the drawer. Evans has been taken off other duties to serve you . . . He was Richard's clerk, and a loyal man. Howard could easily have allocated another clerk to you . . . Then he's suggested that I should act as your personal assistant, which he knew you'd like. Nina's joining us for lunch, by the way.'

We had reached 'The Room'. 'He sounds as though he's been thoughtful,' I said. 'What's concerning you?'

'It's too easy.' He knocked and opened the door.

Howard stood up and came forward to greet me. Mathew, too, was on his feet, smiling. My mantle was taken from my shoulders and I was ushered to Richard's desk. I sat down in his chair. The blotter was virgin white. The silver inkwells had been polished to a high shine.

'I've called a meeting in the boardroom of the senior managers in

161

half an hour,' said Howard, 'just so that you can meet them all, though doubtless you'll want to talk to them individually in due course. Meanwhile, here are a list of our principal clients and the reports, both weekly and daily. The closing prices of stock we hold are listed every night after the markets are closed – like our foreign currency position and sterling balances . . . Ditto Bills of Exchange, both receivable and payable, loans, both lent and borrowed, and . . . '

He went on, giving me a résumé of how the bank was controlled, stopping to remark at one moment: 'It must have been much the same in New York. Their position, of course, is telegraphed to us daily . . . '

I was surprised, despite James's warning. It was as though my quarrel with Howard at Shere had never happened. The managers, too, received me politely when I met them. 'I shall be seeking the guidance of all of you,' I said, 'and I shall be grateful for your help.'

About an hour after my arrival, a client arrived to see Howard. He was a man in his seventies and walked with difficulty, aided by a stick. He had a thin grey beard and wore small steel-rimmed glasses over cold, light blue eyes that protruded slightly in their sockets. 'Good day, Sir George,' Howard greeted him, holding out his hand.

Sir George ignored him, looking instead at me, leaning on his stick. 'May I please introduce Mrs Alexander,' Howard said. 'my poor late cousin's wife.'

'Sir George Brighton is one of our most valued clients,' he explained to me.

'I'm pleased to make your acquaintance, Sir George,' I said with a smile.

He did not respond immediately, still staring at me, appearing almost crouched as he leaned on his stick. 'You mean your cousin Richard?' he asked Howard.

'That's correct,' Howard agreed.

The old man's expression became oddly suspicious. 'But surely he only went a few weeks ago . . . It was a sad business, but what are you doing here, young lady?' he snapped.

'I've taken his place, Sir George,' I answered, 'as I know he would have wished.'

'Good heavens!' he said. 'How absolutely extraordinary . . . '

162

'I should explain, Sir George,' Howard put in, 'that Mrs Alexander worked in our New York office for some years before my cousin met her. So she is, you might say, experienced . . . '

'Experienced!' he echoed, glaring at me now, 'as a banker? What is the world coming to? First they want the vote, now this . . . Is there somewhere we can go, Howard? The boardroom, perhaps? Good day to you, Madam,' he said to me coldly and, turning with the aid of his stick, limped from the room, followed by Howard.

For a few seconds, neither I nor Mathew spoke. I was aware that the colour was high in my face. Mathew was leaning back in his chair, tapping idly on his desk with the end of a pencil, watching me with a slight smile.

'Is he very important?' I asked.

'He's Chairman of about ten companies,' Mathew answered. 'In all he controls assets of . . . about twenty million, I suppose. Certainly'd be important if he took his business away . . . '

'Is he likely to do that?' I asked with concern. Mathew shrugged his bony shoulders. 'Who knows?' he queried.

Howard returned and sat down at his desk without speaking. He rang for his clerk and gave him some instructions. At last I asked: 'What was the result of your meeting, Howard? He seemed a strange man . . . '

'Sir George has decided to patronize another house,' he answered with cold formality. 'He's an old man living in a world that's changing fast. He's accustomed to the time when a widow didn't go out in public for two years, when mourning was a long and formalized process . . . '

'But this isn't going out in public,' I responded. 'It's a private office.'

'I don't think it is to Sir George . . . ' And he bent over his desk to continue his work.

About half an hour later, one of the 'Front Hall Men' came in with an envelope. Howard slit the flap open with a silver paper-knife and read the contents. 'The Governor of the Bank of England,' he said, 'has asked to see me for a few moments before lunch . . . '

Soon after twelve James looked round the door. 'Nina's arrived. . . ' As we walked up to the dining-room on the floor above, he said: 'I'm beginning to understand Howard's tactics.'

'Tactics?'

'They're clever. He's conceding to your wishes in every way he can – and giving you enough rope to knot it round your own neck.'

I found this hard to accept. 'Surely . . . ' I protested.

'Listen,' he cut in, 'the appointment with Sir George Brighton was made only yesterday . . . I've checked with Howard's clerk. That's not like Sir George, he makes plans well ahead. Of all our clients, he was the most certain to be shocked, even if you hadn't been in mourning. Howard arranged it, Quincey. What's more, he knew that the old man was due to call on the Governor of the Bank of England, which'd really put the cat among the birds. So Howard invited him to visit here first . . . '

I stopped walking. 'James that simply can't be true,' I said. 'Howard would never risk losing an important client merely to make a point to me . . . '

'He won't lose him – not if you respond as he expects. He'll just write to him tonight asking him to reconsider. Casually, he'll mention you've thought better of your position.'

James opened the door to the dining-room. Nina greeted me with as warm a smile as she could manage. 'And how did it go this morning?' she inquired. I had an odd feeling I had been betrayed.

Howard was delayed, but we waited for him. When he arrived his face, with his thick eyebrows, was set in a frown. 'Well,' asked Nina impatiently, 'did the Governor have much of moment to speak of?'

Howard sipped from the glass of sherry the butler had brought to him. 'He expressed interest in Quincey . . . Sir George Brighton had called on him after leaving us . . . ' He paused.

'Do go on, Howard,' Nina urged with irritation.

'Quincey,' he said, 'It's hard to understand the City. The Governor doesn't have to say anything, he merely intimates. Usually this concerns some business matter he doesn't favour for some reason – repercussions, perhaps, or a precedent . . . He needs do no more – it's like a command.'

'You make him sound like a king,' I said, and Howard concurred with a shrug. 'And this king,' I went on, 'summoned you behind the huge stone walls of the Bank of England because of me, unimportant as I am . . . Howard, I just don't believe it.'

'He had another matter to discuss,' Howard conceded, 'but you were his real purpose. He and Sir George are old friends. They share the same views. The Governor's concerned about standards, about convention. He made his wishes clear . . . There's no question now that you must reconsider. Don't you agree, James?'

James laughed. 'I can't believe my ears, Howard! Are you really consulting me?'

'I think Quincey might take some note of what you say.'

The two men would never have got on – Howard with his serious aspect, James with his feigned frivolity and undisguised taste for women and horse-racing. Always James had been in Richard's camp. Howard would have dismissed him long ago had he been allowed to.

'Oh, I concede you've cornered her this time,' James said easily.

'Cornered?' I echoed sharply. Suddenly, I could feel Howard's lips on my mouth and the sensation was disturbing.

'You've not got much choice,' James went on. 'Not now.'

'And if, despite the Governor, I insist on staying?' I demanded.

'Despite the Governor?' Howard asked incredulously. 'You couldn't possibly.' He put down his sherry glass and took his seat at the head of the table. 'Quincey,' he said, 'you're not only a woman . . .'

'You're in mourning,' Nina added, '*and* pregnant . . . I don't know how you can be so stubborn – or so tasteless.'

'I think you've got to face the odds, Quincey,' said James, as he sat down opposite Nina. 'You've gone out in the betting now. Wait until next season.'

'And what'll happen then?' I demanded angrily. 'When I'm out of mourning and I've borne a son?'

'A child,' Nina corrected.

Howard was watching me, his dark eyes unblinking. Despite my anger, I wonder if *he* was conscious of *my* lips, if he even remembered his departure from the cottage. 'An accommodation,' he said after a pause, 'of some kind, so long as you're reasonable . . .'

'What's that mean – no desk in 'The Room'?'

He gave a pained shrug. 'We'll consider what's practical. I think you know how I feel about the bank. I'll let no one, not even you,

165

do it damage'.

'Do you think it's not important to me?' I challenged, 'or to its future that I carry?' I met his steady gaze, saw the hint of another shrug. 'I said I *hoped* there wouldn't be a fight, Howard,' I reminded him, 'but don't let's forget who fired the first shot.'

'And what on earth do you mean by that?' asked Nina.

'Howard knows,' I said. I was tempted to continue my resistance, but I knew James was right and limited myself to no more than a rear-guard action. One fact was unchanged: I still owned as much stock as Howard and Mathew did together. No matter what the traditions of the City might be, I could prove an uneasy partner. 'I insist on being consulted,' I said quietly, and Howard conceded with a movement of his head. 'The daily reports are to be sent to me every night when I'm in London,' I went on, and he nodded agreement. 'A meeting with you once a week so that I'm fully informed of the bank's business . . . ' Again, he agreed with a gesture. 'The bank,' I added, knowing this would provoke a different response, 'to acquire the Mason Motor Company at cost and to supply what funding it may need.'

I had taken him by surprise, and he shook his head abruptly. 'Out of the question,' he said.

'I insist.' My anger was growing, more coloured now by bitterness. 'If you want my support, that's a condition, Howard. Otherwise, I'll obstruct you in every way I can – as Richard would have done.'

He was silent for a few seconds. The decision, with its symbolic undertones, was a hard one for him; but Masons, still small, was worth the price of peace – at least for the present. 'Agreed,' he conceded at last, 'under protest . . . '

'This is ours,' I reminded him, taking in Old Broad Court with gesture of my hands, 'not just yours . . . ' And when I said 'ours', I meant more than mine – as Howard realized. I asked: 'You knew Sir George'd be with the Governor today, didn't you?'

Once more, he hesitated, the muted challenge obvious now, for the lines had been drawn. Then slowly, he lowered his eyes – to my lips; my neck; to my breasts even, I felt, under my blouse; to my hands that lay on the table. He seemed to be savouring me. I glared at him, the resentment strong in me, and felt the colour rising to my cheeks. Yet I knew he resented it, too, within himself: the fact that I inspired the savouring, a weakness in the armour. 'Yes,' he answered at last, 'I knew.'

The next day, James accompanied me in the carriage to Waterloo. I planned to stay most of the time in London now, but just then I needed Shere for a few more days. 'I feel responsible,' he apologized. 'I should never have let you make a frontal assault. Next time, we'll attack his flank . . . a series of raids, perhaps . . . '

'There's more than one way to kill a cat,' I agreed, and gripped his hand for a second, grateful for his support.

My train was met at Brockenhurst in the usual way. As we crossed the forest along that road so marked by memories, we passed Stella approaching us in the phaeton she drove herself. She did not wave as she passed, just looked at me blankly for a second, and put the whip to the horses.

I knew as soon as I reached the cottage that something was wrong. The servants avoided my eyes, seeming over-eager to leave me. It was instinct that drew me to the stables. A groom barred my path. 'Good afternoon, Ma'am,' he said. 'Can I be of assistance?'

'No thank you,' I answered. 'I've just come to look at the horses.'

He, too, appeared diffident. 'What's the matter, Harry?' I asked.

'Why, nothing, Ma'am,' he answered.

I moved past him, towards Tamburlaine's stable.

'Ma'am!' he called out, realizing where I was going. 'I shouldn't go to the stallion's box . . . '

I turned. 'Good heavens, why not?' I asked.

'There's been an accident . . .' I looked at him incredulously. 'Miss Stella was here earlier' he said. 'We tried to stop her . . . '

By now I had reached the stable and I could see over the half-door why he had tried to divert me. The horse was lying as he had fallen, partly on his side, his body twisted awkwardly, his legs bent under him. There was not much left of his fine head because she had used a shotgun at close range. For a moment I felt nothing. Then my emotions rose within me—shock, horror, sadness, disgust—and, despite the presence of the groom, I bent down and vomited.

Part 3

Spring 1904

Chapter 9

[1]

Nina stood in the doorway of my office with an expression of astonished disapproval on her face. 'Really, Quincey,' she exclaimed. 'Are you completely out of your senses?'

Often I gained a perverse enjoyment from shocking Nina, but this time I knew her censure had some merit.

The scene before her that morning was offensive, but it was familiar and expected. It was nine o'clock, a time when she often called. As usual I had breakfasted in bed, where I read the *Financial Times*. Then I went to the nursery, where Jonny, now aged fifteen months, was being fed by Nanny Roberts. He still had the flaxen hair and blue eyes of a baby. I was honoured with a smile before a downward thump with a thoughtless hand on a high-rimmed plate directed at me a spoonful of gruel that I only just avoided. I kissed him, avoiding a messy mouth, and went downstairs.

I was sitting now beside my desk, in a housecoat of blue silk, going through my post with Liza, my secretary, while Maisie brushed my hair down my back, as she did every morning for ten minutes. The early part of the day at 18 Grosvenor Square was always marked by informality, since I employed only women within the house. By ten o'clock, when the earliest appointments were made, I would be properly attired – and fully briefed.

The house was alive with activity. In a corner of my office the ticker-tape machine was rattling bursts as it recorded the prices on the continental bourses which, because of the time difference, were already open. The sound of two typewriting machines could be heard from the adjoining room. I was speaking on the telephone to Edgar Smith, Manager of Alexanders Dealing Department, about some sudden overnight buying of copper in Amsterdam. Seeing Nina's face, I ended my conversation quickly. For there was, in fact, one difference from what she usually saw. Despite my *déshabillé*, a young man was leaning against the window, arms folded, surveying us all with a supercilious smile. Steven Mason had arranged an apointment at ten o'clock. He had arrived precisely one hour too soon.

The office in my home was the 'accommodation' of which Howard had spoken after my abortive attempt to claim a desk in 'The Room' in 1902. In fact, inadequate though it had seemed to me at the time, it suited us both – Howard because it allowed me the involvement in bank affairs I had demanded without ruffling traditional waters; me because I could run it how I liked. I kept in touch with the managers by telephone, as well as through James and Howard, and also by regular visits to Old Broad Court which, as I was a big stockholder, no one questioned. If I wanted to work there for a few hours, I used a small private office.

Two years had passed now since Richard had died, and my relations with the Alexanders had grown fragile roots. Once Nina had realized that I accepted her position as wife of the head of the family, she had become amenable, giving me advice that was often helpful – and criticism when she judged that my taste for the unconventional, which she could never comprehend, had gone too far.

As for the others, I had become accepted now as a member of the family, even by Stella. After the Tamburlaine horror, her health had broken down and she had gone to Monte Carlo for a long stay on the advice of her doctors. I knew that really it was me, rather than the horse, she had felt the need to kill. I had wondered often if that terrible act had assuaged in any way the violence in her. I could not tell for certain. After her return she never referred to it, but her hostility had given way, it seemed, to a cool, rather remote acceptance of my presence among them – but that, I suspected, was due to Jonny, whom she worshipped.

Jonny –Jonathan Richard Gilbert Alexander – had been born in May of the previous year in my bedroom upstairs in 18 Grosvenor Square. He had weighed eight and a half pounds and came pelting out into the world in less than three hours as if, so James had put it, there were at least another six runners in the race. His impact on all our lives was immense. Not only was he the heir apparent, being the only boy, but he had a personality that won everyone from the moment he looked at them. He cried sometimes, of course, that being the language babies use, but usually he was giggling, remind-

172

ing me at times of Mrs Schuller, with whom he clearly shared an attitude to life. Anyone who went near him tended to be greeted with a warm, embracing smile or outstretched arms in demand to be picked up — to an extent, I felt at times, that was a trifle indiscriminate.

For me, he revealed a kind of joy I had never suspected. Nanny, of course, provided the vital balance within this enironment of total adoration, insisting on a rigid discipline from the earliest stage. On her day off, though, I would instruct the under-nanny to bring him to me in the morning, and he would lie in bed beside me while I had breakfast, pointing at my newspaper with a demanding finger which I took to be a view that the price of zinc was far too high.

As winter had passed we had spent much time at Shere, where we celebrated his first birthday. By now he had got the measure of us all, even Nanny. He would sit upright in his pram gesturing like an emperor to be transported either to the river, where the birds fascinated him, or to the paddocks, where he liked to watch the horses. He could not walk yet, of course, but the pace at which he could crawl had James watching him with wonder sometimes as though he was a promising yearling — which, in a manner of speaking, he was.

The others were as obsessed by him as I was. Stella regarded him as divinely sourced, and would hold him as though she was partaking in some religious rite. Nina was just as devoted, though at moments I could see he was a cause of sadness. I recall once seeing Emmeline put an arm round her and saying: 'It's a rotten shame, isn't it, Mama, that you've only got us girls — but we'll try to be especially good to make up for it. Hey, Jonny!' she had called out suddenly. 'You see that bird hovering up there! That's a heron. Watch it!' And she had pushed the pram at a run towards the river, with the little boy smiling, fascinated, as the bird streaked down to the water after a fish.

In the mornings in Grosvenor Square Jonny held court, despite Nanny, and never lacked for visitors — which was why Nina was standing in the doorway of my office, scandalized at the sight of me in my peignoir, with Maisie attending to my toilet, in the presence of Steven Mason.

I smiled at her as I hung up the telephone receiver. 'Good

morning, Nina,' I said with a brightness that told her I was on the defensive, for now we knew each other well.

'What in the world is this young man doing here while you're . . . ' She broke off, her gesture encompassing my attire.

'Now that's a good question,' I said, deciding to brave it out.

Ten minutes before, to my surprise, Steven Mason had peered round the door. 'Madame la directrice?' he had inquired, his eyes mocking. He was wearing tweed driving clothes, his peaked cap and goggles held in his hand. Even he, though as arrogant as usual, was embarrassed that I was not dressed. 'Forgive me if I intrude,' he said, 'and for being early, but I have to catch the afternoon boat. The timing's tight, so I was hoping . . . '

'Who let you in?' I demanded coldly.

'You mustn't blame the maid . . . I insisted. I didn't realize, of course . . . ' He broke off, his eyes on Maisie, still brushing my hair. 'You've caught me at an awkward moment,' I said, just as the telphone rang. 'Well, since you're here, you may as well stay . . . ' I pointed to a chair by the window and lifted the receiver.

All the time, as I talked to my caller, I was conscious of Steven watching me. It was a strange feeling. With a man present, the informality became intimate, well chaperoned as I was. Our relations had always been unusual, marked by challenge as though he was smouldering, with a slow match burning in him. He was one of those men whom women see as boys, having a tendency to strut, to hide insecurity beneath the masculine uniform – yet physically he was adult male, strong with hard muscles and a resonant voice.

Yet we enjoyed much together – the same excitement of pioneering a new industry, the same ambitions for the company, the same sheer love of driving, since I could drive quite well by now. We had the trauma of Richard's death in common, too.

I gave my instructions into the mouthpiece about some shipping stock, put the phone back on my desk and hung up the receiver. I met his smile. 'When I watch you at work,' he said, 'I find it hard to believe, especially in the finest silk with your hair down . . . Don't you find it worrying, as a woman?'

'What do you mean?' I said, warning in my voice.

'Giving orders to men.'

174

'Like asking them to win a race?'

It was a sensitive retort – and unfair. 'Oh, I struck a note, didn't I?' he said with a laugh. 'So did you . . . High C. I've yearned to win a race, as you well know, but I've had my orders. Just finish, Father's always said . . . Don't strain anything too much . . . show the car's reliable.'

'You father was right, but now we should win a race.'

'I'll do my utmost to obey your command.' There was a confident smile on his face. 'You're a fine woman, Mrs Alexander,' he said, 'if it's not impertinent for me to express an opinion. A unique woman . . . with the most remarkable eyes.'

I glared at him as Edgar Smith telephoned from Old Broad Court.

Steven did his best with Nina. 'I forced my way in,' he insisted to her gallantly. 'My business is most urgent.'

'Mr Mason's off to France today,' I said. 'An important race . . . You might find it interesting, Nina . . . You've a plan of the course?' I asked him.

She shook her head, incomprehension merging with her outrage. 'We'll speak of it later, Quincey. I just dropped in to see Jonny for a moment . . . ' She left, the wounded aura almost visible.

'I'm sorry I offended her,' said Steven.

'It's I who've offended her,' I responded. He eyed me, gave a smile that was uncomfortably conspiratorial, then laid a map of the race route on my desk. 'It's ninety-eight miles,' he said. 'A few difficult stretches. We've made some changes in The Leopard . . . new cooling system . . . overhead inlet valves . . . '

'You and your technicalities,' I rebuked. 'Will it go faster?'

'Hopefully,' he said. 'More to the point, it shouldn't overheat so easily . . . ' I had grown harder, I thought. I wanted The Leopard to excel. I was not concerned with how.

He spoke of the tactics he planned to employ in the race, of the likely problems, of the competition – four American drivers, including Winton's famous 'Bullet' and Whipple's 'Giant'; three Mercedes entries; Madame du Gast, who had been banned from taking part because of her sex. He dropped that in, hoping to provoke me, but it was too familiar. A Turin firm called Fiat had two entries, one being of seventy-five horsepower.

'Why don't you come to the race?' he asked. 'You've never seen the car in action – not real action . . . '

'I'd have come last year if I'd not been occupied.' He knew that Jonny's birth had coincided with the Paris-to-Madrid.

'That was harrowing, all right,' he said. Five people had died and the contest had been stopped before anyone had reached the Spanish border. 'That's why this is a circuit race,' he went on, 'fenced to keep the public off the course. More interesting to watch, too, because the cars pass several times.'

'I'll come if I can,' I answered.

'You've much to occupy you, I'm sure,' he said coldly, smarting from my dubious answer, adding: 'Madame la directrice . . . '

'How's progress in the commercial department?' I asked. Masons had thrived in the last two years. The expansion of the bicycle side had been a great success and the motor production was now making profits. The commercial section, however, was the newest venture. Already, our vans and omnibuses were on the roads and, within a month, the company would be supplying London with its first motor-driven cabs.

'We've beaten all our targets,' Steven answered, 'But The Leopard's still the crucial part – the symbol of the firm. You're right; it's time to win, as well as finish. I'll do my damnedest. Father wants to switch it to six cylinders next year; he's certain that's the engine of the future. Look, I've got the first design here . . . '

He came round to my side of the desk and laid out the design plan of an engine – a complex of pistons, cylinders, belts, fans. 'What on earth's that?' I asked, pointing to one section of the drawing.

'The carburettor . . . a new sort . . . new position . . . There are many novel aspects to the engine. For example . . . '

I cut in: 'Have we taken out patents yet?'

'We're not quite ready.'

'So this is highly secret?'

'Patenting is technical. It requires care . . . '

'It's also crucial. No delay, please.' That much I had learned from Richard. It was why we, not Stanley Reitson, still controlled The Leopard.

A maid knocked and reported that Howard was waiting in the

hall. He came in and stopped in the doorway, his expression severe at the sight of me in my informal attire and Steven leaning over the desk beside me.

'You've met Steven Mason, I think,' I said.

Howard nodded. 'That was the famous Leopard outside, I presume,' he said with disdain, adding drily: 'The motor that doesn't seem to win.' It was unlike Howard to be sarcastic.

'It sells,' I said.

'It'll win this time,' said Steven, angered by Howard's tone. 'I'll have to hurry to make the boat at Dover. We've two weeks of practice before the race . . . ' He picked up his hat and goggles, folded the plans. 'Oh, Mrs Alexander, I've an odd notion,' he said, with a hesitance that was unusual. 'I was wondering if I could take a favour – you know, like the knights used to in jousts? A glove or something – never know, do you? Might help . . . '

I laughed. His tone was almost winsome after all the 'fine woman' bravado. 'I always suspected it,' I said. 'You're just a romantic youth . . . ' My attention was caught by one of my combs, which Maisie had left on my desk. It was of tortoiseshell, decorated with pearls. 'Would this suit?' I inquired.

'Ideally,' he said. 'Goodbye, Mr Alexander . . . ' He stopped at the door, holding up the comb. 'Nothing'll stop me now – not even Whipple's "Giant".' And he was gone.

Liza left us alone, as she always did when Howard called. She was an intelligent girl who understood the nuances within the family. The daughter of a lawyer, she still bore the traces of her schooldays – an eager enthusiasm that, because it seemed naïve and amateur, concealed a proficiency and even judgement that had impressed me.

'Have you had time to look at the Mason accounts I left for you?' I asked.

'Not at length,' he answered. He strolled to the window and looked out at the square. 'I gathered you want another £20,000 . . . '

'It's justified. We're beginning to do well. The bicycle side's thriving, too.'

'What I always said . . . it'd eat up money like a sponge . . . '

'It's making it. The yield this year should be nudging 30 per cent.

Not many of our investments do that,' I challenged, adding mischievously: 'except oil.'

'It has no roots, no stature. A cold wind'll blow it away . . . '

He paused. 'That young man appeals to you, doesn't he?'

'I like him. He's as keen as his father.'

'More, I think. You were flirting with him quite openly.'

'Hardly flirting . . . '

'The favour, for example . . . '

'A joke, Howard. I don't know why you're so concerned.'

'Why?' he demanded sharply, turning from the window suddenly. 'You're at risk, that's why – and sometimes wilful. Often I wonder if you realize the effect you have on men. You're a single woman, still young and attractive, and there's a hint, too, of . . . ' He broke off ' . . . I don't know how to put it . . . A rich nature? I see men looking at you . . . . Certain kinds of men . . . '

'You're being a bit hard on poor Steven,' I said. 'He's cheeky, but harmless enough.'

'Is he?' Howard sighed as though he did not know what to do about me. 'You're aware of it all, aren't you? With men, I mean. You're just perverse; you gamble; you like to stand on the edge, hoping you can always step back. One day you may find you can't . . . '

'How dare you say that,' I demanded coldly, 'after Paolo Fernandez?'

His wince was fleeting. 'I beg your pardon?'

'No little sermons then about my rich nature, were there?' I taunted. 'You used me as bait, Howard. You put me on a hook and dangled me in front of Paolo Fernandez – and I let you. Perversely, of course . . . Gambling, as you put it . . . '

I had drawn blood. He avoided my eyes. 'You can be mischievous sometimes, Quincey,' he said.

Howard had introduced me to Paolo four weeks before. I had been working in the little office I used at Old Broad Court and had gone into 'The Room' at one moment to ask him a question. To my surprise, I had found him in the throes of a heated argument with a visitor who was angrily reproaching him in a strong foreign accent.

'Nonsense, Mr Alexander!' he had exclaimed, banging the table with his fist. 'I cannot accept your explanation . . . '

'Now, Sir,' Howard pleaded calmly, 'please be patient and allow me to . . . '

'I'll seek instructions from my government, thees very afternoon,' his visitor cut in. 'I've not the leetlest doubt that . . . ' He broke off, sensing someone behind him, and turned in his chair before I could retire. At once, a bemused smile spread across his face. 'And who,' he demanded, 'if I may ask, ees thees delightful unexpected orchid?'

For once, the relief was obvious on Howard's face. 'Why, this is Mrs Alexander,' he explained. 'Quincey, may I please introduce Senor Paolo Fernandez, who is visiting us on behalf of the Dominican Republic, as, of course, you know . . . '

He was an exceptionally handsome man of about thirty, with thick black hair, Latin features and white, even teeth. He stood up, kissed my hand formally, and studied me with intent brown eyes in open, delighted admiration.

'Mrs Alexander is my late cousin's wife,' Howard explained. 'She takes a close interest in the bank as one of our principal stockholders.'

The visitor was still uncertain. 'You mean,' he said, 'that Meeses Alexander's a weedow? For one so young and beautiful, that ees sad.' He noted the papers in my hand, the fact that I wore no hat. 'You help direct the bank, Meeses Alexander?' he queried incredulously.

'Not officially,' I answered, 'but in a manner of speaking . . . '

'But that's wonderful. A lady bank director . . . '

'Would you perhaps like Mrs Alexander to join our discussion?' Howard suggested. 'She's fully acquainted with the details of the loan. If, of course, you're not otherwise occupied, Quincey . . . '

I shrugged. 'If Señor Fernandez would think it helpful . . . ' I said.

'It would be most acceptable, Señora,' he insisted. 'Please allow me . . . ' He held the back of a chair for me to sit down. I looked at Howard. The mask was back, but I was aware of his feelings. He hated men admiring me, but he was entertaining it and even encouraging it, racking himself I knew, as always, for the bank. I wondered sometimes if there was anything he would not do, any emotions he would not sublimate, anything he would not require of me, in that sacred cause.

'As you know, Quincey,' he said, 'Señor Fernandez and I have been negotiating a loan of three million pounds sterling. There's been an unfortunate misunderstanding, which I was just clarifying when you came in . . . Oh, by the way, Señor, I should mention that you have an interest in common with Mrs Alexander. You're both keen followers of the turf. She has some fine horses . . . in fact, I believe you've one running next week, haven't you, Quincey?'

'That's true,' I answered, 'at Ascot. My late husband had a theory that an injection of new Arab blood into the breeding'd prove advantageous. We'll see next week if he's right . . . The first of the new colts is racing as a two-year-old.'

'Perhaps Señor Fernandez'd care to join your party,' suggested Howard.

The intense brown eyes settled on me again. 'That'd be an invitation for which I'd be incredibly obligated,' he declared with a broad smile.

'Allow me, then, to obligate you,' I said.

'I suspect you're teasing me, yes?'

'Perhaps a little . . . ' I admitted with a grin.

We played a kind of game, Howard and I and – as in most games – there were times of high tension with the result at issue, as the players progress towards the finish. In our game, these crises concerned either bank policy – on which we had fought out a rough sort of concord – or now, more often, men.

Indeed, men were the material of the game – the pawns and bishops – and, in that summer of 1904, it was Paolo and Steven and James and even Jonny with whom Howard and I were manoeuvring, as the pace of play increased.

We were locked together, bound to the board – forced, as it were, by circumstances to continue with our moves. Any marriage I made as a young widow, with a big holding in the bank, could have crucial repercussions. Howard, as head of the family, was my protector, and even a surrogate father, a guardian, to Jonny. But he had found that I, as a woman, could have uses to the bank that went beyond the skills I had acquired. In Berlin, he had summoned me into the Cunard conflict to befriend another woman, exploiting what we had in common. In London he had found that, as I was single, he could deploy my effect on men to just as great account. What affronted me was that he was willing to do so if the interests of the bank required it, much though it always pained him.

So if I took risks with men, as he charged that day after Steven had left for France, I took risks with him – deliberate risks, when I was angry, that I knew would punish him. For the basic fact of his feelings for me had not changed, only his need to strengthen the way he contained them.

I was always conscious of him physically, as he was, of course, of me – indeed because he was of me, for I do not think that without this it would have crossed my mind. There had been no more unintentional kisses, for he allowed no contact. He bowed good day or goodbye. Occasionally, when examining papers together, our hands would touch by mistake or, under the demand of courtesy, he would be forced to offer his arm – crossing a road, going in to dinner. We would both know. Sometimes, he would actually flinch.

I had accepted now that I was oddly drawn to him, though he did not attract me in the usual sense. If I had seen him across a room for the first time, I would not have remarked on it, even to myself. I would have noted him. He had authority, presence. But he had none of the humour I enjoyed in men – as Richard had possessed in such abundance, and James, of course, and even Steven in his tortured way.

What Howard really sought was control. When the risk was his, as it was with Paolo, he found it tolerable. When the risks were mine, he resisted them.

'Why do you think I'm more at risk with Steven Mason than with Paolo Fernandez?' I persisted on the day Steven left for France.

'I don't think we should discuss it further.'

'You made a charge, Howard. I want my question answered.'

He looked at me in discomfort, noted my smile. We had been here many times before. In truth I was at risk with them all, though I did not realize how. Nor, in fact, did Howard.

Before he could answer, Bridget came in carrying Jonny, dressed to go out. Bridget ran my household, employed the staff, gave orders to the cook, instructed the chauffeur – the only man on my establishment – and even took precedence over Nanny Roberts. Bridget, too, was a premature widow in her twenties, her husband having died in the war, and we had a bond that reached beyond our respective positions. All were under orders to knock on my door as they passed with Jonny, so that I could swap a quick word with him if this was practical.

'Oh, I didn't know you were here, Mr Alexander,' she apologized.

'Think nothing of it,' he answered, taking Jonny from her and holding him high in the air. 'And how are you, young man?' he asked the giggling little boy. 'A fine chap, eh?' Always, Howard astonished me with Jonny. He behaved with the child as he did with no one else, seeming to lose his reserve. 'He gets bigger every time I see him,' he said. 'Well, he'll need to be big to bear the heavy duty that lies before him.'

'Give him a moment,' I put in. 'He's got a childhood to enjoy first.'

He handed him back to Bridget. 'The hopes of the family rest in that little boy, yours and mine . . . the hopes of all of us . . . ' If we had been standing closer, it would have been hard not to have turned to him then – as I might to a husband, or a father, or a lover, a lover of long standing.

'I think I will attend the motor race at Périgueux,' I said. 'It's the week after next. I might take a party. I'll invite Paolo if you wish. . . . Bordeaux's quite near, so may I take the yacht?'

[2]

The wind, blowing briskly from the northwest, had died as we altered course, running close under the coast of Brittany. So the waters of the Bay of Biscay, so famed for heavy seas were gentle enough. Paolo and I were striding the deck. 'The only time I can be alone weeth you,' he complained, 'ees when we're walking fast enough to catch a train . . .'

'There are arguments in favour of it,' I answered with a smile.

He gave a look of hurt reproach, 'I apologized, didn't I?' he said.

'Handsomely,' I conceded.

We had not won the loan – not yet, but nor had anyone else. It had become a bargaining counter in an overt sexual conflict. Howard had placed me before Paolo as a lure, just as he might have offered a 'sweetener' of an extra quarter per cent commission to encourage new business. And I had cooperated willingly enough, eager to play a central role in a big negotiation.

The dance that resulted between the three of us had developed a certain ritual. The shadow of the loan was always present, but much of the time we pretended to ignore it. It was not hard for me. Paolo's company was amusing, his attentions were flattering and, though straying at times towards excess, were easy to control – at least they were until the 'hour of reckoning', as he had described it with such point.

Paolo had enjoyed Ascot in June. He had remarked with wonder at the high green of the turf, at the number of elegant women in that fashionable crowd, at the royal processions down the course in the open landau carriages with liveried outriders.

I had taken him into the paddock, where the runners were being paraded by the stable boys. He talked to my trainer, Henry Longhurst, and studied my horse. 'He has a fine conformation, ' he declared. 'The Arab's prominent in heem. Can he stay the distance?'

'A mile?' said Longhurst. 'Easily, on the form he's shown in the home gallops, but it's his first time out in public since he's not been sound, so who knows? The going should suit him . . . Likes it firm . . .'

'Then I shall wager £10,000 – on the nose, as I theenk you say.'

'Such a large sum?' I queried. 'Why, you don't even know the odds on offer.'

'They'll be high, since he's not been raced . . . You see, I'm not so stupeed as you theenk.'

'You're an extravagant man, Señor Fernandez.'

'With a beautiful woman,' he countered.

'We must find James,' I said as we strolled back through the crowd towards the lawn in front of the Royal Box. 'Since your bet's so large, he'll have to place it for you. He's well known by the bookies.'

James was ahead of us talking to a handsome woman with auburn hair in a manner that I had now come to recognize. But she was not as young as the girls who usually caught his interest. About thirty, I guessed, displaying great poise and dressed in taste in a white lace gown and a hat to match. 'You haven't met Mrs Alexander,' James said to her as we approached. 'This entrancing lady,' he told me, 'is Mrs Knight . . . You've met Mr Knight at the bank, I think, lucky chap that he is.'

I realized then who she was. Edward Knight was a substantial client, a millionaire, though self-made, with interests throughout the world. More significant, though, was that James had been behaving strangely during the past few weeks. Normally so open, sharing with me his romantic escapades, he had become secretive. He would deflect my inquiries sometimes about how he planned to spend the evening. Now I suspected why. To flirt with single girls, like Daisy Burroughs, or even to seduce Leone was one thing. To dally with the wife of an important client was very different – and dangerous.

I asked him to arrange Paolo's bet before the 'off' and the two men hurried to the bookmakers who lined the rails of the royal enclosure lawn. I noted the way Mrs Knight watched him. It left me in no doubt that she was in love with him.

The horse won, coming from the back in a fast run, and going on so strongly that it was obvious he could make the extra half mile of next year's Derby, which was the aim of every owner. Paolo was so excited that he was literally jumping up and down like a child, shouting encouragement through the roar of the crowd as the horses went past the post. The odds had been long, as he had predicted. With his large wager, he had won £150,000.

He hurried with me to the unsaddling enclosure, and as the steaming horse stood at the coveted winner's place, he joined me in my congratulations to Henry Longhurst and Smith, the jockey.

'Your husband must have been a very clever man,' he said to me. 'First to find such a rare and lovely wife, and then to discover such a stallion as your Tamburlaine. You said he bought heem from the Bedouin? I would like very much to see heem. Is that possible?'

'I wish it was,' I said, and told him how he had died, though without mention of Stella. He was horrified – 'How could anyone do such a terrible theeng?' – but he was fascinated, too, by Richard's breeding theory. 'Judging by his son,' he said, 'that Tamburlaine must have been a fine stallion. What colour was he?'

'Almost pure white,' I answered. 'Richard said he was the most beautiful horse he had ever seen.' And suddenly it was an effort to keep back my tears.

After that, Paolo and I met frequently but almost always at first in the company of others, either on occasions involving the Alexanders, when Howard urged me to invite him, or at functions Paolo attended as a diplomat. He talked to me at times about the purpose of the loan, of what was needed in his country – 'my leetle Careeb paradise', as he would call it. He spoke with his eyes alight of the poverty it would ease, of the sugar plantations they needed to modernize, of the making of a new harbour, of forestry, of the diversion of a river. It made me even more eager to win the loan. 'When are we going to hear if we've been successful?' I asked.

'Soon,' he said, 'but in the Dominican Republic these things take time. There are many considerations. Tell me,' he went on, 'do you enjoy the opera?'

That evening, when we attended *Aïda* at Covent Garden, was the first we had spent alone. After that, his attentions became more ardent. He began to write to me every day – short romantic notes, flowery but unobjectionable, comparing me to flowers or sunny days or the flash of a leaping fish. Then he started to send me presents. At first, these were small but thoughtful – an orchid delivered every hour throughout a day; a Dresden figurine of a beautiful woman, a Chinese powder box that was 2,000 years old. Then, one morning, I was called outside. Standing in the roadway of Grosvenor Square was a white Arab stallion yearling. 'I do not know if he can replace your Tamburlaine,' Paolo had written in the note that accompanied him, 'but I hope you will permit him to try.'

I was greatly moved, but clearly I could not accept the colt, as I wrote to Paolo at once. A reply came back by my own messenger: 'Then keep him for me, if you will and let him make some fast horses.'

Handled with delicacy, as the matter had been, it touched me more than all his elaborate compliments.

As part of my game with Howard I had told him of each of Paolo's gifts, of each letter. If I was to be used as bait, I was not going to let him forget who was holding the rod. It hurt him. He would nod, his fingers turning his gold signet ring, which was how I knew it hurt him. 'That's good,' he said firmly. 'Promising . . . This loan could lead to others. It could be important; Señor Fernandez's father is a man with connections in many countries.'

I viewed Paolo's offer of the stallion colt, dramatic as it was, as more than a preparatory move on our chessboard. My knight, I felt, had taken Howard's bishop. 'What if he becomes too pressing?' I asked.

'I'm sure you'll see that his behaviour is kept within appropriate limits.'

'You mean I should discourage him – perhaps see less of him?'

That bland stare, always with that momentary wince, so fast that at first I had never detected it. 'You should remain friends, of course,' he answered. 'Just friends.'

'It's not easy for a single woman,' I said. 'Shouldn't you ask him his intentions?' I knew he would not do that – nor should he. I was a widow, not a young spinster. 'Perhaps I should marry him. Would you like me to marry him, Howard? To win the loan, I mean?'

'I wish you wouldn't speak like this, Quincey,' he said. 'If you were serious, it might be a different matter.'

'Serious? I'm serious, Howard . . . How do I restrain him? All right, I agree: the loan's not big enough for marriage. We'd want a higher price for that, wouldn't we?' I laughed with a note of affection, putting my hand on his arm and noting the muscles tauten. 'Don't worry,' I went on. 'I'll keep myself for your earl.' That was what he wanted, I knew. If I married an earl, it would add great status to the family and the bank. What he wanted, that is, as the head of Alexanders. As a man, he wanted me.

A week later, it was no longer a joke. During lunch at the Trocadero, Paolo told me he had fallen in love with me.

'You hardly know me,' I responded.

'I'm obsessed by you every minute of the day,' he insisted.

'You really must stop speaking like this,' I said. 'We're friends Paolo, good friends. You know that.'

'Impossible!' he declared. 'Eet's always been impossible from the moment I first saw you . . . '

'In that case,' I countered gently, 'I think Mr Alexander should resume his place in the transactions, don't you? My position has become too delicate . . . '

I took up my bag and prepared to leave the table, but he checked me with his hand. 'No, please,' he said. 'We'll be friends, as you say, just friends . . . ' He paused. 'I've heard from my government. There are matters to be considered . . . Is there somewhere we can go?'

'You can come to Grosvenor Square for tea,' I said carefully. 'We can discuss the terms in my office. But truly, Paolo, there must be no more than that.'

'Didn't I just say I agreed?' he demanded, pained to have his honour challenged.

When we reached my house, I invited him to take a chair opposite me, while I sat at my desk. At first, Liza stayed with us, as I had signalled but he said the matter involved state secrets, so reluctantly I told her to leave us. The result was predictable but skilful. He discussed the loan at some length, eventually taking from his pocket a statement of figures which he placed in front of me. These concerned repayment, which was a key issue. British bankers liked short-term loans that could be renewed; Americans favoured long-term. At one moment, he got up and came round the desk to point to a calculation and before I knew it his lips were on mine. I pushed him away angrily. 'Paolo, you agreed . . . '

He was furious, standing at my side his hands clenched. 'You're playing weeth me. From the start, you've played weeth me . . . '

'From the start, I've made my position quite clear.'

'No woman ever makes anything clear!' he shouted. 'Women

always say no . . . They don't mean eet . . . . They understand . . . .
We understand . . . '

'I mean it, I promise. Now please sit down.'

'I can't live like thees. There can be no loan for Alexanders
unless . . . ' He broke off.

My anger was hard to restrain. 'Unless what?' I asked, very
quietly.

'You are aware of what . . . .' He answered steadily, with a touch
of a sulk.

'This is what you call negotiating?'

'How can I negotiate? I'm desperate, can't you see? There are
other banks to whom I can turn. That'd be wise, I think. Look at
me, Quincey . . . '

'Sit down,' I said, glancing away.

'Look at me!' he shouted, pounding my desk suddenly with his
fist. 'I appeal to you,' he pleaded. 'I throw myself at your feet . . . '

'I wish you'd stop being foolish,' I said, 'and continue the discussion.'

'Is that your final answer?' he demanded, his head high.

'Is that your final condition?' I demanded in my turn. 'Do you
wish it to be written in the contract?'

'The contract?' he echoed, puce with fury. 'You dare to speak of
contracts after the feelings I have confessed to you? What kind of a
woman are you?' He put his hand to his head, took control of
himself with an effort. 'All right, Mrs Banker Lady, so the hour of
reckoning has come. So we draw the line and add the figures to see
if they're in the red . . . Tell me, Mrs Banker Lady, *are* they in the
red?'

'You're holding the ledger,' I said. 'You've added figures that
weren't written there before.'

Liza stood in the doorway. 'You rang, Mrs Alexander?'

'Señor Fernandez is just leaving,' I said. He did not speak. He
looked at me for a second, anger and frustration in his eyes. Then
he took up his papers from my desk and stalked out of the room.

James dropped in to see me, as he often did on his way home from
the bank. He was earlier than usual. 'Hallo, Quincey,' he said, with
a smile that was casual as always, but I could see there was

something wrong. He slouched down in an armchair with one leg cocked easily over the other, his errant lock of hair escaping on to his forehead – and recognized my anxiety as I watched him. 'You can see, can't you? Not much point in pretending . . . I'm in trouble, Quincey.'

'You're always in trouble,' I said, trying to make a joke of it. 'What's it this time?'

'I mean it,' he said. 'Deep trouble that's going to need your help. Mrs Knight's going to have a baby – my baby.'

'Good heavens!' I exclaimed. 'How do you know it's yours and not . . . well, Mr Knight's?'

'Because he's impotent.'

I got up and sat beside him on the arm of his chair. 'Poor James,' I said softly. 'So it's caught up with you at last . . . I got the impression she was pretty gone on you at Ascot.'

'I'm not sure it's quite like that. We attracted each other strongly, no doubt about it. Perhaps that's what you noticed. She's something of an enthusiast, you might say . . . And I'll admit she got under my skin in a way that no woman's done for ages.'

'So she'll be off to Paris, I suppose,' I said. 'That's where they deal with these things with discretion isn't it?'

'Quincey, you don't understand. She's going to have the baby. She insists it's because she loves me, but there's more to it. I think she's using me to hurt her husband . . . That's why she's told him . . . '

'Told him!' I echoed. 'I don't believe it! He'll divorce her!'

James shook his head. 'I think not. She's warned him she'd bring it out in open court – that he can't, I mean. She wants him to live with a child that isn't his – and with the knowledge she's got a lover. She wants it to continue between us, but that's not a goer as far as I'm concerned.'

'Oh James,' I sympathized softly. 'I'm so sorry.' How wrong was it possible to be? It was hard to see that elegant, charming woman as the virago he was describing; and I prided myself on being a shrewd judge. I had been a street dog, had I not?

'There's worse to come,' he said. 'Knight's got his own back – on me, at least. He's taking all his accounts away from the bank, and he's told Howard why.'

'You mean,' I asked incredulously, 'that he's admitted to Howard that he's . . . ?'

'No. He told Howard I'd tried to seduce his wife. Quite astonishingly,' he added with his wry smile. 'Howard believed him. He dismissed me this afternoon.'

My whole body stiffened, anger surging. 'No, James. That he can't do. I won't let him.'

Howard stood in front of my fireplace facing me. Glowering at me with his shoulders hunched and his glass of whisky held close to his body, he resembled an angry bear. 'It's intolerable!' he said. At my request, he had walked across the square to see me after dinner. 'I refuse to accept it, Quincey.'

'You must,' I insisted. 'There are some things between us that are not open to argument. The motor company's one. James is another. Goodness, Howard, he *is* your cousin.'

'What crime would he have to commit,' he growled, a little like his father, 'to lose your support?'

'Crime?' I asked reminding him sharply: 'You're speaking from a glass house, Howard.'

'Quincey, he's lost us one of our biggest clients – through sheer folly! I'm surprised it doesn't offend *you*, since you have this strange liaison with him . . . '

'Liaison!' I echoed sharply.

'Bond – call it what you like. You're very close . . . You spend much time together . . . In fact, it causes talk.'

'Then I trust you do your best to quell it! James is a loyal friend – and has been from the moment I met him. He stays, Howard . . . '

'And if I refuse?' It was almost a snarl.

'Then it'll be war, Howard,' I said quietly. 'I'll fight you. The first chance I get I'll call an annual general meeting – and ensure the press knows there's conflict between us.' It was the old Cunard technique, open to me because of the stock I held. I had used it before, and I would use it again. For Howard was as scared of publicity as any admiral.

'You really would, too, wouldn't you?' he said, 'despite the harm it'd do.'

'As *you* would, for all your talk, if the long-term reasons justified it. As you did with United Mining. You had to pay far more for that than if you'd acted on our telegram, so don't you lecture me.' He had put his glass on the mantelpiece and was turning the signet ring on his finger in controlled agitation. 'Listen, Howard,' I pleaded. 'It's our bank. You have my full support. I even do my best to appeal to men we want to become our clients, but that can misfire. The bait can catch in the throat . . . There's been a confrontation with Paolo.'

Alarm, hardly detectable, came to his face. 'What's happened?'

'He declared himself.'

'You mean he offered marriage?'

I laughed. 'He's a hot-blooded Latin. He was concerned with passion, not mundane details . . . Mind you,' I added, 'he's an attractive man, so what would you have me do? Send him a note, perhaps, admitting I'd been hasty?'

'He'd see that as encouragement.'

'Suppose I said you'd taken over the negotiations – and then kept a distance? That'd be easy if the loan'd no longer be a reason to meet.'

'I don't like it,' he ruminated.

'There are only two other choices,' I suggested. 'We do nothing, or . . .' I paused. 'Just how much do we need the loan, Howard?' I asked him innocently.

'You know as well as I do!' he flared. 'You enjoy this, don't you? You enjoy hurting me. What do you want, Quincey? Do you want me to speak of certain matters of which we're both aware? Is that what you want?'

I felt a moment of sudden shame. I did like to stir his emotions – and it was wilful, as he charged.

'One of these days, if you persist,' he warned, 'I may well speak of it and then, by God, you'll regret you made me to do so – as I will, too.' For a second, his hunger for me was evident. 'We'll talk of Señor Fernandez in the morning,' he declared – and strode towards the door, until I checked him. 'Sorry, Howard,' I said. 'You're right. It's irresponsible and perverse, as you've told me. *Pax*, Howard.'

Uncertain how to respond, he hesitated, then gave a shrug.

'There's more you should know about James,' I went on. 'Were you aware that Mr Knight is buying Allied Steel?'

Shocked disbelief came to Howard's face. 'He can't be,' he said. 'He'd have consulted me on a matter of such importance. He already controls Johnson & Mathews. With Allied as well, he'd become the biggest force by far in the light steel industry. It can't be true, Quincey.'

'He has other bankers, as we know . . . Kleinworts have been conducting secret negotiations. Everything's concluded. Since Mr Knight's no longer our client, what's to stop us buying Allied in the market now? As you say, he's not consulted you, so there's no issue of ethics. I'd hazard a guess that, with that secret knowledge, we could make a cool quarter of a million if we operate with care. The price'll leap as soon as news of the deal gets out.'

He still looked puzzled – and offended. He had liked Knight and had believed he had his confidence. 'Where have you heard this?' he asked.

'From the horse's mouth – or at least from a stable companion . . . pillow talk, I think is the phrase. Cropped up by chance as she spoke of something else . . . No question, James has been absurdly rash, but something, it'd seem, could be said for sin – enough, at least, to forgive him on this occasion, don't you think?'

As it turned out, there was no need for further talk of Paolo. The next morning, a hundred red roses were delivered to the house. 'Please forgive me,' Paolo had written in a note that accompanied them. 'It won't happen again. Let us continue the negotiations . . . '

And we did. We discussed our commission for issuing the loan through the Stock Exchange, the arrangements about the under-writers who would guarantee to provide the money if the public did not buy all the bonds we would be offering, the repayment and the annual interest. Loans had to be made attractive, just like any other commodity that was placed on the market. The matter was not concluded, though. Always he had to report to Santo Domingo. Sometimes he would be buoyant with optimism. 'I'm sure you'll get the loan,' he said. 'I'm doing my utmost on your behalf, I promise. I want you to share with me the benefits that'll be achieved – the changes we'll make to my leetle Careeb paradise. You must come out there and see for yourself the new harbour, the machines in the plantations, the houses in Santo Domingo. I want you to meet my grateful people.'

At a personal level, Paolo had observed his promise. There had been no more embarrassment, which is why he was on the yacht with us, travelling towards Bordeaux at twenty knots, so that we had to stride out against the windstream.

We came to the rails that overlooked the afterdeck, where some of the others were relaxing under an awning — James, whom I thought had needed a break even if he did not deserve it; one or two of his officer friends who were dedicated motorists and keen to watch the race; a couple of bank clients with their wives, invited at Howard's urging. And Frances.

As we stood looking down at them, Frances glanced at Paolo beside me and smiled in mock rebuke. We had not exactly grown close, since confidence was still impossible for me with Mathew's wife, but at a superficial level we enjoyed each other's company, found much to laugh at. There was a frivolous side to me that Frances often stimulated with gossip — not serious gossip that Nina collected for her campaign in the social war; but aimless gossip that was light and sometimes malicious.

Once I thought I had seen her in a cab with a man, but I was not sure. I had asked James if she might have a lover and he had laughed, answering: 'She has the look about her, don't you think . . . as though she's bitten the apple . . .'

'James!' I had rebuked sharply. 'That's an awful thing to say. Do you think people say that about me?'

'Your virtue's unquestioned, I'm sure,' he had answered, 'But you must make them wonder . . . Young widows always do.'

The captain appeared at my side. 'At our present speed,' he said, 'We'll reach Bordeaux about one o'clock. Do you wish to take luncheon at sea, in which case I'll reduce engines, or would you prefer to have it when we reach port?'

'At sea, I think Captain,' I answered. 'We'll eat early. I'm hungry already.'

I leaned back against the rails as he left us and gave a sigh. The dramas, it seemed, were past. Howard had accepted James back into the fold with good enough grace. We had made a big profit from our Allied dealings — 'a nice little killing', as Papa would have said. Paolo was a friend again and we were favourites for the loan. 'It's a happy time, isn't it?' I said to him.

The pre-dawn darkness was eerie as I walked with James and Paolo through the ancient town which, on any other morning, would have been silent at that early hour. Because of the race, Périgueux was awake and expectant. Many had not slept. The cafés had been open all night, crowded because the hotels were full. People hurried over the cobbled streets on foot, on bicycles, in carts. Motorcars, their engine noise heightened by the closeness of the buildings, demanded passage with urgent hoots of rubber horns.

We passed the Roman arena, the jagged ruins of its broken walls outlined against the clear night sky, and approached the medieval sector of the town, a complex of houses dominated by the Cathedral of Saint-Front beneath its five great cupolas.

The starting line was just outside the town to the east, on the road that would lead the competitors into the Limousin Hills, through St Yrieix-la-Perche and Chalus and back to the finish, just north of Périgueux on the route to Limoges – a demanding distance, after three circuits, of 290 miles.

The waiting crowd was thick on either side of the course. In an adjoining field, sheds and tents – interiors illuminated by oil lanterns – had been erected as working bases for the contestants.

Already, the early entrant cars were in position near the start, one behind the other, ready for the flag. Their motors were throbbing, their bonnets open, as mechanics attended to final tuning. The glare of their acetylene headlamps cast dancing shadows as people moved between the vehicles.

The races, on these narrow roads, were not based on the first to finish but on the quickest time, which was why the cars went off in rotation.

We found The Leopard, which was to be fourth away, with

194

Steven sitting at the wheel. He was wearing the close-fitting cap with ear-flaps that was now uniform, his goggles across his forehead. Martin, who would be riding as mechanic, was huddled over the engine with his father.

Steven smiled with surprised pleasure at seeing us. 'Why, Madame la directrice,' he said. 'I never expected to see you at this hour. I thought I might catch a glimpse of you by the second lap, when your toilette was complete . . . '

'I've come a long way to encourage you,' I answered. 'Make sure you win the race for me.'

'I'll win the race,' he said. 'All the same, perhaps we should make certain . . . '

'How'll you do that?' I asked.

'Not me – you,' he answered. 'Kiss me for luck . . . ' A provocative smile was on his face.

'I beg your pardon,' I said, surprised.

'You want me to win . . . '

'You've got my favour . . . '

'Seal it.'

'You go too far sometimes, Steven. That's a little impertinent . . . '

'Yes, Madame la directrice.' He accepted the rebuke with pretended humility. 'You well know I admire you greatly,' he said in a serious tone. 'How'll you feel now if I lose the race? Luck's vital, you know . . . '

'I'll cross my fingers for you, and touch wood . . . '

'It's still quite dark. No one'll see . . . ' He grinned his challenge, and on impulse I leaned down and kissed him quickly on the mouth. 'Now you'd really better win,' I warned, 'We'll be watching from the finishing line . . . '

Dawn broke and the race began. The starter dropped his flag and the first car, a Gobron-Brillié, roared away in a cloud of dust. Five minutes later the second competitor, a Hotchkiss, thundered after it, to be followed in turn after the same interval by a Darracq.

Steven placed his goggles over his eyes, gripped the wheel, kept the engine revving. Martin sat beside him, his face as tense as his brother's as they waited for the flag. Then, signalled, Steven thrust the throttle open and they raced off down the road – a good start, truly like a leopard, except for the car's green paint, the usual British racing colour, which did not suit the name so well as its normal yellow.

We watched some of the others go, released in turn – more blue cars of France, the white of the Germans, the black and yellow of the Austrians, the red and green flourishes of the Americans. After a while, reports began to filter back. A Serpollet had broken a first-speed gear wheel. A de Dietrich was stopped by a jammed clutch. A punctured carburettor float had caused a Panhard to burst into flames. A Mors had skidded off the road after a burst tyre. Nothing was reported about The Leopard. 'No news is good news, Mrs Alexander,' said Mason, and suggested we should all go back into the town.

'In a way I'm sorry the sport's getting so commerical now,' he remarked as we walked, 'even though we're one of the reasons . . . It's hard to believe that only two years ago everyone was shocked by the entry of a professional driver. He was a chauffeur and drove superbly, but embarrassed everyone. All the others were gentlemen, you see . . . Where could the poor chap eat? In this race, there are more than a dozen professionals because winning does so much for sales. It's all become such a serious business . . . '

'But a good business,' I responded, 'with great prospects – the beginning of what you and Richard forecast. Surely it's safer, too . . . '

'Needs to be, with cars that are so much faster.'

The Paris–Madrid catastrophe the previous year had ended the city-to-city races. Now the race roads were banned to other traffic, and the course was wired. Troops were stationed along the circuit to control the public. Horse-drawn tanks had sprayed the surface with a petrol-ammonia mixture to hold down the dust. There were neutralized zones, usually at towns, where officials flagged down cars to conform with the public speed limit. The time-gap between the start of each competitor had been extended to reduce 'dicing', when cars raced together, though such duels still happened if a vehicle had been delayed by trouble.

In the main square of the town, we stopped for breakfast. There was no sign yet of the others in our party, since even now it was barely seven and it would be at least two hours before any cars would complete the first circuit.

We had all arrived late the previous day by train after disembarking from the yacht at Bordeaux. Mason had met us at the station and escorted us to an old château that was now a hotel.

As we talked, we watched a wagon proceeding slowly along the road that cut through the square, driven by a gnarled old man with a beret on his head. A mauve Peugeot rattled into the square behind him, a young woman at the wheel. Impatient at the obstruction, she honked the horn urgently. But the peasant in the cart ignored her, giving no space for her to pass. 'S'il vous plaît, Monsieur!' she called out, to no avail. Lady drivers were unusual and, although she was concealed by her hat and dust-caked veil, I enjoyed the anger in her.

Our café was close to the road, and as she neared us, she saw me. 'Quincey!' she exclaimed suddenly, and at once I knew who it was. 'Why, if it isn't Millicent Russell!' I responded. She drove the car off the road, took off her veil, and ran towards us. I met her and we embraced. 'What are you doing here of all places?' she demanded.

'We've a car in the race.'

'Ah, of course!' she mocked. 'The new frontiers of science! So they've let you.'

'They couldn't stop me . . . The firm's doing well. Our car's named The Leopard.'

'I've heard of it, of course.'

We reached the table and I introduced her to the men. She sat down and took some coffee. 'And why are you here?' I asked. 'The last time you wrote, you were living in Paris.'

'I've returned to London,' she explained, 'to my clinic. You must come and see it,' adding, with the familiar note of sarcasm: 'It's doubtless time you had a salutary glimpse of the really poor . . . '

'Not more lectures, please,' I countered, 'but I'd love to see the clinic.'

'We'll arrange it when we get back. I'm here, though, as a doctor. I've adored motoring since I first rode in a Mors five years ago and the organizers asked me to attend in my professional capacity.'

'Let's hope there'll be no one for you to attend to,' I said.

They had built a kind of grandstand at the finishing line, a rough temporary structure with benches in raised rows and a metal roof to provide shade. Périgueux is in the southern part of France, and it was a hot dusty day. Across the road, vineyards stretched for miles. Nearby was a brass band, playing beneath an awning.

A great cry went up from the crowd as at last a competitor was spotted, roaring down from the direction of Chalus. It was the Gobron-Brillié, the first of the starters, as it should have been since he had a five minutes lead, though this did not always signify. Individual time, of course, was what mattered, not physical position in the race. There was a blast of a trumpet as the car flashed by at over seventy miles an hour before easing speed further down the road at a blue flag, marking the neutralized zone of the town.

'Two hours sixteen point two three,' Mason reported, after inquiring of a race official. 'Not bad, considering the course . . .'

About ten minutes went by before the next entrant was sighted, the long gap meaning that the Hotchkiss was in trouble. Even then, it was not the blue Darracq, which had started third, that came in view but our long familiar bonnet, now painted green. 'He's doing more than eighty,' declared Mason as, to the blare of the trumpet, The Leopard went by, sending up a cloud of dust. Both Steve and Martin were looking ahead grimly. Mason consulted his stop-watch. 'He's well ahead of the Gobron,' he reported. 'Two hours six point seven . . . That's very good . . .'

'That's yours? inquired Millicent.

By l0.15 the sun was high and, even in the shade of the stand, the heat was oppressive. Car after car had raced by. Rumours of casualties were circulating. So far, none had completed the first circuit as fast as The Leopard.

The Gobron-Brillié roared past for the second time, but The Leopard was now only three minutes behind him, which meant that, after two circuits, she was gaining steadily. We cheered as the two boys went by to another blast of the trumpet, but neither gave any indication that he heard us.

The closest to The Leopard's time after the first lap was not, in fact, the Gobron, which Steven was chasing, but a Clement-Bayard, which had been the tenth car to start, nearly an hour later. The Clement had completed the course first time round in only four minutes more than Steve, and there were two more cars within five minutes of his time.

It was about 11.30 when the Clement-Bayard, our main danger, passed the stand at the end of its second circuit. It had cut Steven's lead to two minutes. Both the other cars that were threatening The Leopard's time were closing too. One was neck-and-neck with the Clement.

By noon, the heat in the stand was intense. 'Can't be long now,' said Mason, 'Before the first car finishes . . . ' The race official was already standing at the line, ready to flag down each vehicle as it crossed it.

We saw the distant dust cloud first, as we had come to expect, though it seemed unusually thick. We soon saw why. The blue Gobron raced towards us – but it was not alone any longer. The Leopard was behind it. 'By God, he's caught him up,' said Mason.

The two cars thundered towards us, our green bonnet some fifty yards behind the Gobron, and gaining. It made no difference which first passed the finishing line. Steven clearly had a big lead in time. But they were still racing. Steve was trying to overtake the Frenchman, who was determined to hold him off.

They sped past us, headlamps of both cars almost in line as the crowd cheered and the trumpet blew. 'Six hours forty-two point one!' Mason exclaimed jubilantly. 'That's going to need some beating, by God . . . He must have taken chances on the third lap . . .'

At the very moment he said it, The Leopard's tyre burst – the offside front. The Leopard slewed sideways into the Gobron, seemed to bounce off it, bonnet lifting in what seemed slow motion, forewheels off the ground – then swivelled under the open-throttle thirty-horsepower thrust from the rear before plunging off the road down a small bank into a field of vines. It had disappeared from our line of vision, but we heard the explosion and saw the flames, reaching like busy fingers above the verge.

We ran, all of us, without even glancing up the course – and stood for a second, looking down with horror at The Leopard, which lay upside down, burning fiercely.

Our attention was first caught by Martin, because he was

moving – clambering to his feet unsteadily from some vines about thirty yards away, unhurt, it seemed – catapulted evidently from the car, his fall cushioned by the foliage. But Steven lay on his face, unmoving, close to the flaming car.

Mason and James clambered down the bank towards him, only to be checked by the heat from the red-hot metal. They took off their coats and, using these to shield their heads, approached Steven's body and managed to drag it away from the burning vehicle.

As we went to join them, they turned him gently over on to his back and the shock I experienced when I saw his face provoked in me a violent shaking that I could not conceal. For his forehead, cheeks, nose, chin had all been charred black by fire.

Millicent unpinned her hat, knelt beside him with professional competence and undid the buttons of his jacket so that she could put an ear to his chest. 'He's alive,' she said.

They kept him in the little hospital in Périgueux for two days – mainly, as Millicent advised, to treat his shock. Then we transported him by train to Bordeaux and on to England in the yacht.

He had recovered consciousness after twenty-four hours, and I had steeled myself to visit him in the hospital with his father. They had left his wounds unbandaged, coated with gentian violet, which gave his face an appearance more awesome even than when I had first seen it after the accident. He had not lost his sight but his eyelids were so swollen that he could barely see. He was a monster, his face made shapeless by tumescence.

He could not smile, though his eyes lightened in their puffy slits when he saw me. He could hardly speak because the merest movement of his thickened, blistered lips increased his agony. He tried, though, with the same note of almost insolent challenge. 'I won the race for you then, "Ada la directrice" . . . ' No consonants, just movements of his tongue within his mouth.

I nodded. 'You did, Steve, and I'm grateful. Congratulations . . . '

'Sales 'etter now, eh . . . ?' There was mockery in his words.

'I shouldn't try to talk, old chap,' said his father. 'We'll do the talking. You won the race, and won it well. It's put The Leopard into a new class, and we're all very proud of you . . . '

' "Ada la directrice" . . . ?' Steven queried.

'Especially Madame la directrice,' I assured him. I could scarcely bear to look at him, and when his father suggested we should go, I was greatly relieved – which made me feel ashamed.

I was very quiet on the voyage back to England on the yacht. James assured me that I had no cause for guilt. Paolo sympathized gently. Even Frances said to me: 'Blame yourself if it helps, but it could have happened at any time in the race . . . in any race . . . Even if there was no motor company, there'd still be racing.'

I went to see him every few hours, but it was only with a great effort that I could look at him. And I never stopped wondering if it would have occurred, had I not urged him so strongly to win. 'These things happen,' said James. 'Tyres burst.' But I was coming to realize that, as a woman in my position, I provoked in men an extra element of challenge. If Richard had still been alive, I doubted that Steven would have been so horribly burned.

Chapter 10

[1]

After the horror of Périgueux, I saw a lot of Millicent Russell and we came to know each other very well. There was something about her that touched me deeply. In my two years in London I had made many acquaintances but few close women friends, and certainly none I could confide in. But I would have trusted Millie with my life. Our ideas were opposed, but she had an independence of spirit and a fervour that found an immediate echo in my own aspirations. While I wanted to bring changes to the earth, Millie's driving need was to cure its ills and correct its injustices.

She was a woman of the New World, as I was. She had overcome huge obstacles to become an undergraduate at Oxford and later to qualify as a doctor, reflecting much of my own determination to gain a degree of power.

Constantly, she taunted me, her gamine eyes alight as she watched the effect of her words, but I did not mind. I countered by mocking her socialist panaceas, with their absurdly romantic concepts of equality, their ridiculous notions of state ownership. 'Man must be free,' I insisted. 'He must strive.'

'He doesn't just have to strive for money. You're assuming that people are selfish as a natural state.'

'People are people,' I said. 'Leopards have spots . . . '

'Men'll strive just as hard for an ideal if they're given the chance. Heavens, Quincey, they've died enough times for ideals and there's no lack of patriots ready to fight for good old Blighty, is there?' She grinned suddenly. 'I'll convert you yet, you know.'

That was what I enjoyed in her. Serious though she was, she had an efferverscent gaiety; a comic aspect could occur to her in the midst of the most intense argument and our fiery debates, with their mockery and their jeering, would often end in laughter. In a sense she became my conscience, insisting that the progress I pioneered must be measured against human cost — old human cost, what lingered from before, the old people who were living in the villages that were changed, even destroyed, by new railroads or the

202

bridges I enjoyed funding so much.

'Where do they stop' she challenged, 'those ambitions of yours? Would you finance guns?'

'No,' I answered firmly. 'Guns are negative.'

'What if they're to be used in a worthy cause? Against a despot — say like Genghis Khan?'

'That's politics — your territory.'

'So are railroads. They carry troops . . . take uniforms . . .would they pass muster? The line gets narrow, doesn't it?'

'Not that narrow. Uniforms aren't guns.'

She had been in no hurry to take me to her clinic. I think that this was because she wanted our friendship, unusual as it was in its way, to form a sound base before she exposed me to what she knew would be a shock to me. 'You'll need strong nerves,' she said.

'I'll grit my teeth and smile,' I answered.

We lunched first in a cheap Italian restaurant in Bloomsbury. 'You'd better know,' she said, 'since you're going to meet him. I've got a lover.' There was a challenge in her voice, though we had talked much about free love, embodied as it was in socialist thought. 'In the fullest sense,' she added. 'We've no bonds . . .we're as free as birds.'

She told me more about the clinic which her lover helped her run, and about the opposition she had faced. Based on an experiment in Holland, it was designed to dispel the ignorance of most women about their bodies and to advise them how to avoid pregnancy.

'I was naïve,' she said. 'I saw women old at thirty, so poor that they couldn't even feed or clothe their families. More children could only worsen their appalling conditions . . . ' Anger burned in her eyes. 'Oh, I knew some people'd disapprove, think me indelicate or immoral, but I'd no idea of the forces I'd unleash. They were outraged — doctors, lawyers, clerics, politicians — the whole elite that runs the country. God gave us the sexual instinct to reproduce the species . . . that's what they said. To thwart that aim, even in terrible poverty, was a venal sin. Did you realize you were with a she-devil, Quincey?'

She gave a laugh that was in contrast to the passion that had come into her voice. 'Of one thing I'm sure,' she went on. 'God didn't give us the sexual instinct just to create children. He gave it to us as a sublime gift of pleasure that'd send the spirit soaring, but to say that is heresy, you realize . . . '

'Heresy?' I echoed, thinking of Stella.

'They'd burn me at the stake if they could . . . ' She paused, a sadness suddenly in her eyes. 'Come on,' she said. 'Now it's time for you to see a bit of human sorrow.'

As we left, a man got up to leave. He had been sitting alone reading a newspaper throughout his meal. I do not know why I noticed him.

As Millie had surmised, the clinic was a shock to me. It was in a decrepit shop in the Mile End Road. The interior was clean, of course, and Millicent's trained staff wore crisp white coats. Oh, but it was bleak. The women in the waiting-room were desperately poor, some wearing rags, even without shoes – and the smell was terrible. The thought of such creatures coupling with their menfolk, in beds shared no doubt with children, seemed obscene. I was appalled at my reaction. Had I become so trivial?

She showed me into the room where she gave her advice. 'Well?' she demanded. 'How do you think your bridges's help *them* – or that dam in Egypt you're always on about that'll grow corn in the desert? Do you think it'll stop women like that living the lives they are? Not a chance, Quincey. It'll just line the pockets of plutocrats who are rich already, like Alexanders.'

The door was thrown open and a man stood there, wearing a white coat that, not being buttoned, looked untidy. He was ugly; short and fleshly plump, with straight thick lips, a slightly bulbous nose and unruly black hair that was sparse and receding. For a moment of searing disappointment, I knew he was her lover. It was impossible, I thought, that this was the being who had inspired in her those romantic flights about the sexual instinct.

The reaction was mutual. He stared at me with open hostility. 'Who's this?' he asked.

'Mrs Alexander,' she answered. 'I told you I was bringing her today.'

'Ah yes,' he said, surveying me with distaste, 'the rich Mrs Alexander of the banking family.'

'This is Mr Carl Sandford, who directs the clinic with me,' Millie said.

He made no attempt to greet me. 'Come to view London's poor, have you?' he asked. 'Like going to the Zoo, isn't it?'

I folded my arms and perched on the corner of Millie's desk. 'Do you behave like this to everyone who comes here?' I asked him.

'Please forgive me, Mrs Alexander,' he responded with false remorse, 'if I've offended your delicate sensibilities.'

'Think nothing of it,' I said, 'but I fancy you've got the wrong notion. I wasn't brought up rich. I'd bet that the home I grew up in mostly was a lot more frugal than the *petit-bourgeois* childhood *you* clearly enjoyed.' Millie was always labelling people scathingly as *petit-bourgeois*, yet I guessed this was exactly what Carl was. The son of a lawyer, perhaps, or a doctor.

He glared at me angrily, then turned to her. 'There's someone I want you to see,' he said, and abruptly left the room.

She grinned at me without apology. 'I said you'd need strong nerves.'

The knock was barely audible. The door opened and a young girl in her early teens stood there, wearing a dirty blouse and shawl. She was pale and skinny, the flesh tight on the bones of her face, her hair lank to her shoulders. But it was her young eyes, dulled by experience, that held me. ''E said to come in, Ma'am,' the girl said.

'And who are you?' Millicent asked with surprise.

'Ellen Smith, Ma'am.' In her nervousness, she was fingering a dirty handkerchief with both hands.

'You look too young to be married, Ellen. The clinic's for married people . . . ' But Millicent had guessed that she was pregnant. 'How old are you, child?'

'Fourteen, Ma'am. I'm too young for it, Ma'am, ain't I? The gentleman said you'd 'elp . . . '

'That was wrong of him,' said Millicent. She moved round her desk, sat down in the chair and studied the girl. 'I'd like to help, Ellen,' she went on quietly. 'Oh, I'd like to help so much, but I'm not allowed to. When you've had the baby, come and see me, and we'll get him adopted into a good home.'

It was her sheer control that was horrific. At first she did not even seem to be crying, because her body was still. She stood looking at Millicent, the tears just coursing down her cheeks. 'Thank you, ma'am,' she said, and walked out of the room.

'You see?' Millicent said. 'At fourteen . . . But God chose to put it there, didn't he? That's what they'd say. So God'll find a way to . . .'

The door was flung open before she could finish, and Carl stood there literally shaking with rage. 'How could you, woman?' he demanded. 'How could you send that child away?'

Even Millicent was surprised. 'What did you expect me to do, abort her?'

'Couldn't you have examined her roughly? Probed too far? Couldn't you have found an infection?'

Millie sat for a moment in deep and anxious thought. 'Do you think she could be a decoy? It'd be a way of getting me, wouldn't it? They'd know I'd be tempted because she's so young.'

'Decoy?' he echoed. 'She's no decoy. I know her father. *He's* the father of the child. There's something for you to ponder in the cage, Mrs Alexander,' he sneered at me.

'Oh, stop it, Carl,' Millie snapped in irritation. 'You're being boorish. Makes you think, though, doesn't it, Quincey? Can you really be satisfied with a system that permits such a thing?'

The girl had shattered me. From every aspect, it seemed criminal that she should be forced to bear that baby, but the issue was not as simple as she made out. There were principles to consider. 'I don't know,' I answered. 'It's tragic – and it'll ruin her life, but . . . ' I broke off.

'But?' echoed Millie. 'Tell me,' she asked carefully, 'If you were me, would you do what Carl wants?'

'Would it be dangerous?'

She shook her head. 'Far less than the risk if she had the baby.'

'But it's a crime in law.'

'A cruel, wrong law . . . a child of that age! Her father! It's unbelievable, though God knows I see it enough.' She shook her head in despair.

'You asked me what *I'd* do, Millie,' I said quietly. 'It's terribly hard for you, but I don't think I'd break the law, commit an actual crime – not even a wrong law.'

'Wouldn't you, Quincey?' There was a suspicion of her mocking grin in sad eyes. 'No, I don't suppose you would.' She turned to Carl. 'Is the girl still outside?' He nodded. 'I think,' she said to me, 'you'd better take the cab home on your own, Quincey.'

I stood up with a sympathetic smile. 'Perhaps it wasn't a good idea to come down here,' she said, a bit sadly.

'I hope you don't mean that,' I responded. 'I'm glad I've seen what you're trying to do . . . I admire it very much, Millie.'

Instinctively, we embraced. Carl was holding the door open. 'Have an enjoyable afternoon, Mrs Alexander,' he said sarcastically. I walked past him without a word.

[2]

I stood at bay. That was how it felt – like a stag, like a fox. 'How did you know?' I demanded, as I faced Howard with my back against the wall of 'The Room' – quite literally. 'How did you know where I was?' I had never felt so strong a sense of outrage, but beneath it lay a touch of fear. For I was aware of the answer to my question, and it chilled me. I had been followed. Mathew had put me under surveillance. That Howard should have ordered this, though, revealed an anxiety in him that I found hard to credit.

He watched me, impassive as always in the face of my anger. 'Sit down,' he said, 'So we can discuss it calmly.'

'Discuss it!' I exclaimed. 'Discuss what? How dare you, Howard? And why? For goodness sake, why? There are no men involved, are there?' Whatever his purpose, I knew that would find a chink in his armour.

His arms were flat on the desk, his expression bland. 'Millicent Russell's more dangerous than any man of your acquaintance, Quincey,' he said. If Howard ever killed anyone, that same expression, devoid of emotion, would be in his eyes as he did it. 'She's a revolutionary,' he added.

'She's a socialist,' I corrected. 'Like many respected people – Mr Bernard Shaw, for example, H.G. Wells . . . She believes our society's going to change, but that doesn't mean she's planning to kill the King.'

'Worse,' he continued, 'she's working in a field that's not only offensive to many people, it's on the very borderline of the law.'

I was astounded that his reaction should be so virulent. He had never even seen her. 'Millie's doing an immense amount of good in the East End,' I insisted.

He shrugged. I had missed the point. 'She could be saving a hundred lives a day,' he said, 'But powerful interests are poised against her. When they strike, there'll be a scandal. It's vital you're not involved.'

'Strike? Do you mean prosecute? On what ground could they possibly prosecute?' I demanded, although, of course, I knew.

'You'll find there are grounds . . . '

I was uneasy. 'Even if you're right,' I said, 'I don't see how I could be involved? I'm nothing to do with her clinic. She's just a friend.'

'When mud starts flying, friends can get it on their faces. Touch pitch, as they say . . . I've been warned at high level, so you must stop seeing her, Quincey. You will, won't you?'

I stood staring at him for a moment, deeply troubled. 'No, Howard,' I answered. 'No, I won't stop seeing her.' And I walked out of the room.

[3]

I did not actually tell Millie of my quarrel with Howard, but she detected it from questions that I hoped would sound casual. 'Oh, they've set the dogs on, have they? They won't get anywhere.'

After my visit, we had talked about her work but she had made no mention of Ellen, the young girl at the clinic, and I sensed that she did not wish me to do so either.

It was there between us, of course, as unmentioned subjects always are, but it did not affect our friendship, which continued, with its friendly conflict, much as it had before. She did not mention Carl either. He was taboo as well.

Both of us visited Steven Mason in hospital, and Millie was

following the treatment of his burns with close professional interest. 'The skin grafts were very good,' she said. 'Mr Brown's a skilled surgeon.'

Steven was content to see Millie, since he had known her only as a doctor, but at first, when his bandages were removed, he asked me in his shame to cease my visits. I had declined the request. He had to get used to people, and I was a start. A few relatives and friends had gone there, too, and his resistance was lessening. It was a process of step by step. Then the time came for him to leave hospital. 'Millie,' I said, 'I've been thinking of inviting Steven to Shere to stay for a while . . . rest . . . walk a little . . . perhaps get used to people again, slowly starting with us. Then perhaps one or two he doesn't know . . . singly . . . Aunt Elizabeth . . . others from the Manor . . . Do you think that'd be a good idea?'

'I'd have thought it excellent. Have you spoken to Mr Brown?'

'He approved it – if we could get Steven to agree. So far he's refused. Will you help me talk him into it? His father's trying to persuade him, too.'

[4]

It was after five in the afternoon when the long yellow bonnet of Mason's Leopard emerged from the lane that led through the woods.

Mason was at the wheel himself. Martin was in the back. Steven was the first to get out. He stood waiting, a dramatic figure in the clothes of his tragedy – a wide-brimmed felt hat pulled slightly forward, large-lensed dark glasses, a jacket with a specially broad collar that was turned up with the gap at the front filled by a cravat. Even so, the concealment was only partial. The scarring of his cheeks and chin was only too evident.

'Hallo, Steven,' I said warmly, 'I'm so pleased you've come.'

'It was good of you to invite me, Mrs Alexander,' he answered. Since the accident, we had become more formal with each other.

209

No 'Madame la directrice'; none of the light mockery.

Mason and Martin got out of the car and joined us, then we all went into the house. Meeting the others would be the test.

I had consulted Mr Brown, the surgeon, and in addition to Millie, James was there, since he knew him quite well – and Frances, who, like James, had seen him after the accident and travelled back to England on the yacht.

Also, Frances, being a woman, would demand more of him, but she was sympathetic, easy to talk to, and a member of the family. She was staying in the cottage for the weekend, instead of her own home, in the hope that, after the shock of first meeting, he would become accustomed to her presence.

Strangely, all that day in the cottage, we had avoided speaking of his visit. I am not sure why. Perhaps the others noticed that I did not refer to it and judged it tactful to follow suit. Perhaps they did not want to dwell on it either.

Bridget, my housekeeper, had also sensed my reserve. At one moment when we were in the kitchen discussing dinner, the cook inquired: 'And how many will there be at table, Ma'am?'

'Six,' Bridget answered before I could speak. 'One extra guest.' She changed the subject swiftly. 'I thought I'd take Jonny to the Manor for tea this afternoon,' she said to me. So he would not be there when Steven arrived, I realized. It could be wise, since the little boy might well stare at him. Certainly they could easily be kept apart. The house had never really been a cottage. Now that I had extended it, building on extra guest rooms, staff accommodation and a nursery wing, it was a substantial property.

Bridget's grasp of the situation, with all its conflicts, was almost uncanny, since I had not spoken of it to her. Our relationship, in fact, was remarkable. She gave me her complete loyalty, and ran my homes without apparent effort. I was fortunate to have found her, fortunate also that she, too, was prematurely widowed. We did not speak much of the condition we shared, but it gave us a special understanding of the nuances that stemmed from it in both our lives. She was a little older than I was with a similar background. Her father worked for a wool-broking firm in Halifax, Yorkshire – as a clerk, as Papa had been. She was childless herself, but adored Jonny, who warmly returned her affection.

Bridget was not a striking woman, but she had a certain grace, being dark and rather tall, with a pale, slim face in which the features were as delicate as china.

Sometimes, if I was dining at home alone, she would eat with me, and occasionally, at the cottage, when I had informal company, she would dine with us. Her role as both companion and employee required the lightest touch, as she had demonstrated that morning. Her answer to the cook meant that she would be with us at dinner, which I had not requested. But Steven Mason was better not discussed and she guessed that, at a meal which might be strained, she could be a sheet anchor of a sort.

I led the three men into the big room where the others were waiting. At the door, Steven hesitated. He had not taken off his hat, as the others had, though now he did – with reluctance, revealing that the hairline had been shaven back in the surgery. Much of the flesh of his face was still livid, the colour heightened by its contrast to the pale grafts on his cheeks and forehead. The healing had caused contraction, especially at the eyes and mouth, so that there were tiny creases in tight skin that in places was unnaturally smooth.

'How good to see you, Steven,' Millie greeted him. The word 'see', involuntarily spoken, found response, the merest suspicion of a wince.

'You've met Mrs Alexander,' I said, referring to Frances, 'and you know James, of course.' Frances smiled at him brightly. James gave him the casual friendly welcome that he always did.

I had ordered tea to be brought in the moment they arrived, so that there was something for us all to do. As I served it, I asked Mason about the firm which, if not safe as a subject, was at least what would be expected of me.

'Sales are well up in all departments,' he said. 'Of course, Steven's win at Périgueux has given a big boost to orders for The Leopard, especially from abroad. It's becoming famous – among motorists, anyway. In fact, we're toying with the idea of using it as an insignia on a new line of bicycles . . .'

Dinner, as Bridget had foreseen, was strained. Steven maintained his reserve, answering questions but never asking any. He was carefully polite. I was always 'Mrs Alexander', as I had been before but now it was as though we had just met. Millie was 'Doctor Russell'. He called James 'Mr Stratton' until James could not bear it any longer and burst out: 'Dash it, old chap, I'd prefer it to be James as usual.' Steven looked at him through the dark glasses. 'As you wish,' he said.

The conversation veered repeatedly into sensitive areas. Millie described a man she knew as handsome. James spoke of his current love as pretty. 'Don't you think so, Quincey?' he asked.

'I do, James', I answered, 'very pretty.' Even from me, the word slipped out unnoticed.

Because of the silence that threatened the table, we became desperate to keep talking, falling back on the routine of our lives, but still we found ourselves describing inadvertently the way that people looked.

Bridget, as always, came quietly, unobtrusively to the rescue. She asked Steven about the hospital he had been in. There was nothing artifical about that – or sensitive, since he could have been there for a broken leg – and he responded accordingly. Millie entered the conversation, expanding it to hospitals in general.

Then Frances raised the question of Steven's return to work at Masons, using the word 'when', not 'if', which was good. Then she spoiled it by adding: 'I presume you *will* be going back.' Perhaps it did not spoil it. Perhaps we were wrong to pretend that everything was normal. Perhaps we should have spoken frankly about what life was going to be like, looking as Steven did; although his face might improve with time, it would always be horrific – as he knew and we knew.

'Of course I'll be going back to Masons', Steven answered her. 'I'll be driving again – if that's what Mrs Alexander wants, as I'm sure she does,' he added, with a glance at me, 'for it helps the profits, doesn't it? *And* it helps the company . . . *and* the industry. . . *and*, of course, the bank . . . '

'Steven . . . .' I protested.

'And since the damage is done, there's much less to lose now, isn't there?'

I was shocked and upset by the anger that was clearly raging in him, contained though it was, for this had never been evident in hospital. There, he had changed greatly, at first losing his conceit, and then retreating into himself, becoming morose and hard to talk to. But he had never tried to wound me as he was deliberately attempting now.

'I want you to drive, Steven,' I said, 'only if you want it yourself.'

He was such a serious figure, sitting down the table, gazing at me, unblinking, his facial muscles inert, with none of the rancour in his expression that was in his words. 'They say,' he went on, 'that bullfighters need to be gored before they can achieve the highest skill. Perhaps the same applies to drivers. If so, I'll drive better for you, Mrs Alexander, than I did before . . .'

'For yourself, Steven,' I insisted. 'Not just for me.'

He hesitated, his eyes still on me. 'I'd like it to be for you,' he said. He turned to Frances. 'Do you live in London, Mrs Alexander?' It was the first time he had made a positive move instead of just responding to other people's questions.

The days that followed were hardly easy. The resentment he had revealed at dinner surfaced occasionally. We were walking in the garden, for example, and he seemed content. The sun was shining; birds were singing. 'It's lovely here,' he remarked. 'It's so kind of you to ask me,' but his tone had changed with the word 'kind', suggesting it was not kind at all, but the least I could do.

The previous day, he had apologized for what he had said to me at dinner on that first night. 'It's hard not to be bitter sometimes,' he said. 'Not against you . . . .more against . . . Well, against who? Against God?' At the time, he was looking through the window across the Solent water, his hands thrust deep in the pockets on his jacket. 'There's no point, of course . . . Weakness . . . . Not much pluck . . . And don't think I need your sympathy, Mrs Alexander,' he said sharply. 'I'll manage . . . I'll drive . . . I'll drive faster than anyone has ever driven before . . .'

His moods veered with sudden changes. At one moment he would be cheerful, discussing some experience of the past, and would stop in mid-sentence, a scowl on his face – or as much of a scowl as he could express – and retreat into sullen silence; or the sarcasm would flare in his tone, the sarcasm that was always there like a rock beneath a moving sea, protruding only in occasional foamy glimpses. But none of the others was ever its target. Nor was

God. It was always me.

On the third night after his arrival, I awoke to find him in my bedroom. It was a shock. He was standing by the window where the darkness was less intense, looking out through the glass. For a few seconds I lay watching him anxiously, without speaking, my heart thumping. I found it hard at first to believe he was actually there, then began to puzzle uneasily about his purpose. At last, I whispered: 'Steven.'

'I disturbed you,' he said. 'I'm sorry. I didn't mean to . . . '

I sat up in bed. 'What in the name of heaven are you doing in here?' I demanded, still in a low tone.

'It was hard to sleep,' he said. 'Lonely . . . I wanted to be near someone . . . You . . . I wanted to be near you . . . '

'You really must go, Steven,' I insisted quietly.

'Just for a few minutes, Mrs Alexander,' he said, 'Please . . . '

'No, Steven. Someone might hear us . . . '

'We'll be very quiet . . . talk a little . . . until the desolation goes. Is that too much to ask?' I was silent. It did not seem so much, not put like that. I was troubled, though. His presence there was compromising. What would I do if he did not leave? 'Five minutes,' he said. 'Just five . . . You can time me by the clock.'

I hesitated. 'All right', I said. 'Five minutes . . . ' I struck a match and lit the candle on the table beside me. 'Pass me my nightrobe.' I pointed to where it had slipped from the bed and he handed it to me at arm's length. I draped it round my shoulders over my nightdress, then noted the time by the clock on the bedside table. 'It's ten past three,' I said.

'I'm grateful to you. You're helping, you've no idea how much . . . May I sit down?' I nodded and he looked around him, but the chairs were too far for whispered conversation; so with a glance at me, for permission, he perched on the end of my bed.

In the soft candlelight, the sharp contrasts of his face wounds were not so marked. He tried to smile – the first time I had seen him do so – though this was evident only from his eyes and a slight movement of his distorted mouth.

'I like to see you with your hair down,' he said. 'It suits you. Your eyes are different, too, in the candlelight . . . '

214

They were personal comments. 'You said you want to talk,' I reprimanded mildly.

'It *is* talking. I didn't mean deep talk – not the universe or even the strange ways of God, who selected me for this . . . ' he indicated his face with a slight movement of his hand. 'Talk is contact . . . from inside . . . reaching out . . . It's harder for me to reach out now. Well, who wants me to . . . ?'

'Many people,' I insisted.

'They think they ought to,' he said. 'They can imagine it happening to them . . . There but for the grace of God . . . So they try not to show what they feel – as you do yourself.'

'Steven,' I said, 'That's just not true . . . '

'You know what the hardest part is?' he went on. 'I mean of being . . . well, like this? To know that no woman will ever love me . . . '

'That's nonsense,' I said.

'I've got to face it,' he went on. 'There's no point in pretending. Perhaps you can help me face it, Mrs Alexander . . . '

'You're completely mistaken, Steven,' I said. 'Women don't love a man just for the way he looks. Some woman'll fall in love with you soon enough, Steven, I promise you . . . more than one, I expect. They'll be vying to be your wife . . . '

He did his best to smile. 'You're generous,' he said dubiously.

'Ask anyone,' I said. 'Any woman, I mean. They'll tell you the same. Ask Millie tomorrow.'

The pain of mistrust was still in his eyes. 'Look at me, Mrs Alexander,' he said.

I fixed my eyes on his, trying to blank out from my mind the taut puckered skin around them. 'Don't you want to shudder when you see that face?' he asked. 'If you can call it a face . . . Honestly, please . . . '

'No, Steven, I don't.'

'*I* want to shudder when I see it. I see it every day in the mirror. Parts still grow beard . . . I have to shave . . . '

'Steven,' I began, 'you really must . . . '

He cut in: 'Give me your hand.' I hesitated, then did as he asked. 'I want you to feel my face,' he said. He leaned forward and lifted my hand to his cheek. He guided my knuckles gently over the

215

corrugations. It was an unpleasant sensation, but I knew I must not show it. His face was closer to me now, so that the flickering light of the candle made the ravaged patchwork of his flesh – with so much unaligned, with his eyelids pulled open, each in its own unnatural way – seem more obscene than it had appeared before. He detected it, I knew – the instant of repulsion in my eyes. 'That's what I am, Mrs Alexander. That's me – the me that's now . . .'

His words, half-whispered, touched me through my distaste. I felt a great need to help him, to share in some way his sense of desolation.

'What woman could bear that face?' he asked.

'Many, Steven, I've told you . . .'

'You're just saying that,' he insisted.

'I'm not, I promise.'

'You promise?' I nodded, forcing a smile. 'Then kiss me,' he said. His words, coming suddenly, were a shock. 'Oh, Steven,' I reproved, as though he had disappointed me.

'Kiss me,' he repeated. 'On the lips, like you did at Périgueux . . .'

'It was under protest there,' I reminded him gently.

'Kiss me,' he said.

I hesitated. Then I leaned forward and lightly touched his lips with mine – touched lips of a mouth on which the skin at one corner was drawn sideways by contraction.

'Now you must go,' I said gently. 'The five minutes have passed.'

He did not move. The white of his eyes, only inches from mine, were mapped with tiny veins of red, prominent because of the damaged eyelids. 'That repelled you, didn't it?' he said.

I shook my head. 'Like at Périgueux,' I said softly, warmly. 'Now please leave, as you agreed . . .'

'You've done your good deed, haven't you?' The sarcasm was back in his voice. 'You've bestowed your charity . . . Like giving soup to the poor . . . Why pretend, Mrs Alexander? Does it help me to face it?'

'I told you, Steven,' I said, a little desperately, 'It was like at Périgueuex . . . no difference . . .' His eyes were probing mine for the truth. 'Heavens, Steven, are all husbands handsome? Or all lovers? How can I persuade you of the nature of a woman's love?'

'Like this,' he answered in a whisper, 'Properly . . . ' And his mouth was hard on mine, lips parted in a kiss of passion, of desire, his arms holding me tightly to him. I twisted my head sharply sideways. 'Stop this at once!' I ordered. 'You're going too far, Steven. You always did . . . '

'Can you imagine this face above you in the act of love?' he demanded. 'This damaged, seared replica of a face?'

I was scared now by his intensity. 'You're not being fair to me, Steven,' I appealed.

'Fair?' he echoed, incredulous in anger. 'You speak of fair? Is this fair? Is God fair? Are you fair . . . I won the race for you, didn't I? Now . . . ' His voice was again a whisper ' . . . answer the question. Could you look up into these eyes, these monster eyes, while giving yourself, with a man within you? Could you, Mrs Alexander?'

I put my hands against his chest and pushed him away gently, leaning back against the pillows, breathing heavily. I was in a kind of shock, with my heart beating fast, yet I still felt compassion for him, the pity he so much resented. He did not resist my movement of retreat, loosening the grip of his arms around me – but still maintaining contact, so that his hands slipped up my back to my shoulders.

'Could you?' he repeated. 'Could you make love to a monster?'

I was trying hard to remain calm. 'If I loved him,' I answered. 'And you're not a monster, Steven . . . Now let me go,' I said it softly. 'Please, Steven . . . '

'Experiment,' he whispered, and moved his right hand slowly from my shoulder to my breast. 'Don't do that!' I said sharply. 'I'd never think you'd do that . . . Please, Steven . . . '

'It disgusts you, doesn't it?' he said.

'I'm going to have to scream,' I warned.

'Scream then,' he said. He was brushing the nipple through the silken covering with the back of his fingers. 'What'll you say when they come?' he asked. 'A monster's making love to me, a beast . . . Beauty and the beast . . . Is that what you'll say, Mrs Alexander?' And with a sudden movement, he ripped open my nightdress.

I was very scared. A cry came to my lips, but I checked it, my fear of him still mixed strangely with sadness. 'Aren't you going to scream, then?' he asked. Delicately, he touched my naked breast.

'You see, Mrs Alexander, monsters don't care . . . Monsters have nothing to lose . . . So why aren't you screaming?'

'I don't want to scream,' I answered carefully. 'I want you to show me respect, not treat me like a whore.'

He glanced up at me with sudden hurt surprise. 'Oh no,' he said gently, 'you mustn't say that. I love you, Mrs Alexander . . . I've always loved you . . . I knew you didn't love me, even then when it was possible. Now I know it's laughable . . . Forgive me please, if you can . . . ' And he covered my breast with my gown.

I knew then that it would happen. The need swept up through me with a violence that made me breathless – a desire born of so many things, but mainly of the pain in him, of the despair he felt, of the shame he would later feel, of a compulsion to comfort him like a child. Some instinct, rooted in the way that I was raised, stopped me saying so. 'You must go, Steven,' I whispered.

But he knew. He sensed the change in me. 'I'll snuff the candle if you wish,' he said, 'so you can pretend it's someone else . . . .'

I shook my head. That would defeat the object.

It was the first time since Richard had died two years before – the first man. Steven was gentle, more gentle than I expected knowing the frustration, the violence, in him. He did not kiss me, and I knew this was deliberate. For kissing is too close to see, and it was vital to him that I should see his face.

I have wondered since how it might have ended. The whole direction of my life could well have changed; his life, too. I could have loved a monster, to use his terrible phrase. Everything in me was reaching out to him, as is right in love – until I changed. Even now I do not know what caused that change; not exactly.

I saw the photograph of Richard on the table by my bed. By that moment I no longer had to look at Steven, for there was no more need for proof. I was giving, needing him, enjoying him with a release of passion that enveloped my whole body. My head was moving from side to side on the pillow – which is how I came to catch sight of Richard's picture.

Richard would have wished me well. Gone as he was, he would not have denied me now to another man. But he had *been* there – on that very bed, at many times of such varying quality, from quiet comfort to laughing loving, to the soaring heights of the night that Jonny was conceived.

I stopped moving – just for a few seconds. I held Steven tight within my arms to stop him moving, too. And he misunderstood.

'Just a moment,' I said. 'I need a moment.' He still misunderstood, which was not strange. But, in a way, it was worse than if our joining had been disastrous from the start, as under those strained conditions it might well have been. For I had given him hope, shone a light through all his fears, dispelled the thick mist of his suspicions. He had believed, exulted in my pleasure – and now he felt betrayed, suspecting I had been acting, concealing my disgust. The assurance I had given drained from him and his hardness died inside me.

'Sorry, Steven,' I said. 'It was just for a second . . . A woman needs to pause sometimes . . . Please let's go on.'

He was glaring down at me, supporting himself on his elbows, 'I can't go on . . . You know I can't . . . '

'You can,' I insisted softly. 'Relax . . . Just move a little . . . Kiss me, Steven . . . '

'Bitch!' he snarled suddenly. 'You had me fooled . . .'

'I wasn't fooling,' I insisted. 'Steven, I promise I wasn't fooling. Kiss me . . . '

The desperation was there again in those malformed eyes, which now began to water. Suddenly, a great sob shook him and he slumped on me heavily, crying. I hugged him. I stroked his hair. I pleaded with him to believe me. I said that what had happened did not matter, for he could come to me again.

It had no effect. 'What a pathetic little man I am,' he said. 'Little monster . . . ' He rolled off me.

'Don't go,' I said. 'What you've said's untrue . . . '

He sat on the edge of the bed and looked at me with his monster's face. 'Yes, Nurse,' he said bitterly. 'Nursey . . . Take my head on your bosom, Nursey, so that I can have a good cry . . . Always better to have a good cry . . . '

He got up, bent down to take up from the floor his dressing-gown and pyjamas. He gazed at me, with the bland look of that first dinner, as I lay in the bed. 'Come back,' I said softly.

There was no response. It was as though I had not spoken. 'Mrs Alexander,' he said, 'I really think I hate you . . .' He went to the door and, without a backward glance, strode naked from the room.

It was my turn then. I lay and sobbed — alone, except for Richard's ghost.

By daylight he had left. He had saddled one of the horses, as we discovered, and ridden to Brockenhurst. Then he had caught the first train to Winchester.

[5]

Mason's face, as I walked towards him across the huge lounge of the Waldorf Hotel, was haggard. He seemed much older and smaller somehow. We often met at the Waldorf if we had anything special to discuss. It was a hangover from the past — a sentimental association. He and Richard had first framed their plans there to create the motoring enterprise.

I did not know why Mason wanted to see me. On the telephone, he had just said that it was urgent and serious. But I suspected it concerned Steven.

Three weeks had passed since Steven had left the cottage in such a hurt and angry state. Mason had discussed it with me, though naturally I had kept much from him. Steven had been unhappy, I had said. Perhaps it was too soon yet for him to meet people who were not extremely close.

Mason had known, though. He was a wise man and, over the years, he had seen a lot.

Steven had gone back to work in the factory. He had started driving again, a bit too fast, though, I gathered, and reckless, taking risks.

As I joined Mason, he got to his feet and responded to my smile of greeting with a sad shrug. 'I wish I could be the bearer of better news,' he said.

'What's happened?' I asked. 'I suppose it's Steven . . . ' Then I looked at his drawn features and had an awful fear. Oh my God, I thought.

Mason shook his head, guessing what was in my mind. 'He's left the firm . . . resigned . . . gone to work for Panhard . . . '

In a way it was a relief, but I was surprised. The character of Masons was still a family business, even though the bank controlled it. One day, Steven and Martin would inherit their father's stake in it.

'I'm deeply sorry, Mr Mason,' I said. 'I'm sure he'll think better of it, though. Give him a week or two and he'll be back.'

Mason looked grim. 'I fear there's more to it . . . You know this six-cylinder engine we're working on?'

I nodded. I knew he hoped to have the first test model ready by the winter. 'Panhard,' he went on, 'have applied for patents on some of our key elements of design . . . '

For a few seconds, I could not believe what he was saying, with its appalling implication. 'You can't mean Steven gave them the drawings?' I said at last.

Mason nodded. 'I hoped there was another explanation, but I fear there's not.'

'But surely we've taken out patents ourselves . . . I asked Steven about it when he came to see me before Périgueux. How long ago was that? Four months? Five?'

'We've applied for certain patents,' Mason explained, 'But we've been altering the engine all the time as we worked on it. The carburettor, for example . . . the principle's different now. We've been testing new ideas for the chassis too . . . detachable wheels, for example, so that they can be replaced when we want to change a tyre. Much faster, of course . . . revolutionary, in fact . . . but the hard part's been finding a fixing to the hub that doesn't work loose . . . '

'They've got that, too?'

'Unhappily . . . We only cracked the problem the day before he left . . . '

For a brief moment, I recalled the savage agony in Steven's eyes as he lashed out at me with that word 'bitch'. He had been a little mad, still was a little mad. Gracious, I had been a little mad to do what I had done. 'How much will it cost us?' I asked his father.

'Tens of thousands,' he answered. 'We can't produce the model without infringing their patents.'

'Can we sue them?' I snapped.

'On what grounds?' Mason asked.

'Theft?'

'We could never prove it. They'd say they'd been working on the same lines . . . '

'So much? Surely, coincidence couldn't go as far as that. We could show what we'd been doing over months, call our mechanics as witnesses . . . Call Steven . . . Could we demand his prosecution?'

Mason was shocked. 'Mrs Alexander . . . ' he began.

'Please answer the question!' I said. My fury was scaring me. What more could a woman offer a man than I had? 'Well, Mr Mason?' I asked.

'A set of the latest plans *was* missing after he left,' he conceded. 'But we didn't suspect him, of course, not at the time. I doubt if the police would act – not on the evidence we've got. He's in France, what's more, not here . . . ' He paused, the pain evident in his eyes. 'I wish there was something I could say that was adequate, Mrs Alexander . . . '

I shook my head and forced a smile. 'It must be as bad for you as it is for me – worse, since he's your son. All the same,' I went on coldly, 'we must do whatever's needed to protect the company's interests . . . With the full resources of the bank . . . '

I had intended to go on from the Waldorf to Old Broad Court. There was to be a final meeting with Paolo Fernandez in the afternoon and, since the ministers of the Dominican Republic kept asking for adjustments in the terms of the loan, I had planned to go over the figures with Howard before lunch. But now that I knew the gravity of what Mason had told me, I took the carriage to Grosvenor Square. I needed time to think. I was not allowed that time. When I got home, Howard was there.

Bridget warned me as I entered the front door, knowing that Howard's arrival meant some kind of crisis. He was in my office, sitting in an armchair, reading papers in the motor company file.

He knew, of course. I no longer questioned how he knew.

I tried to draw his fire. 'I see you've got the Mason file.' I challenged.

'You must be upset,' he said quietly. 'You were fond of that boy, weren't you?' So often, Howard surprised me. There was no anger in his voice.

'In a way,' I agreed. 'The accident was terrible. It even shocked you . . . '

'Even?' he queried. 'Of course, it shocked me . . . did you not expect that?'

I sat at my desk, elbows on the table, and rested my head in my hands. 'Can we sue?' I asked.

He studied me. 'That's a woman's anger, isn't it? Anger's the wrong reason for action.'

'Heavens, Howard,' I retorted. 'Don't you understand? They've stolen our car . . . We can't even make it – at least not the way it can be, with such enormous potential. They'll win all the races, outsell the competition . . . Surely we must fight.'

'Always your eyes light up when you speak of your motors,' he said.

His calm stoked my anger. 'Do *you* want Masons to lose tens of thousands?' I demanded. 'Gracious, it's our investment, isn't it?'

'Do *you* want to see Steven Mason in the witness box?' he countered coolly. 'Do you want him branded as a thief, questioned why he stole?' He saw the pain in my eyes. 'You must consider the risks . . . ' He paused. 'Could Steven Mason damage us? In evidence? In public?'

He was right. Steven, with his festering resentment, might well be maliciously truthful in court about our intimacy. The danger was considerable. Howard had sensed there was something for Steven to reveal, something rooted solely in the fact that I was a woman – and his accurate perception riled me. So did the fact that I was powerless. I could not even answer his question, for to say 'no' would be patently untrue, while to say 'yes' would be a confession.

He watched me as I clenched my fists in frustration. 'I think it'd be unwise for us to litigate,' he said. And a sadness came to his eyes.

It was then that Bridget knocked on the door and brought yet another shock on that troubled day. 'There's a gentleman asking to see you,' she told me. 'A Mr Carl Sandford.'

He stood in the doorway with the same expression of distaste that had been evident when last we met. His suit was creased, seeming loose and shapeless on him. His sparse hair was untidy. There were no courtesies. 'I come,' he said coldly, 'on behalf of Miss Russell. Nothing else would induce me to enter this house.' He glanced at Howard. 'I'd like to speak in private,' he told me.

Clearly Millie was in trouble, But it was unwise to talk to enemies alone. 'This is Mr Howard Alexander,' I said. 'You may say what you have to in front of him.'

Carl Sandford studied him with a sneer. 'Well, he'll shed no tears for Miss Russell, will he? Come to that, will you, Mrs Alexander? She thinks so, though I've told her you'll deny you ever met her. I said you'd watch from your carriage window as they took her to the scaffold. "That face seems vaguely familiar," you'd say to your smart friends.'

'Scaffold?' I repeated.

'A figure of speech, of course.' He wandered past me and sat down on the sofa, one arm lying along the back. 'I presume I may be seated,' he said, 'even in this palace of the rich? Why, if that isn't a Gainsborough up there on the wall? And the desk's a Sheraton, unless I'm much deceived. You don't mind if I smoke?'

'We do, indeed, mind,' said Howard. 'And I'd be obliged if you'd get to your feet until Mrs Alexander invites you to sit down.'

Carl was unperturbed. 'Wrath in a pillar of the establishment,' he mocked, adding with false humility: 'Forgive me, kind Sir.' Unhurriedly, he took a crumpled packet from his pocket, placed a cigarette between his lips and, after lighting it with a match, left it drooping from his mouth, observing us both through the smoke with a supercilious expression. 'Send for a footman, Alexander,' he suggested. 'Have me thrown out.' He shrugged. 'You can't, can you? You don't know why I've come. Oh, you've an idea, I expect. You've guessed that Miss Russell's been arrested.'

'Arrested!' I echoed.

'Don't tell me you're surprised, Mrs Alexander – or even you, kind Sir. Only to be expected, wouldn't you say?'

I felt an awful sense of desolation. What he said was true. I was not surprised, no more surprised than a soldier who hears that his comrade has been wounded in action. But that did not ease the sadness. In a way it made it worse.

'I'm so sorry,' I said. The words were inadequate, but it was hard to express sympathy in the face of such hostility. 'Where is she?'

'In a cell in Stepney Police Station. She's to be charged this afternoon.'

'What with?'

'Haven't you guessed, Mrs Alexander? Why, with procuring an abortion, of course. Why else would I be here?' He allowed smoke to emerge slowly from his nostrils as he watched me with amused contempt.

'Mr Sandford,' Howard said, 'I'll tolerate your behaviour no longer. Kindly stand up, put out your cigarette and state your business, or I can promise you I'll send for the police.'

Carl grinned at him insolently. 'I enjoy resolve in a man of power. All right, I'll do what you say, kind Sir.'

Unhurriedly, he got to his feet and wandered to the fireplace where, with his back to me, he threw his cigarette into the hearth. 'Mrs Alexander,' he began in a voice that had no mockery, and turned, facing me, erect in stance, a different man, 'you were at Miss Russell's clinic on the day she interviewed a young girl called Ellen Smith. Is that correct?' He spoke like counsel in court.

'You'll ask no questions, Mr Sandford,' Howard cut in. 'You'll just state your business and leave.'

'Miss Russell is seeking help,' Sandford said. 'Permit me to demonstrate how Mrs Alexander may be of assistance.'

'She can't be of assistance,' Howard insisted.

'In that case I'll leave, as you ask, and convey that message to her.'

I could not let him do that, for I recalled that afternoon very clearly – and the agony of her decision. At least she must know she had my sympathy. 'Let him ask his questions, Howard,' I said. 'What harm can it do? Yes, Mr Sandford, I was with Millie when she saw Ellen Smith – as you well know.'

'Did the girl tell Miss Russell she was pregnant and ask for an abortion?' His eyes were cold, as counsel's would be.

'In effect . . . .She said you'd told her that Millie would help.'

225

'And what was Miss Russell's reply?'

'That it was wrong of you to have said this; that she'd very much like to help but was not allowed to.'

'Did she say anything further?'

'Yes – she said that, when the girl had had the baby, she'd get him adopted into a good home.'

'And then?'

'The girl began to cry and left the room.'

'You were the only witness of this exchange?'

'Yes.'

'And you'd agree, I presume, that the answers you've given could indicate only a refusal to perform an abortion. Since you're a lady of standing and repute, you can appreciate the effect such testimony would have on a jury. That's the help Miss Russell wants.'

For a few seconds there was silence. Then Howard said quietly: 'It's quite out of the question, Quincey. You couldn't possibly testify.'

'There is other evidence,' I said. 'What about the girl?'

'She's grateful,' said Sandford. 'She's saying she aborted naturally. Even if they break her down, who'd the jury believe – a slum child or a witness of your social position?'

'Quincey, I insist,' Howard said. 'There's no way you can be involved in this unsavoury business.'

'But she *is* involved, kind Sir – as a crucial witness. Without her, Miss Russell will go to jail . . . '

At the thought of Millie in prison, I felt a surge of nausea so strong that I thought I would succumb. 'What evidence have they against her?' I asked tautly.

'Her father – bribed, of course . . . Police who were watching for the girl to enter the clinic . . . The doctor who examined her afterwards . . . Conclusive, you see, without your testimony.'

'So the girl *was* a decoy,' I charged, 'though you said she couldn't be.'

He shrugged. 'How could I be sure? It was a risk. There are always risks in the class struggle.'

'Millie's risk,' I reminded him. 'Why haven't you been arrested as a party to the crime? You urged her to do it.'

He stared at me, unblinking. 'There was no point . . . . It's not honour among gentlemen, you know . . . We're not playing cricket . . . Someone has to run the clinic. After all, no one knows . . . .'

'Except me. Why don't you go on with your questions?'

'Because you've given me all the answers I need.'

'I can think of others. I'll ask them for you. "Tell me, Mrs Alexander, what happened when the girl left the room?" Answer: "Mr Sandford entered in a state of anger and demanded that Miss Russell should do the abortion." '

' "And how did she respond?" ' I asked, imitating counsel.

'Answer: "She was greatly affected by the poor girl's plight, especially her youth. We both were. She asked me if, in her place, I would do what Mr Sandford demanded. I said that, tragic though her situation was, I did not think I'd break the law".'

' "What happened then, Mrs Alexander?" '

'Answer: "Miss Russell asked if the girl was waiting outside and, on learning from Mr Sandford that she was, she suggested I should go home alone without her." '

' "And was it your impression that she planned to perform the operation?" '

'Answer: "I cannot be sure, of course, but I thought it probable, in the face of Mr Sandford's fervent urging that she should do so." ' I paused. 'Would you say those answers'd serve your purpose, Mr Sandford?'

For the first time, I saw him look discomfited. 'You won't be asked those questions, for counsel'd have no way of knowing what happened between us in that room.'

'You mean you want me to testify to part of what happened, but to conceal the other part. That, in spirit, would be perjury . . . '

'I'm asking you to save your friend.'

'You're asking her,' Howard cut in, 'to do great harm to the House of Alexander.'

'She'd never have done it but for you, Mr Sandford,' I said bitterly.

'So you're refusing,' Sandford sneered, his poise recovered.

I hesitated, and saw Howard watching me anxiously. 'She is,' he asserted firmly, 'if she cares anything for her late husband, her son, or the bank he will inherit.'

227

'No,' I put in. 'I'm not refusing, but if I testify I'll tell only the truth – which'll fully incriminate you, Mr Sandford. Is that what you want?'

He looked at me with anger. 'It'd incriminate her too,' he said, then shrugged. 'It's what I told her. "Don't count on your fine friend," I said. "She wouldn't even dirty the hem of her dress for you." '

'And what did Millie say to that?'

'That it was a favour she was asking, not repayment of a debt. You see, Mrs Alexander, she still hasn't learned, hasn't lost her childish illusions.' And without another word, he ambled slowly from the room.

I went to the window and watched him hail a cab. 'Well, Howard,' I said. 'I did my duty, didn't I?'

'You did,' he agreed.

'Now I want you to do something for me. I want to see her to explain.'

'That'll be difficult.'

I was watching Sandford's cab as it travelled round the Square. 'I'm sure you know someone who can arrange it,' I said. 'Just for a few minutes, that's all.'

'I am acquainted with the Chief of City Police,' he said dubiously. 'I suppose he might agree to have a word in the proper quarter.'

[6]

She stood in the entrance of the interview room in Stepney Police Station. It had walls of green glazed paint and, because there was no window, the only light came from a single ceiling bulb, beneath a white china shade. There were two wooden chairs at a bare table, used presumably for interrogation of suspects. I was sitting on one of them, facing the door, waiting for her.

She grinned at me. 'Well, for Gawd's sake, just look who's here.'

228

'I had to see you,' I said.

'Good of you to come.' She sat down, elbows on the table, supporting her chin on clasped knuckles.

'Have you heard from Carl?' I asked.

'No, but I knew what the answer'd be . . . I doubt if I'd lie on oath for you, especially if I'd acted against your advice. It was a foolish business. The dangers were obvious . . .'

'It was hard for me to say no.'

'You had others to think of . . . It'd have tarnished the bank with scandal. No doubt about that . . . and why? What's Mrs Alexander doing associating with such a woman?' She held out her hand impulsively and gripped mine. 'Don't worry, Quincey, I understand. We'll still be friends, I hope. What concerns me is who's going to keep an eye on you while I'm locked up, keep those ideals of yours burning clear . . . I always said the process'd warp you, didn't I?'

'Surely there's no sign of that.'

'You said you'd never finance arms. The line's not that narrow, you insisted – remember?'

I nodded. 'There's been no change, Millie, nor will there be.'

'Are you positive?'

'Positive.'

She eyed me for a second, a trifle sceptically. 'I believe you,' she said then. 'They've kept it secret. Have you ever heard of Maxim machine guns?'

'Vaguely,' I answered. 'Didn't they use them in the South African war?'

'They did indeed, for the first time, and changed the face of war. They're amazing, terrible weapons. They can fire 500 bullets a minute. Think of that, Quincey! Eight bullets every single second! No wonder they killed thousands of men. No wonder there's so big a demand for them now. What better means to hold down a revolution? A few machine guns and you can mow down the peasants by the hundred as they charge up the hill. It was bad enough with rifles, but with machine guns tyrants can stay in power for ever.'

'Why are you telling me this?' I asked.

'Has your Señor Paolo Fernandez spoken to you of revolution?'

'No.'

'There's a big threat of it in the Dominican Republic – much unrest, terrible poverty – and a revolutionary leader in the shape of a man named Ramon Caceres. Have you got the loan yet?'

'Not quite,' I answered. 'We expect it to be finalized this week.'

'And what do you think it's to be spent on?'

'A number of projects,' I answered uneasily, for the familiar glint was in her eyes. 'A new harbour, housing, machinery for the plantations . . . construction works on a river for irrigation – the Yaque del Norte . . . '

'And arms,' she put in.

'That's not true, Millie,' I retorted.

'It is, Quincey. Especially Maxim machine guns . . . Vickers Armstrong alone have been promised an order of a half a million pounds. Negotiations are in progress with other munitions companies.'

'I don't believe it,' I insisted.

'I've estimated that half that loan'll be spent on arms,' she went on. 'I'm so glad you didn't know, Quincey, you had me worried. I thought the rot had set in.'

'But how can you possibly be certain of this, Millie?' I asked.

'Uncle Stewart. Remember him with me on the *Lucania*, the first time we met? His firm are brokers to Vickers. The Sales Director told him. I made some inquiries myself, then, with the help of the Party, and learned something of the scale of the Dominican Republic buying . . . ' She paused, watching me. 'So what are you going to do now, Quincey? You're not damming rivers any longer, are you? Or building bridges or railways. Your bank's financing death, isn't it?'

A police sergeant entered the room. ' I fear the time's up, Mrs Alexander.'

We both got to our feet. 'Thank you for coming,' Millie said.

'Good luck,' I responded – and kissed her. At the door she stopped and looked back. 'Toodle-oo,' she said. It was a new phrase, only just in vogue – a cockney adaptation of the French 'A tout à l'heure.' Then she winked, and was gone.

'Has Mr Fernandez arrived yet?' I asked Mr Wells, the immaculate king of 'The Front Hall men', as I strode into Old Broad Court.

'Yes, Mrs Alexander,' he answered. 'He's with Mr Howard now.' My presence in the bank no longer roused interest among the clerks, for I was there too often. As I walked unhurriedly across the pillared marble hall, I felt a deep sense of sadness. Why did I bother? Whatever I chose to do, the obstacles were always immense. If they did not exist at first, as even Richard had not expected with the motor company, they emerged like dark clouds, created, it seemed, in reaction to the thermal currents of my female-ness. It was only a momentary hesitation. I knew why I bothered. As I opened the door of 'The Room', all my doubts were gone.

'Why, Mrs Alexander!' Paolo greeted, effusive as usual. He leapt to his feet and kissed my hand. 'Thees is a great day, ees it not?' he declared, his eyes shining. 'A heestoric day! Have you heard? I've had authority from Santo Domingo to instruct Alexanders formally to issue the loan for the Republic of Dominica.'

'It's been a long negotiation,' said Howard, 'But it'll be most rewarding, I'm sure.'

'So, Señor Fernandez,' I said, sitting on the chair which he held for me. 'Your little Carib paradise'll get its new harbour and your plantations the modern machinery they need.'

'Exactly!' he said, with a delighted flash of white teeth.

'And the hovels of the poor in Santo Domingo will be replaced by good homes?'

'Indeed!'

'And you'll be starting on those works on the Yaque del Norte to divert water for irrigation?'

'Eet'll be magneeficent,' he agreed.

'All,' I went on, 'with the aid of Alexander money. Isn't that a fine thought, Howard?'

He knew my tone. 'You could describe it in those terms,' he responded cautiously.

'To think that, as bankers, we're helping to do so much for the well-being of the Dominican people,' I went on. 'That's really gratifying, isn't it, Howard?'

231

'Quincey . . . ' Howard began, sensing trouble.

'You promised to take me there, Paolo,' I cut in before he could continue.

'That will be a pleasure,' he answered, but even he had detected the steel in my voice. 'Whenever you have the time.'

'You'll show me the harbour – and the plans for the new houses?'

'Of course,' he agreed. 'You must make two visits – before and after.'

'And will you show me the Maxim machine guns, Paolo?' I looked at him innocently, as though we had often spoken of them. 'I look forward to seeing the machine guns. I'm told they're quite ingenious.'

He looked away, embarrassed. 'How did you learn of those?' he asked quietly.

'Oh, we bankers have our sources,' I said in an offhand tone. 'Why didn't you mention them to me, Paolo? Was it so secret? Were you ashamed?'

'I couldn't speak of everything we needed – and war ees a man's concern.'

'War, Señor Fernandez? This is business to a banker, like harbours. I'm told you're spending half the loan on arms.'

'No, that's quite untrue, Mrs Alexander,' he said, with a shocked expression.

'How much then? Half a million? A million?'

'Well . . . ' He gave a Latin shrug, all hands, and then grinned sheepishly like a small boy. 'In that region, I suppose,' he admitted.

'A million?' I demanded in confirmation.

'You must know, Mrs Alexander, that we face great dangers in the Republic . . . We live under constant threat from enemies to our people . . . '

Howard intervened. 'I don't understand the questions,' he said firmly. 'The Dominican Republic have invited us to raise three million for them by way of loan. It's an honour for the House of Alexander. How they propose to spend the funds has nothing to do with us.'

'It may have nothing to do with you,' I snapped, 'but it certainly has something to do with me – as Señor Fernandez has understood well enough, or he wouldn't have deceived me with his romantic tales of new harbours and houses for the poor.'

'It's you who don't understand, Mrs Alexander. There are pleasant things that governments have to do, and not so pleasant things that I don't like to speak of to ladies . . . We *are* planning works to the harbour . . . '

'I'm sure you are,' I said bitterly, 'but the fact is that, if we issue the loan, you'll be killing people with the aid of Alexander money.'

'We'll be protecting the legitimate government of our country,' he responded hotly.

'No you won't, Señor,' I said, shaking my head firmly. 'Not with Alexander money.'

'I must explain, Señor Fernandez,' Howard put in, 'that Mrs Alexander's very upset today. This morning she had news that distressed her greatly . . . ' He turned to me. 'Quincey . . . ' he began.

'No loan, Howard.'

'Then it'll just go to another house,' he reasoned, 'and the Dominican Republic will get the arms just the same. Any bank in London'd jump at the chance.'

'Then let them. I didn't come into banking to fund guns, Howard. Nor, I believe, did Richard. He'd have fought you just as hard.'

'Are you saying that we must approve the purpose of every loan we make? Would you refuse to fund a dreadnought for the Royal Navy?'

'I'd rather not.'

'Even though Britain'll be threatened if we don't match the sea power of Germany?'

'There'll always be finance for such things, you've just said so. There'd be finance for anything from some quarters, no matter how degrading. I'll give you a better argument, Howard, a banker's argument. If the danger of revolution in Dominica's so great they need to spend a million pounds on arms, then they're hardly a good risk, are they? The security is flawed. What if the rebels win?'

'We shall defeat the rebels, Mrs Alexander,' Paolo declared stoutly.

I stood up. 'I insist we decline, Howard,' I said. I did not have to elaborate. He knew what I would do if he refused. We had been here before, when he had dismissed James.

'Quincey,' he argued calmly, 'I'm sure Señor Fernandez won't mind my saying that revolutions are not rare in the Dominican Republic – which is why the U S government is securing the loan. The Board have already approved the project.'

'Then you'll have to explain that circumstances have changed.' I turned to Paolo. 'I have to tell you that I don't like being made a fool of.'

'Won't you permit me to explain, Mrs Alexander?' he pleaded.

'I don't think there can be anything to add,' I said. 'Good afternoon, Señor Fernandez.'

In the carriage going home, I thought of Millie. She would have been charged by now. They would have taken her to Holloway Women's Prison to await her trial. At least, she would have approved of what I had just done. And Howard? How would it affect my relationship with Howard? There would be change. There always was. The new positions of the chessmen would offer scope for advantage or expose weakness for a future move. Would the game be won? Could it be won, now that I was part of his life and he was part of mine? It could – but on that winter afternoon of 1904 neither of us knew how. Not even Howard.

Part 4

March 1907

Chapter 11

[1]

The March day was bright, with a thin sun striking through light, fleeting cloud. We were at Shere and Jonny was playing in one of the pools in the mudflats that emerged below the reeds when the fast tide drained the river. I was sitting on the bank, my skirt to my knees, luxuriating in the sight of him as, with intense expression, he explored the riches left there by the receding water. He was almost four now and clearly Richard's son, with the same sensitive mouth, laughing eyes, animated features. 'Look, Mama,' he cried excitedly, peering into the little shrimping net he used for his explorations, 'I've got a fish.'

He hurried to me, eager to share his find, and together we examined the soft mud at the bottom of his net. He dug his fingers into the slime. A minnow squirmed. 'That's a fish, isn't it, Mama?'

As we bent over the net, our heads close, we were suddenly in shadow. I looked up, surprised to see Howard surveying us. From that perspective he seemed even taller than he was – a gaunt figure in his long black overcoat and top hat.

'I was just passing,' he said.

He was never just passing. The act of impulse was not in his nature. 'You're down early from the City,' I said, getting to my feet, smoothing my dress, 'even for a Friday.'

'Look, Uncle Howard,' Jonny exclaimed. 'I've got a fish.'

Howard examined the net, as expected of him. 'Are you going to have it for your tea?' he asked gently.

We strolled across the lawn towards the cottage and I wondered why he had come. He spoke of some papers he had brought for me to look at, but I sensed there was a more important purpose. 'Are you doing anything for dinner tomorrow?' he inquired, continuing when I shook my head: 'The Earl of Lydborough's coming and I'd like you to meet him. He might appeal to you. He's got an interesting scheme which I'll leave him to tell you about. He's unmarried, by the way . . . about thirty-five, I suppose. Title goes back four generations – granted by George III. There's a family seat

– Lydborough Castle near Nottingham – but I wouldn't think he was rich.'

It was all there in those few words. The scheme he spoke of might be attractive, but it was his lordship himself who was the purpose of Howard's visit. And he was not guessing about his means, as he suggested. Mathew would have reported his resources to the last penny. The situation was well established. American heiresses were always marrying aristocrats of diminished fortune. As a wealthy widow I was in the same position, only I had greater obligations. There was the bank, and Jonny, whose future was inextricably entwined with the bank, and the Alexanders, to whom I owed allegiance, for it was because of them that I was rich. I was not a free agent, as Richard had always said I could not be – not a George Sand, not an artist living on the Left Bank in Paris. This was business, not romance. With Alexander money, the Earl would be able to live as earls should, and the prestige would wash back much benefit to the bank. The title would enhance the Alexander Board, and that of other companies where Howard might deem it wise to place him. And Jonny's mother would be a countess with an eighteenth century title. Certainly, he would not be ragged at Eton, as Howard had been, for being a Johnny-come-lately.

'So you've found my earl for me at last,' I said with a smile, touched with melancholy. I had often teased him about the earl I would make my husband, though it had never amused him.

'I wouldn't put it like that.'

'How would you put it? Do you want me to marry him?'

He sighed. He did not want me to marry anyone. 'I suppose you'll want to consider marriage sometime,' he answered. 'It's five years now since Richard died.'

In a sense, I was to be 'bait' again – as I had been with Paolo and several others since – but this time his sights were not set just on a useful admirer. He was aiming at the marriage bed, with all that this implied for him. He was offering me in totality, the me he had wanted for years, as we both knew and tried to ignore, except when I was being perverse and dancing near the flames. Now, as we sat waiting for tea to be served in the big front room of the cottage, I wondered if it would be worse or better for him to make me into a countess with a husband I did not love – or possibly even like – than to give me to a man with whom I could have shared the joy of passion. It was academic. Richard had made my standards high. In the five years since I had been a widow I had met no man I would have wished to marry.

'What's he like?' I asked.

His unhappiness was evident for barely a second. 'I don't think you'll find him objectionable,' he said. 'There's much to be said in his favour.'

I smiled bravely. 'I look forward to meeting him,' I said.

I wondered sometimes what would have happened between us if Howard had been a different sort of man – more adventurous, less controlled, less dedicated to the bank, for which he felt the bounden duty of an anointed king. Would he have revealed his feelings in a weak moment – even tried to make love to me? And what would I have done if he had? Laughed it off? Reprimanded him as a married man with a wife I daily met? Succumbed, perhaps – to an extent, at least, if he had chosen the right moment? I did not know. I was not in love with him, of that I was positive, but there was a bond between us that was constantly changing, evolving in both intensity and character. Our deep mutual concern for Alexanders never changed, but we fought our battles over it and I was still an adversary in the sense that I carried Richard's standard. Had I been a man, I would have contested the leadership, as he well knew.

The fact that he was unchallenged as the head of the bank and the family affected me subtly. There were times when I yearned for him just to touch me, put an arm round me perhaps, and others when his sexual need for me shone from him like a homing beacon with such power that it was hard for me not to respond. He was the authority in my life – what I had known as a small girl in my father, what I would have known in an older husband. But I did not deceive myself. The ruthless figure I had first met on the yacht, the cold antagonist to my husband, was still there. And should the need arise, I knew, he would reappear, surface like a sea monster, and attack with pitiless and single-minded purpose – attack me, no matter what his feelings were.

Over the past five years, though, we had become accustomed to each other. Our conflicts had become assimilated, the rough edges

239

worn down. We had given ground and taken it — middle ground that both of us could afford to concede. Together, we had watched Millie go to jail, and he had sympathized without referring to his warning of the dangers of our friendship. He had accepted the loss of the loan to the Dominican Republic — which had proved fortunate, for as predicted it had been racked by revolt — and advised me well over Steven Mason, assuring me that the motor firm would survive despite his betrayal. In fact, it had thrived, despite the bitter sight of Panhard's racing victories. It was old Mr Mason who had been savaged most, for Martin had followed his brother and now the old man spoke to neither of his sons.

At a personal level, my bond with Howard was deeply embedded now by constant usage, the cord that linked us becoming concealed by the moss of daily contact. So most of the time we could ignore it, except on occasions like that day in March 1907, when we spoke of marriage to my earl. For marriage was for ever, and I knew a sense of dread. 'What time will you be dining?' I asked brightly, continuing before Howard could reply: 'I think I'll wear my black gown, designed by Mr Worth. Do you think that'll be suitable — the sort of gown a countess might wear on such occasions?'

James came down for the weekend and, in the carriage as we drove to the Manor the following evening, I experienced a sudden pang of fear. 'Do I really have to do this, James?' I asked. 'Can't I stay a widow for ever?'

'You can,' he said dubiously.

'I mean, there are plenty of widows, aren't there?' I said. 'Even widows who are still quite young, like me . . . Well, aren't there?'

'Yes', he agreed, with the same note of doubt.

'Do I have to, then?'

'I can't guide you,' he said. 'Not on this . . . You know the benefits. As for the sacrifices . . . ' He gave a sigh. 'Well, you'll soon be in a better position to judge, won't you?'

'Thanks,' I said with a rueful smile. 'Next time you push me off in my own canoe, please give me a paddle.'

I handed my cloak to the butler in the hall, walked into the big drawing-room and, for the first time, saw my earl.

Peregrine Lydborough, could have been worse. That was my first thought. In point of fact, he was in his thirties, neither plain nor handsome – just ordinary.

My main impression of him was of physical immaturity. He was lanky and not, it seemed, totally in control of his body, as is evident sometimes in youths who have grown too fast. As he stood up to greet me, doubtless as anxious as I was, he appeared to uncoil awkwardly, a nervous but amiable grin slowly coming to a small square face. He wore steel-rimmed spectacles, had straight strong black hair that was brushed across his forehead – presumably because it refused to remain further back on his head – and an over-ample moustache that seemed untidily to overlap his upper lip.

He shook my hand with a limp grip and said what a pleasure it was to meet me. 'I've heard lots about you,' he added with a big smile, marked by an enthusiastic innocence.

We were placed next to each other at table. The conversation veered to politics and I asked him if he had spoken in many debates in the House of Lords. 'Not jolly likely,' he said with a laugh. Howard mentioned a company of which he was a director, and I inquired what it manufactured. 'Do you know,' he answered with his good-natured beam, 'I'm not absolutely sure.' We spoke of fox-hunting, of the days when hounds met at Lydborough Castle, and he admitted with a sheepish chuckle that he was 'a bit of a mug on a horse'.

Howard noted my response of dismay. For there seemed nothing of substance behind this man, who displayed the unashamed naïvety of a schoolboy. To have the privilege of a seat in Parliament and never to enjoy it; to direct a company without interest in its purpose? Glory, what was Howard asking of me? Stella, too, had seen my misgiving and I noted the satisfied quality of her smile. 'Lord Lydborough,' Howard put in idly, 'why don't you tell Mrs Alexander of the project you've submitted to us?'

'Really?' he inquired and his wide-eyed vapid smile. 'Wouldn't it bore the lady?'

I was thinking that, regardless of its benefits, this marriage would be impossible if I was to retain my sanity, when he began to speak about his enterprise. He changed. In front of my eyes, he became a different man, enthralled suddenly by what he was describing.

For my part, I could hardly believe what I was hearing. It was the most exciting venture that had been put to us in years – a rail link to be built from Buenos Aires in Argentina to Valparaiso in Chile, between the Atlantic and the Pacific. It would not only open up the interior of the vast South American continent, as the railroads had at home; it would reduce the need for the long and hazardous journey round Cape Horn.

We were being asked to finance only a section – 500 miles – because another consortium had dropped out, but it epitomized my ambitions and, for all Howard's bland exterior, I knew it thrilled him just as much, if only for the prestige it would carry. Certainly it transformed my view of Peregrine, vesting him with a certain panache. I guessed that he was part of the syndicate because of the weight provided by his title, but there was no doubt that he was informed of every tiny detail – the problems the engineers would face in terrain that was often rugged and how they would solve them, the cost per mile of laying track in varying conditions, the bridges that would have to be built across rivers and marshland, the labour and skills that would be needed, the hostile Indian tribes that might be encountered in the forests. He had even ridden by mule over much of the terrain with the surveyors.

When I commented on his knowledge, the bright smile I had found so irritating came to his face. 'I've dreamed of it since I was a boy,' he said. I realized then what sort of man I was being asked to marry. Peregrine, for all his unfortunate manner, was a pioneer. Well, I supposed, one could do worse for a husband than a pioneer.

Over the next few weeks, under Howard's orchestration, I saw a lot of him. I took Jonny and Bridget to visit his castle, which sorely needed restoration, and the three of us stood on the ramparts, imagining it under siege. I attended meetings at Old Broad Court where we discussed the detail of the loan which, at £5 million, was a big one. Howard and Nina began to entertain more, and Peregrine would usually be at the table.

But the prospect of marriage to him remained appalling. It was not enough to be a pioneer, especially since I soon realized that even this was a reflection of puerility. He was like one of Lord Baden-

242

Powell's boy scouts. He was playing with trains.

'Do I have to go through with it?' I asked James in panic, suddenly robbed, it seemed, of any power to make decisions of a personal nature.

'They can't force you.'

'But you think I should, don't you?'

'Well, obviously,' he said, putting his arm round my shoulder, 'It'd be a help to the family – and I wouldn't have thought Peregrine'd be hard to handle, would you?'

Howard surprised me with his persistence. He was gentle and understanding, but he was set on the marriage. He would negotiate it in any way I liked. I could make my own terms. As a duty, it should not be too onerous. Peregrine and I would have to be seen together at times for appearances' sake, but he would travel frequently.

'And the conjugal rights?' I demanded suddenly, resenting as always his willingness to deploy my value as a woman. 'Perhaps he has qualities as a lover I haven't glimpsed, a capacity for passion that he's kept concealed. What then, Howard?'

He looked back at me steadily. It was part of our ritual dance. 'He'll be your husband,' he said simply.

I was saddened, the fight draining from me. 'I feel as if I'm about to go to the scaffold,' I said.

Peregrine went through the motions of courting me. He escorted me to the theatre and we dined out in restaurants. He proposed, as required by the play we were acting out. I said I needed time to get to know him better, but wondered why I was prevaricating over a marriage of convenience. Quite apart from the interests of the family and the bank, it would have much personal benefit. As a countess I would have more freedom than I enjoyed as a widow, the social rules for wives being less demanding. There was only one real disadvantage: I could marry no one else.

Howard and Peregrine continued their plans as though I was not involved. A date was set, though postponed a couple of months to accommodate my feminine sensibilities.

But no bells rang for the wedding. I was at Shere on the day my nuptial prospects ended. It was another Friday and raining heavily from clouds so dark that, though it was late spring, I had turned the lights on in the cottage by early afternoon. I was alone, for Bridget was away for a few days and Nanny Roberts had taken Jonny to tea with Aunt Elizabeth at the Manor, where the maids had gone as well. Life was less formal at Shere than in London and I liked the silence of the cottage when I was alone in it, so I often relieved the staff of their lighter duties.

I was standing at the window watching the Solent on that dark wet afternoon as the waves built up under a freshening wind from the southwest. I was thinking of the South American loan issue that was to be launched the following week. Arrangements were complete – contracts signed with the underwriters, prospectuses printed, advertisements booked, staff warned at Old Broad Court for the all-night marathon required to handle applications from the public.

My thoughts were disturbed abruptly by heavy knocking on the front door. I opened it to find Howard standing there, rain dripping from the brim of his top hat – and one glance at his face told me that something grave had happened. I led the way into the big front room and, without being asked, poured him a brandy from a decanter on a side table. I brought it to him where he was sitting on the sofa. 'Well?' I asked.

He did not make much of it. He was too shocked. 'We've had an escape, Quincey,' he said quietly, 'that was so narrow I can hardly believe it . . . hours only . . . '

'Escape? From what?'

'Fraud.' His effort at control, usually so concealed, was manifest. 'The rail project's a fraud. It doesn't exist.' He lifted the glass to his lips and swigged it like ale, which was most unlike him. 'Quincey, I've been a banker for thirty years, but I'd never have believed a fraud like this was possible – and it was such a close-run thing.' He closed his eyes as though trying to obliterate the thought.

'Tell me,' I said. 'Please . . . what happened?'

He drank again, sipping this time. 'The scheme was clever,' he replied. 'Forged certificates . . . forged contracts . . . forged land grants. They knew we'd investigate locally and they'd set up everything . . . offices with staff in Buenos Aires, officials in long-established banks whom our agents actually interviewed on bank premises . . . Properly accredited papers, supporting correspondence . . . God knows how they arranged it all, but the prize was large . . .'

There was the nearest expression to fear I had ever seen in his eyes. 'How did you find out?' I asked.

'Chance,' he answered. 'That's what's unnerving. If it hadn't been for a jealous woman, we'd still be proceeding . . . Ladyfriend of one of Peregrine's colleagues. He'd strayed to someone else and she wanted retribution. She didn't know much but she'd overheard enough to alert Mathew. He was following it up at the bank all through last night . . . Paris . . . Berlin . . . New York . . . Constantinople . . . and BA, of course. By early this morning the telegrams were coming in and the picture was forming . . .'

I poured a brandy for myself then and sat beside him on the sofa. By now, as I began to absorb what he was saying, I was badly shaken, too. 'I wouldn't have thought that Peregrine had the wit for such ingenious crime,' I remarked quietly.

'He was probably just a figurehead,' Howard responded. 'Possibly he was being blackmailed . . . That's if he knew at all . . . Either way he'll probably be jailed – as indeed we might have been if we hadn't found out.'

'Surely it couldn't have been as bad as that,' I said.

He shrugged. 'We were backing the issue . . . at best our reputation would have been shattered . . .' He drank again and gave a long sigh. 'Well, at least you've been saved from the scaffold.'

I smiled at him, in shared relief. I had not yet thought of that. What if I had not prolonged the issue? By now I'd have been married to a criminal. Suddenly I felt as though, with Howard, I had escaped a fatal accident – a train at a crossing, a runaway horse. I even began to perspire, a knot of fear in my stomach, a quicker beat to my heart. It was as if, together, we had just avoided death. I am not sure if it was I who needed the reassurance, or if I felt an urge to offer it, but I reached out to press his hand that lay on his knee – and put a flame to combustible elements that had long been smouldering.

The explosion that consumed us was both unexpected and shocking in its intensity. We were inured to control, accustomed to a private knowledge that was never mentioned or even recognized, and we had lived with this for so long now that we took it for granted — which was why, I suppose, we allowed our guard to drop.

. I do not think that either of us said anything at that moment. I do recall that, as our hands touched, the change in our situation was immediate — by which I mean that, at one second, we were as we had been for years and at the next his mouth was on mine, and I was clutching him to me as though I was about to drown. All caution went — all thought of consequence, of danger, of concern for others. The demand in me was blinding. I cannot remember taking off my clothes, nor even running, as I must have done, to my bedroom. Yet later I was undressed and on my bed, and my gown and other garments were strewn over the floor, torn and ripped. I recall with precision his lips, his tongue, his hands on my breasts, my thighs, my ankles even. To this day I can feel him thrusting into me so hard it hurt in a pain in which I revelled. I remember arching to him with a strength that I did not know I had. I can taste the blood drawn from my lips by his teeth, so tight was my grasp upon his head.

There was no art to this coupling — no skill, no tender touching, no gentleness, no love. It was savagery — a desperation that began to ebb only when at last we lay, with me sobbing like a child and him, heavy on me now, panting as though he had run at least a mile.

I do not know how long we lay there. At one moment, I became vaguely aware that the servants might return, or Nanny with Jonny. They would not enter my bedroom, but they might see Howard leaving it. Oddly, I did not care. I was in a strange state of emotional numbness.

Howard sat up, his head in his hands — not in regret, I do not think, nor even in guilt, but in a kind of exhaustion that was both physical and emotional. Neither of us spoke. What was there to say?

At last he stood up and began to dress, collecting his clothes that were scattered on the floor. I noted that his body was sturdy, thick and firm, as I imagined that of a Russian peasant might be, except that he was tall. I lay watching him, my attention caught by his movements, until at last he picked up one of my petticoats and handed it to me. I saw that the lace of the hem was torn from the silk.

Then I, too, got up and went to my wardrobe to select new

clothes. I sat at my dressing-table and tried to create some order from the chaos of my hair. I studied my reflection in the big mirror. I looked like the same woman – my colour, perhaps, a little high. Conscious of my body, I smoothed the bodice of my dress, moving the palms of my hands down firmly from my neckline, over my breasts, to my waist. It gave me a certain satisfaction, a sense of containment. My eyes seemed very blue. Then I realized he was no longer there.

I found him in the front room, sitting on the sofa in the place he had occupied before. He was staring ahead of him, turning the gold ring on his finger gently and slowly, with none of the controlled agitation that was sometimes evident in this habit. There were two glasses of brandy on a side table by him, and as I approached he handed me one without speaking. I stood watching him for a few seconds, my glass at my lips. Then I sat beside him. Our mood was strange – a certain unison, the aftermath of deeply shared experience. There was no guilt in me, either, no wishing it had not occurred; but already I had recognized the danger. Forces of that strength could be devastating in their damage. Howard held a position of probity in the City. I was a woman of unquestioned reputation. Our situation held a potential for scandal that was as great as the fraud from which we had so narrowly escaped. We had, I told myself, known a few minutes of madness – almost in the class of hysteria.

I spoke at last. 'That cannot happen again,' I said.

'No,' he agreed.

We were not looking at each other. 'Perhaps I should go away for a while,' I suggested. 'New York . . . Take Jonny to visit his grand-parents.'

'That would be advisable, perhaps.'

He drained his drink and stood up, his shoulders rounded. 'I'll leave now,' he said, but then he hesitated. 'I'd like to say . . . .' he began, but broke off. 'I don't know how to say it . . . . or even what I want to say.' He shook his head, turned and left the cottage.

[2]

It was a fine cake. Everyone agreed on that. My cook had excelled herself, creating a work of art with icing a quarter of an inch thick and the words 'Happy Birthday Jonny' piped on it in blue. Bridget brought the cake into the dining-room herself. 'Look, children!' she called out. 'Just look at this!' The chattering faded. A dozen youthful eyes were directed at her as she stood in the doorway. She held the cake high like a trophy, the four flickering candles lighting up her face.

'Happy birthday to you,' she began and the children quickly joined her in the singing as she moved forward, with the cake still held high, towards the table. 'Happy birthday, dear Jonny,' they chorused as she placed it reverently before him, ending with a final shout of childish voices: 'Happy birthday to you!'

'Now blow, Jonny,' Bridget urged.

'All at once, mind you,' declared Nina.

And my son, flushed with excitement, filled his lungs and directed one big breath at the candles, managing to extinguish the four of them at the same time. We applauded, all of us – the grown-ups standing round the room and the seated guests, clapping as children do with their hands stiff. Jonny looked at me with a buoyant grin. 'I did it, Mama,' he insisted, 'I did it, didn't I?'

'You did indeed, darling,' I agreed, smiling 'you did it beautifully.'

It was a happy occasion, a kind of sunny peak in the years of truce that had existed between me and Richard's family since his death – and an important one, graced as it was by all the Alexander wives and daughters. Even Howard had planned to attend, which showed the weight he attached to a birthday of the Crown Prince to the Alexander throne – but there was a crisis at the bank which prevented his attendance. Instead he had come to lunch with his offering of a beautiful red tricycle.

I knew of the crisis. Our tankers carried the produce of the Romanian oil-fields, one of the largest producing areas in the world. Rumours had reached us that they would not renew their contract, due to end next year. John Trevor, head of our oil department, had been in Bucharest, exploring to see if these reports were based in any truth.

'Trevor got back this morning,' Howard had said at lunch. 'The news isn't good. The Romanians are under heavy pressure from our competitors – especially Standard and Rothschilds, who are acting in unison.'

I watched him as he elaborated on the situation in his grave tones. I wondered what he felt now about the 'happening' at the cottage only three days before. Had he blocked it from his mind? Surely this would be impossible, even for Howard. The memory of that emotional explosion must be there – still vivid with high colours, intrusive, demanding, tempting possibly. He had not referred to it in any way, not even obliquely – not even when I had remarked that I had booked passages to New York at the end of the month. The familiar screen was back, his behaviour to me unchanged – reserved, a little formally polite, occasionally impatient. For me, it was an odd sensation to have shared an intimate experience that was so violent and demanding and still to know that nothing outside us was changed, that the facts of our lives were unaltered. It upset me to look at him, conjuring as it did strong images that were marked with shame and a touch of fear because of the power that had been released within me, because of my failure to control it.

'What exactly will it mean if the Romanians don't renew the contract?' I asked.

'We'll have to lay up half the tanker fleet. The losses'll be heavy. I'd better get back now, if you'll forgive me.'

Jonny rushed into the hall as Howard had prepared to leave. 'It goes wonderfully, Uncle Howard,' he had exclaimed of the tricycle, his eyes bright. 'I've been trying it in the garden.'

Howard nodded, ruffling the little boy's hair. 'You be careful, young man,' he had said with a sad expression, 'and don't eat too much cake.' I wondered then if what had happened at the cottage had been a dream.

After the ceremony of the birthday cake, Bridget had been opening the curtains – drawn previously to give effect to the candles – when

249

one of the maids entered and whispered to her. She left the room, returning almost immediately. 'I fear you've got a visitor,' she told me. 'I said you were occupied but he insists that his business is urgent.'

'Couldn't he make an appointment?' I asked.

'He's leaving for Liverpool tomorrow, and sails for America in the evening . . . says he met you some time ago, though you might not remember . . . Bit of an odd character . . . '

'What's the name?' I asked.

'Smith,' she answered. 'O'Sullivan Smith.'

It seemed familiar, being unusual, but I could not at first remember him. Bridget saw my perplexity. 'Perhaps I should have sent him away,' she said, 'but I had a feeling you'd want to see him.' As usual, Bridget knew, with that extra sense of hers. We had grown even closer over the past three years. As a team we had become more efficient, more comfortable, meshed like the wheels of a well-oiled clock.

I remembered then where I had encountered him – a very brief meeting, five years before. He was the veteran oil-driller who had approached me on the SS *Lucania*.

As I entered the library, he was looking out of the window into Grosvenor Square. I noticed that his jacket was creased and ill-fitting, seeming to overhang his shoulders. He heard the door and turned – and I was looking at the same gnarled face like an old walnut, covered with a straggly beard, topped by a head of thick grey unruly hair.

He noted my response to his crumpled trousers, to his tie that was awry with one corner of his high collar turned over, and gave me a grin of crooked yellow teeth. 'I don't reckon the good God intended me for respectable drawing-rooms,' he said.

'No doubt he was liberal with other gifts,' I suggested.

He raised his eyebrows. 'It's good of you to receive me, Ma'am, what with me not having written to request an interview.' He spoke in the same strange mixture of accents – a bit of Irish touched with Cockney, overlaid with Southern American.

I gestured towards an armchair and he lowered himself awkwardly into it, sitting on the edge, his hard weathered hands on his knees. 'Shocked to hear about your husband, I was,' he went on.

'Terrible tragedy . . . You were a true delight to witness together, you know. I said then that I'd come to see him sometime, didn't I? Well, the good God had other ideas, so it's you I've come to see.'

'Mr Smith . . . ,' I began.

'O'Sullivan Smith,' he corrected. 'I know . . . you wish me to state my business. Well, on board that ship I told you there was oil at Paulina in Oklahoma. No one believed me then. Hardly anyone does now, but if there's one single thing in the world I really know about it's oil. I've worked in the field in Philadelphia, Kansas, Texas . . . I've drilled in Borneo, and Sumatra . . . I can 'smell' it when it's hundreds of feet below the earth, like an animal senses danger. These days, men laugh at the 'wild talent', as we call it, just as they laughed at the old gold prospectors, but it ain't a joke, Mrs Alexander. There's oil at Paulina . . . I'd go to the Cross for it . . . They could cut off my arms and legs. There's a fortune just waiting there to be brought up to the surface.'

'Then why hasn't someone exploited it?' I asked.

He gave a slight shake to his head. 'They don't believe it – the experts, I mean . . . the jolligists . . . ' Again, one of those nightmare grins came to his face as he spoke of 'geologists'. 'I'd more land when we met before, but I've still got leases on a hundred acres, which ain't much out there on the fringe of the prairie, but it's enough. Granted to me by the Cherokees, for it's In-*di*-an territory.' He spoke it as a word of three syllables, emphasizing the middle one. 'The In-*di*-ans have gone crazy about oil.'

He paused, a sad half-grin on his old face. 'There's been times of hope . . . a while ago, some local people put up the cash for some test drilling . . . yielded nothing. We had an inspector down from the US Government Survey in Washington, a jolligist if ever I saw one. He said there couldn't be oil in that kind of territory. Eventually, I sent for Standard Oil, which shows how desperate I'd got. Another jolligist . . .said the same . . . Marshy land in the wrong place . . . Contours of the land most adverse. Not a chance in Hell, he said. Most folks believed him . . . '

He broke off, watching me with a strangely impish expression before adding: 'Except one, that is – a jolligist at that, but not locked up in his mind like most of them. They're always looking back, you see, and with oil they ain't got far to look . . . Pennsylvania in the '60s . . . That's when they hit the world's first well, barely fifty years ago, yet with the rock they find the oil in, you're talking about millions of centuries. That's why jolligists get it wrong so often. They got it wrong in Texas, Virginia, Kansas . . . same in Burma and Malaya . . . Sometimes they think there's oil and there's not. Often there's only a bit. Why, Royal Dutch almost went broke in Sumatra because suddenly it was salt water coming up the pipe at Telega-Said and they'd got ships waiting at the port to carry oil that had disappeared. One day the jolligists may know, but they don't know yet . . .'

'But *you* know,' I challenged sceptically.

He shrugged his bony shoulders at my jibe. 'I know like a Christain knows . . . What jolligist could prove that God exists? And there's two of us now, I'd remind you – me and my jolligist . . . Name's Hampton, Bill Hampton . . . By the time we met he'd already figured out a theory that no one ever taught him in college. He was working out in the field in a salt mass, salt being his speciality. He came to reckon that where you got salt and sulphur and sand all together, then you were also likely to get oil, though he didn't know why . . . Well, I got all three at Paulina – which got me Bill Hampton.'

He stood up and walked over to the window. 'When I met Hampton,' he said, 'I was near cleaned out – selling my leases off in bits – time was telling . . . Then Hampton made me an offer for my drilling rights on the land I'd still got. The deal gave me 10 per cent of the take . . . I accepted and now he's drilled, too, and *he's* failed as well . . .'

'And your faith's still not shaken?' I asked.

He turned; for a moment I saw yellow teeth. 'Nope,' he said. 'We just ain't got deep enough – and remember we're talking of Oklahoma, where there's more oil than any other part of America. Why, my land's only a hundred miles from Glenn Pool, which even made Spindletop in Texas look small . . .'

'And Mr Hampton?'

'More convinced than ever . . . Mind you, he's had a bit of support. Professor of Minerology at the University of Minnesota got the same theory . . . Wrote an article in one of those journals scientists read . . . He figured too that ancient volcanic ash had a bearing. Well, we got volcanic ash at Paulina, so that's something, ain't it . . . And something's better than nothing, you'll agree . . . '

I could not help laughing at his buoyant, hopeless optimism. 'Why have you come to *me*?' I asked.

'You're my last resort,' he answered. 'Some people here got interested, so I saved up enough for the fare. Same as when I saw you last, except that time it was the Germans . . . Same result, too . . . Then I heard that you'd got problems, too . . . '

'I have?'

'Alexanders . . . you've always been open to trouble, as I told you on the *Lucania*. You got tankers, but not much supply. You got a field in Malaya which ain't exactly turned into the oilderado you'd hoped, and a big deal to carry the Romanians' oil that ends next year . . . The Paris Rothschilds are leaning on them not to renew because of their own oil from Baku. The Nobels are, too . . . so is Standard, who've loathed your guts ever since your first ship sailed through Suez. They all want you out, Mrs Alexander. They'll go back to savaging each other soon enough, but just for now the heat's on Alexanders . . . soon you could well have ships but nothing to carry – as I'm sure you know.'

For a moment I could say nothing, astonished that this unkempt old man could be so well informed. He grinned again. 'So here I am, like an angel of deliverance,' he went on. 'Consider your position if you struck oil big at Paulina . . . Why, you could kiss goodbye to the Romanians and laugh at Rothschilds and the others.'

The vision he drew was tempting, since half the bank's profits came from oil, but I knew it was absurd. 'Mr Smith,' I said.

'O'Sullivan Smith,' he reminded me.

'My apologies – but you've no good reason for believing we *would* strike it big. Just vague unproven theories, and hunch . . . '

He gave a sudden laugh. 'Hunch ain't so bad a reason . . . Hunch was why you're now in tankers . . . Hunch put you into motors when they was just a game. Sure, it's a big gamble, but even if it fails, what'll you lose?'

'Well, what *will* we lose?' I asked.

'A hundred thousand pounds, give or take a few quid. And what's that kind of money against what'll go down the drain if the Romanians pull out? Or what you'll win if my hunch is right?'

What he was asking was breathtaking. He was proposing that we should stake a small fortune on the turn of a wheel. It was exciting but, even if I agreed, I knew I could never persuade Howard or the other directors. Or could I? There was logic to the old man's argument.

'Mr O'Sullivan Smith,' I asked, 'what exactly is your proposition?'

I saw the hope light up in his eyes. 'Take over my leases,' he said, 'and put up the money to drill real deep . . . Fifteen hundred feet, maybe two thousand, even two five . . . enough holes to be really sure. Employ the best drilling team in America, The Williams Brothers. They got a new type of rotary drill that could get through diamonds. That was Bill Hampton's problem, you see. He hadn't got the money, but you have . . . I'll want five per cent up to a thousand barrels a day. After that, we can negotiate . . . '

'What about Mr Hampton?' I inquired. 'You said you'd given him drilling rights . . . '

'Only for two years,' he answered, 'and that's up in July – seven weeks' time . . . Anyways, he's as broke as I am. He'd be happy with a share of what I get . . . '

To my amazement, I was half convinced by him. 'Have you anything factual to support your hunch?' I asked. 'Anything I can show our Oil Department?'

'Drilling logs of the holes we've dug,' he answered. 'Brought them with me, since I thought you'd ask that question. We've had problems I ain't mentioned and they're clear in the reports . . . '

'Problems?'

'Well, quicksand for example, and that's a devil to get through . . . and the piping's kept breaking – gas pressure . . . It's not easy hundreds of feet down. The earth fights back . . . ' He saw the look on my face. 'Don't you worry,' he insisted. 'The Williams Brothers'll handle that . . . '

I hesitated, my thoughts in turmoil. 'Leave your logs with me,' I said, 'and come to the bank in the morning at 10.30. I'll see if anything can be done . . . '

'Mama!' I heard from behind me, and turned to see Jonny standing there, a paper hat on his head. 'The clowns are soon . . . ' he said. 'Aren't you coming?'

I smiled. It was time for the entertainment provided by Harrods. 'I'm coming now,' I answered. 'This is Mr Smith – Mr O'Sullivan Smith . . . '

Jonny approached him and held out his hand. 'How do you do, Mr . . .' He broke off, perturbed by the complications of 'O'Sullivan'.

The old man laughed. 'How do I do?' he replied. 'Why, I do a lot better than I done when I arrived, young fellow-my-lad.'

[3]

I do not know what Uncle would have thought. It was not banking business. Even 'speculation', which he always condemned so roundly, was an understatement. Yet there was Howard the next day considering the proposal quite seriously – and John Trevor, who had studied the drilling logs and even discussed them with a 'jolligist' we consulted sometimes in Broad Street nearby.

There were some grounds, the expert had said, to support Hampton's theory, and that of the Professor of Minerology. Also, the logs indicated shale under conditions that might be favourable, but he could hardly advise expensive exploration on the data offered. Oil was found in rock – in porous 'traps' like huge sponges locked within massive layers of impermeable stone – and there was no rock of the right kind at Paulina. At least, if there was, it might be as deep as a mile below the surface.

Despite this cautious view, John Trevor was in favour of proceeding and Howard was veering towards agreement. What was influencing them was the argument with which Smith had won me. Our loss, if it failed, was minimal against the huge investment we already had in oil. But if the gamble, dubious as it was, should be successful, then it would transform our prospects. Smith had lived with his land for ten years. Clearly, he was experienced. Perhaps there were times to back a hunch, even for a bank in the heart of the City of London.

O'Sullivan Smith was shown into 'The Room' by one of the Front Hall men and, when I saw him standing there with his ill-fitting clothes and unruly grey hair, I thought that their view might change. He was hardly impressive – not when a hundred thousand pounds was at stake. But they found him convincing. John Trevor was in his forties, a dapper, meticulous man, which always surprised me, because he had worked in the field, supervised drilling operations and lived for long periods with rough characters like Smith. He knew his job and he grilled Smith closely about his land at Paulina, taking him through his logs, querying the juxtaposition of different strata below ground that his drills had bitten through.

Howard, sitting motionless in his chair as though he was made of wax, watched the interrogation, then asked further questions about costs and transportation in the event of oil being found. When he raised the question of experts, Smith shook his head. 'It's sniff you want, Mrs Alexander – not jolligists,' he said. 'It's sniff I'm offering.'

At last, Howard leaned forward. 'All right, Mr O'Sullivan Smith,' he said. 'We accept your proposal. Arrangements will be made by our New York office. I'll telegraph them today to expect you. They'll check out your leases, arrange the necessary funds and draw up our contract with you. There'll have to be a drilling agreement with the brothers Williams . . . that is, if they can take on the project. Then, if we want to start work before the rights of your colleague Mr Hampton expire, we'll need his formal waiver. Now . . .' He hesitated, thinking for a moment ' . . . Mrs Alexander will sail for America next week with Mr Trevor to supervise expenditure . . . ' He looked at me inquiringly, the old blandness on his face. 'I trust that's not too soon?' I shook my head and he turned back to the old man. 'There's a railway at Paulina?' He asked.

'One train a day from Tulsa,' the old man answered, a bit proudly.

'And a hotel, I take it?'

Smith confirmed the fact with a vigorous nod of his head. 'It ain't exactly grand, but Mr O'Reilly, the proprietor, is most demanding about cleanliness . . . and Godliness . . . and gentlemanly behaviour.'

Howard stood up and held out his hand. 'Let us hope, Mr O'Sullivan Smith, that our venture will be attended by success.'

'Have no doubts, Mr Alexander,' Smith answered firmly. 'No doubts at all.'

Howard and Bridget travelled with us to Liverpool. I had asked if I might take James as well as John Trevor, feeling that two men as escorts might give less cause for speculation in a frontier town. Nanny Roberts and Jonny were going to stay with my parents in Brooklyn.

We were sailing on the *Mauretania*, one of the two advanced ships of which Uncle had spoken with such hope during the Cunard battle, and we stood on the boat deck, all five of us, arms raised in farewell, as tugs towed her from the dock. On the quay, a smiling Bridget waved with an excess of energy at Jonny, who was standing beside me, his hand in mine. He responded with equal vigour, a happy grin on his face.

Howard had taken off his hat and was holding it above his head. Our experience together had still remained unmentioned. 'I trust you'll enjoy a good crossing,' he said in his formal way – almost exactly the same words he had addressed to me when first we had met aboard the yacht. Watching him now, standing as he always did on such occasions as unmoving as a statue, I felt a sudden poignant sadness.

They were soon out of sight and the *Mauretania*'s great turbine engines were thrusting her at increasing speed through the waters of the Mersey River and we were heading for America.

Chapter 12

[1]

We arrived at Paulina at six o'clock in the evening after travelling for two days from New York. At Ohio we had changed on to the Rock Island Railroad, which cut south through the Great Plains to Abilene in Kansas and on by way of Oklahoma to San Antonio in Texas. I had never before been beyond the East Coast states where I was raised, but Papa had often dealt in railroad stocks during those heady days of the '90s, when he had fired my imagination for the market. Together we had studied on the map the ever-growing network of tracks that spanned the North American continent, paving the way for new townships — for pioneers in search of gold, silver, copper; for homesteaders, cultivating still-wild country; for men like Smith who were drilling for oil; and for the stores and merchants that served them.

From the windows of my statecar I had gazed at the prairies, stretching like a green sea to the horizon before at last we crossed the edge of them and then there were hills and ravines and isolated, often coloured houses; woods of cotton trees and elms and hickories; red earth and golden corn; even, at times, big squares of tidy fencing — and, once or twice, a nest of cone-shaped derricks.

At Tulsa we had abandoned the private and privileged comfort we had known until then, and boarded the little train that once a day traversed the fifty miles to Paulina. Sitting on hard wooden benches together with the tough kind of Westerners I had heard about — one or two even wearing revolvers, as in the bad old days — I reflected on my return to America.

As always, coming home had been an emotional experience that was discomforting. My parents now occupied a house in which I never lived, but the streets and the people and the smell of Brooklyn had not changed much. This was my childhood, my roots, as Howard had once said. Mr Morgan had honoured his promise five years before to Papa — who had executed his assignment in Berlin, though other factors had checked the banker's plans — and he had set up in business again in a modest way, combining broking with a bit of dealing. It was not the high-flying speculation that once we had known but, so far, within its limits, it had been successful. He still spoke with extravagant optimism, but Wall Street was in one of its weak phases and offered little scope. Their new home hardly compared with our old big house on the Heights, but it was pleasant enough, with a maid to do the rough work and a bit of money to spare.

My mother was bedridden now. Aunt Abigail was over eighty but still ruling the family, dispersed as it was, like a retired but revered colonel. I had to face, though, the fact that there was the chasm between us that I had always feared there would be. My sisters' husbands were still clerks and they kept house with the kind of budget a clerk could afford. They worried about such things as being behind with the rent or how in due course the children might possibly work their way through college.

'At least,' I had said, 'Let me pay for that when the time comes,' but it was an old battleground of pride on which I was always repulsed. 'Thanks very much,' Laura had said, 'but I think we can manage without depending on charity.' Her strong response had been hurtful, especially since she would often sneer that I was spared the anxieties of ordinary mortals.

The others, though not so outspoken, shared her attitude. Both my brothers-in-law, suspecting patronage, had refused to consider positions in the Alexander Wall Street office – even, on one occasion, when Elmer, Mary's genial husband, had been out of work.

The mood of reproach lapped over to the younger generation and Jonny found it hard to understand the resentment that emerged at times in his relations with his cousins. The only children he had ever known lived in homes that were fully staffed with servants and travelled in their parents' carriages or chauffeur-driven motors. In fact, he got on well with my youngest nephews, both near enough his own age – especially Thomas, Mary's boy – but in the inevitable childish quarrels, their taunts would reflect what they had heard at home.

There was a price for everything and wealth, too, had to be paid for, as I was thinking when, with bell ringing, our train slowed to a halt in the little township of Paulina. There was quite a crowd waiting, together with a few wagons backed up to the track, but through the window I saw O'Sullivan Smith elbowing his way through the throng towards us, a broad smile on his lined old face.

'It's a real pleasure to welcome you to Paulina, Mrs Alexander,' he said as soon as we had stepped down from the train. 'Hope the journey's not been too tiring.' He shook hands vigorously with John Trevor and James before winking broadly at Maisie. He had arranged for a couple of men to cart our luggage, and we walked from the track along the sagging timber sidewalk of Paulina's Main Street. It resembled the photographs I had seen of frontier towns – a few buildings in brick, but mainly wooden clapboard, some of them single-storey with false fronts to make them seem bigger than they were. The place was busier than I expected, possibly more than usual because the train had just come in. There were a lot of people on the sidewalks – hurrying, chatting in groups, going in and out of shops – and a good deal of traffic on the pitted dirt road that formed the street: horsemen riding easily, one or two buggies and wagons, an odd Sulky.

On our way to the hotel we passed Smith's Clothing Store and the Lone Star Saloon and the Citizens' Bank and the Alamo Saloon and Mills' Tonsorial Parlour and Rowdy Helen's Saloon and Jones's Hardware Store and the Long Ranch Saloon.

'Bit of a change from those big cities you're accustomed to, Mrs Alexander,' said Smith, elbowing a passage for me through the people on the sidewalk. 'But Mr O'Reilly's done his best to make your rooms as comfortable as possible.'

'I'm sure they'll be satisfactory,' I said.

'Twenty years ago,' Smith continued, 'there wasn't a house standing here in Paulina. It wasn't even a cattle halt, though the old Chisholm Trail passed close by . . . The Chisholm was one of the routes north for the herds from Texas. Two and half thousand head usually – 800 miles to the terminus at Abilene for shipping to Chicago. The railroad south stopped all that – and Texas fever, which the cattle brought with them, so they weren't exactly welcome among the local ranchers . . .'

He saw me noting the number of saloons. 'They'll all be closed when Oklahoma joins the Union in November, then we'll be a dry state – in theory, anyways . . .' He flashed me one of his grins.

'Mind you, we've got pretty respectable now . . . We got a theatre and a church, of course, and a school and a courthouse . . . Not like it used to be . . . ' He broke off once more to demand room for me to pass.

'It was the run of 1891 that made this funny little town,' he went on. 'Hundred thousand men lined up in Old Oklahoma, then galloped like the devil to stake their claims. My leases weren't staked, of course . . . *your* leases, rather . . . As I said, they're on In-*di*-an land – in the reservation about ten miles out of town . . . '

I sensed there was trouble. The old man was talking too much. I had been disturbed, in New York, to learn that the strings of our enterprise were not all tied. Smith's title to his leases was proven – at least as far as it could be, for the laws on Indian land were obscure – and our contract with him was signed; but the Williams Brothers were occupied, so we needed other drillers. Also, Bill Hampton, Smith's partner, was away, so his waiver for us to start work before his rights expired had not been executed.

Bankers do not like unsettled details, but what concerned me most as we made our way towards the O'Reilly Hotel was that Smith, for all the fascinating history, had barely spoken of our project.

'Mr O'Sullivan Smith,' I said as we reached the hotel, 'What's gone wrong?'

He looked at me then. 'You guessed?' he asked. 'Well, it's sort of hard to understand, but, well, the fact of the matter is that Bill Hampton's sold his rights . . . '

'But they've only got five weeks to run,' I responded in astonishment.

'That's true,' he agreed, 'as true as God made little apples.'

'You mean,' I pressed, incredulously, 'that someone's bought the right to drill for only five weeks?'

He nodded. 'Well, seven,' he corrected. 'The rig's been there a couple of weeks now . . . Makes no difference though . . . '

'And *could* they strike oil in so short a time?' I asked.

'Hardly,' he said with a laugh. 'I been trying for ten years . . . Hampton for two . . . '

'But it'd be possible,' I persisted.

'Just, I suppose,' he agreed, 'If they spudded in exactly the right

261

place first time . . . if they hit no trouble . . . if they could get deep enough . . . Chance in a million, even for a team that really knows their business.'

'And *do* they know their business?' I asked. 'I mean, as well as the Williams Brothers?'

He looked down at his feet, embarrassed. 'Mrs Alexander,' he said, 'they *is* the Williams Brothers . . . '

John Trevor and James had caught us up. 'We have competition.' I told them. 'Someone's gambling they can strike on our leases before the rights revert.'

'Good gracious!' exclaimed Trevor. 'That's impossible.'

'They've been drilling for two weeks,' I said. 'Got the Williams Brothers.'

Trevor looked as though he had detected an unpleasant odour and shook his head. 'They'll have to average fifty feet a day at least,' he insisted, 'and there's not much chance of that – not with moving sand and the granite they're bound to hit. Even as a gamble it's insane.'

'Some people back horses at very long odds,' James reminded him. 'They don't *always* lose . . . This chappie must be a really wild plunger . . . '

I turned back to Smith. 'And who is this wild plunger?' I asked, a trifle acidly.

'Name's Charles Taylor,' he answered. 'From New York . . . . Wall Street . . . . Made a fortune out of copper, so the story goes. Took on Standard Oil in Montana and made millions out of them. Not many men have taken on Standard and gotten away with it.'

The entrance of the hotel was crowded – mainly, so Smith said, because it served as an information centre. There were notices on a board about land and livestock for sale. Men were huddled together in groups with serious expressions on their faces.

'That's him, if you're interested, over there,' said Smith, pointing beyond the lobby to an adjoining room where four men were playing cards at a corner table. 'Charlie Taylor, I mean,' he added, 'wearing the hat on the far side of the game . . . '

I am not certain what I planned to do at that moment; I think that in the back of my mind was the belief that we must reach some kind of agreement with him. It was important to avoid delay in our own operation, and I was not as convinced as Trevor that he would fail.

I strolled towards the four men but the card-players, intent on their game, did not appear conscious of my approach.

Taylor was sitting askew to the table, his feet, ankles crossed, resting on the seat of the chair beside him. He was about forty with broad muscular shoulders and a strong square jaw, the lines deep on his forehead and beside his mouth. His hands caught my attention, since he was holding his cards high – large and hard like the rest of him, but with sensitive tapered fingers that provided an odd contrast. He was wearing a black suit which, despite his relaxed posture, was obviously well cut in a fine broadcloth, together with a stylish, flowing tie and a waistcoat with pearl buttons. On his head was a hard black straw sombrero, pushed back to reveal thick greying curly hair.

For a moment, as I stood beside him, he was studying his cards with great concentration – until suddenly he looked up at me with eyes that were as blue as mine and a brazen, confident grin on his face. 'Don't tell me,' he said without moving, 'let me guess . . . It's Mrs Alexander.' I knew he had looked at many women in that amused steady way and doubtless they, too, had resented it; for there was an arrogance there, an assumption that was unpleasantly intimate.

He did not stand up, or even suggest I took a seat until he could give me his attention. 'I'll raise you ten,' he said to his neighbour. 'No, damn it, we'll make it a hundred.'

'A hundred?' the man asked in surprise.

'A hundred,' Taylor insisted firmly, glancing at me again. 'Maybe Mrs Alexander here'll bring me luck.'

'She won't if *she* has anything to do with it,' I said sharply. 'I'd like to speak with you when you can spare a minute, Mr Taylor. Meanwhile, I hope you lose the lot . . .'

I turned and walked towards the lobby, where Smith was waiting with Mr O'Reilly to conduct me to our rooms.

Two hours later his visiting card was brought to me by one of the girls Mr and Mrs O'Reilly had attracted from the East to work for them in a town where men outnumbered women by seven to one – including the 'soiled doves' who were hardly wife material. Inscribed on the card were the words 'Charles Taylor, 14 Exchange Street, New York City'. Above them, he had written by hand: 'You only asked for a minute, but I could spare longer if you wish.' At the bottom, he had added: 'You *did* bring me luck – muchos gracias!'

Our accommodation was surprisingly comfortable, considering that many of the O'Reilly patrons were required at busy periods to share their beds with strangers. One room had been converted into a parlour with a sofa, armchairs complete with antimacassars, a desk and a table, on both of which stood rather fine ornate brass oil-lamps. It was here that I was talking to James and John Trevor when Taylor's card was brought to me.

I was tempted to decline to see him, in view of his behaviour to me, but I told the girl to ask him to join us.

As he entered, I saw that he was a bit shorter than he had seemed at the card table, but stocky, all muscle, seeming oddly light on his feet, like a boxer ready to dodge. I noticed that his nose was slightly crooked, suggesting that once it had been broken.

He had deigned to remove his hat, and held it by the brim in front of his body with the fingers of both hands. Standing in the doorway, he displayed a shy, almost boyish hesitancy, though the smile that had piqued me downstairs was still evident.

'I fear I've upset you, Mrs Alexander,' he said.

'Oh, not really, Mr Taylor,' I answered, the sophisticate from London, adding: 'Well, just a little perhaps . . . '

'I'm truly sorry,' he said. 'There's nothing I like worse than to offend a pretty woman, but it's hard for a man to break off in the middle of a poker hand.'

'So it's I who should be apologizing?' I inquired, conscious that he could easily have continued his play with a modicum of good manners towards me.

'Oh, apology's hardly necessary, Mrs Alexander' he answered, taking the initiative from me without the slightest effort. 'A small misunderstanding . . . Perhaps I may come in?'

'Please do,' I said coolly. 'This is Mr Trevor and Mr Stratton . . . James, I'm sure Mr Taylor'd appreciate some refreshment . . .'

He sat leaning forward informally, elbows on parted knees, cupping with both hands the glass of Bourbon James had brought him. He was studying me, quite openly, the glint of amusement still in his eyes.

'It's been quite a surprise for us, Mr Taylor,' I said, 'to learn that you've acquired Mr Hampton's rights.'

'Likewise,' he answered. 'I was taken aback when I heard of your own interest. I'd planned to deal with Smith when he got back from Europe . . .Hampton said he was broke. But then, when I thought about it, I found it reassuring . . .'

'Reassuring?'

'Well,' he said, 'I figured that, if Alexanders were prepared to invest in Mr Smith's little bit of country on the scale that I was told, then they must know something I didn't . . . .' He raised his glass to his lips, watching me as he sipped the whisky. 'So even with only seven weeks to play with, it made the horse worth backing as a long shot. Think of the pot if he won . . .'

I smiled a little sleekly. 'And if I told you that we've no more information than you have?'

He shook his head. 'I'd think you were gambling pretty wildly for a bank . . . Something'd seem to be missing.'

'You mean,' I challenged sharply, 'you suspect me of lying . . .'

He laughed and sat back in the chair. 'Why should I think you're lying, Mrs Alexander? There'd be no purpose to it, would there?'

'I suppose I could be pretending. It might make you a little more . . . what shall I say? Uneasy? Anxious perhaps? I mean, since your time limit's so narrow?'

Again, he grinned broadly. 'Well, aren't you devious, Mrs Alexander?' he mocked lightly. 'Clearly, I must tread with care – but I don't think you're lying and it wouldn't matter if you were, because the point is you're here in Paulina . . . You're talking to me . . . I take it there's business you want to discuss. Now, if you were pulling out, then that'd be different. Then I'd be getting nervous . . . As it is, I think of my team drilling away out there among the Cherokees and feel a warm glow of anticipation.'

'But only a short time to enjoy the sensation.'

'Who knows?' His shrug was elaborate, his eyes laughing. 'The timing's a trifle tight,' he admitted, 'but it could be bonanza.'

'The odds against it are high,' I said. 'Five weeks . . . . So surely,' I suggested, 'both sides'd benefit from some kind of accommodation, Mr Taylor?'

'Perhaps,' he agreed. 'but I doubt it.' He leaned forward again and drank from the glass. 'Why, Mrs Alexander?' Suddenly, he was serious – no challenge, no mocking. 'Makes no sense. What could possibly lead a London bank to risk that kind of money out there among the Indians . . . ' he stabbed his finger in the direction of the window ' . . . on such limited evidence? There's no oil within a hundred miles. Oklahoma's a large territory . . . *Why*, Mrs Alexander?'

'We need an oil source, Mr Taylor,' I answered. 'Badly – a bonanza, like you said . . . There was something about Mr Smith that made us back him.'

He eyed me – shook his head incredulously. 'The wild talent? Not the wild talent, Mrs Alexander? That's medicine man stuff . . . I want to believe you, but when you tell me that back there in London they're making decisions by rubbing lamps or flipping coins, then it does get a bit harder.'

'Not flipping coins,' I answered. 'Judging a man, which is what bankers do all the time, and a bit of hunch, I suppose . . . '

'Now that's real music,' he said. 'If an outfit as successful as Alexanders get a hunch, then I figure it can't be too doggone stupid to ride along with it. Maybe if I'd lost that hundred bucks downstairs just now I might start thinking different, might wonder if you were lucky for me, but I won, didn't I? So maybe,' he pointed again at the window, 'I'll win out there . . . '

'No chance, old chap,' said John Trevor. 'Not a glimmer of a chance.'

Taylor, surprised by the intervention, turned to him. 'Then why are we here?' he asked innocently.

'Because the situation's untidy,' I said, 'and you're holding us up . . . Mr Taylor, is there a figure at which you'd sell your contract?'

He looked back at me with that sudden grin. 'Lady, there's a figure at which I'd sell anything . . . what kind of price did you have in mind?'

'Ten thousand dollars,' I replied.

He did not respond for a moment. Then he said lazily: 'I have to confess that you're not exactly tempting me.'

'Well, what are you looking for, Mr Taylor?' I asked.

He settled back heavily in his chair. 'I'm not keen on selling, you understand . . . I've got interested . . . . but I *would* sell, I suppose, for something in the region of . . . ' He paused, watching me. ' . . . one million dollars.'

For a couple of seconds, no one spoke. I became conscious of the sound of people in the lobby below, a tinkling piano in some distant room. 'But that's ridiculous!' James exclaimed suddenly. 'Why, the horse hasn't even got four legs, for all we know.'

Taylor looked at him with his healthy boyish grin. 'You're entitled to your opinion, of course,' he said amenably. 'Mrs Alexander just asked me a question – and I gave her my answer.'

'Have the drillers found anything,' asked John Trevor, 'to suggest there's oil in the ground at all?'

'They haven't seen anything like paysand, if that's what you mean,' Taylor answered, 'but they've got the smell all right – like Bill Hampton and old Smith . . . '

I intervened. 'Perhaps we could be a bit more realistic. I take it there's scope for negotiation, Mr Taylor, other aspects we could explore – a royalty perhaps, or . . . '

He checked me with a slow shake of his head. 'No,' he said, 'it's a million cash . . . or I'll just leave the chips lying there on the table, like they are at present.'

He got up to leave. 'Good evening to you all,' he said. 'It's been a pleasure.' At the door, he turned back to me. 'I'm going to Tulsa for a couple of days, Mrs Alexander, but if you'd care to visit the rig on my return, I'd be happy to drive you there.'

The trail ascended gently, and as we reached the top, he reined in the horse. 'There it is,' he said, 'over there.' He pointed to a low hill across sweeping, undulating land, mostly wild red earth marked with boulders and clumps of trees, but parts that had been shaped by man. A long stretch of corn, tall and high yellow; a cotton field, dappled white, that reached for miles.

It was a single rig that he was indicating – a bit like a windmill without sails, but black and made by rough unfeeling hands so that it was ugly, which windmills rarely are. Around its base were a few shacks and what looked, at that distance, like a couple of wagons. One day, I thought, that may have grown into a boom town like Titusville or Beaumont, or perhaps it would become derelict, collapsing slowly as it rotted, chipped to pieces by winter winds. 'There's my jackpot,' he said, 'or yours . . . or no one's . . . '

He had collected me in a surrey, gleaming with fresh varnish and complete with a fringed canvas hood that was welcome enough, since it was a scorching day. The harness on the well-groomed horse was obviously new. He himself was in a light grey suit, beautifully cut like his black one, Texas boots polished until they glistened, and a spotless big white hat. The sheer perfection of his clothes and his vehicle made him look as though he was about to go on stage at the Madison Square Garden.

As I came out of O'Reilly's Hotel he smiled broadly, and stepped down to greet me. 'Only the best, you see,' he declared, 'for Mrs Alexander.' He handed me into the surrey and clambered back into the seat beside me. 'Of course, some people'd call it flashy, wouldn't they?' he said, urging on the horse with a slap of the reins. 'Speaking personally, I like to think of it as style . . . I hope it doesn't perturb you.'

I laughed. I am not sure of what I expected of him. Both our previous meetings had been marked by confrontation. 'Would it concern you much if it *did* perturb me, Mr Taylor?' I asked.

He shrugged with a grin. 'I'd prefer you to appreciate it,' he answered, 'But . . . well, I guess I *am* that kind of horse . . . You can train a horse, but you can't change its nature . . . What kind of a horse are you, Mrs Alexander?' He was looking ahead of him down the street.

'I've been described as wilful, Mr Taylor,' I answered.

He grinned, still without looking at me. 'That figures,' he said approvingly. 'A wilful streak . . . Never pays to relax in the saddle – a sudden buck, a leap sideways – but there's no doubt *you've* got style, Mrs Alexander. And I'm an expert on style, I can tell you . . . Exposed to it at an early age . . . and to vulgarity, expensive vulgarity. The line can be narrow – not with you, of course, but I know *I* push it close . . . '

'And where,' I asked, taunting him mildly, 'did you gain this special knowledge?'

He glanced at me, sensitive to my tone. 'Bell boy,' he said, 'at a hotel in Philadelphia . . . I was fourteen . . . Life with Pa wasn't easy – the demon drink – so Ma walked out with lover-boy. Luckily, I'd an uncle living in the city and he was shocked to his boots by what his sister had done, so he took me in and got me a job in a hotel where he was a waiter . . . the Splendide, with an 'e' . . . was pretty splendid, too . . . '

'You must have looked appealing,' I remarked indolently,' 'in a pillbox hat and buttons.'

'I saw a lot of rich people close to . . . That's where I learned that there's an art to being rich, as well you know . . . '

'And how,' I asked, 'did a bell boy get the chance to deploy such an art?' There was a trace of sarcasm in everything I said to him, though I did not know why. Perhaps it was a way of maintaining distance. This was a different man from the one I had met before.

He looked at me, his body swaying under the movement of the surrey, with a kind of hurt perplexity. 'We can talk of something else if you'd prefer,' he said.

'Please go on,' I said. 'You were starting to tell me how a bell boy made a fortune . . . '

He was still uncertain, studying me intently for a second. 'There was an old lady who lived in the hotel' he went on, 'Mrs Blackstone . . . Sometimes I had to take messages to her and run the odd errand. In time, we got talking. No one ever came to see her, so she was a bit lonely and she'd detain me often just for the company. It grew into a kind of friendship . . .

'She told me a bit of her life, and I spoke of my ambitions . . . especially about a young friend of mine named Ed Walters, who worked as a clerk in an attorney's office. This was in the dazzling days of the '80s, and Ed's eyes were fixed firmly on Montana . . . copper . . . . He knew a bit about copper because his firm had a client who invested heavily in Montana mineral stocks. Ed had read all he could about mining legalities, but Montana wasn't due to be a state until '89 so the laws there were still a little primitive. One day the client came into the office with a mining engineer who was working for him in the territory, and this fellow urged Ed to get out there . . . Fortunes waiting, he said, for young men with initiative and nerve and a little bit of cash. That was the problem, of course – cash . . . . '

'So you talked the old lady into parting with the cash,' I said.

The slightly wounded expression returned, and touched me. 'You really don't have much of an opinion of me, do you, Mrs Alexander,' he said seriously – then grinned. 'Oh, I'd have tried to talk her into it if it had crossed my mind, but when you're a bell boy your horizons are limited . . . The difference in our stations was gigantic. Horizons are what hold people back. They can't see over the next hill, and you can hardly aim for something you can't see. But I did tell her about our hopes, how Ed and I met in my evenings off and spoke of what we were going to do . . . how we'd buy a lease and mine it and strike copper and be rich . . . '

'I'd have said that was well over the next hill,' I interposed, 'for a bell boy.'

He shook his head. 'It was dreams, looking at the stars . . . Ed had a hundred bucks. I could hardly have raised ten. That didn't stop us making plans, of course. I was going to join a mining camp to discover the practical side . . . Ed was going into an attorney's office . . . He was very definite about learning the Montana laws, such as they were – and he was dead right . . . '

The horse was slowing down as we began to climb the hill, and Taylor cracked his whip and called out 'Gid-up!' but it was hot and Taylor did not press the issue.

'I was nearly seventeen,' he went on, 'when one evening the old lady sent for me. "Charlie," she said, "I've been thinking about this plan of yours with your friend Ed . . . I've decided to lend you two thousand dollars . . . That'll give you a chance to get started, and you can pay me back when you get rich." In fact, there was to be no repaying, for she was dying and she knew it, and she left me the two thousand in her will, so the debt was cleared . . . '

He halted the surrey so that we could look across the valley at that single derrick – the symbol of what he had demanded a million dollars for. 'Come a bit of a way since then,' he went on, and I thought what a pleasant voice he had. 'Into competition, for example, with Alexanders.' And he looked at me with those eyes that were as blue as mine – and I felt a stab in the pit of my stomach that I had not felt in years.

[4]

'Pete up there?' he asked one of the 'roustabouts', as the men who worked around a rig were called.

'Who wants him?' said a man in a deep voice, appearing at the top of a platform. 'Oh, it's you, Mr Taylor . . . I couldn't see you for that big hat of yours . . . And who's this young lady?'

'This is Mrs Alexander. She's bought Smith's leases. I said you'd show her around if we asked you nicely . . . '

Pete gave a great booming laugh. He was a huge man with an enormous chest and a big red jowly face. 'Come on up, Lady,' he said. 'It's a pleasure to meet you . . . '

That day I was in a simple cotton frock and sun-bonnet, beneath the shade of a parasol, and faced with the sweaty masculinity of the men of that rig, I felt completely out of place. However, I climbed the short ladder, which was not easy in my skirt, and Pete reached down an immense hand to help me surmount the final rungs.

'You might get that dress a bit soiled, Lady,' he apologized, 'like Mr Taylor's fancy suiting . . . ' He threw him a friendly, if mocking, glance ' . . . but I'll do my best to keep the damage to a minimum . . . Well, now you see that big wheel that's turning there. We call that the bull wheel and, as maybe you can see, it's clamped on to a

271

small pipe that's turning too. At the end of that pipe, deep in the earth, is the drilling tool, which is wider so it makes a bigger hole. That's how, as we go down, we can drop a larger pipe in sections to form a casing that stops the hole from caving in . . . At least, that's the idea . . . . Doesn't always work, because of gas pressure or moving shale or sand that can break through the steel of the casing, and then we lose everything below the breach . . . '

I watched that huge revolving wheel, and found oppressive the throbbing of the engine in the hot confines of the platform. I looked up to the top of the gantry where there was a set of blocks, threaded with loose hanging ropes and wires.

'We send water down the casing,' Pete went on, 'To wash the debris from the hole the tool makes up through the inside of the drilling pipe – as you can see up there where it's spilling down the chute into the slush pit. We watch that stuff pretty close because it can tell us a lot about what's going on down there – clay, sand-stone, granite, shale, gravel and other things that our old earth is made of . . . '

'What are the chances,' I asked, 'that there's oil down there?'

'Good . . . fact, I'm certain . . . . The real question is how far we got to go . . . and whether we're drilling in the right place.'

'*And* how long it takes you,' I countered.

Taylor laughed. 'August first,' he said. 'Peter knows that if he brings it in by then there's one huge bonus . . . '

'You mean July 3lst,' I corrected. 'Midnight – just over four weeks now . . . Perhaps I should double the bonus if he doesn't . . . .'

'You see, Pete,' said Taylor, 'the lady sometimes thinks a little naughty.'

Pete grinned, opening his big mouth like a lion. 'We'll have to do better than we did yesterday, Mr Taylor . . . We hit real hard granite . . . Blunted two drilling bits . . . In the end we had to torpedo . . . . '

'Torpedo?' I inquired.

'We take the drills out and pour nitro-glycerine down into the casing to blow our way through . . . '

'That sounds dangerous.'

'The explosions's hard to control,' he agreed, 'but there are dangers on a rig that are maybe greater . . . . A parted wire can take a man's head off . . . A kicking brake can put him out of action for weeks . . . '

He went on talking in his deep resonant tones about the twelve-hour 'towers' they all worked, meaning 'tours', which is what they called the shifts, and how he or his brother were on the rig all the time so that drilling never stopped. He spoke of the poor efforts of the 'slum-burner', the bunkhouse cook – 'unless you happen to like rat stew' – and of the 'donnybrooks' on pay nights when the men who were not working that 'tower' would go into town and come back with sore heads and blackened eyes.

Then Taylor and I went back to the surrey and Pete waved cheerily to us from the platform as we drove off. 'I thought you might like some lunch now,' Taylor said.

'That's a good idea,' I responded, looking around me at the deserted landscape. 'Which restaurant did you have in mind?'

'A little place I know,' he answered. 'The *maître d'hôtel* is a friend . . . '

I found it hard to associate him with the man I had met before, and on both those occasions he had differed, the offhand ill-mannered poker player seeming to have little in common with the hard outrageous bargainer who had nevertheless been courteous and even diffident. Now, as an escort, he was amusing in a flamboyant way, without the boasting or preening so often displayed by that sort of man. He was flattering, too – not so much by anything he said but by his behaviour and the way he looked at me. I felt consciously attractive as we travelled along that dirt road under the awning of the surrey.

He turned the horse off the trail and headed for a clump of green cottonwoods on a hillock about half a mile away.

'Bit of a bumpy ride, I fear,' he said, 'but it's not too far . . . '

When we got to the trees, he reined in the horse in the shade. From the surrey I could see that about fifty feet below us, at the foot of an easy incline, was a small ravine and some persimmons beside it. 'Just a short walk now,' he said.

A little uncertain at the unexpected turn of events, I followed him down the slope. And then I saw why we had come. For laid out on a reach of the ravine bank that had been hidden before by a low bluff was a scene like a painting. Rugs had been stretched out on a piece of flat ground beside the water. Arranged on them was a bottle of champagne in an ice cooler, two settings, complete with cutlery, glass and napkins, and a variety of serving dishes that had obviously been positioned by someone with a gift for conformation.

Taylor had moved ahead of me and, as I approached, he was standing beside his display, rubbing his hands together like a restaurant manager. 'Good morning, Madam,' he said, with a gracious smile. 'If I may conduct you to your table . . . ' With an elaborate sweep of his arm, he beckoned me to sit down at one of the places laid on the rug.

For a few seconds I could not speak because I was so moved by the surprise, and his easy humour, and the immense trouble he had so obviously taken. I just stood there and gazed at all that was laid before me, registering details I had not noticed before – like a jar of caviar. 'Oh, Taylor,' I said softly, 'it's beautiful . . . ' It was the first time I had called him 'Taylor', but 'Mister' seemed inappropriate and 'Charlie' too informal.

'If Madam would kindly take her seat,' he said, and taking my hand, he helped me lower myself to the rug.

'I have to concede, Taylor,' I said, 'that this is style.' I found calling him 'Taylor' rather appealing.

He shrugged with a half smile. 'All I'll say for it,' he responded, 'is that it's all real. The champagne comes from France and the caviar comes from Russia and the Scotch salmon comes from Scotland and the wild turkey comes from Oklahoma . . . '

'How did you get it all to Paulina?' I asked, 'and why, for goodness' sake?'

'Why?' he said as he popped the cork from the bottle, 'because I felt like it . . . . How? Well, there's a wonderful new invention called a train.'

He filled our glasses and sat opposite me on the ground. 'What shall we drink to?' he asked. 'Williams bringing in the well on time?'

I shook my head. 'Not likely.'

'To honour between rivals, then,' he suggested.

'I'll accept that,' I answered, and lifted my glass.

We started to eat, and I asked: 'If Williams does bring in the well in time for you, what'll you do with the oil?'

He shrugged. 'Sell it,' he said.

'To us?'

'Who knows? Depends on the deal you offer . . . Tell me, Mrs Alexander, do you always talk business through lunch?'

I nodded. 'I guess I'm just that kind of horse,' I said.

'I'm sure you win a lot of races.' He held my gaze.

'I win a few,' I answered carefully.

'I'd stake money on you any time,' he said. His eyes were soft as he studied me with such obvious pleasure that for a moment I thought he was going to attempt to kiss me – but I should have guessed that Taylor was not the kind of horse that rushed his fences.

Sitting there in the shade of the persimmons, with the noise of the running stream, I felt absurdly happy – but, oddly, a trifle embarrassed, uncertain, ingenuous, as though I was sixteen receiving my first beau.

He seemed to detect my feeling, to share it. 'If I was to tell you,' he said, 'that what I'd like to do at this moment is to take off my boots and put my feet in the water, would you think it too childish to contemplate?'

I laughed. 'Why not? It's a warm day.'

'I was afraid you might be too grand.'

'You weren't . . . you knew exactly what I'd say . . . .'

He laughed easily. 'The gift of second sight . . . Well, there's no one here to see us, is there? No one to be shocked.'

'Not even the horse,' I said, 'since there's no view from up there. Just as well, perhaps, for I'd judge he's a respectable horse.'

'You know, I think you're right there,' Taylor agreed very seriously. 'Mind you, I'm not positive about his opinions, but I'm told his table manners are beyond reproach.' And we both burst out laughing – infectious, silly laughter.

So we did. We sat on the bank of that creek that looked red because of the colour of the bottom. I drew my skirt to my knees and we kicked, splashing the water like children, and we looked out for fish and talked with wide-eyed fear of rattlesnakes and poisonous lizards and other sorts of frightening things that fascinate young minds. It was cool, because the sun was filtered by the branches of the trees above us. 'Mrs Alexander,' he asked idly, 'are you content at this moment?'

'Utterly, Taylor,' I answered.

'You'd not prefer it if we were talking business?'

'I'd prefer it,' I answered, 'if you were going on with your story. You only got to two thousand dollars and, being a man with a taste for champagne and caviar, I wouldn't have thought it sufficient for your needs . . . '

'It got a little more difficult then,' he said, the laughter going from his voice. 'Ed and I headed out for Butte, Montana, just as the old lady intended, and we did what we'd planned, with me joining a mining camp and Ed studying the law. That's where I learned a bit about the nature of men – and mining, too, of course . . .

'We met up with the engineer that Ed had talked to in the attorney's office in Philadelphia and he told us we mustn't trust anybody. He said that what we had to do was to find a hill that was likely to be metal-bearing and then tell him and he'd come and check it out for us before we put out any money on it . . . He gave us a kind of quick course in geology so we knew a bit about what to look for – and we spent all our spare time doing just that . . . '

He paused, kicking the water with one foot. 'We were lucky. Beginner's luck, I suppose . . . We found a place that seemed hopeful and we told the engineer and he confirmed we were right – as far as anyone could be at that early stage. But of course we hadn't leased the land and we soon found that in some mysterious fashion the news had spread and someone else had got in first.

'That mine became a high yielder, so next time round, we leased the land at the start. Actually we leased a mine from a man who had got into trouble and couldn't afford to keep it going. But he was certain there was a good vein there somewhere and we guessed he was right, so we staked him on a partnership deal that enabled him to keep on working it . . .

'That's how we made our first real money. By then I'd seen men using marked cards . . . I'd had cash stolen at night from under my pillow . . . I'd been held up at gunpoint, beaten silly, and cheated. Perhaps Ed and I had not got too hardened. We fell out with our partner in the mine and then after a while Ed and I took to quarrelling, so we broke up, too . . . After that, the deals went on . . . . Sometimes they worked and sometimes they didn't. I got rich and I lost it all . . . Got rich again and lost it all again, almost going right under that time. Now I'm rich once more – so rich that I can afford to hold you off in that little speculation back up the trail . . . ' He smiled at me, enveloping me with his eyes in a way that made me feel I was melting. I had to clasp my hands together to stop them shaking, and knew I must get him talking again. 'I gather,' I said, 'that you had a battle with Standard – and won.'

He gave a short laugh. 'You can never be sure you've won against Standard,' he said. 'Not until you're dead . . . I'll tell you about it one day . . . Now, it's time to go home, Mrs Alexander. The restaurant's closing.'

We left what remained of our picnic where we had found it and walked back to the surrey. He hitched up the horse and we set off back to Paulina . On the journey, he said little. I did not want to speak much either.

[5]

I had planned to go back to New York, for there seemed little for me to do in Paulina for a month. But I delayed my departure without quite knowing why. In fact, I was rather enjoying the place. It was a quaint little town, I thought.

I saw a bit of O'Sullivan Smith, who kept me up to date on progress on the rig. They had reached 800 feet, he said. Yesterday they had brought up some oil sand, but only three feet of it before they were into blue clay and then hard limestone. I listened to his long discussions with John Trevor about the significance of the strata.

Once Bill Hampton came with him to see me. He was a tall lugubrious man with bags under his eyes. Hampton was not hopeful that the drilling would succeed, at least not in the time nor, he suspected, in that spot.

I did not see Taylor for three days after our picnic lunch. Then his card was delivered to me by one of Mr O'Reilly's girls, with a scribbled message asking me to dine with him.

During the next couple of days, I saw quite a bit of him. We had two or three meals together and went out riding. He did not offer to tell me any more of his past, and I did not seek to ask. Then he said: 'I'm off to Oklahoma City tomorrow . . . Can't be certain how long . . . . You likely to be here when I get back? Or are you leaving for a while?'

'I've been planning to go to New York,' I answered, 'but I've been feeling lazy . . . '

The next day, James returned to Paulina. He had gone back to New York the day after we arrived since, in view of our unexpected situation, it seemed wise to learn more about Taylor's background.

James had compiled a dossier. 'The form's not good, I fear,' he said. 'He's been in jail . . . '

'Jail?' I inquired with surprise.

'Mexico City in '97 . . . He appears to have cheated every partner he's had. One of them committed suicide – a man who'd leased him a mine near Butte. Then there was a young law clerk he went into business with named Ed Walters . . . They'd known each other in Philadelphia, but it seems that Taylor learned more about the law than Walters did . . . Walters had put up the money for their first venture together . . . '

'Walters had? Who told you this, James?'

'A pretty reliable source who deals in mining stocks. He was out in Butte at the time . . . ' James saw the expression on my face and gave a horrified sigh. 'Oh no, Quincey,' he said. 'Not him.'

'Of course not,' I said, but James knew me well.

He did not comment further, merely read out the other information he had gathered: crooked deals, exploitation, bribery, including a judge, share pushing, misrepresentation. Once, he had ordered boiling water to be poured down the mine shaft of a competitor. He was suspected of fraud though never charged, had been connected with a killing that was never proven, and at one time had been made bankrupt. Well, he had more or less admitted that last. 'And women, of course,' James added pointedly, 'by the dozen, one or two of whom brought suits against him.' And that

278

did not completely surprise me either.

'Marvellous with crowds, apparently,' James went on. 'Regular Mark Antony . . . provoked a few riots but always made sure that he said nothing that anyone could charge as incitement. Your Mr Taylor's not stupid, it's obvious . . . Also, he always paid his workers over the odds so they, at least, held a high opinion of him.'

Oddly, that worried me most of all. The rest was too much, easy to disbelieve. Had I really been sitting on the bank of that ravine with the Devil incarnate? But James's report about the workers had been gathered from the same sources as the other horrors, and that gave it credence. And strangely the worst of these, if true, was not that he might have committed murder, but that he had lied to me about old Mrs Blackstone and the Splendide Hotel.

'And Standard?' I inquired.

'That was brilliant – and the one thing no one condemned him for. He knew the Montana mining laws and he discovered that years back it'd been found to be legal to follow a vein of copper from the apex wherever it took you, even below someone else's mine . . . Standard had the property adjoining . . . . When he was under them, they broke through his shaft and he sued them. It was a long and bitter battle, but he won. They bought him out for big money, and with the proceeds he moved to Wall Street . . . Done one or two spectacular raids in the market, but by and large he's gone respectable . . . '

'The Mahogany Bar at the Waldorf-Astoria?'

'No doubt,' James agreed, watching me closely. 'Quincey,' he said. 'even if it's not all accurate, some of it most certainly is . . . '

'It's a question of which parts, isn't it?' I responded.

'Let's go back to New York,' James suggested, looking more anxious than I think I had ever seen him. 'Right or wrong, he's dangerous, Quincey . . . Seriously. This really *would* be a disaster . . . Let's go tomorrow. John can stay here to keep us informed . . . We can come back at the end of July.'

'I'll think about it,' I said.

Later that day, I was wandering along the street when I saw O'Sullivan Smith driving a buggy. 'I'm just off to the rig, Mrs Alexander,' he said, 'to see how things are going . . . Want to come with me, or are you busy?'

I needed something to take my mind off what James had reported. 'I'd like that,' I said, and climbed in beside him.

The journey may not have been conducted with the style of my last trip along that trail, but old Smith was a comfort. He was a warm man, a bit like a loving grandfather, and colourful in his way, with an endless stream of often aimless chat. We passed a group of Indians on horses. 'Comanche,' said Smith. 'Ever seen a Comanche before? The warriors . . . Like to travel . . . Did you know they mounted their horses from the other side?'

We drew up at the rig. 'Why, Sullivan, you old rascal!' Pete Williams bellowed from the platform. 'Oh, hallo, Mrs Alexander . . . You gotten the pull of the black gold, eh?'

Smith led the way up the ladder. They were not drilling, but working with a wire cable from one of the blocks at the head of the gantry, hauling something from the hole with the aid of a motor-powered winch. It was not coming up smoothly, seeming to be held down by some obstruction. The winch operator put the machine into reverse to loosen the wire – and once more put it into forward motion. The wire tautened.

'That's enough,' said Peter after a couple of seconds. 'Enough!' he repeated a bit louder. 'Ease it, Mike, for Christ's sake!' he shouted.

'She's stuck, Pete!' Mike cried out in alarm as he wrenched at a lever beside the winch. 'The gear's bloody stuck!' I saw that the winch was still turning the wire round the barrel.

I heard a whine. 'Watch it!' Pete yelled. 'She's singing!'

I was flung to the ground very suddenly and I heard a great crack, then the sound of breaking timber, and the rig seemed to lurch. A heavy male body was across me as I lay face down in the oil and mud on the platform.

It took a few seconds for me to orientate myself. The man who had flung me to the ground lifted his weight from me and, shaken, I got to my feet. Others, too, were getting up, the fear evident on the platform of narrowly avoided disaster. To my surprise I saw Taylor, whom I had not noticed before because he had been standing at the back hidden from me by several roustabouts, and realized then that it was he who had thrown me down. He was brushing himself down with his hand, but it was not doing much

280

good to the oil and mud on the smooth linen of his suit.

He was glaring at me, his eyes the colour of steel. 'You little fool!' he said.

'What happened?' I asked.

'The wire parted . . . They sing when they're going, as everyone here knew except you, so they get down on their faces as fast as they know how . . . Just see what it's done to the rig!'

I realized then, as I looked around me, that the wire had whipped back as it broke and cut through a whole side of the timber structure. There were great jagged gaps in the protective walls of the platform. Planking was splintered, broken wood hanging in pieces at angles from nails.

'That could have happened to you,' he said angrily,' 'So you'll please get off my rig, Mrs Alexander, and stay off unless you're invited, which is extremely unlikely . . . And the same goes for you, Mr O'Sullivan bloody Smith.'

'I'm sorry,' I said abjectly. 'I thought you'd gone to Oklahoma City.'

'Do I have to tell *you* every time I change my plans?' he demanded. He was pale with fury, his eyes wide. 'There's no place for a woman on a rig. It diverts men engaged in dangerous business. So off – *Now!*'

I was tempted to insist he accept my apology, but Smith jerked his head to indicate that we should go, and started down the ladder.

'And another thing,' Taylor called out to me when I was halfway down the steps. 'I don't want you making any more inquiries about me. You want to know anything about my life, you come and ask me and if I choose to, I'll damned well tell you!'

I looked up at him as he leaned out from the platform, his body tense with rage. 'I understand why you're angry,' I said calmly, 'but I don't think you should swear at a woman – especially when it's me.'

Then I joined Smith on the buggy. 'I never seen that happen before,' he said, 'a winch jam in motion, but I've heard about it.' I nodded, my lips tight. 'He's a real mean man, that Taylor,' he said.

That evening I did something foolish. I realized that Taylor might have saved my life, but I had been deeply hurt by his abuse. As I sat silently beside Smith on the buggy as we returned to Paulina, my resentment grew with every mile. All that James had reported began to gain credence in my mind. By the time we reached the town I felt cheated somehow, betrayed even, as though he had made some promise to me that he had flagrantly dishonoured – which is why, when I saw him playing cards a few hours later at the usual corner table, I went up to him. I had not planned it. I was responding to an emotional impulse. I was careful, though – just strolling across the crowded smoke-filled room with a slight smile on my face, as if the matter I had to speak about was unimportant.

And I had learned, too, from the past experience. When he glanced up at me, I urged him to finish his hand. So he did – and won it, scooping the cash towards him with easy unhurried movements.

As I stood beside him the sound of voices began to fade, as though the others there sensed that something untoward was going to happen. Taylor took his time, stacked the notes he had won with neat precision. Then he said: 'Well, Mrs Alexander, what can I do for you?'

'You told me, Mr Taylor,' I said in a clear voice, 'that if I had a question about you, I should ask you . . . Well, I have . . . '

He shrugged. 'Ask away . . . '

'Just *why* were you in jail?' I demanded.

He won, of course. He always won – at least, with me he did.

Chapter 13

[1]

James and I left for New York on the train the next day. I was looking forward to getting home to Brooklyn. I needed familiar faces, familiar streets. I looked through the window at the endless plains and suddenly I asked James: 'Do you believe what he said?'

'I don't know,' he answered. 'We can find out fast enough if it's true.'

In fact, Taylor had not said much. He did not even seem to be surprised. 'Jake,' he ventured lazily to one of his companions at the table, 'perhaps you'd care to answer the lady's question.'

Jake wore a full beard, grey and stained yellow by tobacco. He grinned as he stacked the pack. 'Always did think you were pushing your luck out there, Charlie . . . Only got mixed up with you because you've got that persuasive way. Lady, he offers you Brooklyn Bridge, don't even start to discuss it . . . '

'She wants an answer, Jake,' Taylor said, 'not a judgement on my character . . . '

'I only mentioned it,' Jake answered, shuffling the cards as he spoke, 'since it was the only time in your life I can think of that you weren't doing something for money. You just took exception to Porfirio Diaz and his way of running Mexico . . . ' He lifted the corner of the pack, spilling the cards past his thumb, and looked up at me. 'Charlie got real worked up about Diaz, which isn't like Charlie. He's never gone in much for that kind of thing . . . He even got associated with some people who shared the same opinion and were expressing it a little strongly from hideouts in the mountains.'

He began to deal the cards to the others. 'Of course, there were some people,' he went on, 'who said that Charlie was selling them guns, but personally I never believed that story. It wasn't his line and anyway, I'd have known, since I was seeing a lot of him at the time. And then, well, he just got careless, I reckon . . . Anyone's careless that ends up in a Mexican jail – or unlucky. Only there a few weeks, so far as I recall. Then he talked them into letting him escape – and into buying Brooklyn Bridge, I shouldn't wonder . . . '

He gave me a warm, hairy smile, then turned to the serious business of studying his cards. 'You mean,' I said, 'That he was jailed for a political offence?'

'Political?' Jake repeated, a puzzled look coming to his face. 'Would you call it political, Charlie?'

'Yes,' said Taylor, 'I'd call it political.' And he looked up at me and winked.

It was good to be back in New York – though hot, with temperatures way up in the nineties – and for the first time for a while, I got a chance to enjoy my son. We strolled in Central Park, fed the ducks, had ice cream in the open in the McGowan's Pass Restaurant. With James, and Mary's son Tom, we went to the new Luna Park that had replaced the old familiar amusement centre on Coney Island that had been destroyed by fire, and visited its circus on water, walked in its Japanese Tea Garden, slid down its helter-skelter. Both boys were too young for the magnificence of the place – for the sideshows that took you to the moon or allowed you to experience burning buildings or full-scale battles at sea – but there would be time enough for that.

I had long talks with Mama and Aunt Abigail, who was avid for every detail of my life in England. I discussed Wall Street at length with Papa. He still had an instinct for the nuances, except the most important one of all – the smell of the smoke when a market is smouldering.

James and I went to dinner with my sisters. Laura said she was sure the food was not up to the standard we were accustomed to; Mary was unassuming and generous as always, making us feel that both she and Elmer were delighted to see us.

I spent time in the Alexanders' office, taking over the room where I had first met Richard and discussing the projects of the bank with dear Mr Etherington, now sixty-five, who was still in charge. When I had first returned on a previous visit, he had found it difficult to call me Quincey – as did the few girls who had been in the office alongside me. But I refused to be addressed as Mrs Alexander. Not there.

Together with James, I checked over his information on Taylor, studying his sources and going with him to meet one or two of them. I had a long conference with the Pinkerton investigator whom James had dispatched to Butte before he had returned to Paulina. Always, though, the more serious charges against Taylor defied confirmation.

Occasionally, it seemed, he had been generous in his business relations, in one case cancelling a signed contract with a man who had suddenly died, so that his widow would not be burdened with its obligations. As usual, there had been suggestions that Taylor had cheated the bereaved woman; but she denied this firmly, insisting that he had behaved in a most generous fasion.

It was vital, I kept repeating to James, that we must find out exactly what kind of man he really was. We might be forced to deal with him if the Williams Brothers brought in the well. 'Yes, Quincey,' he mocked, 'we must indeed,' But it had struck him, he said, that I seemed far too pleased when the darker suggestions were found to have no grounds. 'Of course I am,' I snapped. 'If we're to do business with him, I'd prefer him to be honest.'

'Honest?' James said incredulously. 'Quincey, he may not be a killer, but there's no chance he's honest.'

'You've no right to say that!' I flared.

He looked at me sadly and then put his arms round me. 'I've the right, Quincey,' he said, 'because I care for you very much. I'm on your side whatever you do – which is why I want you to take care. Look the horse over well before you rent him, because he's not sound . . . He really isn't . . . '

I looked at him coolly, aware that in all logic he was right. But I wanted Taylor to be sound. As James had guessed, he had been on my mind a great deal since I had arrived in the city. Too much, in fact. I had even found myself waking in the night and lying awake thinking of him for quite long periods, content enough to be sleepless. Despite his behaviour to me on the rig, despite his easy rejection of my challenge in the hotel, I was missing him badly. 'Have you found Ed Walters for me yet?' I snapped at James.

'Yes,' he answered, with his easy grin. 'As a matter of fact, I have. He's back in Philadelphia, working in an attorney's office.'

'Telegraph him,' I ordered, piqued by his attitude. 'Say we'd like to talk to him but don't tell him why . . . We'll stay at the Splendide and we could meet there.'

Walters was a surprise. I suppose I was looking for someone with the bravura or mystery of his ex-partner, for Taylor had spoken as though Walters was the enterprising one. But Mr Walters looked like an old man. He was short and bald and grey, and already his shoulders were very slightly bowed.

He had a pleasant smile — though his eyes were bright behind steel-rimmed glasses — and the kind of solicitous manner morticians deploy for the bereaved. 'You're wondering why we wanted to see you,' I said. 'It concerns Charles Taylor, who was once a partner of yours, I think.'

'Charlie?' he asked, with a laugh that carried an unexpected note of affection. 'I haven't seen Charlie in years.'

'I believe you went to Montana together,' I said, 'to prospect for copper.'

'That's true,' he said. 'Butte . . . quite a rough place it was then . . .'

'So I hear . . . what interests me, Mr Walters, is . . . well, how you got started . . . . I mean, you could hardly have gone out there without any resources at all . . . .'

'It's no secret,' he said with a soft smile as if recalling a boyhood prank. 'We had two thousand dollars. Charlie got it in this very hotel from an old lady who lived here . . . Seemed an awful lot to us at the time . . .'

The relief I felt was a shock to me. I was more than pleased, as James had taunted. I was so elated I found it hard to concentrate further. So Taylor had not lied to me.

'There was talk, of course,' Walters went on. 'People suggested he wheedled it out of her, but he didn't . . . didn't have to . . . why, Charlie could sell anyone Brooklyn Bridge without really trying . . .'

'So it wasn't you, Mr Walters, who put up the money,' I persisted, eyeing James pointedly, 'and he didn't cheat you out of it?'

He nodded. 'He didn't cheat me out of *that* . . . he cheated me later. Well, I suppose you might call it cheating . . .'

My spirits ebbed. It was the picture that was now familiar. No sooner was one charge against him quashed than another took its place.

'How do you mean, Mr Walters?' I asked.

He pushed his spectacles back to the bridge of his nose. 'Well,' he said, 'We'd done pretty well with the first mine we'd got our hands on. Our modest success had whetted our appetites. This time we were going to make it big . . . We leased a lot of land with the help of large mortgages. Then one day, Charlie came to me with a proposal. 'I'm tired of being a partner', he said. 'I want to go solo. I'll sell you my share or I'll buy yours . . . *You* decide . . .'

'I opted for the land – and bought him out, using every spare cent I had . . .'

'And what happened?' I asked, though by now I could guess.

'The land, it turned out, was not such a good buy as we'd thought. We'd had it surveyed, of course, before we took it and the findings were hopeful, but suddenly a few months later the bank got jittery and called in another expert. He condemned it out of hand . . . No hope, he insisted, so the bank foreclosed on the mortgages and, since I'd bought Charlie out by then, I was the one who went bankrupt.'

'So how did he cheat you?' asked James.

'I've got no proof,' he said, with the strange tolerance he displayed about Taylor, 'but it's possible he could have found out that the second report was adverse and guessed the bank'd foreclose. He was friendly with the man who ran it . . .'

'But Mr Walters,' I put in, 'he offered you either course . . . What if you'd decided to sell to him instead of buying?'

Walters laughed. 'That was the risk he took, Mrs Alexander. Charlie was always a gambler. Want to hear the end? Doggone if he didn't buy it back from the bank and . . . I expect you've guessed . . . There was copper down below all the time. Lots of it . . .'

'I'd have said that added up to cheating,' said James, deliberately avoiding my eyes.

'I'm not positive,' Walters said. 'Charlie had his own rules – and it could be that the cards just fell right for him. They often did. And if he *did* plan it, I reckon that wife of his had a lot to do with it . . .'

'Wife?' I echoed. Suddenly, I felt so cold I shivered – there in high summer. 'I didn't know he was married,' I said calmly. Somehow he had never seemed married.

'He wasn't for long . . . Few months only . . . She was a minx, that one, but he'd an eye for women, of course. He liked them spirited like his horses, but at times he could be susceptible . . .They could get him doing things he'd never have done on his own.'

'Was there a divorce?' I asked, though I knew the answer. It was a wild faint hope.

'In Montana?' Walters echoed incredulously. 'No, Mrs Alexander . . . Not that it makes much difference . . . I shouldn't think he's ever seen her since . . . .'

I went back early to Oklahoma. It was a sudden decision since, short of a summons from John Trevor, I had intended to arrive there on July 31st, a few hours before the deadline. Somehow, though, I yearned for the place – and, as at last I was forced to admit, for Taylor. I found that he was in my thoughts almost all the time – his voice, his mocking, the hard callused hands with the sensitive fingers, the eyes like mine with their fast-changing expressions. Even the vivid image of his fury that day on the rig no longer seemed to offend me. He interfered when I was working, when I was talking to people, shopping in stores, even playing with Jonny. The last was the hardest for me to face. I had leisure to spend with Jonny, but I was prepared to forgo the opportunity.

I had tried to look at the situation as I had learned to judge an investment. You set out the facts, considered the options and made a decision. By any standard, Charlie Taylor was the poorest investment anyone could make. Although he had not lied to me and nothing was proved against him, his background was clearly suspect. He was obviously a womanizer of the worst kind. He was married. His discourtesy had been gross. Anyway, I hardly knew him, so the foolish thoughts that were lurking in my mind could have no basis – and his recent behaviour allowed no suspicion that they might be shared.

Despite all this, there was still a week to go before the end of July when – after leaving an anxious James in New York to finalize unfinished matters – I arrived in Paulina. I was in one of the front cars of the train and, through the window, I saw Taylor before it came to a halt. He was standing – feet apart, hands on hips – with the crowd washing round him as though he was a permanent fixture. He was in a dark suit, perfectly tailored and pressed as usual, with his hard black sombrero.

He did not see me until I stood at the head of the steps of the car. Then he moved towards me unhurriedly through the crowd, with an easy smile on his face. 'Welcome back, Mrs Alexander,' he said.

I was astonished. When I saw him, I had assumed that he was there to welcome someone arriving in the town. I had not thought it would be me. 'How did you know I'd be on today's train?' I asked.

'I've been meeting them every day,' he said. 'Figured you were bound to be on one of them . . . '

I wished then that he would kiss me. Oh, how I wished he would kiss me, despite all the people around us. But it was hardly fitting. However, his eyes were bright with pleasure as he ordered a man to bring my luggage and strolled with me along the sidewalk. 'You know, Mrs Alexander,' he said, 'I been feeling badly about that last day you were here.'

He was walking beside me in his characteristic way that I had recalled so often in New York — hard and compact, like a fighter, almost on his toes, elbows bent and close to his sides as though ready at any moment to dart out a punch. Always he imparted a sense of contained strength.

'Hoped you'd realize it all started with me being anxious about you . . . shocked, I guess, and it sort of grew . . . . Also, I suppose I'm that kind of . . . '

'That kind of horse?'

He nodded. 'A bit ornery sometimes . . . I feared you'd refuse to talk to me.'

I was feeling quite absurdly happy, but angry with him, too. Did he really think he could so easily wipe the slate clean? There was no doubt about the answer to the question. 'Taylor,' I said as we approached the hotel.

'Yes, Mrs Alexander?'

'I think I'm in the market for Brooklyn Bridge.'

[2]

The lights were crude, casting harsh moving shadows as the men worked on the drilling platform. Even though it was night, I found

289

the air oppressively hot. There was something claustrophobic about the noise of the bull wheel as it was turned by the chain, the beating of the engine, the sound of the slush as it came out of the ground. Every now and then, I had to go out and breathe the air of that fine Oklahoma evening.

We were all as tense as cats, for there were only two hours left to midnight. 'She's making hole,' said Pete, 'but only just. Anyone'd think it was steel down there we were having to cut through . . . '

He had joined his brother on the derrick even though it was not his 'tour'. Hampton and Smith had been there since dawn, both refusing to leave the platform even to eat. Hampton, for all his persistence, looked as gloomy as a bloodhound, shaking his head slowly whenever anything happened that was remotely adverse. John Trevor was there, too, seemingly unmoved – containing, as the English could, any sense of excitement he might feel. Bankers, after all, were concerned with results, and as yet there were no results.

Taylor and I had been out twice that day already – on horses because they were quicker than his surrey. Fresh ones each time, so that we could gallop. He had refused to stay on the rig for long. When he was gambling with men, he could be as cool and unhurried as a Mexican peasant, but the earth made him frustrated and impatient – especially during the long breaks when the crew were attending to the drilling equipment.

The past days had been dramatic. The Williams believed they were close. Several times they had hit oil sand, with a fairly rich content, before once more biting through gravel or soft clay. Then they had struck rock so hard that they could not get through it and Pete had said he had a hunch that this was the lid of the oil pool – for they called it a pool even though a well was more like a hard sponge filled with oil. That is, if there *was* a pool, for oil sand was not a definite indication. There could be oil sand without any well.

By that morning, the Williams had tried every way they knew to get through that massively tough rock stratum – including 'pile-driving', which was like trying to hammer in a nail instead of the rotary action of a bit, and even 'torpedoing', which was always a last resort because the explosion was hard to control and you could do great damage to the shaft without achieving the object. At last,

Pete had taken a train into Tulsa in the hope of obtaining a new kind of bit he had heard of. He had got back with it only twenty-four hours before that tense evening. With its aid there had been progress, slow though it was. Certainly, Taylor's speculation – which had seemed so hopeless five weeks before – could be promising now, *if* the Williams could break though the rock by midnight. Otherwise, of course, it would become promising for me.

On our first visit that last morning of July, we had ridden out to the rig as the sun was rising. We had watched operations with the new drill, but it was not long before Taylor had suggested impatiently that we should leave and come back later. At first, we had walked the horses in silence. He was in a quiet, introspective mood. It was a hot day with a cloudless sky and the corn in the field, which had so impressed me the first time he had brought me out in the surrey, was bright golden. 'Why am I trying so hard?' he said. 'Either way, I win . . . you, I mean . . . Even if you get the well, I win you,' adding: 'Don't I?'

'That's what I've been telling you,' I answered.

'So I'm not gambling . . . I don't have to kiss the dice or beg the help of the spirits . . . ' He smiled a bit sadly, his body moving unresisting with the horse. 'You've taken the fun out of it, Mrs Alexander. No risk!'

'No risk?' I asked incredulously. 'Are you out of your mind, Taylor? You're taking the biggest risk you ever did . . . . Gracious, I'm hungry for breakfast . . . .' I put the horse into a flat-out gallop, shouting over my shoulder: 'Bet you a thousand dollars I can beat you into town!'

During the week I had been back in Paulina, I had wondered at moments if I was sane. I had loved Richard and felt the strange magnetic pull of Howard, but I had never known a man with the raw toughness of Taylor – in all its senses. I knew he could have walked for days in the desert without food and survived, that he could kill if he had to without qualm. I knew he was completely opportunist – that even if he had not cheated Ed Walters or the widow in Butte, he would have done if the motive had been strong enough. For him there were no real limits, as there were for

Howard, who would be curbed at the end of the day, I suspected, by the code within which he had been raised. Howard was a king who might order the execution of his rivals. Taylor was a bandit who would shoot them in the back as they left him for dead.

None of it ranked in my scale of priorities. I knew only one thing: I needed to spend the rest of my life with him more than I had ever needed anything. I knew, too, what the price of this would be. At least, I thought I did. For I was fully aware that, to the Alexanders, Taylor would be anathema — with good solid reason. The fight, when I got back to London, would make anything I had experienced so far seem like a minor skirmish. My eyes were open, so I thought, but in fact I did not know the half of it.

I think that when I had left New York, I was responding to a demand within me that I had found hard, well, impossible, really, to resist — and I was not proud of it. Always, I had cast myself in the role of my own woman. Yet there I was travelling west like a lovesick seventeen-year-old just to be near a man whose treatment of me had been callous in the extreme. Near? Just to be in the same town, the same territory. What in the name of heaven had happened to my self-respect?

Then he had been waiting there in the crowd when the train pulled in — just like it was in those ten-cent romances — and gave every sign that my tumultuous feelings for him were reciprocated.

Yet by four days after my return he had not even held my hand nor made any declaration of . . . . well, love, or even admiration.

Nor had he left my side — except at night. We had taken every meal together, spent every hour in each other's company. Our relations were completely changed. He looked at me with those intense blue eyes as a man does when he is overwhelmed by a woman. He complimented me continuously — on my hair, on how I was looking that day, on my features. The unusual curve of my lips; the shape of my nose; my dimples, for which he had a particular partiality; my freckles, which had been so disdained in London; and my blue eyes, which must have been flashing out my need for him as though they were connected to electric wires.

He praised my intelligence, too. I had an unusual mind, he said — which of all his compliments I knew I deserved because I could often out-argue him being, in general matters, better informed.

And, although he had me lassoed and down on my side with all four feet tied up in rope, this was one feminine ploy I never sank to. I did not let him win. I did not restrain myself to allow him to feel superior. He was superior in the one way that mattered. He was like a rock, with all his moral flaws – like a rock that was not smooth but flawed, with bits chipped off by erosion and winds and rain and frost and sun so that it was jagged and stark.

Behind everything he said lay the assumption that our life in the future would be together, that we possessed special insights about each other. If he asked a question about my past, it was only to elaborate on knowledge he already had – as though he, too, had a dossier but his had been given him by God, for he was aware of things that no man could have revealed.

I knew about him, too – far more than I had read in James's report. At moments, I felt as though he had been a part of my life for years. I had an understanding of him – at least I felt I did – that wives must know after decades of marriage. Often, before he spoke, I knew what he was going to say and how he was going to say it, what inflections there would be, what words he would use.

There was no question that we were lovers, but we did not make love – not in a physical sense. At the end of our first day together, being a forward hussy, I had taken his hand and drawn him towards me to kiss me, but he had shaken his head with a smile and said: 'Not yet' – which, darn it, is what women, not men, are supposed to say.

The only aspect that did not change was his attitude to his stake in the oil concession – at least not until the final morning, when he was in so strange a mood. He was just as demanding as ever he had been that the Williams should bring in the well before the midnight deadline, even doubling the bonus he had promised. When I asked why it mattered any longer and, in jest, even offered once more to negotiate a deal, he became serious. 'My price,' he said sharply, 'is a million dollars, Mrs Alexander.'

It was on the fourth day after my return that, as we were riding back from the rig, he said suddenly: 'Why don't we go down to our ravine?'

I laughed. 'Got a spread down there like last time?' I asked.

'No,' he answered, 'But the ravine's the same.'

We cantered towards it, left the horses in the shade of the cotton woods and ran down to the creek. This time, I was in the rough clothes I had taken to wearing for riding – a stetson, shirt, split skirt and Texan boots. As before, we sat on the bank with our feet in the water. To start with, he did not say much of moment – talked about the last occasion we had been there, ruminated about the future, about the ambitions he wanted to fulfil. But it was 'our' future he was speaking of, I knew. 'You got to live in England always?' he asked suddenly.

I nodded. 'A lot of the time,' I said.

He moved one of his feet in the water, making a slow pattern on the surface. 'I liked England,' he said. 'They've got style in England, no question . . . . Gets gaunt in winter, and rains in summer. Maybe we could go somewhere in the summer . . . . Italy, France, some place the sun shines . . . Back here, maybe?' Suddenly, he kicked violently, as though raging against the stream, splashing us both. 'It's hopeless, isn't it, Mrs Alexander? You know I'm married, don't you, with all your inquiries . . . ?'

'Yes, Taylor,' I answered. 'Ed Walters told me.'

His smile of response had the same affectionate quality that Walters had displayed. 'Seen Ed, have you? How's he doing?'

'He's no millionaire,' I said. 'Law office in Philadelphia . . . .'

'Where he started, eh? Ed never liked Enid. "Poor material," he'd say, "even for you, Charlie . . . Got spirit, I grant, but what's the value of spirit if it's not from character? All you got then is a mean horse." He was right, too . . . ' He looked at me suddenly, 'What'd you think when he told you?'

'I wished he hadn't.'

A puzzled look came to his face. 'Doesn't seem to have made a lot of difference.'

'Nothing'd make a difference, Taylor.'

He watched a fish jump. 'I've been trying to get free . . . . hasn't mattered till now . . . Offered her a quarter of a million . . . .'

I was amazed. 'That's a high price, Taylor,' I said quietly, 'for a mean horse.'

'Turned me down. She may be mean but she's no fool . . . . and where'd we be at the end? I'd still be divorced . . . Still wouldn't go down well in London town.'

He had thought it all through without even mentioning it — all that lay ahead. Tears came into my eyes. We looked at each other with a hint of despair and he leaned forward and kissed me gently on the lips.

It was not a passionate kiss and he sat up again at once. 'Wish there was a different way,' he said, 'of making love to you.'

'Different, Taylor? Why?'

He was looking across the ravine at the far bank.

'I'd be treating you just like all the others, wouldn't I?'

'Perhaps that's not so bad,' I said.

There was a serious expression on his face. 'You don't understand, do you? There've been a lot . . . over a hundred, I'd say. None has mattered . . . Never thought any woman'd matter. I'm forty-one, Mrs Alexander . . . . Jesus, you'd think you'd know by forty-one . . . What I'm trying to say is . . . .the coinage is debased . . . '

This was a side of him I had never seen. Tough rough Taylor was talking like a schoolboy. 'That's like saying you can debase speech by talking,' I said.

'Talking's not loving.'

'I'd say talking's been loving these last few days. For goodness' sake Taylor, just treat me like a woman. Unless you're scared that is . . . '

'Scared? He snapped, suddenly angry.

I met his gaze. 'Lusting's easy,' I said, 'because there isn't any giving . . . ' I lay back on the grass with my feet still in the water, and looked at the trees above me. 'Love's taking away the shutters,' I added, 'revealing secrets . . . You can get trapped by loving, ensnared . . . Am I that frightening, Taylor? Am I a siren? Will I lead you to destruction?'

'I think you well might,' he said. He was lying beside me, supporting himself on one elbow, looking down at me. 'You've got your theory, Mrs Alexander. I've got mine, and it's not flattering, but I'm going to tell you just the same. What's more, it's crude — cruder than swearing — but when it comes to it, when we lie together, how do I know it'll be different from the others — even the good ones? How do I know that what we've got, what I've known with no other woman, won't just crumble to pieces in my hands?'

It was crude, but that was not what hurt. How could he possibly think it would be like the others? The thought was inconceivable. I was hopelessly, wonderfully in love with him. His doubts seemed absurd. 'Why don't you test me out, Taylor,' I asked quietly, 'by easy stages – like dipping your toe in the water?'

He was smiling down at me softly, with love, with desire – but also with male confidence, like an actor slipping into an accustomed role. 'All right, Mrs Alexander,' he said, and was bending down to kiss me when, under some involuntary impulse, I was on my feet and running for the horses . . .

I heard him shout: 'Don't you want your boots?' – which was the first time I had realized I was not wearing them. But I did not stop, barefoot as I was. I mounted the horse quickly and put him into a gallop, leaning forward urging him to go faster, with the wind blowing my hair.

He caught me up after a mile or two. He was carrying my boots and my hat. 'You can't go into town without your boots,' he said. 'People'd think it funny.'

It was half an hour before midnight – the crucial July deadline – and Taylor was pacing the platform like a caged tiger, chewing on the end of a cheroot. It was crowded with us all waiting there under the lights with the drilling crew, and even though we were just standing watching them as they worked, the sweat was pouring down us from the heat on the rig.

At last Pete stood up from examining the slush chute, wiped the dirt from his eyes, and said: 'I could be wrong, but I've got a notion we're getting close . . . I think maybe you should all leave the rig. It'll be messy if she blows.'

Taylor looked at his watch, which he took from a jacket pocket, glanced at me, then moved to the head of the ladder. I followed him to the ground. 'Let's go to the ravine,' he said. 'If it goes, we can hear it there as easy as here.'

So again we got on the horses and rode to the creek. The moon was full, so it was almost as clear as daylight, throwing our shadows ahead of us as we approached the cotton woods. When we got there we just sat on the bank, with our boots on this time.

He did not talk much, just kept looking at his watch, which he could see clearly by the light of the moon.

For all appearances, nothing seemed to have changed since the last time we were at the creek, though we had not spoken of it. We had spent most of our time together, as we had before, and laughed at the same jokes, but we had not talked of the future. I still did not really know the reason for my rushed departure. I suppose I had feared suddenly that his doubts might well be justified.

'It's two minutes to midnight,' he said, and stayed looking at his watch as the second hand went round. 'One minute . . . . The last throw . . . I'm kissing the dice . . . ' We sat in silence except for the sound of a cricket in the grass. 'You've won, Mrs Alexander,' he said, putting away his watch. 'It's the first of August . . . . My luck's not running . . . '

'You said you won either way . . . .'

'I won a side bet – big one, granted, if I *did* win it. But I lost the main play . . . '

We heard it then – like a great crack of thunder followed by the continuous roar of the gusher. He did not move. 'You just struck oil, Mrs Alexander,' he said. 'by two minutes. I'd say *your* luck was running.'

I did not answer – just put my arms round his neck and pulled him down on me, lying back on the grass, as I had the last time. 'We've got to find out sometime, Taylor,' I said. 'What's wrong with now?'

He took it slow, being practised, as he said; very slow, just kissing me gently to start with – my mouth, my eyes, my ears, my neck, my palms, my fingers. He let it build at its own pace, the urgency of his kissing growing as he parted my lips, but keeping it always within his control. He undid the buttons of my shirt without hurry and kissed my breasts. I felt his hands on my legs within the split skirts, my thighs, myself. All his movements were controlled as he undid my belt and slid my skirt from under me.

It was never a great flaring. I did not lose myself as I lay there loving him with the moonlight slanting through the trees. But it was deep with roots that had already taken a strong hold. It was right – and all I would ever want to the end of my life.

'Is it like all the others, Taylor?' I asked softly. 'Is everything crumbling to pieces in your hands?'

He lifted himself, so that his weight was on his arms, so dark against the silverlight that I could only just make out his eyes. 'You ask some stupid questions sometimes, Mrs Alexander,' he answered.

'I've got another, Taylor,' I whispered. 'When are we leaving for London?'

Chapter 14

It was reminiscent of another dinner five years before on the yacht in the Irish Sea, when, as a young and unexpected bride, I had been displayed before the massed ranks of Alexanders. This time, though, it was I who sat at the head of the long gleaming table with the hand-cut crystal glasses, the Queen Anne silver cutlery and the Minton china dinner service.

The tactics were the same, too. The Alexanders would meet Taylor as a group, as they had met me. I had decided to take them by storm – a surprise attack – though I did not really hope for success. It was just something I had to attempt.

I had sent no warning of my return, telling Mr Etherington I was going away for a few days to explain my absence from New York, and travelling across the Atlantic under an assumed name.

When we arrived unannounced at my house in Grosvenor Square, Bridget was astonished to see us. Impulsively she threw her arms round my neck, then lifted up Jonny and hugged him to her, and welcomed Nanny Roberts and James.

'This is Mr Charles Taylor, Bridget,' I said. 'He'll be staying with us for a few days. So will Mr Stratton . . . .'

Taylor met her inquiring glance with his easy smile, looked at her in the way he looked at women, and she was conquered. 'I'm delighted to meet you at last,' he said.

I asked her to have the main guest room prepared for him and then to come and see me. I was sitting at my dressing-table when she entered. I turned and smiled at her. 'Oh, it's good to be back,' I said, 'but it's battle stations!'

She sat on the bed as I indicated. 'He seems very pleasing,' she said, 'and handsome . . . Does Jonny get on with him?'

'They adore each other. Taylor tells him about the West, about how they break the mustangs, about killing rattlesnakes with a whip . . . On board the ship they went for long walks on deck together and he explained all about the dolphins . . . '

She was looking at me shrewdly. 'I gather you expect some

resistance from the family.'

I gave a sad little nod. 'He's a millionaire, Bridget – a successful figure on Wall Street – but he hardly comes from one of the Founding Families.'

'They can't stop you marrying him,' Bridget said, 'if you're set on it.'

'There's another problem,' I added.

She guessed at once. 'He's married?'

'Twenty years ago, only for a few months . . . ' She was looking at me incredulously. A man who was married, she knew, would appal them even if he had come from one of the Founding Families. 'Bridget,' I said, 'I'm going to stay with him, even if we can't marry for a while, even though some discretion may be needed – no matter what the odds . . . '

Her smile was affectionate. 'There's nothing I can say,' she said, 'except "good luck" . . . '

She stood up. 'When do we prepare to repel boarders?'

'We don't' I answered. 'We invite them aboard as soon as possible. Tonight, ideally . . . Find out what they're all doing, then I'll send notes of invitation. Tell cook she must prepare the best meal she's ever done in her life. We'll have the finest wines in the cellar . . . '

'And what time do I order the trumpeters? she asked.

I laughed. 'Oh, I'm glad I've got you, Bridget,' I said.

Somehow, that afternoon, we retained the secret. They all came in to see me – Nina, Stella, Frances. They were intrigued by my sudden return, of course, and suspicious. Nina and Stella, disturbed that the oil success at Paulina might strengthen the power I already wielded within the bank, suspected some Machiavellian ploy. Frances, as always, was on the right track.

Howard dropped in, too, on his way home. It was strange to see him again, though there was nothing in his demeanour to suggest that he even recalled that dark wet afternoon at Shere. Oddly, I felt nothing for him. For a few minutes – or was it hours? – he had been my lover. For that short period, he had possessed me totally. Was it possible to feel nothing for a man who had shared so volcanic and intimate an eruption? But it was gone like a sudden summer storm.

I wondered then if it had been a kind of preparation, an awakening, if I would have fallen so deeply in love with Taylor if it had not occurred.

Howard knew also, of course, that something lay behind my unexpected appearance in England, and he groped for it. I must be pleased by the events in Paulina, he said, remarking how strange that someone (a Mr Taylor, was it?) had bought Hampton's rights for so short a period.

'Can we kiss the Rothschilds goodbye?' I asked, using Smith's colourful phrase. 'Do we care if the Romanians renew their contract?'

'Well,' he answered cautiously, 'the last telegram from Trevor put the yield at 800 barrels a day . . . If that holds, it'll certainly strengthen our position.' He was watching me closely. We were not really talking about oil or yields. I was staking everything on the hope that he knew nothing yet about Taylor and me; that Mathew would not have considered he merited investigation from London; that for a few hours I held the initiative.

No trumpets blared that evening, but the impact made by Taylor was as great as if they had. We were all standing there in the drawing-room before dinner, talking of Oklahoma and events at home in my absence, as families do at such times. It was an informal Alexander occasion, and no guests were expected.

Then he walked in.

He was not the Taylor I knew, but he looked marvellous – superbly elegant in his tails, relaxed with an air of authority that contained an element of deference. With his thick greying hair, he could have been a senator visiting a Rothschild – as important in his own way, but in the home of his host. His smile was a trifle shy, suggesting that there was in him an inherent diffidence that he had managed to overcome.

As I introduced him, he made the appropriate remark to everyone and told Howard what an honour it was to meet the head of so renowned a family.

I had overdressed a little for a family occasion – deliberately. I was in my best dinner-gown – décolleté and white, in layered lace, with earrings and a necklace of pearls. As I walked in to dinner with

Taylor on my arm, I was amused at the change he had made to himself. I wondered what they would all have thought if they had seen him playing poker, with his feet on the chair, in O'Reilly's Hotel.

My plan was finely calculated, with a modest aim. I sought a degree of toleration. No more. His surprise presence would alarm them, but I wanted them to like him before they learned about his past, to blunt the prejudice that was inevitable. Then there would be a slim chance that something could be saved from the fire. And I had not deluded myself. It would be a great big blaze. Even so, if they liked him, they might just possibly accept him as a visitor – in my own home, at least. Until he was divorced, that is, but we could consider that situation when we came to it, if we came to it.

During that dinner, I felt like a circus trainer in a cage with tigers. There were areas of discussion that it would be wise to avoid, so I had planned diversions. By way of preparation, I told them a bit about him over the *truite marinée étoile*, speaking of the fortune he had made by outmanoeuvring Standard Oil, which I knew would appeal to them; of his skilful operations on Wall Street; of his uncanny instinct for opportunities that had so nearly been successful at Paulina.

There were moments of crisis, as I had predicted. I had said nothing of his start as a bellboy and, when Howard inquired politely where he came from, he handled the question with easy skill. 'Philadelphia,' he said, going on at once to speak of a Wall Street speculator who also came from Philadelphia – which led to anecdotes of other colourful characters on the Exchange that fascinated the Alexander men.

There were a few delicate seconds when Nina asked if he was married. He replied that he was. 'My wife lives in Montana,' he explained. 'She doesn't enjoy New York, where naturally I have to spend much time.'

'A country girl,' said Nina coolly.

Following leads from James, Taylor spoke about his travels, and recounted amusing experiences. To say he flirted mildly with Stella and Frances was not quite accurate – though he was a little outrageous with Aunt Elizabeth – but he moved close to it, making them laugh a lot.

Cook had done well with the *canard en daube* and the *estouffade de bœuf*, matched in turn by a superb Château Lafite and a Romanée-Conti. By the time the *baba au rhum* was placed before Howard – whom I had seated at the head of the table opposite me – he was growing increasingly cordial to our guest. In particular, the seven-week gamble at Paulina fascinated him. Taylor responded to his questions with the familiar grin that was both confident and modestly deprecating. 'I have to admit it, Mr Alexander,' he said, 'I like to speculate at times.'

I laughed at the understatement. 'Remember the price he asked from us?' I said to Howard.

'A million dollars, wasn't it?' he answered, pensively swirling in his glass the Château Yquem that had been served with the dessert. 'You've a cool nerve, I grant you, Mr Taylor,' he said. 'I envy it.'

I suggested then that the ladies should retire. The dinner seemed to me to have gone well. As we went up the stairs, Frances gave me a wink. 'Pretty smart horse you've reined in there,' she said.

'Do you know what his father did?' Nina asked, which I had never thought to investigate.

It had been a bold, desperate plan but, if anyone was fooled at that dinner table, it was me. After we had left the men, so I learned later, and the port was passed round the table, Howard inquired if Taylor was in London for business or pleasure. He asked about his plans and sought his views on the state of Wall Street, which had been depressed since March. 'Further to go, would you say?' he asked.

'I think it's about to turn,' Taylor replied. 'I'm buying.'

For a moment, Howard sipped his port reflectively. 'Mr Taylor,' he said at last, 'you'll understand, I'm sure, that I feel a certain responsibility for Mrs Alexander as my cousin's widow . . . '

'Of course,' Taylor responded cautiously.

'So I hope you won't consider it untoward of me to ask . . . Well, to put it frankly, what your intentions are with regard to her?'

'Intentions?' Taylor asked with surprise. 'As you heard, I'm a married man.'

'Not *very* married, I gather, from what you said earlier . . . '

Taylor smiled. 'Are there degrees? Mrs Alexander and I have certainly become friends . . . '

Howard became quite still. His elbows were on the table and he was holding his glass delicately between the fingers of both hands. 'Tell me,' he said, 'if you were in my position, what view would you take of such a . . . of such a friendship?'

'I'm amazed by your question, Mr Alexander,' said Taylor.

'Given, of course,' Howard went on, 'that I know a good deal about your past.'

I had been wrong. Mathew had regarded Taylor as worthy of investigation. 'Would you not, in my place,' Howard continued, 'be wondering, for example, about the untimely death of Mr Spencer of Standard Oil?'

Taylor faced him out, as he had faced out men with guns. 'Would you not in my place,' he answered in Howard's words, 'find that remark offensive in the extreme? I'm sure you know that Mr Spencer was killed in a riot.'

'A riot deliberately provoked by you,' Howard pressed, 'who happened strangely to have been seen close to the house at the time of the killing.'

'That's a charge that's only ever had one source,' Taylor said in a calm tone. 'And that was Mr Mason, also of Standard Oil . . . My God, Mr Alexander, haven't you fought Standard yourselves? You know how they work . . . How dare you make such an allegation without further evidence?'

Howard was unmoved. 'I made no allegation . . . . I asked a question . . . '

Taylor leaned back in his chair informally, one leg cocked over the other. 'I'm inclined to tell you to go to hell,' he said, 'but that'd embarrass Mrs Alexander, so I won't . . . . I was mining under Standard's land, quite legally, following my own vein of metal. They tried to stop me and I sued – successfully, which amazed their attorneys, who thought I'd got no case. They counter-sued before a judge they'd bribed. That wasn't difficult in Montana at the time. He declared in their favour, of course . . . . At the same time, Standard bought the town's newspaper, which started printing calumnies against me. Now, in *that* situation, what would *you* have done?'

'Appealed the court's decision,' Howard said, 'and sued for libel.'

Taylor burst out laughing. 'In the Wild West, Mr Alexander?' he inquired incredulously. 'You've struck oil in Indian country, so you're going to have to face it—even now things aren't the same out there as London or New York City, let alone the time you're talking about, when Montana'd only just become a state. I *did* appeal . . . Meanwhile, gangs beat up my workers. They poured boiling water down the mine shaft. The newspaper went on printing lies about me . . . No one in Butte liked Standard, but a lot of people depended on the company for their income. I had only one advantage: I paid my men well, and this made me popular with the workers in the district. So, to answer the press campaign against me, I deployed the right of free speech. I held public meetings and told the men the truth. Standard didn't like it and broke up a meeting, which caused feelings to run a little high . . . '

'As you intended,' Howard put in.

'I didn't intend them to kill anyone . . . Why should I? But the men didn't want Standard to ruin the one employer who paid them decently. They *did* riot, as you said, but they wouldn't have done if they hadn't been attacked first. They hadn't rioted before . . . '

Howard turned to his brother. 'What do you think of that explanation, Mathew?'

Mathew smiled in his cold way. 'Mr Taylor's known to be persuasive,' he said.

Taylor ignored the barbed comment. 'I won the appeal, of course,' he went on, 'which is why Standard had to buy the mine and pay me to leave the territory. That fact isn't even open to question, as I expect you know, so I await your apology . . . '

'Apology?' Howard repeated.

'You implied I'd been party to a murder, though no one ever charged me with the crime – no officer of the law . . . I'd say that merited apology, wouldn't you?'

Howard nodded. 'I apologize.' He held the decanter over Taylor's glass. 'It doesn't answer my question, though, does it?' he said. 'Your record's been colourful, I think you'd agree – too colourful, we feel, for the escort of an Alexander widow who owns a large holding in our bank. You'll appreciate our view, I'm sure.'

Taylor leaned back in his chair and surveyed the Alexander men with a supercilious smile. 'No,' he said. 'I don't appreciate it. I'm not the President of the United States, I'd concede, or a Lowell, or even an Astor, but I've done pretty well despite Standard's lies, and I'm not ashamed of it. I'm a man of means, accepted to a point in New York society . . . Even from where you sit, I can't see much harm in my relations with Mrs Alexander. After all, she's not seventeen, is she? She's a woman of maturity, a mother – old enough, I'd say, to choose her own friends.'

Howard did not seem to have heard him. 'There are two courses open to us, Mr Taylor,' he went on – elbows on the table, the ring on his finger turning. 'We can offer you our help – funding, should you need it, on beneficial terms, or the kind of favour that's in the gift of a bank such as ours . . . Our support, shall we say . . . Or we can warn you that, if you continue your friendship with Mrs Alexander, you'll find us a formidable opponent in all your dealings on the Wall Street exchanges . . . You understand me, I assume?'

'I understand only one thing,' Taylor answered. 'You're insulting me.'

'I'd urge you to consider what I've said,' Howard concluded and stood up. 'Now we'd better join the ladies.'

We made love that night. He needed it. 'Am I too colourful?' he asked at one point. 'Vivid,' I answered, 'which is how I like you.' As I returned to my room, I saw Bridget coming up the stairs in a white cotton nightgown. 'I couldn't sleep,' she said, 'so I went down to the kitchen to get something to eat. I suppose you couldn't sleep either . . . ' She gave me a meaningful smile.

The next morning I went to see Howard at the bank. I was furious with him, of course, but I was determined to be calm. 'I hear you tried to bribe Mr Taylor last night,' I said.

He shrugged. Unpleasant actions were indeed sometimes forced on men of responsibility.

'I'm going to spend my life with him,' I said, 'one way or the other . . . '

He shook his head. 'That's impossible, as you're aware . . . .'

'I'll be discreet,' I insisted. 'We'll have separate homes. If ever it becomes practical, I shall marry him . . . '

306

He shook his head. 'I could never permit that, Quincey.'

'You're jealous,' I challenged, and regretted my words at once. Another shrug – a disappointment, it seemed, that I should employ such weapons. 'Perhaps you'd tell me,' I demanded, 'exactly what you've got against him.'

'You know it all yourself. He's shady, Quincey, unprincipled – a gambler looking for the main chance. Would you really want him involved with the bank? Would you choose him as father for Jonny?'

'Whom would you prefer?' I asked. 'The Earl of Lydborough? I hear you actually accused Mr Taylor of murder . . .'

'I apologized . . . I believed what he told me, but he could have killed, Quincey. He's a brigand made good, gone respectable . . .'

'Wasn't that what your own grandfather was?' I flared.

'Yes,' he agreed, 'and I wouldn't want you marrying him either – or having a liaison that might become the talk of London. Our situation's different now. We're a family of some standing, of wealth, of power and, in consequence, of duty . . .' He paused, watching me as I glared at him. 'Oh, I can understand his appeal,' he went on. 'He's an entertaining, lively fellow. He's got inititative and drive . . . The ladies all found him most attractive. But you must break with him, Quincey.'

'I won't,' I responded. 'Howard, I love him more deeply than I've ever loved a man before.'

He glanced at me incredulously. What had love got to do with it? 'Except Richard, perhaps,' I added, 'but that was different. I was younger then . . .'

'I know it'll be hard,' he said quietly, 'but . . .'

I was on my feet. 'I won't do it, Howard!'

'Quincey there's no alternative.' Then, seeing my determination, he sighed wearily. 'Don't press me,' he said, 'to drastic measures.'

'Don't *you* press *me*, Howard Alexander,' I retorted, and walked out of 'The Room'.

Two days later, I took Taylor to Shere. We sat on the terrace and looked across the water. We walked in the woods. We rode in the forest. We made love in Richard's bed and I felt his ghost was smiling.

We behaved with care, and filled the cottage with people. James had come down with us, bringing a couple of friends and his latest *amour*, a rather pleasant girl called Diana. Bridget was there, too, as well as Nanny Roberts and Jonny.

As Taylor left my bed one night, I said: 'I hate you going.'

'I don't think I should be here in the morning,' he responded with a smile. 'Do you?'

'Can't we go away somewhere on the Continent?' I said. 'Somewhere no one knows us, so we don't have to bother about what people'll think . . . Somewhere like Paris?'

'Perhaps,' he said, but he did not really mean it. He knew we could not opt out. I knew it too, really. He began to open my door – and immediately closed it. He was very fast, a man accustomed to danger. He signalled to me to snuff the candle. I could not see him but I knew he was standing there by the door, listening. After about ten minutes, he opened it gently again and left. The next day, he told me there had been someone in the passage.

The following week we returned to London. This time, in view of Howard's hostility, he took a room in Claridges Hotel, which was close to Grosvenor Square. The mood of the family was strange. None of the women came near me – nor Howard nor Mathew. There was a sense of isolation that was unpleasant. I did not remark on it to Taylor, but I knew he felt it too.

On Friday morning of that week, at about 10.30, Frances sent me a note by cab, which was a strange method, but I realized that if she had sent a footman, my staff would know who it came from. 'Meet me in the park,' she had written. 'It's urgent . . . I'll be among the trees on the way from the Serpentine to the north carriageway. Tell your chauffeur you just feel like a stroll. He won't be able to see us. Say nothing to anyone, of course . . . '

I was amazed, both by the secrecy and by the fact that it came from Frances, whom I did not meet often except with all the family. I did not delay, however. I ordered the car – the newest model of The Leopard – and put on a hat and a light coat.

She was sitting on a bench behind some thick trees and bushes. It was a pleasant sunny morning. She smiled. 'Hallo, old thing,' she said, 'sorry about all the drama . . . Come and sit down. The going's getting hotter for you, I fear . . . Now listen: you must take

Jonny to Liverpool as fast as you can and leave for America – on any ship that's not British . . .'

'Good heavens!' I exclaimed. 'What's happened?'

'Howard's applied to the court to take Jonny under its protection as its ward . . . .'

'Can he do that?'

'On certain grounds . . . . As the only boy in the family, he's due to inherit a large fortune and a responsible position. The argument is that he should be in the care of a proper person, and certainly not a . . .'

My heart was beating fast. So this was why the family had shunned me. 'Not a what?' I asked.

'Quincey,' she said, putting her hand on mine. 'You've got to face it . . . They're alleging his mother's an immoral woman . . .'

I was utterly shocked. Howard had threatened drastic measures, but I could not believe he had applied to the court on such grounds – and even if he had, where would be his proof? She guessed what was in my mind. 'Bridget,' she said. 'She's signed an affidavit . . .'

'Bridget?' I exclaimed and felt a moment of the same terror that I had known in New York when I realized Mr Johnson was dead. If there was one person I trusted implicitly it was Bridget. 'Bridget would never do that,' I said.

'Money can buy nearly anything, old dear,' she said, 'especially in the hands of two determined women like Stella and Nina, who've always hated you. Bridget's testified that you were in the same room as Mr Taylor late at night on a number of occasions. I suppose she's telling the truth . . .'

I nodded. She smiled with compassion. 'I thought she probably was . . .'

'But surely,' I said, 'that'd be a far bigger scandal than anything that could happen if I married Taylor, or even had a discreet liaison.'

'Only for you, old thing. The family would appear as righteous, cutting off a dead branch. And it'd be quick, while the damage they think you could do with Mr Taylor would continue – insidious rumours, jokes after dinner over the port . . . That's the theory. . .'

She saw the tears in my eyes – tears of anger and humiliation. 'Now listen,' she said. 'Howard's no idea you've been warned. The hearing's not for two weeks, but if he suspected you were planning to leave the country he could ask a judge to issue a restraining order. So you've got to act before he realizes.

'It's the start of the weekend, which is a help. But what's important is to get Jonny from the house on his own without anyone suspecting. Just think of an excuse to take him out this afternoon in Mr Taylor's car – not your own. Claridges'll hire one for him. Say you're going for a drive in the park, perhaps, and on to the Zoo or to Harrods – something that won't make them suspicious. That'll buy you three hours or so. You should be well on your way to Liverpool before they realize what you've done. If you pay your driver well, he'll say what you tell him to . . . .'

'But there's Jonny's packing – and mine . . . '

'Take nothing . . . . That's vital, Quincey. And if you see Bridget before you go, behave quite normally so that she doesn't think you've scented trouble.'

'That'll be hard,' I said bitterly

'You must . . . . it's crucial . . . Once you've left port on a foreign ship, there's nothing they can do. You'll be outside the court's jurisdiction. Waste no time, old dear, and good luck. Now, stroll slowly back to your car . . . . I hope next time we meet, it'll be on a happier occasion.'

'I don't know what to say, Frances,' I said. 'Why have you done this? You've taken a big risk . . . '

'Perhaps I understand the predicament . . . . Birds of a feather . . . Off you go now . . . .'

I walked away, turned back for a moment to look at her, still sitting there on the bench. She gave me a little wave.

I drove at once to Claridges. Taylor was marvellous, as I knew he would be. 'Got to admire that Howard,' he said. 'He knows how to deal the cards, but we won't go to Liverpool. They'd catch up with us at the port. We'll go to Dover. It's much closer and the ferries leave far more often than the liners. By the time they guess we've left, we'll be on a French boat heading for Calais. We'll cross the Atlantic from Cherbourg . . . .'

The plan did not go quite as smoothly as Taylor had suggested. He had said he would call for us at 2.30. I had told Nanny, who responded coldly. She did not approve of Taylor, I knew. I wondered then if she had heard, through the servant's grapevine, of Howard's action against me. 'Jonny's to be ready to go out at 2.15,' I ordered firmly.

Bridget's behaviour to me was unchanged. 'We're going on an outing,' I said. 'I think Harrods is on the schedule, but we're in Taylor's hands.'

'You should visit the Pet Department,' she responded. 'They've some fascinating new miniature pigs – from Australia I think . . . Might interest Jonny. I'm told that Harrods'll even sell you an elephant,' she added pleasantly, 'but perhaps Jonny's still a bit young for that.' Her performance was consummate. No one would have guessed what she had done.

'I think we'll leave it a year or two before we buy an elephant,' I agreed and, with a huge effort, forced a smile. 'After he's learned to ride a bicycle, perhaps.'

We had just finished lunch when Stella arrived and suggested she should take Jonny for a drive in the park. Her performance was not as good as Bridget's. The malice was showing. She had come to gloat, even though she did not think I knew what lay in store.

'It's kind of you, Stella,' I told her, 'but Mr Taylor's invited us both for an outing.'

'Well, I'll sit down for a minute,' she said. I feared then that she might suspect what we planned. Had she guessed? Had she been warned by Bridget? Perhaps my performance had not been convincing. Stella had always seemed to have an extra sense that I did not trust. Bridget, too, had lived very close to me for a long time.

Taylor was late, which made me anxious. As ordered, Nanny brought down Jonny, dressed to go out. Her face was grim and I told her she could leave us.

'Are you taking the tricycle?' Stella asked.

'No,' I answered. 'I think we're going to Harrods, though I'm not sure what Mr Taylor has in mind. It's an outing – a surprise, he said.'

She looked at me uncertainly. Something was up, she was sure. 'I didn't see the car outside,' she said.

'Mr Taylor's collecting us,' I responded, and it was obvious that she thought this odd.

He arrived at last, only fifteen minutes late, though it had seemed like hours. If he was alarmed by the sight of Stella, sitting there so firmly, there was no sign of it in his expression. 'Why, good afternoon, Miss Alexander,' he greeted warmly. 'Have you heard? We're going on a little outing – and it's all,' he added with his eyes on Jonny, 'a big secret! I'd toyed with going to the moon, but I figured we'd be late back for supper, so I've settled for a more modest arrangement.' I wished he would stop wasting time.

'I'm consumed by curiosity, Mr Taylor,' said Stella. 'Won't you please satisfy it – in a whisper, of course?'

Taylor raised a finger to his lips, acting again apparently for Jonny's benefit. 'I said it was a secret, Miss Alexander,' he reproached. 'Jonny'll tell you about it later.' Goodness, I pleaded silently, would he not stop this aimless repartee.

'You know, you've really made me wish I was coming with you,' she said.

'Next time, Miss Alexander,' he countered with his grin, 'we'll make it a party.'

Taylor's relaxed behaviour did not remove her doubts, I could see. She was positive that something was not as it should be, but she could not put her finger on it, 'Well, are we ready?' he went on to me. 'We've got a Rolls Royce. Have you been in a Rolls Royce before, Jonny?'

'Goodbye, Jonny,' said Stella. 'Have a nice time.'

'Goodbye, Aunt Stella,' he said.

Her eyes settled on mine and I knew what she was thinking: just you wait.

At Victoria Station, Jonny became anxious. He knew that this was not the way to Harrods, that trains took you far away. He was anxious that we might be home late, that Nanny would be cross. We had changed our plans, I said. Nanny would not be concerned. We were going on a lovely trip to France, which made him sad that he had left his teddy bear behind – and he was not really consoled by the idea that we would buy another for him in Paris, a beautiful new one. He would have preferred the old one, which had lost an ear.

Behind Taylor's idle banter with Stella, he had been as worried about her as I had. From the carriage window, he watched the head of the platform until the train began to move. 'No sign of anyone,' he said to me.

At Dover we boarded a French ferry and Taylor was quiet as we stayed on deck, watching the quay before we cast off. Despite the fact that we were on a foreign vessel, he would not feel secure until we were at sea. The Alexanders had ways of evading rules when it suited them. As the sailors on the jetty were releasing the mooring lines, a police vehicle emerged from beside the harbour buildings and headed for our ship. The car came to a halt and officers got out. I never knew if we were the reason they had come. Whatever their purpose, they were too late. For there was a long blast of the ferry's siren and we were under way.

'Will we see any dolphins, Uncle Taylor?' asked Jonny.

'I don't think so, Jonny,' he said. 'Not on the way to France. When we sail for America, perhaps.'

From the deck, I watched Dover's gaunt chalk cliffs as they faded in the evening haze and wondered when I would see England again. I would return, I knew. Some kind of reconciliation with the Alexanders was inevitable. I owned nearly half the bank. Jonny would be Howard's successor at its head. But what would be the price of such artificial concord? The Alexanders were scarred veterans of many battles, as once again they had just demonstrated. It was not by chance that they had acquired such power. I sighed. Already, the bitterness was in my soul.

Chapter 15

[1]

It was on a beautiful morning in late September that the silence from London ended. I had travelled to the Alexander office in Taylor's gig, polished as always to a shine you could see your face in. There was a chill in the air and I was wearing a fur hat and a coat with a high collar. Taylor had a Studebaker and a couple of carriages, but he liked to think of me in the open gig, spanking along on its high wheels with the horse stepping out – stylish, he said, especially when I was dressed in fur.

I went down to Wall Street several times a week to read the telegrams and keep informed of the bank's affairs – encouraged by my staunch ally, Mr Etherington, whose warm and friendly greeting on the quay in New York when we had arrived is something I will never ever forget without a surge of intense gratitude. He knew few details of my break with the Alexanders, but he had realized how serious it was from a wire concerning me from London: if I was to request it, I was to be given what money I needed to live in the style he would expect of a Mrs Alexander, but I was to have no access to capital funds, nor deal on the market without Howard's personal sanction.

Mr Etherington considered the edict humiliating to me. I thanked him for his sympathy. 'You've got to obey your orders,' I said. Meanwhile, any business proposals I had were channelled to London through him, as though they were his own.

I heard regularly from James. His own position seemed unchanged. From France I had telegraphed him to dismiss Bridget instantly, give notice to the rest of the staff and close down the house. Since then we had corresponded often and he had urged repeatedly that, for the time being, I should leave all initiatives to Howard.

James knew this would be hard for me – as did Howard. I preferred pitched battles to a waiting strategy. And as the weeks went by, the inaction began to concern me – no recriminations, no demand that I should observe my duties as a mother and an

Alexander. I was being left, as Aunt Abigail put it stoutly, to stew in my own juice.

I knew it would not continue, of course. In fact, on the journey downtown on that bright fall morning, as we sped past Tiffanys and Altmans and Macys, I was uneasy. Perhaps I had developed a defensive instinct, rooted in the dangers of my position. For within an hour the speculation ended.

On arriving at Alexanders, I was greeted by the staff in their usual friendly way and I went upstairs to the visitors' room, next to Mr Etherington's, which I always used. I opened the door and stopped in sudden shock, my heart thumping – for there, behind the desk, sat Mathew.

For a few seconds he just stayed seated, the usual sardonic smile on his face. Then he rose to his feet. 'Good morning, Quincey,' he said. 'I trust you're keeping well.'

He guessed that I was wondering why no one had warned me downstairs of his arrival. 'I wanted it to be a surprise,' he said. In the fact of their silence, I knew again that familiar sense of betrayal. The Alexander power could be levered with so little effort.

'Won't you sit down?' he suggested. 'I gather this is *your* desk.' He indicated the chair behind it. I unpinned my hat and he helped me off with my coat. I took my place, as he suggested, and he sat down himself in a small armchair. 'Now, Quincey,' he said, 'I think we'd better have a little talk.'

I had made a life with Taylor in New York under conditions that were not easy, renting a large apartment on East 52nd Street, two blocks north of his brownstone house that was sumptuous, with only occasional lapses in the taste that concerned him so much.

I employed some staff, including a coloured governess for Jonny called Polly – a real fat mammy from the south, to whom the little boy became attached – and began tentatively to dig some roots. Taylor put all his carriages and cars at my disposal, together with Harry May, his coachman whom he had first met in Butte. May was a taciturn old man with a narrow craggy face who doubled as a bodyguard and carried a small gun in his waistcoat.

Our first weeks in America had been as happy as they could be under the shadow of a situation in London that was unresolved.

Howard might bide his time, but he was not going to do nothing for ever. Jonny, of course, missed England at first, but he soon made friends. Taylor and I would take him often into Central Park, which, with its zoo and bouldered hills and tree-bordered lakes, offered more scope to an agile young mind than London's formal Hyde Park. The patrolling mounted police were more exciting, too. Unlike their sedate British equivalents they rode their horses like cowboys, often at full gallop.

He got to know his cousins better, despite Polly – for there were no Pollys in their lives – and saw a lot of my parents. In fact Polly, with her ebullient sense of humour and stories of the south, soon became a favourite with the whole family – and with me, though my searing experience of Bridget had made me wary of favourites.

Life with Taylor was hardly like being married again, but it was close. When Taylor entertained, I acted as his hostess and we were often invited out together. One or two wives were a little outraged, but since we were discreet – and I maintained a separate home on some scale – we did not encounter too much criticism. Even if we had shocked the entire city, though, I would have made little change. Nothing was going to keep me far away from Taylor.

One evening we were dining with a party at the roof garden of Sherry's when I heard my name called. I turned to see the lively eyes of Mrs Schuller. 'Quincey!' she exclaimed. 'I didn't know you were in New York . . . You must come and see me and we'll talk about Berlin . . . ' And she gave me her address.

She was a welcome friend, wise and sympathetic woman that she was. When I told her about Taylor and our hasty flight from England, she broke into one of her strange giggles. 'So you're an immoral woman,' she said. 'Well, I've been an immoral woman for much of my life, and it's not too bad.'

Since leaving England, there had been time to consider my position. My weakness, the point where I was most vulnerable – as had been so painfully emphasized – was Jonny. But he was also my strength. Jonny was vital to Howard, so vital that it scared me. It seemed melodramatic to think he might try to abduct him back to England, but it was good to know that Harry May was never far from the boy whenever he left the apartment. Taylor joked about it.

Like me, he knew there were other easier weapons Howard could deploy.

I got a hint of these the day we arrived in New York. 'London have asked for a list of stock owned by Mr Taylor,' Mr Etherington told me unhappily. It was confidential information, of course, but not too hard to gain. Taylor's brokers would have it – and, more particularly, their clerks and others concerned with his business. I knew the reason, for the tactic was an old one. Alexanders would start buying into the companies Taylor was most heavily invested in, slowly building a position – perhaps dealing with other large stockholders, taking options, offering opportunities. Then suddenly they would unload. Prices would plunge. Others, knowing who was selling, would get out, too. The value of Taylor's holdings would be halved, quartered – and the pressure would then go on from creditors, associates, bankers.

That evening, I said to him: 'I think you should start going liquid, even at a loss.'

He laughed, as he always did when I spoke about the market, for my knowledge of it still intrigued him, as it had intrigued all the men I had ever met. 'This isn't business, Taylor,' I said when I saw the doubt in him. 'It's personal . . . They're out to damage you – or rather me, through you. I'm the prize – together with Jonny – and they won't mind what it costs.'

He leaned back, one leg cocked over the other in his lazy way, a grin on his face. 'Oh Taylor,' I said unhappily, 'perhaps I was a siren after all.'

He held out his arms and I ran into them like a child, dropping to my knees because he was sitting down. For a few seconds he held me very tight, then kissed me with gentle passion. 'If you're a siren, Mrs Alexander,' he said, 'then I sure succumbed to your song . . . You still make destruction seem worthwhile, but I think it can be avoided.'

I eased myself from him and looked into his eyes. 'Go a bit liquid at least, Taylor,' I said. And suddenly I remembered saying much the same words to Papa all those years before.

Mathew's sudden arrival in New York marked the end of the first phase of our new situation. 'You know,' he remarked, 'we're missing you in London.'

'What do you want, Mathew?' I asked sharply.

'No courtesies, eh?' he said with a smile. 'Howard would like to know if you've been happy.'

'What's he expect after what he's done?' I snapped. 'Goodwill?'

'He's tried to make life for you here as comfortable as possible,' he replied. 'I'm sure you'll grant him that.'

'I'll grant him nothing,' I retorted. 'Because of Howard I had to flee the country like a criminal.'

He shook his head as though in sorrow. 'About Jonny and the legal suit,' he said. 'There's room for negotiation . . . . The boy could live with you, of course, so long as you'd accept Howard as a kind of trustee. After all, you are a woman living alone,' adding pointedly, 'in a manner of speaking.'

'You mean he'd have control of Jonny?'

'A measure,' he agreed. 'Not much, providing you . . . .'

'No, Mathew,' I cut in. 'No conditions.'

He sighed. 'The realities before you are stark, Quincey . . . .'

He paused. 'Go on,' I said, the dread growing within me.

'We've several options. Your income, for a start . . . . That'll stop . . . '

'You've no right to do that,' I said.

'Right?' he inquired with that cold smile. 'Who's talking about right? I'm speaking of realities . . . '

'I'll sue,' I warned.

'That's what I mean . . . You'd be a litigant who didn't dare set foot in Britain. Your case'd be heard by a hostile judge. There'd be adjournments . . . Then appeals . . . Could go on for years . . . '

I felt very cold suddenly. 'Why should the judge be hostile?' I asked. 'My case'd stand on its merits.'

He looked at me with sad wonder. 'Judges don't favour immoral women, Quincey. There are other things we could do . . . You won't be permitted in the office here . . . James'll have to go . . . . We'll be selling the motor company . . . .'

'You can't do that – any of it!'

'The directors can do what they like. You *could* summon a

318

meeting of the shareholders, but it'd take a while and who's going to support you? As for your Mr Taylor, well, we did warn him in London . . . ' His voice softened. 'Come home, Quincey, and all will be forgiven.'

'Forgiven!' I echoed. 'How dare you, Mathew? I told Howard: I'm not parting from Taylor . . . .'

The expression of mock sadness came once more to his thin, gaunt face. 'I was afraid you might say that. Taylor said it, too . . . .'

'You've seen him?'

'Wouldn't listen . . . Perverse, like you. . . '

Elation pierced my anxiety like sunshine. That was my Taylor. 'I know he's rich,' Mathew went on. 'Doubtless he'd give you money if you want to be a kept woman. But how long will he stay rich, Quincey?'

I did not answer, staring in front of me grimly. I knew that already the Alexander holdings in his companies would be substantial. Mathew stood up. 'You can contact me at the New Plaza,' he said. 'Or here, of course. I'm sailing for home on Friday.'

At the door he turned. 'Oh, there *was* one more thing, Quincey. Jonny's a great favourite of Howard . . . You know that, don't you? He's very fond of the boy, always had great plans for him, but your stubborn refusal to be reasonable has caused him to reconsider . . . '

'Reconsider?' I asked suspiciously.

'Jonny's always been regarded as the only boy in the family, hasn't he? But in a sense that's not quite true.'

I felt as though I had suddenly been punched in the stomach. 'What in the world do you mean?'

He leaned on the back of the chair on which he had been sitting. 'Has anyone ever spoken to you of Paul Andrews?' he asked, and saw the answer on my face. 'I thought not . . . We don't speak of him much . . . . He shares a great-grandfather with Jonny . . . '

I began to tremble. 'That's impossible, Mathew,' I said. 'I'd have heard of him, surely . . . Why's Howard always talked of Jonny as the only Alexander who could succeed him?'

'Well, young Paul's not an Alexander, is he? Not in the male line. The poor lad suffers from another problem . . . . Well, so far, that is.'

He was playing with me, as he had years before over the Mr Johnson affair. 'And what's that?' I asked.

'Has anyone ever told you that Old George Alexander, our grandfather, had a mistress?' he inquired. 'I wouldn't think so . . .It was a long time ago. She was a French lady called Marie Bellon. She had his child.'

'You mean this boy's illegitimate?' I asked.

'Not young Paul, but his Great-grandmother was . . . He's got as much of old George's blood in his veins as Jonny has. And he could change his name to Alexander, couldn't he? Legally, I mean, by deed poll. Howard's thinking of adopting him . . . insurance, you could say . . . .If he does, he'll leave him some stock in the bank and wants me to do the same. What'd you do if you were me?'

I did not answer at once. Then I asked quietly. 'How old's this boy?'

'Fourteen.' He could see I had absorbed the significance, but he spelled it out. 'He'd be well established in the bank by the time Jonny was old enough to join it, wouldn't he? Means another battle, I suppose, like Howard and Richard all over again. Not to be desired, would you say?'

I stared at him almost without seeing him. 'You're trying to force me to choose, aren't you?' I said. 'Taylor or my son?'

'That's always been the choice,' he answered. 'Ever since Oklahoma.' And he closed the door behind him.

I did not see Mathew again before he sailed, but I had a note from him, brought by Mr Etherington the morning after his departure. It just said: 'Dear Quincey, Oh what a pity — Yours, Mathew.'

'I've been told to give you until Monday,' said Mr Etherington, 'then I must act.'

'You mean stop my income?'

'And bar the bank's premises to you. Mathew said they'd be dismissing James Stratton when he got home, and selling Mason Motors.'

I was silent. 'I suppose they're still buying into Mr Taylor's companies?' I asked.

He nodded. 'Much more heavily now.' He heaved a big sigh. 'I fear that's not all, Quincey. Mathew's got interested in your

320

father . . .'

'My father?' I asked nervously. 'I don't suppose he's holding much of a portfolio.'

'Not his stocks, Quincey, his clients, who might be open to persuasion – and creditors . . . You know how it'll be done, how I'll have to see that it's done . . . Better terms, better deals, the chance of favours, tip-offs, not even directly from us . . . nothing overt or clumsy, but the message'll get through . . . I can't tell you how I hate this business, Quincey. In all my years as a banker, I've never been involved in a personal vendetta on this scale. I thought of refusing but, well, they'll get someone to do it, won't they, and if I'm in charge at least we'll know what's happening . . .'

Impulsively, I pressed his hand. 'I owe you so much, Mr Etherington,' I said. 'The debt's getting big . . . tell me, couldn't I raise a loan against my shares in the bank?'

He shook his head. 'That crossed my mind, too, so I checked. Under the Articles, you can't pledge your stock because you can't sell it – at least not without offering it to the family first . . .'

'Which is what Howard's always wanted me to do,' I said grimly, 'but I'm not going to, Mr Etherington. I'll die before I let Howard have a single share.'

Mrs Schuller's eyes sparkled from across the luncheon table as she listened. 'It'd be funny, wouldn't it,' she said, 'if it wasn't so serious. In England you're a rich woman. Here, you're a pauper.' She giggled. 'I'll see you don't starve, Quincey.'

'It'd all stop if I gave up Taylor,' I ruminated gloomily. 'They'd take the pressure off him then, wouldn't they? Is it fair of me?'

'Have you asked him?' she mocked. 'Unless, that is, you're having second thoughts yourself . . .' She laughed at my appalled response. 'I didn't think you were,' she said.

'It'd kill me to leave him,' I admitted. 'I'd die . . . That's how I feel, quite literally, but there's Jonny to think about, too . . .'

'Oh fiddlesticks, Quincey,' she said in irritation. 'That's like speaking of Little Lord Fauntleroy. You stick to your guns,' she added firmly. 'However, I do see you're in a bit of a pickle . . . I think that for a while you should do nothing, see what happens . . . . For the time being I'll lend you what you need. Then, if

Alexanders do anything drastic ... Well, we'll have to think again.'

[2]

Two weeks later, like the coming of a sudden storm, the market broke – and Howard acted. He ruined Taylor in four days flat. Sooner or later he would have struck anyway, but the Crash of 1907, as history was to know it, made it simple for him – and cheap.

Alerted by me, Taylor had taken defensive measures. He had sold some options, which meant that the shares were not traded in the market, with the resultant drag on prices, and reduced some of his borrowings. In fact, though, he thought he could ride an Alexander attack. He would just hold on, he said. In time, the value of the stock would rise again. But he had not predicted the torrential conditions in which he would have to fight for survival. Nor had anyone else. Not even J.P. Morgan.

It started, as storms do, with a ripple, with an attempt by speculators to manipulate the stock of a copper company – which was a bit ironic, since Taylor had made his fortune out of copper. The operation misfired and a small bank, which had funded it, was forced to close. The snowball began to roll, for that little bank was in debt, too, to other banks, which had loans from even more banks.

Suddenly, right across America, the rumours grew. Banks became suspect and depositors in their thousands tried to withdraw their cash – and the banks could not cope, as they never can, under a wholesale demand for repayment.

Within hours, in many US cities, angry crowds were gathering in the streets outside banks that had locked their doors and the stock market sank like a lump of concrete in the Hudson.

Howard was relentless. He knew Taylor's bankers and the stocks that were his collateral. Under pressure from London – and in those taut days, not much was needed – the prices of Taylor's holdings were forced even lower than the market had taken them

322

and his loans were called in without notice.

For Taylor it was the end of another fortune. By the time J.P. Morgan checked the panic by announcing a rescue operation by the biggest financiers in the country, it was all over for the man I loved. Everything went — the brownstone house on East 50th, the carriages and the Studebaker, even Harry May. Taylor moved into the apartment of a friend who was away.

'Give me a week or two,' he said to me with a grin, 'and we'll be back up there again.' But the crisis, though its peak had passed, had left a mood of fear and caution. And the word was out, too: it was known that Alexanders would not look kindly on anyone who supported Taylor. This might not have deterred the big banks, but it had their sympathy. If one of their womenfolk, with a big holding, had done what I had, they would have responded in the same way.

They were terrible weeks that followed — similar in many ways to the period following Papa's débâcle. To start with Taylor continued going to the office, but gradually there was no longer anything to do. The rejection he encountered daily from previous friends began to sap his confidence, if not his courage. He became like a fighter who had been knocked down time after time, who had a broken nose and two black eyes and still managed to stagger to his feet and go on hitting — but, though I admired the bravery and suffered every blow that struck him, there was no doubt that he was losing. He still wore the fancy clothes, but the spirit was being eroded and, with it, the style that was vital to him.

The distress was hard for me to bear, for the solace I could give him was so limited. The tension was always there in him, which is why he began to drink. It eased the strain, like making love. There was a new element of need in that, too, and I was gratified there was. It was a contribution I could make, like no other kind of sharing, but it could only be a balm. It did not change the facts.

'I've hit harder times than this, Mrs Alexander,' he would insist. 'You watch — I'll clamber out of the pit.' He spoke to convince me, as though I was doubting.

'You're rolling with the punch, Taylor,' I assured him, using one of his sayings. 'You've got your hands over your ears as he batters you and you're just waiting for the opening . . . ' Again, I was employing his words.

'You believe I'll get the opening, don't you, Quincey?' he said. There was no appeal in his tone. It was more an assessment of me, of my courage.

'The opening always comes,' I answered, quoting him still. 'You just have to be ready for it – one quick jab and come out fighting, and then wham!' And I punched the air in front of me.

He laughed. 'I'm glad I'm not having to square up to you, Quincey,' he said. Suddenly, his mood changed and he became very serious. 'Do you think maybe we should part for a while?'

'Part?' I echoed in horror.

'Just till I get back up there and come for you in a carriage with Harry May at the reins . . . . Just for the moment I'm a liability. Not just to you, but to the boy as well . . . .'

It was the exact opposite of my question to Mrs Schuller. He was not just being selfless. He hated me seeing him as he was. In front of me, he only wanted to be rich and powerful.

I put my arms round his neck. 'Taylor,' I said, 'You're still the same man who had the nerve to demand a million dollars from me in Paulina. I love you, Taylor . . . .I love you when you've got the world at your feet and I love you when it's trying to trample you into the ground.'

He eased me from him and looked at me, his eyes soft. 'You're a great lady, Mrs Alexander,' he said. 'I'm a lucky feller.'

'Sit down at the table just for a moment,' I said. 'I've got an idea.' Suspicion came into his eyes. He knew what I was going to suggest, but I did so all the same. 'What if we raised some money,' I said. 'Privately, I mean. Just a few thousand dollars. You could get started again, deal on the market a bit.' I was thinking of Mrs Schuller, of course, though I had not mentioned it to her.

He shook his head. 'Thank her very much,' he said, 'but I wouldn't feel right taking that kind of help from a woman.'

'You took it from old Mrs Blackstone at the Splendide Hotel,' I reminded him.

'That was different. I was a kid.'

'I'm taking it. It's only a loan, after all.'

'You can pay it back. With you it's just a matter of geography.' He did not appear upset. 'It was a kind thought and I appreciate it, but no . . . .'

I gave up my apartment so that my living standard dropped with Taylor's. I went to stay in Brooklyn with my parents, keeping Polly only of my staff to look after Jonny while I helped Papa with his business.

The pressure was on him too, and in a sense he was in deeper trouble than Taylor, who I knew would get back somehow – not all the way, perhaps, but off the ground. Even without the Alexander intervention Papa would have been in trouble from the crash. In fact, though the crisis marked the end of an era – and in time the unfettered power of the great financial moguls – it did not last for long. The Morgan rescue operation gave strength to the market. Gradually confidence returned.

Even so, Papa's clients had suffered, and all had become as nervous as cats. The message had reached them: they would be well advised, advantaged even, to seek new brokers. Certainly, scorched as they had been, they wanted no big enemies.

Suddenly, too, Papa's own loans from a Brooklyn bank were revoked. I called on the manager as Mrs Alexander, but I made no headway. 'I'd like to accommodate your father,' he said, 'but I've got my orders.'

I wrote to Mr Thompson at Morgans, my old adversary from Berlin and Papa's one-time friend. He invited me to lunch at the Café Savarin, but revealed an eager partiality for twenty-eight-year-old widows that I had not suspected; and, much though I needed his help, I was not on offer.

As always, I fell back on Mrs Schuller. She, too, could be persuasive. The old clients were replaced by new ones, including herself. When I asked her for the kind of help I had hoped that Taylor might accept – just so that I could support Papa's small holdings in the market until prices rose – she introduced me to Diamond Jim Brady, one of Wall Street's most colourful figures, who wore big diamonds instead of buttons. Miraculously, he said, he had gone liquid just before the bottom had fallen out of the market and had a lot of cash around.

'I'm bullish,' he said to me, 'buying . . . I'd have said that Mrs Alexander was a pretty good place to put my money, wouldn't you? Some of it, leastways.'

'I can offer no security,' I reminded him.

'It's a personal loan,' he said, 'and you personally will answer for repayment. I'd reckon that was a pretty safe investment.'

I managed to keep Papa afloat and urged Taylor to let me speak to Diamond Jim for him, as well, but he refused as he had before. If he was going to borrow, it would be against his own collateral.

The passing weeks were marking him badly now. The rock was being chipped. He had always been a drinker – proud, like so many men, that he would take it without being too affected. Now, just a couple of times, I had found him so drunk that he had fallen on the bed and slept in his clothes. It was not like the Taylor I knew.

Several times a week, we dined together in the apartment he had borrowed – as we did one evening early in December. I enjoyed cooking for him and often, as on that occasion, I would let myself in with my own key before he got home.

'How did things go then?' I asked brightly when he returned, busying myself cutting carrots so that I did not have to look at him. I had to ask the question, though I dreaded the answer.

'Usual,' he said. 'I met McKinley, though. Remember me telling you about McKinley? He said he'd got something coming up – a copper-mining interest. Just up my street, he said.'

It was his stock answer to my stock question. The names just changed. It was better than saying that absolutely nothing had happened. I was never quite sure whether he was pretending only to me or to himself as well. 'Sounds like the opening,' I said, referring to the moment for the fast jab when he would come out fighting, 'like it's always happened before.' That was what we both clung to. He had lost fortunes before and come back, so he could do it again. But I had never before been there to watch, and this made a huge difference to him. Oh how he wanted to bring me back some small prize – something really solid that could be a first step back to the time when again he could excel before me.

'It's time I got a good hand,' he said. 'Maybe McKinley's the ace.' He sat down at the kitchen table and I poured him a drink. I was extra sensitive to his moods now and I detected that this evening's was different. Something had happened during the day that he had not told me about. It was not that good or that bad but McKinley, I

326

suspected, was just a smoke screen that he had put up to give himself time to think. I knew better than to press him.

He took a drink and put the glass down. 'Want to hear a joke?' he asked.

'If it's funny,' I answered carefully.

'Oh, it's funny,' he said with a cool smile. 'Mrs Alexander, I'm free to marry — least, I will be . . . .'

I stared at him in disbelief, trying to contain my excitement. There had been a note of sarcasm in his tone that made me distrust it. 'It's not a joke, is it?' I asked. 'You wouldn't joke about a thing like that, Taylor?'

He shook his head. 'It's the truth. Enid wrote me today . . .wants a divorce. Knows there isn't a quarter of a million any longer . . . Jesus!' he said. 'A quarter of a million! That was a different world, wasn't it? No, Enid wants it for herself . . . There's a man in mind and she's pregnant . . . . She's gone to Nevada, where they divorce you fast . . . Ironic, isn't it?'

'Ironic?' I exclaimed, 'Taylor, it's the most marvellous news I've ever had!' And I rushed into his arms.

He held me for a moment. 'Not so fast, Sugar,' he said gently. 'I don't have the money to marry you — remember?'

'What's money matter, you silly old idiot?' I said. 'Why, we could go back to England, couldn't we? If we were married, that'd weaken their hand, surely. They'd have to lift the embargo if we were married, wouldn't they?'

He eased me from him, looking into my eyes. 'Sounds simple, doesn't it?'

'It *is* simple,' I said.

'I don't think I was made to be kept by my wife,' he remarked.

'Taylor,' I scolded. 'This is not time for that kind of nonsense. I shan't be keeping you. I'll lend you a little capital . . . You'll make another fortune, and repay me every cent you've borrowed . . . Oh, Taylor, I've never wanted anything so much in all my life . . .Please, Taylor . . . '

'We'll think about it,' he said.

We were married secretly, for when at last my euphoria subsided, I realized care was needed. For the first time since my bitter struggle

327

with the Alexanders I would no longer be an immoral woman, but they had evidence that I had been. What would a court make of that? I needed the best legal advice in London. Whatever I felt about the Alexanders, I did not underestimate them.

So the wedding was a quiet one in the Catskill Mountains, at a little Dutch church near my uncle's farm outside Denning. All the family came up to attend it – including my mother in her wheel-chair – and even Mrs Schuller. 'I want to see this Taylor make an honest woman of you,' she said. Jonny came, too, with Polly, though I do not think he realized what was happening.

There was snow on the ground, but the morning of the wedding was fine and crisp and we drove away after the reception in my uncle's home to spend a few days alone at a mountain inn. 'Take some getting used to,' Taylor said, 'being Mr and Mrs Taylor – got a sobering ring about it.'

It was a short but ecstatic time, with walks and snowballing and roaring log fires. Then we went back to New York.

Just for the moment, until I heard from London, we agreed that we should continue living as before and my parents' home should remain my address.

It was a nervous, uncertain period for me as I waited for news from the English lawyers, but it came to an end at last about ten days after we had returned to the City – and in a manner that was devastatingly unexpected. I arrived at the apartment in the evening, a bit later than usual, when Taylor was sure to be there. But as I opened the door with my key, the place seemed oddly quiet. All the lights were on, though, which suggested that Taylor must be home.

'Taylor,' I called out, but there was no reply. I moved uneasily towards the living-room door.

Cautiously, I opened it. Taylor was not in the room, but sitting in an armchair, reading a newspaper, was Mathew. He put down the paper. 'Good evening, Quincey,' he said. 'Always popping up like a jack-in-the-box, aren't I?'

I was scared, as always when Mathew was unexpected. 'What are you doing here, Mathew?' I asked. 'How did you get in? Where's Taylor?'

He sighed. 'Gone, I fear, Quincey.'

'Gone? How do you mean – gone?'

'Skedaddled.'

Ice was in my stomach. 'He can't have gone,' I insisted.

'He asked me to give you this note.'

I did not believe what was happening. I was asleep and dreaming. I would wake up and Taylor would be there as usual. It was not me who opened the envelope that Mathew passed to me. It was someone I was watching. 'Dearest Mrs Alexander,' he had written, using the name he had not dropped with our marriage. 'Sorry, but I'm being an ornery horse again because I figure it's the best for all of us. Try to understand. Love – Taylor. P.S. By the way, they don't know we're married. Thought you might like to keep that up your sleeve for now.'

I felt nothing – except the cold. Outside in the street the temperature was under twenty. It could have been as low in the apartment. I was shaking, numb. I knew what had happened, but I had no emotion, no tears, and by then not even anger. 'How much did it cost you?' I asked at last.

'A hundred and fifty thousand,' Mathew answered evenly.

'Did he drive a hard bargain?' I felt oddly remote – curious.

'You could say so. At first, he wouldn't entertain it . . . Said you were worth more than money to him . . . Nothing's worth more than money, of course – contradiction in terms – but it may be some solace . . . '

'Oh, it is,' I replied. My tone was not sarcastic, for there was still no emotion in me – just deadness. 'You went in too low, I suppose,' I said. 'Did he talk of a figure at which he'd deal? A million, perhaps? He liked the sound of a million.'

'No, he told me I was insulting him.' There was no concern in Mathew as he answered, but no antipathy either. He was just giving a report, as he might of any transaction.

'So you doubled the offer?' I suggested. 'What did you start off at? Fifty?' I was dead on, for I had planned strategy with them often enough. 'No point in going up by ten or twenty, so you went straight to the hundred. That ought to make him sit up, you thought, given his situation . . . A man like that – a brigand, as Howard called him? Why, he could do a lot with a hundred grand, couldn't he . . . ?'

'What's the point of this, Quincey?' Mathew inquired coldly. He

329

wanted the business over.

'Because I'd like to know my value in the market!' I snapped. 'Did he weaken at a hundred?'

He shook his head. 'Not noticeably.'

'So you went to a hundred and fifty and that began to tempt him . . . You could see he was dealing so you knew you could stick – and offer favours instead of cash. You'd broken him, as he was only too aware, and you could help him back, as you pointed out . . . . What'd have happened if he'd kept his nerve? Would you have gone much higher?'

'Oh yes,' Mathew answered. The half smile I loathed came to his face suddenly. 'You were cheap at the price.'

I knew a moment of hatred then. Still nothing violent. Cold, in fact, like everything inside me. 'One day,' I thought,'you'll find I wasn't cheap at the price, that there are some things worth more than money.'

'Where is he?' I asked.

'On his way to the West Coast . . . I saw him off myself from Grand Central Station . . . .'

'Why, Mathew?' I asked. 'Why all this? Wasn't Paul Andrews up to the mark on closer inspection?'

He shrugged, his clothes as always seeming too large. 'We'll take him into the bank when he's old enough. We're going to need other young blood as well as Jonny . . . '

'Insurance against a wayward mother?' I asked bitterly.

'This situation had to stop, Quincey. Your Mr Taylor was the cause of it. Now that he's gone you can come home . . . .'

'So everything'll be hunky-dory again?' I mocked icily.

'You could say that . . . The legal action'll be withdrawn.'

I looked at him. He had not enjoyed what he had done. I rather wished he had, but there was no real malice there. Nor had it troubled him. No sympathy, nor regret at the pain it might cause. It had just been a job, like buying a parcel of stock. I turned and walked out of the apartment, stopped a cab and went to Brooklyn.

I did not sleep that night, mainly because my mind was too active. The pain was slow in coming, partly because of shock, but mainly because I could not believe it. I could not accept that Taylor was no longer in my life, that in only a few months the Alexanders had systematically ruined him and then bought him. I could even see Howard issuing the order in 'The Room' — sitting back in his chair, hardly moving — as I had seen him give so many orders. And Mathew had obeyed. I wondered if he had taken a note, written it down, perhaps as an item on a list of things he had to do, so that he did not forget. My response was still unfeeling — intellectual, even self-mocking.

Dawn was just starting to break, the sky lightening behind the curtains, when the effect of the chloroform began slowly to wear off. Then the need for him pierced the stupor in which I had been enveloped like a cloud since I had read his note — not too sharply at first, but it was a harbinger, I knew, of an agony that was to come; an agony, I knew already, that would be greater than anything I had yet experienced — worse, far worse even than I had endured after Richard's death. I was capable now of more pain. For each great pain increases the capacity for the next. I was older, too; more developed. I had borne a child. The hurt in youth is acute, but not so deep as later it can become. And there was another difference: God had taken Richard from me. Taylor had left of his own accord. Taylor was there, still living, somewhere on a train, getting farther from me all the time. But there on earth, on the American continent. Taylor I loved as I would never love again.

I did not cry — I was beginning to feel the wound, the humiliation, the remorse — but no tears came. It was like injury in an accident. Women can bear physical pain without tears. Women may scream in childbirth, but they do not cry. Perhaps, too, I feared that once the weeping started, it would take a long time to stop. And how would I explain it all to Jonny? Literally how? Could I put it into words? What would be the effect on him of all the sobbing?

I left Brooklyn that day. I did not go far. Just to Long Beach, where I had gone often as a child. There were miles of sand, deserted because it was December, and stark trees bending before the icy wind, and huge angry white Atlantic rollers, and one hotel that I had thought might not be open. But it was. They never closed, they said.

That is where I bore it — though the full impact did not come for several days, and after that was a long torture I will never ever forget until the moment of my death. I knew the time only by the light. I did not sleep. I wept and wept and wept. Every day I walked for miles, breasting gales, tears streaming endlessly down my cheeks. I ate little and spoke to no one. I thought of dying, of walking into that cold sea and allowing myself to be swept out to oblivion by those huge withdrawing waves. But even in those depths of deep despair I knew there was Jonny — and I felt, too, the start of the anger that a doctor might have said was the beginning of recovery. Just then it dominated me — anger at everyone: Howard, Mathew, Nina, Stella, Taylor. Oh, Taylor. I had known him from the start for what he was. In a sense I forgave him, making the excuses for his conduct that rejected women always do, accepting that he had left because he could not stay with me as a husband who was poor. This was a brief moment of hope. Perhaps he would return once he had made his fortune with the money Mathew had given him. But even then I knew I was reaching for the sky, conjuring dreams that had no roots in any reality. And all the time images of him haunted me — insistent against my efforts to banish all thoughts of him from my mind. Kicking his feet in the stream; waiting, legs apart, on the platform at Paulina; playing cards with his boots up in O'Reilly's Hotel; acting a man of repute at my own ...ner table; making love in the moonlight — even the bad moments, like the time he had ordered me off the rig; or returned so often to the apartment with that look of rejection on his face.

The anger turned to bitterness, to a yearning for revenge, and this, I knew, I must control — for that was the way to self-destruction. I walked faster along the beach. I began to eat again — and even to sleep. I talked to the few people I encountered, mainly staff in the hotel. I was emerging, renascent, from the ashes. Someone different. Well, a bit different — cauterized, the anger cold once more, my thinking more rational. I did not seek revenge now. I sought protection. I felt used, exploited. My rights had been mocked by Mathew with his talk of realities. There must be no more mockery, nor exploitation; never again must I have to fear the British courts or flee the country, or consider a threat to Jonny's future; my son must follow Howard unchallenged, as head of Alexanders — all of which meant one thing:

I must win control of the bank

But how? As I strode through the soft sands of Long Beach, with those bitter winds tearing at my hair, I considered the situation of the stock. This was where the essence of power resided and I owned a lot of it, which gave me an obvious base from which to manoeuvre. My holding was matched by Howard and Mathew together, and between us we owned nearly all the shares in Alexanders – but not all. There were a few, a tiny percentage, owned by others – so few that I had never thought to explore who their owners might be. Now, though, they loomed importantly in my mind. Would they sell to me? If not, could I create conditions in which they would always vote with me?

How could I be certain? Then one of Papa's sayings from way back came into my mind. I was standing, looking out to sea, waves reaching towards my feet, the dampness in the shore fading each time with their retreat. 'There's always a key to a man,' he had said, 'and if you can find it and tap it, he'll nearly always deal. With a rich man, it may be a son . . . With others, it may be ambition or status . . . The motives are legion – guilt, women, God, fear, ideals, greed . . . Search for the key, Quincey . . . . like a terrier in the sand.' Water swirled round my ankles from a sudden, larger wave, penetrating my boots, soaking my stockings. I hardly noticed. What was the key to those few stockholders who had just began to interest me – the key that Papa had said was always there?

What, for that matter, was the key to Howard and Mathew? For if this could be identified and touched, was their own stock – or the use of it – as unobtainable as I had thought?

If Papa was right, I swore to the wind, then I would find that key in all of them. I would use any means, any weapon. Nothing, but nothing, would be sacred.

That was to be the plan, though as yet I had no idea as to how it would be executed. I did not know the facts. But then, as I turned on that December day and walked back along the beach in boots half-filled with water I hardly cared. For I had acquired a sense of purpose, an aim, so determined that I knew it would dwarf any other aspect of my life.

When I returned to my parents' home in Brooklyn, there was a letter from the London lawyers waiting for me. My marriage made all the difference, they advised. No court now would insist on

Jonny being its ward.

It was almost Christmas, which I intended to spend with the family in Brooklyn, but I gave Howard good notice of my return, telegraphing him that we would sail in January. Then I wrote him a letter saying that I was grateful for what he had done, for clearly I had been in a temporary state of madness. The lying words came easily off my pen. Truth did not matter. Nothing mattered except my plan. I wrote to James, too, to start assembling the facts that I would need.

We had a good Christmas, but we had known better. I tried to enter into the spirit, even being generous to Laura. But my heart was not in it, I had returned from the dead, I was too serious – dedicated, as I had now become. It was only when the liner was steaming down the Hudson, for what was likely to be a stormy crossing, that I felt alive once more.

Part 5

January 1908

Chapter 16

[1]

It was raining as we docked in Liverpool. He was standing on the quay, unmoving as usual, beneath a black dripping umbrella. None of the family was with him, and he looked a lonely figure. His presence there was an indication of what lay ahead. He had travelled from London to meet me — taking the trouble, in short, that was appropriate to the status that I had regained.

'Look, Mama,' Jonny exclaimed. 'Isn't that Uncle Howard there?'

'That's right, darling,' I said. 'That's Uncle Howard.'

I had looked forward to the voyage. I had planned to speak to Jonny of the dolphins, as Taylor had done, and of whales and icebergs, on which I had informed myself. I had hoped to arrange a visit to the bridge, which I had avoided on previous crossings since, unmarried as Taylor and I had been, it seemed unwise to ask favours of the captains.

My plans had gone awry, for we had both been sick as dogs — and Ireland had been in sight by the time the gale had eased.

With the resilience of the young, Jonny had recovered fast. 'That was a bad time, wasn't it, Mama?' he said, as if we were soldiers who had survived a battle. He had been buoyant with excitement as the liner steamed up the Mersey and was rewarded by the sight of Howard's familiar figure.

Jonny hurried down the gangway and ran ahead of me. Howard lifted him up in his usual way — one of the few extrovert actions he ever performed, which is why it always seemed awkward. His pleasure in the boy was obvious — and reciprocated.

As I approached, his look was questioning. How bitter would I feel? 'Welcome home, Quincey,' he said.

'Good morning, Howard,' I answered, and kissed him on the cheek — what he would expect after my letter, surely. All the same, for all that had happened between us, it was a strange sensation to kiss an acknowledged enemy.

He had reserved a whole first class compartment so that we

could talk freely without being overheard. I knew he wanted me to be the first to speak of what had happened in America, but I avoided the subject. 'You must understand,' he said at last, 'how much I regretted what we had to do.'

'I'm sure you acted as you considered best,' I said, adding quickly: 'How's the yield holding up at Paulina?'

'Growing daily,' he answered. 'They've brought in three new wells . . . . There've been strikes by other people, too . . . .'

So it was becoming a boom town, as Taylor and I had pondered. 'What about the Romanians?' I asked. 'Are they renewing their contract?'

He nodded. 'After Paulina, the pressure was taken off. The point was gone. We were strong enough to survive without them . . . .It's proved a great success, Quincey . . . .'

He was complimenting me; placating me, one could say.

'Nina's arranged a reception for you this evening,' he said. 'I hope you won't be too exhausted by the journey.'

I smiled to myself. A triumphant return, as though I was a successful Roman general. 'That's kind of her,' I said.

It was all very English. Despite what had happened between us, despite his regret, this was the man who had destroyed a part of me, like a surgeon taking off an arm. I would never be the same again. But we had interests in common and, on the surface at least, Howard wanted a return to the status quo, to apparent normality. He had a need, too, to appear magnanimous in victory. He had brought me to my knees and he sought, as the whole family would, to make amends – but this was one thing I would never grant them. He could have his status quo, though – for the time being.

That evening, I stood in the doorway of the big drawing-room in what had once been Uncle's house. All the family were there, as well as a few close friends. As soon as she saw me, Nina left the person she was speaking to and, forcing a smile to that severe face, came to greet me. She kissed me on both cheeks and said: 'How nice to see you, Quincey.'

Stella joined her. 'How good to have you both back,' she said. I wondered what the price had been of Bridget's betrayal. Less, I supposed, than was needed to buy Taylor. Like a store, really. Gold

338

fetched a higher sum than silver plate.

'I've missed London,' I told them. I did not smile. I was playing a woman who had been deeply hurt but realized it was wise to let bygones be bygones.

'Not bad,' said Frances, who had been watching, as I kissed her, too. 'No one would know that you hated their very souls.'

'Not hated,' I responded. 'That's too strong . . . Almost anything's too strong . . . .'

'I felt for you,' she went on, 'as the news filtered back . . . . I wished I could have done something to help . . . .'

'You did more than you should have done,' I said.

She laughed, and I thought what a lively, pretty woman she was. 'Anyway, you're home now,' she said, with light sarcasm, 'in the bosom of your family . . . Come to tea tomorrow and tell me all about it. Look at Emmeline there . . . . Grown into quite a beauty, hasn't she?'

Howard's eldest daughter was approaching us with leisured movements, marked a little by the self-consciousness of youth. At eighteen she had become willowy and graceful, though a little tall for a girl, due presumably to her father's height. Also she had inherited his intense brown eyes that, though often troubled and almost sinister in him, were striking in her young face. 'Hallo, Aunt Quincey,' she said with an easy smile. She was the only one of the younger generation who had dared to speak to me. What could you say, after all, to an aunt who was a scarlet woman? In fact, I soon discovered, she sought in me an ally – which had a certain irony. 'I'd love to come and have a talk with you, if you didn't mind,' she said. 'Papa's being very difficult just at present. I want a career – in the bank, if it's practical. He doesn't think it's proper for a woman, he says, but look how successful *you've* been . . . .'

'I'm not sure he'd agree with that,' I said.

'We're at the start of a new age, aren't we, Aunt Quincey?' she asserted, the faith flowing in her eyes. 'I mean the suffragettes are doing sterling work, don't you think?'

'I'm not sure that chaining themselves to railings and blowing up post-boxes'll have the results they hope.'

She smiled suddenly. 'Aren't you being a bit cautious, Aunt Quincey, for a woman who struck oil in Oklahoma? I've joined them, you know – the suffragettes, I mean – but don't tell Papa, will you?'

I smiled at her fervour. It made me feel quite old. 'Come and see me whenever you like.'

I was happy to be an ally of Emmeline. I hoped, too, for closer relations with Frances. Both would be friends in the enemy camp. They could be a vital source of information. There were other ways, too, they might serve 'The Plan', as James and I had called it in our letters. Nine months ago I would have have been appalled by this calculated thinking, but I was appalled by nothing now. My morality had been stripped from me in an apartment in New York and taken a train to California.

Mathew wandered up to talk to me and, even to him, I was agreeable though distant. I thought with a grim smile of the conferences that would have preceded my return. How should they all behave, in view of my stock and my son? Mathew, who had seen me mortified, would have judged my conciliatory and deceitful letter as a tactic. Howard would have urged that my gesture should be welcomed even if it was insincere. When my wounds had healed it could provide a bridge to true *rapprochement*.

So the policy had been to please me. James had been reinstated. Plans to sell the motor company had been abandoned. Nina had even invited old Mr Mason to her reception, as a sop to me.

I exchanged a few warm words with him. 'What news of Steven and Martin?' I asked.

'Steven's still alive,' he said. 'At the new track at Brooklands the other day, he had a burst tyre when he was going at over a hundred miles an hour. He still won, though Lord knows how even though it was near the finish. It's a miracle that he survived at all, that he ever survives the way he drives. That's how he wins, though, why his reputation never stops growing . . . .'

'It's a sad business, Mr Mason,' I said.

'He'd be a great asset,' he agreed. 'What I always hoped – but it's something that can never be.'

I squeezed his arm in sympathy and looked round the room. Had I convinced them, I wondered? Would even Mathew have guessed the scale of what I intended?

James and I did not waste time. The next morning, we had our first meeting about 'The Plan' in the office of my home in Grosvenor Square, which he had prepared for my arrival, employing staff — including some of the old servants like Cook and a couple of maids — and Liza who, in addition to her secretarial duties, would control domestic affairs until I had appointed a housekeeper.

It was with the old sense of challenge, of excitement, that I studied the list that James had handed me. It consisted of the names and addresses of the seven people who owned shares in Alexanders. It was written on a sheet of my own notepaper and I held it with delicate care, for already it had for me a symbolic quality. One day I might frame it and hang it on the wall.

My own name was there, of course, as were Howard's and Mathew's but my attention was concentrated on the other four stockholders. They did not own many shares, as I knew — just 60,000 between them, a mere 6 per cent of the total — but they could be vital to me. All were women and I had heard of none of them, not even a Margaret Alexander, who was the most important of them, since she owned half the stock that interested me so much.

'That's Aunt Margaret,' James explained.

'Your aunt?'

'And Richard's of course . . . Uncle's sister, but they loathed each other, so she never saw the family . . . Lived in Ireland . . . Engrossed by her horses . . . I went over to visit her once after Mama died. I knew from the letters I'd found among Mama's things that she felt my grandfather had been unfair to her after the elopement. They were sisters, of course, and quite close. She was friendly enough but I didn't have four legs, so she wasn't very interested.'

'I wonder why Richard never mentioned her,' I mused.

'I don't suppose it crossed his mind. He hardly knew her . . . None of us did.'

'But she's got 30,000 shares.'

'So few that they were irrelevant . . . Until Uncle died his control was absolute — just as yours and Howard's is today, if you choose it to be . . .'

I studied the others on the list. Bettine Laffont, who lived in Paris; Helga Petersen, whose address was in Stockholm; Jocelyne Andrews — presumably Paul Andrews's mother — whose home was near Lyons.

'Who are they all?' I asked.

'Descendants of Marie Bellon . . . She was my grandfather's mistress for years . . .'

'You mean he actually left shares in the bank to his mistress?' I inquired incredulously. That was something Mathew had not told me.

'He didn't intend to originally. He planned to leave both his daughters 30,000 shares each outright . . . I think he wanted them to have some independence of the trust even though the trustees had discretion to provide for their needs; then, when Mama eloped, as you know, he was so bitter that he cut her out of his will and left her shares instead to Marie . . .'

'Wasn't that a strange thing to do?'

'It happens . . . He was an old man and still loved her — *and* Thérèse, her daughter . . . *His* daughter, of course . . . It was romantic — except to Mama and me. He met Marie when he was in his early twenties, just before he made his fortune. She was seventeen, a dancer, so she was hardly an ideal wife for an ambitious young man, set on founding a dynasty . . .'

'He really was an old rogue, wasn't he?'

James gave a tolerant shrug and pointed to the list in my hand. 'They're the result — Marie's grandchildren, except young Helga who's the next generation . . .'

I thought for a moment. 'Surely,' I asked, 'Howard must have considered negotiating with them after Richard died? He wouldn't have had to take nearly so much account of me . . .'

'You don't understand,' said James. 'They've always embarrassed the family, so they've just paid up the dividends and pretended Marie never existed . . . The others didn't like being treated like lepers. They deeply resented both Uncle and Howard . . .'

'Then that should give us an advantage,' I suggested.

He grinned. 'It should,' he agreed, 'but Howard's shrewd, as you've discovered often enough. As a woman with an equal holding, he guessed he could control you, as by and large he could. Once he finds out what he's facing now, though . . . Well, you know Howard . . . He wouldn't be deterred by past resentments. As Richard always said, if he had to, he'd deal with the Devil.'

[3]

The road to Old Kilcullen was narrow, but, even on that wet February morning, it was picturesque. Fields stretched away on either side of us across Kildare's green hills, broken into sections by walls of old grey stone. The cab we had hired at Sallins, where we had left the train from Dublin, had made good progress. It was not yet midday. As we came to the brow of a rise in the road, James said: 'You can see the house now, up there on the high ground near the wood.' It was about a mile away – white and rambling under a slate roof – lying at the end of a long drive between paddocks, enclosed by timber fences.

As I gazed at it, I felt exhilarated. It was our first objective in 'The Plan'. That was one good aspect of dedication. Nothing was unimportant any longer. Everything I did, every hour of the day, was measured against the long-term aim.

Secrecy was vital at this early stage. For as soon as Howard discovered what I was attempting, then battle would commence in earnest. By then, my position must be as entrenched as possible.

Our visit to Aunt Margaret was a cautious opening probe. So far we knew little about the other stockholders, so James had initiated inquiries about them in France and Sweden. We wanted to find out as much as possible before we made contact. What was important to them? Where was the weakness we might exploit, the desire we might satisfy – the key, as Papa would have said? Money might not rank high in their priorities. Their holdings in the bank, small though they were, would make them fairly wealthy.

Aunt Margaret, we had assessed, might well be sympathetic, divided as she was from a family for whom she had never had much time, and fond as she had been of James's mother. At the very least, James judged, she would stay silent about our visit.

The cab turned off the road and progressed up the long drive.

343

Horses of quality were grazing in paddocks on either side. At close quarters the house was less impressive. As the cab came to a halt before it I noted the peeling paintwork, the rusty broken gutters, even slates missing from the roof. No one would have guessed that Aunt Margaret was a woman of means.

James had to knock several times with the big brass lion's head before there was any response. 'All right, all right, no need for such commotion,' said a voice within as the heavy front door, warped with age and inattention, was slowly swung open on creaking hinges. A woman stood in front of us. She was about sixty, her hair uncombed, her apron filthy with unwashed stains.

'Miss Alexander is expecting us,' said James.

She gave a nod. 'Come on,' she said gruffly, and led the way into a room that adjoined the hall. 'I'll tell her you're here,' she said, and left us looking around in astonishment. It smelt like a kennel. Beneath a chandelier, in a corniced room of elegance, there were some seven dogs lying on the sofa and in the armchairs. They did not bark, but stared at us with expressions of muted malevolence.

Aunt Margaret came in then. She was seventy-eight, as I knew, but she looked younger – a wiry little woman, so thin that her skin was tight on delicate bones. She was wearing riding breeches and calf-length stockings. Her hair, like her servant's, was unbrushed. However, she greeted us as brightly as a sparrow, entering with quick, lithe, rather awkward movements. 'You must be poor Richard's girl,' she said to me. 'Sad business – best seat I'd seen in years . . . . Do *you* ride?'

'Not in Richard's class, I fear.'

'Well, some can't, some can,' she declared. 'I'm as hungry as a horse . . . . Isobel!' she shouted. 'Food!' She turned back to us. 'Lazy old trout.'

'It's a pleasure to see you again, Aunt Margaret,' said James. 'I thought you'd like to meet Quincey. You've not seen her before.'

'Well, I've met her now,' she said. 'Nice girl she seems . . . What else do you want?' But before he could answer, she shouted again, 'Isobel! Food!' She looked sharply at James and said: 'You're not a bad-looking boy now . . . What I'd expect of course, being Ivy's son, but you were a bit sallow before. Odd – I'd been thinking a lot about Ivy when I got your letter . . . Pater was hard on Ivy . . .

Isobel!' she called out once more.

'All right, all right,' said the old woman, appearing in the doorway. 'No need for all the fuss . . . It's on the table . . .'

'About time,' Aunt Margaret retorted. 'Always have to keep after her,' she said to us. 'Oh, but I'm hungry . . . Come on, fellows . . . '

She stalked, like a walking bird, through the doorway and we followed her across the flagstones of the hall to a dining-room, accompanied by all the dogs. We sat down at a long table with Aunt Margaret at its head. Isobel, grumbling to herself, placed soup before us with such deliberate carelessness that it slopped over the rim of each plate on to the table.

Aunt Margaret sipped noisily. 'Well, James,' she said. 'You haven't answered . . . What do you want?'

'It's not me, Aunt Margaret,' he replied, 'but you could help Quincey if you'd be willing to . . . She's been having a bit of trouble with the family . . .'

'Not surprised,' she declared. 'That Howard's a toad, like his father . . . Julius was a toad – a real toad, even though he was my brother . . . What trouble are you having, girl?' she asked me.

Her abrasiveness was daunting and I did not know how to start. 'I've been a widow five years,' I began.

'Oh,' she snapped, 'so it's a man.' Again she drank deeply of her soup. 'To be expected, I suppose . . .' she eyed me as if I was a horse. 'Good-looking girl . . . nice eyes . . . mouth too big . . . What happened with the man? The toad didn't like him, I suppose . . .'

Her distaste of Howard seemed a good sign. 'He was a little unconventional,' I said, 'and Howard had to consider the bank . . . My son's the only boy in the family . . . '

'Got a boy, have you?' she said. 'Nobody told me you'd got a boy . . . Why didn't you tell me she'd got a boy, James? Well, go on, girl . . . What happened?'

'I take a small part in the bank's affairs,' I explained hesitantly . . . .and I went to Oklahoma to supervise a wildcat oil exploration . . .'

'You must have ridden there, girl . . . Mustangs, weren't they? I'm told they're mean . . . The Spanish blood, I wouldn't

345

wonder . . . So that's where you met this man that the toad didn't like. What was he – a cowboy?'

'No,' I answered, 'he was a millionaire. He'd made a fortune out of copper . . .'

'And lost it, I expect . . .'

I nodded with a smile. 'And made it again . . .'

'And lost it again?' she darted at me with her bright sparrow eyes.

'And made it again,' I insisted, finding it suddenly important. I was surprised at the strong need I felt to defend him. My eyes watered and I was forced to blink. She looked at me with a wise but sympathetic smile. 'Oh, one of those,' she said. 'Gambled, too, I suppose . . . Terror with women . . . Attractive, that sort of man, but perhaps the toad was right . . .'

'Howard broke him,' I said. 'Ruined him quite deliberately . . .'

'Then paid him to desert you, I suppose, . . . How much did it cost him?'

'A hundred and fifty thousand dollars,' I answered.

'Phew!' she said. 'You could buy half a dozen Derby winners for that . . . Must have been desperate . . . Was he *that* bad?'

'He was my husband,' I said, 'though Howard didn't know that. I'll never forgive him,' I spoke quite quietly. 'Never.'

'Don't blame you, girl,' she agreed. 'But where do I come in?'

'Quincey,' said James, 'thinks she needs protection . . . They cut off all her income and threatened that another boy'd be given precedence over her son . . .'

'Another boy?' she inquired. 'What other boy?'

'The great-grandson of Marie Bellon . . . '

'Good heavens!' she exclaimed. 'The toad ran you a hard race, didn't he? They never even talked to any of that lot . . . This fellow of yours must have scared them to death. Was he a criminal, or something?'

'They've always wanted me to marry well . . .'

'And he wasn't marrying well?' She smiled. 'No, the toad wouldn't like a speculator. He'd want a lord . . . So how are you going to . . . what was it James said? Gain protection?'

'By getting control of the bank,' I said simply. 'By acquiring more stock, if possible . . .'

'Richard left Quincey all his shares . . .' James put in.

'Did he, by George!' Aunt Margaret exclaimed, putting down her spoon and studying me for a second. 'So that gives you as many shares as the toad and his brother, if I remember correctly?' She eyed me shrewdly and I nodded. 'And you hoped I might dispose of my little lot?' She paused for a moment, watching me carefully. 'Cost you a small fortune . . .'

'Name your price,' I said. She stared at me without expression – then laughed. 'It's tempting . . . but it'd cause no end of trouble. Too old for trouble . . .'

'Surely . . .' I began.

'The toad'd be over here before you could say Jack Rabbit . . . Then *you'd* be back and there'd be one devil of a tussle . . .'

'But Aunt Margaret,' James put in, 'if you definitely sold to Quincey, there'd be nothing left to tussle about.'

'There's always something to tussle about . . . No tussles . . . Now let's change the subject.'

We were not the best conversationalists for the rest of that meal. It did not matter, because Aunt Margaret chattered on without pause about her horses and what they could do, or why they failed to meet her standards because they were lazy or badly bred or lacked spunk.

After lunch, she came to see us off at the front door. Dogs were swirling round us like a pack of hounds. She looked at me for a second with a serious expression on her face. 'I like you, girl,' she said. 'Sorry I had to say no . . . wasted journey for you, I fear, but I've enjoyed meeting you . . .' Instinctively, I leaned forward and kissed her on the cheek.

We climbed into the vehicle and the cabbie had cracked his whip when she suddenly called out: 'Wait!' She came to the window. 'Tell you what,' she said, 'If it comes to a fight with the toad, I'll abstain . . . I won't vote at all . . . Knowing that'll help, won't it?' She grinned suddenly, pleased with herself at the solution. 'That'll help, eh?'

'It could be most important,' I answered. 'May I take it that's a promise?'

'A promise,' she assured me. 'Shake hands . . . Gentleman's word's his bond . . .' She slapped her palm against my hand. 'This lady's bond's as good as any gentleman's.' She stood back. 'Drive on, cabbie,' she ordered.

As the cab went down the drive, James looked at me. 'Tell me,' he asked idly, 'would you say that was a wasted journey?'

He was teasing, of course, for what she had suggested removed her 30,000 shares from the contest — one half of those that were our target. This was not as good as my owning them, for Howard and I would still control equal votes, but it left in issue only the other 30,000, the stock that had gone to Marie Bellon instead of James's mother. That meant that any shares I could gain over 15,000 would give me the majority I needed. I still faced a formidable objective, but it was now much smaller.

'No, James,' I said. 'I wouldn't call it wasted.'

Chapter 17

[1]

Howard looked inquiringly in turn at each of the men sitting round that long polished mahogany table, all in black coats and wing collars, most of them bearded. 'Are there any other matters for us to consider?' he asked and, when no one spoke, he said; 'In that case, I declare the meeting ended. When's the next one, Brown?'

'June 2, Mr Alexander,' answered Edward Brown, secretary to the bank.

'Until then, gentlemen,' Howard said, adding courteously: 'and Mrs Alexander, of course.'

I would never have believed it possible. There I was at an Alexander Board meeting – not as a director, in that male world, but in a role of 'consultant'. Howard was my advocate. No wonder I was wary. 'Oklahoma's made all the difference,' he had explained. 'We need you.'

I did not believe the bank needed me, though Oklahoma had changed much. Two more wells had been brought in since my return, raising the yield to 4,000 barrels a day, a level far beyond the wildest hopes even of O'Sullivan Smith. As promoter and director of the venture, I had gained the credit.

Even so, the reward was exceptional. When Howard had first mentioned it, we were sitting in 'The Room'. I contained my surprise and thanked him coolly. Then I leaned forward and kissed him on the cheek, my lips not far from the corner of his mouth. I felt him flinch with the contact of our skin – and resumed my seat.

We were playing games again . . . but the rules had changed. I do not know how much he had guessed of the ruthlessness that had grown in me, fed by the bitter winds of Long Beach. He was uncertain of me, though, which gave me the initiative. Howard was trying to rebuild the bridge between us, and was not sure to what extent he was succeeding.

I knew him very well. Beneath that façade – the distinguished benevolent figure of power – was a man of passion for whom I was a weakness, an underbelly where the shell was thin. I was exploiting this casually – not mischievously, as I had sometimes in the past, but with calculation. I allowed our hands to touch. On suitable occasions, I kissed him in a manner that, though seemingly innocent, I knew to be arousing. When we walked together – into dinner or even in the park – I would allow the outside of our arms to brush, appearing not to notice his instant recoil. It was easy for me now, for my emotions were numb.

I was not yet certain how I would deploy the weapon I was honing, or if I ever would, but I knew it would make harder for him the conflict that lay ahead.

Most of the time this was strangely easy for me, for the objective was so strong. I could have done anything to anybody, just as an actress can portray roles that may conflict sharply with her nature. But there were times when, despite all my efforts to fight it, I knew hate – usually after nights when I had slept little, when I had been haunted by vivid pictures of my life with Taylor, when he would resist every ploy I knew to force him from my mind, and just stand there laughing, with his sombrero pushed back on his head. Always he was laughing – not at me, of course, but with me. We had indeed laughed a lot, for it was his way of responding to almost any situation until those last weeks in New York, when the laughter had soured and the anger was always there.

It was not strange, I suppose, that on such dawns I would rise in the morning with a need for violence so great as to be, I knew, extremely dangerous. Success could come only from a cool head. I pandered slightly to my emotions, ensuring that Howard detected my bleeding, that he glimpsed the ravages he had caused. Once, in fact, he had said: 'You look so sad sometimes, Quincey.'

'I'll give you three guesses why,' I responded – not tartly, but quietly brave.

'Is there anything more I can do?'

My God, had he not done enough? 'I'll recover in time,' I answered. 'Thank you for your concern.' There was no derision in my tone.

I knew his regret, as a man, was genuine. But his invitation as the head of Alexanders to attend the inner councils of the bank was puzzling, even disturbing. 'Is there some aspect I've overlooked?' I had asked James that evening. 'Can he really believe the fight's gone out of me?'

'It's shrewd,' James answered. 'If you share the power, you'll have less reason to resent it.'

'The power's unchanged.'

'It's a gesture, at least—an offer to help him run the bank, to have more influence than you've ever had before . . . He wants you back . . . The whole family does . . .'

I glared at him as though he was on their side. 'Well, I am back, aren't I?'

'I don't think they're positive.'

Suddenly, the anger swept throught me. It came with force at unexpected moments, like a freak wave, so violently that I had to stop myself breaking the nearest object within reach. 'Have you heard any more from the agent in Stockholm about Helga Petersen?' I asked sharply.

'Not yet, but I had another letter from Paris about Bettine Laffont.'

'And?'

'There are still unanswered questions.'

I clenched my fists with frustration. 'Oh, it's all taking so long, isn't it?'

'Only a month so far,' he reminded me. 'Caution, you said . . . Full information, you said . . . Make no move towards them until we're absolutely ready, for then Howard'll soon find out, and we'll have lost the initiative . . . You were right, too.'

I was silent, suddenly cold, my feelings dampened by his logic—*my* logic. 'I wasn't made to be a schemer,' I said. 'I like an open fight, but this is the only way, isn't it?'

'If you want to have any hope of winning.' His expression was sympathetic. 'Shouldn't be much longer now,' he said in comfort.

'Mrs Alexander,' Howard said formally as the directors prepared to leave the meeting, 'I wonder if you could spare me a minute of your time.'

We walked together from the boardroom through that great hall, where so many clerks were bent over their tall desks. We sat down in 'The Room' and Howard looked at me pensively for a moment from behind his desk. 'I think,' he said, 'we should be considering Jonny's education . . . After all, he's five now, isn't he? I suppose Eton's probably our best course . . .'

I wondered why he had raised the matter then at the bank, when we could more properly have discussed it at our leisure in Grosvenor Square.

Then I got an inkling of his reason. One of the Front Hall men entered and said that Mr Roland Andrews had arrived to see him. 'Ask him to come in,' said Howard. 'Mr Andrews may interest you, Quincey,' he remarked. 'He lives in France . . . Partner in a motor business which has a few problems, though basically it's sound enough . . . I thought there might be scope for a merger with Masons' since the French motor industry's so far advanced. Also his wife's got a few shares in the bank. There's a vague family connection . . .'

'You mean he's Paul Andrews's father?'

'That's true,' Howard answered, with some surprise. 'How did you hear about young Paul?'

I stared at him, surprised by what he said, but his expression was bland. 'Oh,' I answered idly, 'Mathew said something about him in New York.'

'The Andrews are hoping we'll take Paul into the bank. I've said we'd consider it . . . I think you'll like Mr Andrews,' he added. 'He's a merry fellow.'

What was Howard up to, I wondered? Had he raised the issue of Jonny's education at the moment when Mr Andrews was announced to remind me that there was still an alternative to him, still a threat? Had he already discovered 'The Plan'? Was he promoting the idea of a merger as part of the price of the Andrews' support? I was mystified.

Roland Andrews fitted Howard's description. He breezed into the room, appearing breathless as though pressed for time. He wore country tweeds and carried a driving hat. His face was round, resembling a large red happy apple, topped by sandy hair that, like his bushy eyebrows, was unruly. 'Morning, Alexander,' he declared, shaking Howard's hand with a vigour that almost took him off his feet. 'This must be Mrs Alexander,' he said, turning to me, beaming. Though obviously English, he lifted my hand to his lips in the continental fashion. '*Enchanté*, Madame, as we say in

France . . . Did you know I had a French wife?' I knew all right. There was not much about the Andrews I did not know, for our agent in Lyons had reported fully. It was strange to meet him, especially since he was being so cordial. But I did not delude myself. He was in the enemy camp, based there firmly because of Paul. There might be some way I could switch his support to me, but neither James nor I could think of anything that could equal the promotion of his son — and that was one avenue along which I was not prepared to travel.

He sat down without invitation, one leg cocked over the other, holding his calf with both hands as though for support. 'Alexander's told me of your keen interest in Masons,' he said. 'Well, they're a sound business . . . Fine piece of machinery, that Leopard . . . Mind you, we've got a car that'll soon be running it a good race. Then, by George, you'll have to watch out . . .' His round scarlet cheeks bulged into a boyish grin. 'Mainly, though,' he went on, 'we concentrate on commercial vehicles — lorries, vans, that sort of thing . . . Don't do badly, do we, Alexander?'

'I'm sure you'll find the figures impressive,' Howard said to me.

'Positive we should get together,' Andrews went on. 'Have a marriage . . . A corporation straddling the Channel . . .'

'Perhaps a meeting with Mr Mason could be arranged,' Howard suggested. 'Informally, of course.'

I was still perplexed, suspicious of this keen interest by Howard in the motor business, but I realised that I must humour it. 'I'm sure Mr Mason'd be glad to meet you, Mr Andrews,' I said, 'and show you the factory.'

'Marvellous,' said Andrews, standing up, with one hearty clap of his hands. 'You must meet my wife, Mrs Alexander, and my son Paul . . . You were abroad, I think, when they were here last year . . .'

'I'd enjoy that,' I said.

'Blood ties are important, don't you agree?' he declared.

I wondered if the comment was pointed, but his good-natured grin seemed sincere. 'Without question,' I said.

For a second, Frances paused in the doorway, a bright smile on her face. I saw a lot of her now, as I did of Emmeline, for whom I had become a champion in her career ambition. In fact, I met all the Alexanders more often than I ever had before. They behaved as though Taylor had been forgotten, the slate wiped clean, treating me almost like a prodigal daughter who was now penitent.

Not Frances, of course. She knew I was no penitent, and her secret role in my escape with Taylor formed a bond between us that encouraged confidence. By her. Not by me. I was not confiding in anyone in the family – no one except James.

That morning she was clearly in high spirits. 'I can't tell you how glad I am that we're all being urged to be nice to you, Quincey,' she said. She sat erect on my sofa, mimicking a great lady, one arm outstretched on the handle of her upright parasol. 'I hope you won't be angered,' she went on, 'but I've arranged to be collected this morning. I wanted you to meet him . . .'

'Him?'

'Major Thomas Alnutt of the Brigade of Guards . . . Oh, I hate the secrecy, Quincey. I'd like to share Tom with everyone . . . Sometimes, I get an almost irresistible urge to stand up in Hyde Park and shout "I love Thomas Alnutt" . . . Gone a little mad, you see, but I hoped you'd agree to meet him, since you know what it's like to be a little mad. Then I could talk about him occasionally and you'd know who he was . . . Do you mind very much?'

I could not help laughing at her look of concern. '*I* don't mind, but I do have servants.'

'I've told him to ask for you.'

'You mean that, with my reputation, another gentleman caller'd be unlikely to attract surprise?'

'Hardly, Quincey. After all I'm here as chaperone, aren't I?' She giggled. 'Don't you think that's ingenious?'

I sat beside her. 'How long's it been going on?' I asked.

'A couple of years. He's married, too, of course . . . There's no future for either of us. He just makes me unbelievably happy. When I'm with him I'm a different person . . . You of all people must understand that . . . You do, don't you, Quincey?'

'As long as you're ready for the pain . . . It's got to end sometime, hasn't it?'

Concern for me suddenly clouded her evident happiness. 'Oh, I'm not being fair, am I? Not suffering as you must be, though you keep it to yourself . . . I'm so sorry, Quincey. Forgive me, please, but you see you're the only person I can talk to about Tom . . . .'

'Has Mathew any idea?'

'Not the slightest . . . At least, you can never be certain with Mathew, but I'm sure I've given him no reason to suspect a thing. If he found out, I daren't think what he'd do.'

'I don't suppose he'd divorce you, not with the family and the bank.'

'There are worse things than divorce, as you discovered . . . Mathew's capable of almost anything, you know . . . Anything . . . '

The intensity in her voice alarmed me, with its implications that even I could not believe of Mathew. 'Surely,' I began, 'you don't mean . . . ?'

'It's happened . . . At least, I'm fairly certain. The situation was critical to the bank . . . An accident a long time ago . . . ' She saw my expression. 'Oh, *I* wouldn't have an accident, don't think that. It just shows what he can do if he has to . . . No, there are far better ways of paying *me* back. No one suspected, of course . . . I only learned by chance, and I didn't believe it . . . But I know him better now.'

'Then,' I asked gently, 'are you positive it's worth the risk?'

'Oh yes,' she insisted with quiet passion, 'without question. Oddly, you know, it was Mathews's ruthless streak that first attracted me. I liked the hardness. He was rather handsome then, in a quiet way – and considerate . . . He's still considerate . . . ' She smiled suddenly. 'I said I was mad, didn't I? You'll understand when you meet Tom.'

I doubted this. The objects of great loves rarely seem equal to it. Probably Taylor had appeared ordinary to others. Certainly Major Allnutt seemed ordinary to me.

He stood before me, erect as to be expected of a soldier, and said what a pleasure it was to meet someone of whom he had heard so much from Frances. He had charm and good looks and even presence. No doubt he had courage, too – the kind of courage required to lead a cavalry charge. If ever Mathew discovered who was dallying with his wife, then that courage would be fully tested.

They did not stay long after he had arrive. Frances had only wanted me to meet him, not to entertain him for hours that were sparse and precious. Then they went, leaving me in vacuum of grey, aching sadness.

That night, James dined with me. It was our last evening before the crucial stage of 'The Plan'. Within days, Howard would know my intentions. Dramatically, we drank a toast to our mission, as conspirators surely always do – though not invariably, perhaps, in vintage Bollinger. The final inquiry about Marie Laffont and Helga Petersen had been answered by our agents. The letters, seeking permission to call, had been dispatched. I was going to Paris. James was sailing for Stockholm. By the time we both returned, I might control the bank.

[3]

It was a glorious spring day, so I decided to walk. The Ritz Hotel in the Place Vendôme was not far from Madame Laffont's address at 125 rue St Honoré. I had never been to Paris before and I was captivated by the city's elegance and sense of space, by the noisy throngs in the outdoor cafés and the wide avenues busy with open carriages, cabs and motor taxis.

For a second, I imagined Taylor walking beside me in that way he had, almost on his toes like a boxer. Taylor would have loved Paris. I would have loved Paris with him. Then the truth pierced through my thoughts and I was so devastated that I only just managed to stem the tears.

I found this happening quite often – this momentary lapse in memory – at special times and places that we would have enjoyed sharing. If he had been there, of course; if he had not gone to California with Howard's money.

I quickened my step, my resolve strengthened by the unhappy

musing, but I knew I must check the bitterness before my meeting with Madame Laffont. She was a very important lady. I must take care.

The apartment was magnificent. It had high ceilings in spacious rooms, furnished in the ornate Empire style, and tall windows that overlooked the formal gardens of the Tuileries, once the home of the kings of France.

The door was answered by a maid, who asked me to wait while she informed Madame of my arrival. There was a picture on the wall over the fireplace that portrayed Desdemona in *Othello*. I presumed it to be Madame Laffont, since I knew from our report that she was an actress, aged forty-three. Clearly, the painting had been executed when she was younger and her expression was agonized, as demanded by the role. It revealed an attractive woman with long dark hair and a rather gaunt but ethereal face.

I searched the picture for clues. Where was the key? I already had a theory. With James, I had examined all the material we had amassed and, like detectives studying the habits of a criminal, we had tried to draw conclusions. She had never married, the 'Madame' being a courtesy, but I knew she had a lover, that in the past there had been others. As an actress, she had played important parts but never a role of stature in the proper company.

Intent on the canvas, I did not hear her enter. 'Mrs Alexander', she said from behind me. 'You must forgive me for keeping you waiting.' Her soft English was perfect though marked, as to be expected, by a French accent. She looked younger than her age – in her mid-thirties, perhaps – and her spare face, though showing some lines of living, was touched still by the fragile quality of the painting.

'Let us be seated here by the window,' she said. 'You know, I've never been bored by that view of the Tuileries Gardens. *C'est magnifique, n'est-ce pas? Vous parlez français?*'

I shook my head in apology. 'Your English is excellent,' I said.

'When I'm sad,' she went on, 'I often think of Marie Antoinette walking in fear with her guards along those paths . . . She was held in the Tuileries for a while – she and the King . . . I've played her in the theatre, so I feel *sympathique* . . . An apéritif, perhaps?'

357

We sat down at a small table by the window and she filled two glasses from a bottle of Vermouth that she held with slender fingers. Her ease of manner was appealing and, as I was to discover, she had a humour that, though oddly resigned, would sparkle from her suddenly.

'Are you in a play at present?' I asked.

She shook her head. 'I haven't acted for months . . . I've hopes, of course . . . Actresses always have hopes, but for me there's never been one like this — a role that I was fashioned for by God . . . A role,' she added with a sad smile, 'I've little chance of gaining now. But let's speak of more amusing things. Have you been in Paris before?'

'Please,' I insisted, 'May I ask the nature of the role . . . or is it a secret?'

She shrugged, self-mocking. 'Why not? It's ambitious — ridiculous really — nothing less than Catherine the Great . . . Don't you think I'd make a fine Catherine?' She held herself regally erect, then broke into laughter that had an attractive but sarcastic gaiety.

'Why are you so pessimistic?' I asked.

She gave another self-deprecating laugh. 'Men . . . who else? It's always men, isn't it? They give and they take away, like the *bon Dieu* . . . *Hélas, mon brave, mon chéri, mon chevalier sans reproche* . . . He is in no mood for charity at present — not to me, at least. Why not? *A cause d'une petite fleur . . . une actrice* . . . eighteen years . . . *Tres belle* . . . The familiar story . . . ' She smiled suddenly and stood up. '*Maintenant, le déjeuner . . .* You have an appetite? I hope so, for I have an excellent cook . . . '

She led the way into her dining-room. I felt for her, impressed by the good humour with which she clothed her distress. 'Tell me,' I said, when we had sat down, 'I don't understand . . . Surely a young actress could hardly play Catherine the Great . . . '

'*C'est vrai,*' she agreed, 'she wouldn't want the part, but she wouldn't want *me* to have it either . . . Nor would Marcel . . . I'm history. A painful reminder, perhaps the source of a little guilt . . . He'd fear scenes . . . Still, it's sad, for this actress who plays Catherine will be making history.'

'History?' Surely she was exaggerating.

'I'm speaking of a film. Not what's come before . . . Not a little reel for nickelodeons . . . Not a peepshow, but a film that is the length of a play. The first major work on film . . . You see an audience at the theatre always leaves. Their memories die. But a film of this stature in the hands of Marcel Didier, who I have to admit's a genius . . . why, that'll be shown in cinema halls throughout America, England, Germany, Russia . . . it'll be there for our grandchildren and *their* children . . . You see now why I'd give anything to play the role.'

'Anything?'

'My life, even . . . ' Her laugh lit up her face. 'Well, not my life, perhaps . . . Now tell me: to what do I owe this honour? A visit by an Alexander . . . why, it's never happened before. We're the *troisième classe* of the family, the poor relations, you would say . . . '

'Hardly poor, madame,' I corrected, indicating, with a gesture, the luxury of the apartment.

She giggled. '*Touchée* . . . That Marie, *ma grandmère* . . . She was a naughty one, wasn't she? But my question . . . it's a delight to receive you, *mais pourquoi?*'

'We have similar problems, Madame Laffont.' And I told her about Richard dying and Jonny and Taylor and the method the Alexanders had used to remove him from my life.

She looked at me with sympathy. '*Ma pauvre* . . . No *petite fleur* but worse, perhaps . . . That Monsieur Howard has much to answer for, *n'est-ce pas?* He's why you're here?'

I nodded. 'You own 10,000 shares in Alexanders. I'd like to buy them.'

She stared at me with astonishment. '*Mon Dieu!* It's happened . . . My father always said it would . . . '

'They're worth a lot of money, of course . . . '

'But Papa didn't foresee this – not a fight by a woman against Monsieur Howard, not a battle for her son.' A big, excited smile came to her face. '*C'est drôle* . . . Like Jeanne d'Arc – alone against the might of the British . . . '

Her enthusiasm was encouraging. but I had been here before, with Aunt Margaret. 'So you'll sell?' I asked hesitantly.

The smile faded from her face. 'I'd like to,' she said, 'but my father made me promise . . . He was far-seeing and very bitter at the Alexanders, especially your Monsieur Howard, whom once he met. When the trust is broken there'll be a big conflict, he said . . . It'll be our turn then. We'll have the power even with only our few shares . . . The Alexanders'll have to consult us, ask our opinion, invite us to meetings. Our votes'll count . . . Swear to me, Bettine, he said, that you'll never sell. I swore, of course, so how can I disobey my father, Madame?'

I understood the dilemma. How could she? Then, as I prepared to leave, I glimpsed an avenue of compromise – just a possibility. She came with me to the door and I said: 'Tell me, Madame . . . I'd like to make history, too . . . If I could speak to Monsieur Didier . . . If I were an influence, shall we say, and he were to offer you the role of Catherine, as he once intended?'

'If you . . . ?' She broke off. 'Mrs Alexander, it's quite impossible, I promise . . . '

'Why are you so positive? After all, what stands between you and that opportunity? Your talent? No . . . Your fitness for the role? No . . . Then what? Why, just *une petite fleur* . . . Madame, every day bankers face problems far greater than any *petite fleur* . . . '

Hope came to her eyes, but she did not trust it. 'You make it sound so easy, but . . . '

I interrupted her. 'What would your father have thought if he knew you'd made history with the first great role on film? Would he not be proud?'

'More than proud . . . he'd be ecstatic!'

'Wouldn't he have considered that a fair exchange for the sale of your shares in Alexanders?'

She clapped her hands and laughed. 'Mrs Alexander, you're incorrigible . . . *mais ravissante* . . . You think like a . . . ' She searched for the word ' . . . like a clock.'

'Well, wouldn't he?' I pressed.

'Perhaps,' she agreed.

'Then if *you* have the will,' I said, 'and *I* have the will, I know that *Catherine the Great* will be an enormous success.'

Marcel Didier, I could see, was wondering if he could seduce me. We were at a corner table in the smaller room at Maxims and he was sitting informally, one arm hanging over the back of his chair, his eyes fixed on mine with an intensity that must have led many a young actress to succumb to him. I suspected, though, that his desire was rooted more in the nature of our meeting than in my charm. I doubted if he had done business with a woman before — this sort of business — and to make love to a woman who had negotiated as much as £15,000 for the rights in a manuscript would be piquant, even unique in his thick catalogue of sexual conquests.

The sale, I knew, had provoked a conflict within him. His ambition for years, since he had first worked with Louis Lumière and later Charles Pathé, had been to make *Catherine the Great*, to create the first major work on film. It had been a vision that could have been turned to reality only in France where the future of the cinematograph industry, seen elsewhere as an extension of the fairground novelty business, had long been appreciated.

He was an attractive man, about forty, with thick, black hair and brown eyes that seemed to flash whenever he grew excited, as he often did. He talked fast as ideas caught him, illustrating what he was saying with hands that were always moving — until he would stop suddenly, remaining as still as stone, and just gaze.

We were near the end of a complex duel, though the final thrust of the rapier still had to be made. I had called at his office the previous day well prepared. I knew by then that he was not only a director of talent but part-owner of Didier Frères, a fast-expanding company that made films and owned cinema halls, including some in America — and was in such heavy debt that, like so many growing firms, its future was in question. My position, therefore, was a strong one. They needed every centime they could raise.

I had wasted no time, just said at once that I wished to acquire the performing rights in *Catherine*. I would want him to continue as director, I said, and Didier Frères as producers. Alexanders, I explained, wished merely to make an investment that they believed would be fruitful.

'But Madame . . .' he began, intending to insist that the rights were not for sale, until I said; 'Twelve thousand pounds.' That checked him, stopped him dead in the middle of the road, for no one had ever offered such a sum for the rights to anything, let alone a venture as speculative as a film.

I was in a hurry so I allowed him, in his pride, to bid me up to

£15,000 on the condition that the matter was completed within twenty-four hours, after which I was due to leave Paris. Astonished by his stroke of fortune, which still left him artistic control, he invited me to lunch the next day. I accepted with a smile. 'I'll have the contract prepared for signature,' I said.

He had been waiting for me at the table at Maxims when I arrived. He stood and kissed my hand – and then invited me to join him in an apéritif. I placed the contract on the table before us, suggesting that we should complete the business at once so that we could relax over our meal and talk of other things, but he was horrified. 'Madame!' he protested, in a shocked tone, 'what is the haste? Here I am in the company of a woman who is not only beautiful but also rare – unlike any woman I've ever met before. Is it asking too much that I should be permitted to enjoy so unusual an experience, that I should be allowed to savour it to the full, to taste it, you could say . . . Perhaps to become a little intoxicated by it, before . . . Well, before being forced to consider such mundane matters of commerce . . .'

I could not help laughing at his absurdly elaborate compliment, and my obvious amusement did not displease him. He began to laugh with me. Then he held up his glass in silent toast. 'I'm becoming lost,' he said, 'drowning, it seems, in the deep, deep blue of your eyes.'

And so the luncheon proceeded. I found it amusing, even a little flattering, though I guessed that he behaved like this to all the women he met. At one moment he took my hand in his and said that it was impossible to believe that we had known each other only for one day. He had a collection of *art nouveau* in his apartment that he insisted I must see. Was I not moved by the sheer sensuality of Beardsley? He hoped, indeed he pleaded, that I had some free time that afternoon.

I was ashamed of my response to him. I was actually luxuriating, like a cat being stroked, in his nonsensical extravagance. It was time, I decided firmly, to curb it, to speak perhaps of the film. What actress, I inquired, did he have in mind for the leading role?

He looked at me as though I had displayed an error of taste and shook his head in sad rebuke. I was incorrigible, it seemed, even insensitive, but since I was insisting, he would reluctantly concede.

'I hoped,' he said, 'that Madame Sarah Bernhardt would consider the new medium a challenge, but her commitments made it impossible for her to accept. That left me, I decided, with two alternatives.'

'May I ask,' I inquired, 'if one of them was Bettine Laffont?'

The lazy smile left his face. 'What made you think of Bettine Laffont, Madame?'

'Oh I met her the other day. She impressed me. I'd have thought she'd be ideal as Catherine.'

'It is strange,' he said, 'for I was considering her for the role at one time.'

'And now?'

'I'm doubtful . . . I think there are other actresses who might be more suitable for the interpretation I have in mind.'

I did not press him. There was no point. Once he had signed the contract and I owned the rights, my control of the cast would be secure. That would be a surprise for him, I thought.

In fact, it was *I* who was to be surprised. We had finished the meal and were toying with coffee and a liqueur when I ventured once more to raise our 'mundane matter of commerce'. 'Perhaps now,' I said, 'we should brace ourselves to the signing of the contract.'

'Ah!' he said. 'Madame, I do not know how to say this to you, but I have to confess now that today I've not been completely honest. I must freely admit it . . . I've been indulging myself in the pleasure of your company, which you'd have refused me if I'd told you . . . '

Anxiety knotted my stomach. 'Told me what?' I demanded.

He shook his head, looked down. 'Someone else has acquired the rights to *Catherine*.'

For a few seconds, I just stared at him. 'It's impossible,' I said. 'Utterly impossible . . . Who could have acquired them? Why didn't you explain this yesterday?'

'Because they had not been acquired by the time we met.'

'You mean . . . ?' I began incredulously. 'Monsieur, we came to an agreement . . . Are you trying to tell me that you've reneged on that agreement?'

He looked at me sadly. 'I have partners, Madame,' he said. 'My brothers . . . I'm not the sole arbiter in the matter . . . I can assure you that if I had been . . . '

'You said nothing of brothers yesterday,' I cut in. 'You spoke of no need for consent.'

'That's because the situation was unique . . . I knew they'd be delighted, as they were . . . Madame, I must ask you to try to understand . . . ' Through my anger, I was trying to think. How did Howard know? Had he had me followed?

'It was two hours after you left my office,' Monsieur Didier continued. 'A gentleman called. He was from Paris, an *avoué* – a lawyer . . . He, too, said he wished to buy the rights in *Catherine* on behalf of a client. I said that I had already disposed of them, at which moment my brother Pierre came into the room. The lawyer asked if contracts had been executed and I explained the position. He said he would pay five thousand pounds more than I had agreed with you . . . '

'You told him the figure?'

He shook his head. 'He didn't care what the figure was. You see, Madame, no one could have predicted such a thing. Two people in one day offering these unheard-of sums for the rights in *Catherine* – and leaving the production in our hands . . . He made only one condition: we must sign a contract at once. He had it with him, already prepared, only the amount being left blank . . . '

'So you said yes?' I accused.

'Indeed, Madame, you wrong me. I said No . . . very firmly . . . *Non, sûrement pas*, I said, but my brother Pierre said yes. Five thousand pounds, he insisted, was a great difference. He fetched our brother Jacques and he said yes, too, so I was outnumbered . . . I could do nothing . . . You understand, I hope, Madame?'

I did not speak. I felt so cold I almost shivered. 'And was that the only condition, Monsieur Didier?'

'There was another,' he answered, 'but he did not mention it until the contract was signed and he could then dictate. He, too, required Madame Laffont to have the leading role. Madame Laffont seems suddenly to have inspired an amazing strength of support. Would you perhaps know why this should be, Madame?'

'No, Monsieur Didier,' I said, 'I haven't the faintest notion.' I stood up. Again he formally kissed my hand. 'Will you forgive me for not telling you sooner?' he asked softly. Before, he had seemed rather attractive in his ridiculous way. Now he reminded me of a spaniel.

'I'm sure women always forgive you, Monsieur Didier,' I answered with a sparse smile, and walked out of the restaurant.

[4]

I stood on the deck of the ferry boat, staring grimly at the English cliffs only just visible in the light sea mist, and wondered how it was that Howard always won — and with so little apparent effort. But he would not go on winning. Of that I was determined. He might win some battles — and I could not deny that he had brilliantly outflanked me — but not the war. Not in the end. I clenched my fists. 'Somehow, I'm still going to win,' I declared to the wind, alarmed suddenly as I realized I had uttered the words aloud. I glanced at some people standing near me. One of them, a man, gave me a cheeky grin. I did not really care that he had heard me, for my mind was fixed on important things. Winning would be harder now. I had needed Bettine's shares. If James in Stockholm had persuaded Helga Peterson to sell, it would have given me victory. Now I was on the defensive. Helga's stock was vital to me just to retain parity, and that still left the Andrews, who were certain to side with Howard unless . . . well, unless I could offer something that he could not.

I wondered if Howard would make any mention to me of the ease with which he had parried my first stroke, but it did not surprise me when he did not. He was courteous and considerate and there was no change in the thoughtful behaviour he had displayed to me since my return to England.

It was hard sometimes to believe we were locked in a struggle — except for Emmeline, who provided a constant reminder.

Like Frances, Emmeline had taken to calling on me several times a week. She would sprawl on my sofa in a way that would have appalled her mother, chattering amusingly about the minutiae of her life, including what she had heard during meals at home.

Usually, she would realize her indiscretion and swear me to silence. 'Cross your heart and hope to die, Aunt Quincey,' she would say.

'Cross my heart,' I would answer, with a smile.

She understood my conflict with her father, but she was on my side. We were women standing together against the unjust world of men. I had learned in this way that Howard had spoken often to Nina of the need to reach accommodation with me, and had assessed my response to his approaches. Emmeline believed, on what she knew, that he had behaved disgracefully in America. 'He was doing what he thought was best for the bank,' I explained, 'as you'll have to.'

'If ever I get the chance.' She looked glum.

'You'll get the chance . . . We'll wear him down together.'

I had learned from her, too, what was discussed of Roland Andrews. 'Papa said the merger of the two companies would be sound business, regardless of the other advantages. I wasn't quite sure what he meant by these . . . '

'He meant,' I said, 'that if it came to a fight between us, he would be assured of the Andrews' support.'

She frowned. 'I suppose it *will* come to a fight, Aunt Quincey?'

'I fear so, Emmeline.'

It was two days after I had returned from France that she was eating my cucumber sandwiches from her usual position of recline, idly asking questions about the Paris fashions, when she suddenly sat up. 'You were up to tricks there, weren't you, Aunt Quincey?' she challenged, with an impish expression. 'With Bettine Laffont.'

I smiled. 'Some more tea, Emmeline?'

'I hear you've been to see Great-Aunt Margaret, too . . . What's she like?'

'A nice old lady . . . '

She stirred her cup, watching me. 'Uncle James is in Stockholm, isn't he? You said he was going to Paris with you, Aunt Quincey, that he'd stayed on to see a friend. I wish you hadn't lied to me.'

'I can't tell you everything, Emmeline.'

'I may be young, Aunt Quincey,' she reproached, 'but I'm not a fool. I know my father . . . If there's a fight, will I still be able to come and see you?'

'I should hope so. Whoever wins, we'll all still have to meet a

366

lot . . . '

'Even if Papa does?'

'I'll still be a large stockholder, Emmeline. We're all locked together. The fight's about control, about the final word . . . I've experienced the power that the family can lever on me. It changed my life, and still threatens Jonny. It's not going to happen again, not if I can help it, not if I can gain enough shares to outvote your father should the need arise . . . '

As the bitterness emerged I was not far off tears, and she embraced me. 'Oh, Aunt Quincey . . . '

'Sorry, Emmeline. I just get a bit upset when I think about it. How did you hear about Paris?'

'Father was telling Mama last night at dinner. He said you'd thought up a skilful way of negotiating, but I didn't hear quite how because Uncle Mathew arrived suddenly with a crisis . . .'

'I haven't heard of any crisis.'

'Some woman's threatening to blackmail them. A Mrs Edwards . . . Apparently it goes back a long time and Uncle Mathew says she's got no grounds, but you know how terrified they are of even the smallest whiff of scandal.'

'And?'

'I didn't hear any more because they went off to Papa's study . . . '

She stood up to leave, a smile on her face that touched me – she looked very pretty, with all the eagerness and energy of youth.

'I'd like to say I hope you win,' she said to me, 'but I suppose it wouldn't be loyal, would it?'

I stood up and kissed her. 'It's none of your business, Emmeline . . . not really . . . Come again soon.'

I went to my desk and sat there wondering about what she had just told me. The name 'Edwards' seemed familiar. Then I recalled why: I had asked James about what Frances had told me – Mathew's possible connection with an accident way back in the past. James had thought for a second and then remembered hearing about one of the managers who had fallen from an upper floor window of Old Broad Court, in the '90s before James himself had joined the bank. Someone called Edwards had been arrested but then released without being charged. The coroner had ruled that it was death by misadventure. There was a heat wave and the windows were open. 'I think the name was Edwards,' James had said. 'Something like Edwards.'

It was strange that Mrs Edwards should appear at this time, but it was a common name. Bankers made enemies quite often. I had not really believed Frances's suspicions of Mathews, callous and unprincipled though he was. This kind of accident happened in America, of course. Companies like Standard stopped at nothing. But not in England, surely. Not in the City of London. Perhaps James could find out more, I thought.

Meanwhile, I was more concerned with the other things that Emmeline had revealed. Howard seemed to know every step I had taken in the cause of 'The Plan'. It was unnerving. I wished that James was back, and for the hundredth time prayed fervently that he had won Helga Peterson's stock.

Chapter 18

[1]

Even if James had not had a weakness for women, Helga Petersen would still, I suspect, have made an impact on him like a flash of lightning – as he admitted when reporting later. Her mother, another sister of Bettine Laffont, was dead, as was her father, who had been a timber millionaire; so Helga, an only child, would have been wealthy even without the Alexander stock.

Helga was not only rich. At twenty-three she was beautiful, still single, and a shining star in Stockholm's *jeunesse dorée*, maintaining a suite of rooms in the Grand Hotel that overlooked the old town across the waters of the Saltsjön.

With blonde hair piled high and a small round face that made her look like an alert but wayward child, she was outrageously avant-garde, smoked black cigarettes and was constantly eager for stimulating diversion.

I knew all this from our agent's report, so I could not complain at the result. I had deliberately sent James into the den of this young lioness because he would clearly be more persuasive than I could ever be.

There was a party in progress when he arrived at her hotel suite. She greeted him effusively with the smile of an angel. 'So *you're* cousin James!' she declared, her English touched only by a slight Swedish intonation. 'We *are* cousins, aren't we?'

'Distant cousins,' James agreed.

'Then it's proper for you to kiss me. We *must* be proper, mustn't we?' She proffered her cheek to him, then stood back and studied him with critical detachment. 'You know, you're rather handsome, Cousin James. You may kiss me again.'

She slipped her hand within his arm and led him among her guests, asserting in English that 'this is my distant cousin James from London . . . Don't you think he's handsome? Are we not a fine-looking family? James and I have just found each other. Like lost souls . . . we're on a voyage of discovery, as Ulysses was . . . Or was it the Flying Dutchman? Whoever it was, it's certain to be exciting, isn't it, James?'

'Already,' James assured her, 'My pulse is racing.'

'You see,' she declared to the company, as though he was an interesting piece of porcelain, 'he's charming, too . . . Now we'll dine.'

Some twenty people sat down to dinner. Helga positioned herself at the head of the table, and placed James beside her. 'Now I can't wait to hear,' she said, 'why you've come all the way from London to see me? As a matter of fact, I'm a trifle offended. Why have you not come before? Wouldn't *you* be offended?' she asked the girl sitting on the other side of him. 'We had the same grandfather,' she explained, 'which means we're not too close, doesn't it? Why, we could get married . . . Shall we get married, James?'

'Why that's a capital idea,' James responded.

This was too much even for Helga. 'You should be more cautious, James,' she warned. 'You've just proposed to me – before witnesses . . . But perhaps you're married already?' He shook his head. 'Then why are you not?' she demanded.

'I've been waiting for a mysterious, beautiful girl from the North.'

She eyed him evenly for a second. 'You joke too easily about important things.' Then a smile lit up her face and she raised her glass of schnapps. '*Skoal!*' she said, and drained the glass in one movement.

'*Skoal!*' he said, and did the same.

'Why,' she praised, 'you did that just like a Swede. Now, we must be serious for a moment . . . Why have you come?'

'To ask if you'll sell your shares in Alexanders.'

She stared at him. 'Now that's something I'd never have guessed. Have you spoken to Aunt Bettine?'

'Mrs Alexander is negotiating with her now.'

'Or my Uncle Roland . . . not that I care about my Uncle Roland . . . How much will you pay me?'

'A good price.'

She hesitated, a frown clouding that innocent face. 'I don't know . . . I'm not keen to sell, but . . . Well, perhaps you can persuade me . . . ' Her laugh was wicked and she squeezed his hand. 'Now, I know what we'll do. We'll go to the Humle

Gardens . . .Listen, everyone!' she called out, still in English, since in Sweden it was spoken commonly. 'The Humle Gardens? No autos . . . Open carriages in the light of the moon . . .'

For James, it was an astonishing night. When they went downstairs, the carriages were lined up in front of the hotel. 'You come with me, James,' she said. 'Sven!' she snapped to the coachman who, without any show of surprise, stepped down from the box and helped her climb to his place. 'Come, James,' she ordered. 'You'll ride beside me as footman.'

It was still early May and quite cold. She had donned a dark green velvet cloak with a hood, which she wore over her head. She looked a dramatic figure with the reins in her hand. '*En avance!*' she called out and urged on the horses, handling them with confident skill.

They drove to the Humle Gardens – Stockholm's central park – in a chain of open carriages, shouting to each other as they progressed. As they reached the gardens, someone started to sing a Swedish song and the others took it up. It was romantic, driving through the park in the night, with the trees and the grass lit only by the lamps on the carriageway, and everyone singing.

Then one of the other carriages overtook them. Like Helga, one of the men guests had taken the reins and they went by at a brisk trot, the occupants all laughing as they passed.

Helga accepted the challenge and whipped her own pair. For a few seconds the two carriages were alongside, going at a fast trot. Then without a thought, it seemed, she put her own horses into a canter, which became a gallop with everyone in both vehicles laughing and urging encouragement.

She was just ahead as they approached the Engelbrekst Gaten, a main street that bordered the park. She stood up like a charioteer to check her horses quickly and hauled back on the reins. Even so, she took the corner too fast into the wide road and one of the animals slipped. But she pulled him back on to his hocks, whipped him sharply and had him back on all four feet before he fouled the traces. It was a dangerous moment, brilliantly handled. She sat back on the seat, laughing gaily. 'Why, Cousin James,' she said, 'I do believe I gave you a fright. With me, you must get used to frights . . . Now champagne . . . ' She was on her feet again, turning back towards the other carriages. 'Champagne!' she called out, and the others joined in the cry: 'Champagne! Champagne! Champagne!'

As they turned towards the hotel and progressed down the Sodra Blasieholms-Hamen which bordered the Saltsjön, she said wistfully: 'The water looks beautiful in the moonlight.'

Early in the morning, as the guests began to leave her suite, she motioned James to remain behind. Then, when they were alone, she put one hand on each arm of his chair and suspended herself above him. 'Now we will talk business,' she said softly, her face not far from his. Her eyes were a high blue, aquamarine. 'Tell me your proposal.'

'As I said,' he rejoined, 'I wish to buy your shares.'

'For how much?'

'Ten pounds each.'

She lightly kissed his lips. 'It's not enough,' she whispered.

'What would you accept?'

She kissed his lips again. 'Thirty pounds.'

'No,' he said, 'I think that's . . . ' But she stopped him speaking by kissing him once more.

'You were saying?' she asked.

'I was saying . . . ' He checked her chin with his forefinger, so that she could not repeat the tactic. ' . . . that thirty was too much. But there's room for negotiation . . .'

'There's room for negotiation,' she repeated, mocking the way he said it. 'You're very English, Cousin James . . . Here I am kissing you and you speak of money . . . '

'You spoke of it first . . . '

She smiled and put her lips to his again, this time without removing them. He responded, tried to pull her down on to him, but she stiffened her arms to hold her position above him. 'Twenty pounds.'

He shook his head.

'Twenty pounds is good, isn't it?' she said. 'How many shares do I have?'

'Ten thousand.'

'A bagatelle,' she shrugged, and kissed him again. 'So we're agreed?'

'Not at twenty . . . Fifteen perhaps . . . '

'You're not gallant, Cousin James. You should tell me: "Yes, twenty . . . twenty-five . . . whatever you say as long as you continue to kiss me with the most beautiful lips in Stockholm" . . . '

'I *am* honoured, but fifteen is a good price, Helga . . . '

She kissed him lightly. 'Sixteen.'

'Sixteen,' he agreed. 'It's settled?'

'I think so,' she said, between kisses. 'We'll talk of it more in the morning.' She put her lips to his mouth, this time allowing him to draw her down on to his knee. Then she got up suddenly and said briskly: 'You may take me to luncheon tomorrow.'

They lunched at a restaurant she suggested in the Humle Gardens. 'I've changed my mind,' she said. 'I've decided not to sell my shares.'

'I thought it was settled.'

'It was but now it's unsettled – like the weather . . . ' A tiny laugh rippled from her.

'Why, Helga?' he asked.

'Oh, I don't know . . . Those Alexanders . . . They're so superior . . . They were most unkind to my grandmama . . . *and* my Mama, for that matter . . . '

'They weren't very kind to *my* Mama either. If they *had* been, she'd have owned the shares I'm asking you to sell . . . '

Helga laughed again, her face bright. 'That's amusing . . . isn't that amusing?'

'Not to me. And Quincey's not one of *those* Alexanders, as you call them. She's as much against them as you are – more, for she has more reason . . . She's the widow of my cousin Richard.'

Helga looked at him intently. 'Are you in love with her?'

He laughed. 'No, but we're close – as I was with Richard. I was like his younger brother . . . '

She studied him sceptically. 'She's like a sister?' She shook her head. 'You're in love with her, Cousin James, and I'm devastated . . . I thought you were in love with me – and don't tell me you are, for I shan't believe you. You tease of serious things.'

'You were teasing yourself . . . '

'How can you know?' she demanded with genuine anger. 'We

373

only met last night, so how can you be so sure?' She laughed again. 'Join us tonight. We're dining at the Hasseblacken.'

'I'd be pleased to, though I can't stay long in the city.'

That evening she again placed him beside her at dinner. 'Why can't you stay long in Stockholm?' she asked. 'We're becoming close too, aren't we? You and I? Like with your Quincey.' Her tone was mocking again. 'Like brother and sister . . . so what's the haste?'

'We're in a fight . . . Every day matters . . . '

'Eighteen pounds,' she said without blinking.

'Will it be settled then? Or like the weather?'

'It'll be settled.'

It was not settled, though. For a week, she kept James in suspense. She flirted with him, kept him constantly by her side, insisting he become a part of the frenzied social whirl that was her life. Often she would change her mind several times a day, at one moment offering to sell and an hour later remarking that now it seemed unwise. The price moved up and sometimes down, depending on whether she was petulant at some shortcoming in his attentions or if he had especially gratified her.

Advanced as she was, she had suggested they should make love and, while actually joined, changed the price three times, whispering the figures in his ear among endearments and guidance to what pleased her and even screams of ecstasy.

Poor James, I thought when I heard. No one could say he had not done his duty. It had been an arduous task indeed.

At last, he decided that their game must end, one way or the other. He placed before her the papers needed to transfer her stock and said: 'I leave tomorrow. The price is twenty pounds. You must decide now . . . Sell or don't . . . '

She reproached him playfully. 'You sound so stern – like a schoolmaster . . . Are you teaching me a lesson?'

'I can teach you nothing, but the time has come . . . '

She saw that he was serious and shrugged. 'You have a pen?' she asked. He took one from his pocket and handed it to her. She was about to sign when she hesitated and looked up. 'I'm going to miss you, Cousin James . . . '

'I shall miss you, too, Helga . . . '

'I think I love you a little bit. Not a lot, you understand, but enough for my life to be left a little empty, a little marked by wanting . . . '

'You have a life that's full . . . Parties, champagne, midnight races . . . '

'That's all on the surface, Cousin James. I thought you knew that . . . I felt you understood me, even in a few days . . . ' Her lip trembled slightly and she put down the pen. 'I don't feel like selling today . . . Goodbye, James.' She stood up and embraced him, holding him tight to her, then looking up at him with eyes that were wet with tears. 'Come back soon . . . Without any papers to sign.'

The next morning James left Stockholm for Gothenburg, the port from which the steamer sailed. The train had just begun to move from the platform when Helga joined him, together with a trunk, six suitcases and her maid. 'I've decided to come to England with you, Cousin James,' she said.

[2]

Helga may have had the look of an innocent child, but no one could question her instinct for timing. She could not have arrived in London at a moment that was more favourable to her. She was vital to me to gain the ground I had lost, as she was to Howard if he was to retain the ascendancy Bettine Laffont had given him.

We were poised like cats to spring. The pretences were over – my performance as a wounded angel, his attempts to repair the damage from a clear cold decision that, given the same facts of Taylor, he would certainly have made again.

We had not yet faced it out. I had, indeed, been charming to him. We had even lunched alone together in the bank, since Mathew was elsewhere that day, and I had looked at him with the parted lips and soft eyes that I knew disturbed him so much. If ever there had been a need to weaken him, to open the holes in his defences, it was now. He had realized what I was doing, but this did not diminish its effect, which – like a plant, exposed to continued sunshine – was growing stronger all the time. It still made me an uneasy opponent, tempting him to pull his punches, which was my purpose.

We spoke of our contest, using other words, as people often do. 'I hear that Mason and Andrews have made progress,' he said. 'The merger seems practical.'

'Mason doubts the benefit,' I countered, keeping my eyes on his until he was forced to glance away. 'So do I.'

'Mason's getting old . . . Andrews is ambitious . . . He sees himself as the head of what could be a huge motor company, bigger than Panhard or Peugeot or Benz . . . Isn't that just what Richard planned?'

'Not like this, Howard, as well you know . . . ' I switched the subject to the one that neither of us had mentioned. 'There'd be scope for us in a film company I discovered in Paris,' I remarked, watching him, wondering if it would provoke him into speaking of what he had done. 'Didier Frères,' I went on. 'They're expanding fast, but they've got big debts . . . They need capital badly . . . '

'For us?' he queried incredulously. 'Films? Penny gaffs? Nickel-odeons? Not even you'd recommend it surely.' There was no hint in his bland expression of the tactics he had deployed so successfully in Paris.

'Films are going to be an important industry, Howard,' I said. 'Bigger than the theatre and even publishing . . . Once they're made, they can be shown without actors, transported easily . . . One day there'll be cinema halls in most of our major cities here, throughout America, Europe . . . There'll be plays on films . . . Epic stories,' I paused, then added carefully 'like Catherine the Great.'

He glanced at me in his remote way and for a moment I thought he was going to refer to Paris, but evidently he decided not to. 'Perhaps one day it'll be as you say – many years ahead . . . '

'Richard would have been urging it if he'd been here.'

He stood up. 'I have much to do,' he said. The mood in the room was expectant. We were like opposing generals dining together before a battle. 'I hope you know, Quincey,' he said, 'how attached I am to you.'

'Attached?' I repeated, smiling at the word. 'I'm attached to you, Howard, too,' I said and kissed him goodbye – on the lips.

*

She was playing with Jonny, on her knees behind my desk. He was on the floor, too – hiding, waiting with obvious anticipation for her to leap from her position. 'I'm coming,' she warned. 'Are you ready, young man?' He tried to smother his giggles, and she rushed round the desk. 'Got you!' She held him to her, both of them laughing. She was sitting on her heels on the floor with Jonny in her arms when she saw me in the doorway.

She gave me a friendly smile. 'This must be your Quincey,' she remarked to James, who was leaning casually against the mantel-piece. 'I've been having a game with your son,' she told me. 'He's a delightful little boy. Aren't you?' she said, kissing him on the forehead.

'He's a scallywag,' I responded fondly. 'Don't *I* get a greeting?'

'Say please,' he ordered, pouting.

'Please.'

'Promise you won't send for Nanny to take me away.'

'What's this? Negotiation?' I demanded. 'All right, you can stay for five minutes . . . As long as you're as quiet as a little mouse.'

'Not a squeak,' he agreed. 'That's a very nice lady, Mummy.'

'The nice lady,' James said as I put Jonny down, 'is Miss Helga Petersen. She couldn't decide about our proposal, so she insisted on coming back with me to meet you . . . '

Helga had a grin like a nine-year-old. Her hair, I thought, should have been in plaits. 'I'm glad I came, Mrs Alexander.'

'I am, too,' I said. 'Why don't we sit down? James'll ring for some tea . . . How are you, James?'

'Exhausted,' he answered. 'Miss Petersen lives a fast life.'

Helga was studying me, quite openly. 'It was ingenious of you to send him,' she said. 'A good ruse – and successful . . . He's captured me . . . I've become his slave . . . '

'But you've resisted his persuasion?'

'Oh, he's persuaded me,' she insisted, her eyes wide. 'Often he's persuaded me – and often I've succumbed. And then I get away from him, and I ask myself: Helga, is this a wise thing to do? To be persuaded for what are, perhaps, the wrong reasons?'

I glanced at the cause of this fatal attraction, which was not quite fatal enough, but he was avoiding my gaze.

'What would be the right reasons?' I asked her.

'Well . . . ' she began, almost flirtatiously, 'Before I decide I think I should speak to Mr Alexander, don't you? He's not been kind to us, I fear, but perhaps such sentiments are not of relevance in a matter of business . . . I suppose it's possible he'll refuse to see me, as he refused my uncle on one occasion, in which case . . . '

'He'll see you,' I assured her.

'Of course,' she went on carefully, 'if James was to become my husband, the situation'd be different . . . '

'Your husband!' he exclaimed in amazement. I got the impression that, with Helga, James was always at least three jumps behind.

'Well, don't look like that, Cousin James,' she complained. 'You proposed to me the very night we met . . . You said I was the mysterious girl from the North you'd been waiting for . . . I told you not to be hasty. After all, I didn't know you then, but now I do and I think it was a good idea of yours.'

'It was not my idea, Helga,' he insisted. 'She's joking, Quincey, I hope you realize . . . '

'Why should I joke? Is it so amusing? Mrs Alexander, do you think I'd make so bad a wife?'

'I'm sure you'd be a perfect wife,' I said.

'Then James and I'd be sharing everything, wouldn't we?' she said. 'Including my shares in the bank.'

'Helga,' said James, 'You must stop being mischievous.'

She seemed hurt. 'Who are you trying to convince, James?' she asked very seriously, 'Me? Or your Quincey, who is like a sister to you?' She flashed at me an ingenuous smile. 'He said you were close to him like a sister,' she explained. 'So you wouldn't object to us marrying?'

I shrugged with a smile. 'If that's what he wishes.'

'It's not what I wish,' he insisted. 'I don't wish to marry anyone . . . And you don't either, Helga. Not yet . . . She's always playing these games,' he said to me.

She got to her feet suddenly. 'It's not a game . . . How can you say it's a game?' She seemed near to tears. 'You're being most unkind, James, jeering at me here in a foreign country in front of your own sister . . . I didn't realize you were so cruel, or I wouldn't have come here with you. I'd have stayed in Sweden, where every-

378

one's always kind to me . . . ' Her indignation seemed genuine as she stood, like an angry doll, glaring at James. 'I'm sorry, Mrs Alexander,' she apologized, 'but I think I must go. I must compose myself . . . ' She forced a brave little smile ' . . . It's been a pleasure to meet you.'

'Helga!' said James, as she started towards the door.

'As for you, Cousin James,' she declared angrily, 'I wouldn't sell you my shares at a hundred pounds each!' And with the flounce of a child, she left the room.

'It's a charade, Quincey,' he assured me as the door closed behind her. 'Don't take any notice.'

I was not as sure as he was. I had seen the way she looked at him. 'Follow her,' I said. 'Make sure she gets a cab, at least . . . It'd be a disaster, wouldn't it, if she meant what she said.'

'Why's the nice lady gone so soon?' asked Jonny as James hurried out of the room. I had forgotten he was still there.

'Your Uncle James has made her cross,' I explained. 'He's gone to make it up with her now.'

Helga *did* mean it, and she was in no mood to make anything up, refusing even to speak to him as he handed her into a cab. She did not recognize his existence again until she returned at noon the following day to the entrance hall of Claridges, where he had been awaiting her all morning.

'I'm glad you're here,' she said imperiously, 'I want to speak with you.' She led the way to her suite, told him to sit down and stood before him, as pert as a young schoolmistress. 'Now listen to me. I've just been to your bank. Your Mr Alexander could not have been more courteous to me. He's made me a good offer for my shares – better than you did . . . *Much* better . . . '

'Helga . . . ' James began.

'Please don't interrupt, James,' she said sharply. 'Your Mr Alexander has agreed to pay £2 per share more than anything you or your Quincey may choose to offer. What's more, I have it here in writing . . . '

She took a paper from her reticule. 'Don't you think I've been clever?' she taunted, flourishing Howard's document in front of him. 'He's won, hasn't he?' she leaned down so that her face was inches from James's. 'You've lost, James.' She began to skip in a circle, chanting: 'Howard's won! Howard's won! Howard's won!' She stopped, looking at him like a proud kitten. 'So's Helga, except that . . . ' She broke off wistfully.

'Except that what?' said James.

'I think you are too modest James . . . You think I am joking when I say I'm in love with you. You look at young rich beautiful Helga, with the world at her feet, and say to yourself: "How can she possibly love poor little James when she has so many men to choose from?" But you're wrong. It's *you* I have chosen, James . . . It's *you* I want . . . I always get what I want . . . So we'll get married, yes?'

James shook his head with a smile. 'I think you're enchanting, Helga, but I'm not the marrying sort . . . '

She eyed him with a frown. 'You're in love with your Quincey,' but before he could answer, she mimicked him: 'No I'm not – we're just close as if she was my sister,' challenging in her normal voice, 'A fine sister . . . a *really* fine sister . . . With those beautiful eyes, elegance, poise, wit, *je ne sais quoi* . . . Oh, a fine sister . . . Have you not been tempted to incest, Cousin James?' Again, she became the wounded little girl with a trembling lip. 'You've misled me. I think you've been most unkind, James . . . '

'I haven't misled you, Helga,' he said. 'How can I convince you?'

'Marry me!' she retorted. 'Just marry me.' And when he sighed his decline of her proposal, she went on: 'All right, you don't want to marry because you want to be free. You want other women. Well, you *can* be free . . . I can be free, too, of course . . . We'll both be free. We must make love sometimes because I want your children . . . You won't mind making love sometimes will you? I pleased you when we made love, didn't I?' She was a little doll once more, sinking to the floor beside him, holding his knee to her with her elbow, even fluttering her eyelids in parody of an ardent maiden.

He put his arms around her. 'No, Helga,' he insisted gently. 'You delight me utterly, but no . . . '

'All right!' She was on her feet, furious. 'I'll sell to your Howard. You've had your chance – a chance that hundreds of men would have paid for with their lives. It's over . . . I'll walk out of your

380

life . . . I'll sign the transfers at the bank tomorrow at ten, as I've arranged, and take the ship from Tilbury.'

I listened to James's account of what had happened with Helga with growing dismay. 'Are you sure you wouldn't like her as a wife?' I asked carefully. 'She has all the qualities that most men want – in abundance. Your life wouldn't be dull, would it?'

He was standing looking out of the window, with his hands in his pockets. 'And we'd control the bank together,' I went on. 'We could even appoint you Managing Director.'

It was an attempt at a joke, though I did not feel like joking. Possibly it was in poor taste, for James did not have the standing to replace Howard.

He turned slowly and looked at me with a hurt indignation I had never seen in him before. 'Is there anything you wouldn't do for control?' he asked. 'I mean anything?'

'James . . . ' I began.

'Answer,' he snapped.

I was not sure how to respond to him in this unusual mood. 'I've been hardened, I admit . . . ' My tone was calm, reasoning ' . . . as you know, Helga's stock is crucial . . . '

'I know it's crucial, Quincey . . . I know *why* you need it . . . I asked about the limits . . . Would you kill for it, Quincey?'

'James, please . . . If I've upset you . . . '

'You were serious, weren't you,' he said. 'It wasn't just a jest. You'd like me to marry her . . . '

'Only if she'd make you happy.'

'And if she wouldn't? That'd be a price worth paying . . . That's right, isn't it?'

'James,' I pleaded. 'Dear, dear James . . . '

He could hardly contain his temper. 'I won't marry!' he shouted – literally shouted. 'I'll do almost anything for you – things that many people wouldn't do for anyone . . . I'll investigate for you. I'll get secret information. I'll bribe. I'll threaten – not openly, of course, for we don't act openly, do we? I'll dig into the past of anyone you want, in search of dirt we can exploit. I'll even go to Sweden and make love to Helga Petersen. But I won't marry – not even for your blessed issue of control that seems to have obliterated

381

every decent thought you ever had . . . '

'Stop this, James,' I insisted. 'Please stop speaking like this . . . '
Despite myself, I was close to tears.

He saw it, too, and the fury eased in him. 'You've got cause, I
grant you . . . You're fighting a war, but there's no morality left in
you, is there? A person's lost without morality because it forms a
frame. Even criminals have a morality. I hope it'll come back,
Quincey, when all this is over.'

'It'll come back, James,' I said, taking his hand, 'when I've got
control.' I kissed him gently on the cheek.

Ironically, it was then that the notion came to me. There was no
morality in it, I had to admit. Certainly, it was classic – what
women had been doing since the start of time.

[3]

The clock on the mantelpiece showed the time to be 8.45 when
Howard arrived the next day – the hand put back by twenty
minutes. I was still in a housecoat, as usual at such an hour, going
through my post with Liza while Maisie brushed my hair.

'You're early,' I said.

'Am I?' he inquired. 'A few minutes, perhaps.' He glanced at the
clock.

'You must forgive me for not being ready for you,' I apologized,
with a gesture at the informality of my attire.

'It becomes you – as usual,' he said tonelessly. Liza and Maisie
left the room, as they always did when he came, and he moved to
the fireplace. Lifting his coat-tails, as though there were coals
burning in the grate, he surveyed me from a distance.

I stayed at my desk. There was nothing abnormal about our
situation. He had often seen me in a housecoat with my hair down,
calling in sometimes before he left for the bank. That morning,
though, it was a special gown – in peach silk, with a collar of
abundant lace that dipped to buttons down the front. The two top
buttons had been left undone. There was a touch of perfume
behind my ears. It would not fool him, I knew. We had been playing

the strokes ever since I had returned to England, but until then I had always stood behind the line. I planned today to approach the net. He would know why, but it would still affect him. For how long? That was the only issue.

'Some tea, perhaps? Or coffee?' I suggested.

He shook his head. 'I can't stay many minutes. I welcomed your note, though. I was going to suggest myself that we had a . . . well, that we spoke to each other openly . . . Clearly, we can't continue like this . . . '

'Like this?'

'You know about Miss Petersen?' I nodded. She was due to meet him at the bank at ten as James had told me. Her ship would sail from Tilbury at 11.30, so she would not have much time. Nor did I – and it was what I needed now. For situations can change with time – if, for example, the mercurial Helga went on to Sweden without signing the transfers – but time is the hope of desperate people. Well, I was desperate but, idly scribbling on a pad in front of me, I hoped it was not obvious. 'So it's all settled, Quincey,' Howard said. 'Perhaps now we can return to normal.'

'What's normal?'

'We must work together again, as we used to. We share important interests . . . You've been sly, Quincey . . . '

'Sly?' My eyes were on the pad. I was drawing a little man, shading in his hair.

'Pretending you were prepared to forgive . . . '

'But not that I'd forget.' I spoke quietly and looked up at him. 'What do you want of me, Howard?'

'The cards on the table.'

'Surely they're lying there now.'

'I want an end to it, Quincey . . . I want peace between us.'

'Victors always do . . . ' He was not the victor yet, but he soon would be – unless Helga left the bank before he reached it, unless I could delay him. 'No question you were a victor in America, Howard,' I said. 'My defeat was total, wasn't it? A real Bosworth Field . . . Of course, peace has less appeal to the vanquished. They dream of fighting another day . . . '

He looked at me curiously. 'There can't be another day, Quincey . . . not now . . . '

'There can always be another day.' I got up unhurriedly, wandered to the front of my desk and leaned back against it, facing him with my whole body. 'So this is the confrontation,' I said softly. 'I suppose that if it was a hundred years ago and I was a man, our swords'd be crossed by now. The duel'd be about to begin . . . '

'It's been fought and won,' he insisted. He was holding his shoulders back, with his chest forward like a fighting cock.

I folded my arms. 'It's strange, isn't it? By rights, I should loathe you, but I don't . . . We're enemies . . . '

'Not enemies, surely . . . '

'Oh, we're enemies, Howard,' I insisted, 'But it doesn't alter the strange force that draws us, does it? The candle to the moth . . . The iron to the magnet . . . You feel it, too, don't you?' I said, going on softly: 'I know you so well, Howard . . . All your moods, your fears, your hopes, your desires . . . Howard, do you ever think of that dark afternoon at Shere? Or have you banished it from your memory, pretended it never happened?'

'I recall it sometimes,' he said. 'With shame.'

'Why shame?' I began to wander slowly towards him.

'I do have a wife.' He was watching me as I moved within the silk. I saw him swallow. That was the only outward sign. 'I don't suppose you're the only married man in London who's succumbed to passion . . . '

I was near him now – but not too close. I leaned against the mantelpiece, my forearm lying on the cold marble. His eyes dropped for a second to the two buttons undone at the top of my gown. Then he looked away, stood up straighter.

'I ought to be on my way, Quincey . . . '

'Don't go for a moment. We need to talk, don't we, about our differences . . . Tell me, Howard. Isn't it good to be overwhelmed at times, at rare moments, to let the spirit fly?'

'It can never be good to lose control. What do you wish to suggest about our differences?' He looked me straight in the eyes and I knew he was testing himself, proving he could stand near the fire and remain unburned. His hands were at his sides and, holding his gaze – challenging it, in fact – I took each of them in mine. He did not respond – nor remove them. I leaned forward and kissed him gently on the lips, but he did not kiss me back. 'That wasn't

384

wise, Quincey,' he said.

'Tell me,' I whispered, 'when you issued those orders from London to Mr Etherington – to buy, to sell, to warn off my father's clients – did you think of me as the woman you knew?'

He just stared at me. 'Could you still feel the touch of my skin?' I said. 'Did you remember my breasts, my lips?'

I had shocked him. 'Quincey,' he began, but I went on: 'I cried, didn't I, that day? . . . When the moment came, I cried . . . Did you recall that then as you were dictating the telegrams? Did it make it harder or easier? Or did you pretend I was someone you'd never met, never known on a dark afternoon?' My pause was less than a second. 'Or did you think of the hurt you'd caused me? Did you grieve a little, say to yourself: "Poor Quincey, but perhaps she'll understand one day that I must do this"? Was that how it was?'

I reached out both arms, keeping them straight with my hands clasped behind his neck, and looked at him. His answering gaze was steady, but he did not speak. 'Or did you hate me?' I went on softly. 'Did you enjoy the pain you were causing? Did you hate Taylor because he'd got what you wanted but couldn't enjoy because of Nina, of scandal, of the bank . . . What you still want, don't you . . . ?'

His expression did not falter, but after a second he drew me to him slowly but firmly, and kissed me violently, his grip on me so tight that he almost squeezed the breath from me. Then he pushed me from him, holding me still by the shoulders. 'Yes, I remembered,' he said in a matter-of-fact tone, as though discussing business. 'Yes, it was hard. No, I didn't hate you. Yes, I want you, but it's a desire I can endure . . . I have it under control, like a monk . . . Now I'm going . . . ' I was touched by his words, even knew the beginnnings of the old wanting.

He walked past me towards the door. 'Please,' I said, 'Don't leave yet . . . Not after this . . . '

He turned. 'I'm sure you know I've an appointment with Miss Petersen, though now it's later than we planned. She's taking a different boat, going home by way of Copenhagen, where she has a cousin, I believe . . . So you can put your clock forward to the proper time . . . '

I could not help laughing. I was a good loser. The British always admire a good loser. But I had not lost for ever. I would never have lost for ever.

'We need a truce, Quincey,' Howard said, 'for the sake of us all – you, me, the family, the bank, Jonny – and even Paul Andrews.' The door closed behind him.

[4]

Oddly, at the very moment that Roland Andrews called to see me that afternoon, our file on his family was on my desk. I do not know what kept drawing me back to it. The Andrews had never been a real prospect for me, since Howard's sponsorship of Paul was an incentive I could hardly equal, but occasionally I had wondered if there was not another key to their support that I had not detected. Now, however, with the loss of Helga's shares as well as Madame Laffont's, there was no real point in exploring the question further, for the Andrews could make little difference. Even so, I was intrigued to know what he wanted, so I did not keep him waiting.

'Mrs Alexander,' he declared with an embracing beam, hurrying into the room as though he was late for a train, 'it's most generous of you to receive me without warning, but I was nearby unexpectedly and there's a small matter I thought we might usefully explore.'

I got up from my desk and, after having my hand kissed in his exuberant fashion, gestured towards an armchair. He was the untidiest man I had ever met. Stout as he was, he slumped heavily on the cushions, his jacket twisted so that the material was pulling at his buttons, his tie askew, his hair uncombed.

'Now how do I raise the matter I've come to discuss?' he asked, grinning at me with the bulging red cheeks of a schoolboy. 'My mission, dear lady, is delicate . . . Not easy for me. I'm a blunt man . . . No good at dainty footwork . . . Still, can't put it off, can I? So it's into the water headfirst . . . You and Mr Alexander . . . You'd seem to be engaged in . . .' He broke off ' . . . well, in a bit of a tussle . . . Or am I misinformed?'

What in the world did he want, I wondered. 'We *were*,' I

answered cautiously, 'but I think he's proved the winner.'

'Well, *has* he?' Andrews's eyes were alight, as though he was about to impart some exceptional news. 'That's why I'm here, Mrs Alexander. You think you're counted out, don't you? You think you're lying out flat on the floor of the ring. Well, I've come to tell you how you can stand up and deliver to your adversary nothing less than a knockout blow. How? Simple . . . My wife's shares in the bank . . . Now, if these were available to you . . . ? Well, surely I needn't elaborate . . . '

I was astonished. 'Are you saying they're not pledged to Mr Alexander?'

'Nothing's signed. Terms are agreed, of course – most attractive terms, I'd add, for my son, for my company . . . All our interests have seemed to lie with Mr Alexander. Until now, that is . . . '

I felt a strange sympathy for Howard. This man was venal. 'How's the situation changed?' I inquired.

'Our position has become crucial. Before, there've been others to consider, but now – since your late husband's Aunt Margaret has declared she'll abstain from any voting – there's just my wife. She can give to either of you more than 50 percent of the remaining Alexander stock . . . In short, control of the bank is in our gift . . . '

'I'm not sure you understand the latest position, Mr Andrews,' I said. 'The fact is that both Madame Laffont and Miss Petersen have now disposed of their holdings . . . That amounts to 20,000 shares against your wife's 10,000 . . . '

He was undeterred by my news – just shook his head, his red face creasing into a broad, knowing smile. 'Not quite true, dear lady. Madame Laffont, my sister-in-law, has a memory that you might say was faulty. She finds it easy to spend money. She's extravagant, generous – especially to those gentlemen who win her favour – but as to where that money comes from . . . well, that she finds tedious, unimportant . . . So she appears to have forgotten that a few years ago, affluent though she was, she fell short of funds. I rallied to her cause. She was, after all, my wife's sister . . . I loaned her the money she required against the security of her stock in the bank – a secret loan, of course, unknown to Mr Alexander, a loan that's never been repaid. We've never foreclosed on the security, of course, but we could at any time we choose . . . In short, Madame Laffont has disposed of stock she had no right to sell. So for all practical purposes we control, not 10,000 shares, but 20,000 — which, if you and I found basis for agreement, would give you the majority you need . . . '

I eyed him cautiously, but I felt a sudden hope. He might be venal, but what he said was right. I knew that Howard, cold and pragmatic as he was, would be willing to deal with him under these conditions — just as, cold and pragmatic, he had smashed my life with Taylor. So why should I be more restrained? 'Are you holding an auction, Mr Andrews?' I asked.

He slapped his knees with his hands. 'Ha! Thought that's what you'd think. Almost right, but not quite . . . Well, not for money, anyway — not mainly . . . No, I'm thinking about what we could create together, Mrs Alexander . . . about what you might describe as a tie between our families.'

'Surely Mr Alexander is in a better position to give you that . . . '

He raised his eyebrows dubiously, shook his head. 'No . . . You can provide something he can't, as well as everything that he can . . . That is, if you gain control . . . '

'I'm mystified,' I said. 'Does it concern the merger?'

'Dead on the nail, Mrs Alexander. I've always hoped to build the biggest motor enterprise in Europe. Now at last it's within my grasp. The elements are there . . . Two to three years, that's all . . . But, to do it, I need the merger, the base that our two companies together can provide. What's vital, too, is that I gain the best men — the best brains, the best skills, the best designs . . . One man in particular has all these combined. He's to be my closest associate, and I'd like you to talk to him. May I call him in? He's waiting outside . . . '

'Of course,' I said, still wondering what lay behind this astonishing negotiation. Then I got a notion, for Mr Andrews's partner stood in the doorway, and I was looking at the same ravaged face that I recalled so well.

'Well, Madame la directrice,' he said. 'Surprise, eh?' The high colour that had marked his face had gone, but the scarring and the malformation remained — and the eyes, of course. The eyes were the same. It was the eyes that really brought that night at Shere flooding back into my memory — the fear I had seen in them, the

388

desolation, changing to hope, becoming despair; the eyes that had made me take him into me to give him the assurance that, child-become-man, he so desperately needed. It was the eyes, too, that had later branded on my consciousness that searing sense of betrayal.

Anger rose in me so violently I thought I was going to strike him. 'How dare you enter this house, Steven?' I demanded.

My fury did not disturb him. 'Andrews,' he said, in a tone that was almost bored, 'perhaps you'd answer Mrs Alexander's question.'

Andrews advanced like a welcoming grocer, his hands clasped in front of him. 'Dear lady,' he said, 'I must beg your forgiveness . . . I should have warned you, perhaps, who would be with me, but Mr Mason thought you might refuse to see him.'

'He was right!' I was on my feet, glaring at them both. 'And I'd like him to go at once!'

'Now, Madame la directrice,' Steve cautioned, 'Not too much haste, surely . . . We're not in a race, are we?' His deformed smile was mocking. 'You know, you're even more fetching than when I saw you last, though you could hardly say that for me, could you?' But there was none of his previous bitterness. 'You were right about the women, though . . . No shortage there . . . My face seems to help. Different, I suppose . . . After all, handsome men are three a penny. *And* the speed . . . I think they're stimulated by the speed, the danger, the risk . . . '

'Mr Andrews,' I said sharply, 'Will you please ask Mr Mason to leave this room before I . . . '

'Now wait, dear lady,' he begged. 'Just hear me out, that's all I ask . . . You're opposed to Steven, I know – doubtless with excellent cause – but we must be practical, surely, must balance the pros against the cons. He's essential to my plan, which means he's vital to any arrangement between you and me about the Alexander stock. Now is all that worth risking for what, if you'll forgive me, may be emotional reasons . . . ?'

I was caught. This funny clown-like man, with his sprouting hair and winning grin, had my hands tied up behind my back.

'So you see,' Steven put in idly, 'we're bound together by mutual interest . . . Ironic, wouldn't you say, Madame la directrice?'

'Will you stop calling me that!' I snapped. 'Mr Andrews,' I asked, '*why*? Why are you asking me to accept this one man whom you knew I'd object to most strongly, whose own father won't even talk to him?'

'Because he has the qualities, dear lady. As a driver, he's brilliant. . . Holds the record for almost every circuit in Europe. He understands engines better than anyone I've ever encountered. He has an ambition that's demanding, ideas that are original . . . '

'Enough!' I cut in. 'Have you not exposed Mr Alexander to this person with all his virtues?'

'No.' Andrews was almost smiling. 'I'm a realist. Mr Alexander would never stand a chance of gaining your agreement . . . or persuading old Mr Mason . . . '

'He could order it,' I said, 'if he controlled the stock.'

'In theory,' Andrews agreed. 'Not in practice. For a start, you'd fight us like a tigress. You might challenge the Board, involve the press – as you threatened once before, I'm told . . . As for Steven's father, he'd resign without your help and I need him as chairman of our new corporation. He has a high reputation that'd have great value to us . . . '

I looked at him curiously. He seemed so unlike the role he was playing. 'Let me get this quite clear,' I said. 'You're offering me your wife's stock in the bank so long as I accept Steven Mason?'

His cheeks bulged again, his eyes shining. 'Simple as that. Twenty pounds a share . . . That's all we'll ask . . . In an auction you'd go much higher. Also, only *you* could persuade Steven's father. Mr Alexander could never do that in a hundred years . . . '

It was clever, but there was a missing element. 'There's something you haven't told me, Mr Andrews,' I said. 'Steven Mason couldn't possibly be worth that price, even allowing for everything you've said . . . '

'Oh, there's more to come,' drawled Steven, who was lounging in an armchair that I had not invited him to occupy.

The grocer's smile spread across Andrew's ruddy face. 'He does own some patents, too,' he admitted. 'Important ones.'

'Where did he steal those from?' I demanded.

'Oh please, Madame la directrice . . . ' Steven lifted the back of his hand to his head in mock despair.

'Does it matter, Mrs Alexander?' said Andrews. 'The fact is he *has* them . . .'

'Do they include any of ours?' I asked angrily.

Steven examined his nails. 'One or two,' he conceded airily.

'Believe me, I understand your feelings,' Andrews said to me, 'But the patents are wide in spectrum. They'll enable us to produce a car that's revolutionary, like nothing on the road today in Europe or America . . . With Masons and Andrews together, with all the capital we need from the bank, why, there'll be no company in Europe that'll even smell our exhaust . . . You see how crucial you are to me, how important it is that Steven should be accepted . . .'

I made no comment, but sat down at my desk and once more read the report on the Andrews family. 'And your son Paul?' I said at last. 'Where does *he* fit into this grand scheme?'

Andrews approached me with a persuasive beam as though he was about to introduce me to a new variety of jam. 'Well now, Paul's ten years older than your son. He's fourteen . . . In three years' time, he could join the bank. That's what Mr Alexander has offered . . .' He hesitated.

'Please continue . . .'

'Mr Alexander's forty-four as you know. At sixty, he plans to play a smaller role. Paul will then be thirty . . .'

'After being groomed to take over?' I inquired. 'After serving as a director for years? Howard Alexander's right-hand man?' Andrews shrugged agreement. 'Jonny will be only twenty then,' I went on, 'too young to challenge him . . . Not bad, Mr Andrews . . . So what's your proposal now . . . if you make a deal with me instead?'

'Is the same impossible?' he asked cautiously.

'Completely, utterly impossible.'

Andrews looked genuinely perplexed. 'But why, Mrs Alexander? Jonny'll have control through your holding. He'll always have more actual power than Paul, and in due course, he can take over . . .'

Andrews was wily. He had considered all the aspects, fitted them together like a jigsaw. But I did not like it one bit. If I agreed, Paul would remain a major threat. Power, as I had learned in a bitter lesson, did not lie solely with the owners of shares. Heads of banks could lever it in many other ways. And if Paul was anything like his odious father, then I had good reason for concern.

My choice was hard. If I approved his proposal, I would gain the vital stock. If I refused, Andrews would be forced to deal with Howard – and then, with the support of a majority holding, there would be no way Paul could be challenged for the leadership of the bank.

Much thought was clearly needed. Anyone who supped with the Devil required a long spoon and that, it seemed, was what I might be forced to do. 'Mr Andrews,' I said. 'I need time to consider your proposal . . . A few days perhaps . . . '

'Very well, dear lady,' he agreed, 'but the matter's pressing, as you understand . . . May I expect your answer by the end of the week?'

'I hope so,' I answered.

He looked at me uncertainly. 'Until then,' he said, and made a formal little bow. He glanced at Steven, still slouched in his ungainly way in the armchair, expecting him to leave with him, but Steven gestured to him to go on alone.

For a moment, Steven remained watching me with a derisive grin. Then he got to his feet in a slow movement that seemed casually offensive. 'Oh, Madame la directrice,' he mocked, 'is the issue *really* so hard?' I just stared at him coolly without reply and he shrugged his shoulders, sauntering to the doorway, where he turned. 'Is it as hard, for example,' he continued 'as giving yourself to a monster?' And he was gone before I could respond.

When Emmeline arrived twenty minutes later, I was still sitting at the desk staring in front of me. 'Goodness, Aunt Quincey,' she declared, 'you're looking serious. Has anything happened?'

'You could say that, I suppose,' I answered, 'but don't expect me to tell you about it.'

'That means it concerns the fight with Papa,' she said, reclining on the sofa. 'I'm dying to know, Aunt Quincey . . . It's obviously frightfully important . . . I won't breathe a word, I promise . . . '

'It was you who spoke of your conflict of loyalties – and rightly, too. I don't want to add to them . . . ' I got up with a slight sigh and perched on the arm of the sofa, 'Now tell me,' I said, briskly, 'what have you been up to since I last saw you?'

She ignored my question, studying me curiously. 'You know, Aunt Quincey, I was thinking this morning about your Mr Taylor . . . I mean, there wouldn't have been a fight with Papa if it hadn't been for him, would there?'

'No,' I agreed, 'I don't suppose there would.'

'Do you still miss him terribly?' Emmeline asked, and the question was like a sudden blow in the stomach. She noted my response. 'Sorry,' she said, a bit helplessly. 'I shouldn't have asked, should I? It was impertinent, even though I do feel we're close now . . . Forget it I said it – please . . . You will, won't you?'

I smiled a trifle sadly. 'Of course I miss him,' I answered. 'Feelings as strong as that don't just end like turning off a tap. I miss him far too much. I wish I didn't.'

'Would you take him back if he returned?'

I looked at her with shocked surprise. How could she ask such a thing? But I had forgotten how young she was, how acute emotions were in a girl of her age, but also how quick recovery could be. She could see she had touched strings I tried to keep concealed. 'Oh, forgive me, Aunt Quincey . . . I've done it again, haven't I? Where angels fear to tread . . . I just wondered, that's all . . . because I've come to care for you so much. From now on, I'll try to keep my foolish mouth shut . . . '

I put my hand on her shoulder in reassurance. 'You don't need to feel badly,' I said, 'but he's caused me more pain than I ever imagined I would have to bear . . . So how could I trust him? How could I be sure he wouldn't just go off again when it suited him? And then I'd have to endure it all once more . . . I'm not sure I could . . . Not a second time . . . '

My words had moved her, and there were tears in her eyes. 'Oh, Aunt Quincey,' she began, and was about to get up and embrace me when there was a gentle knock on the door and Jonny's little face appeared around it. 'Are you busy, Mama?' he inquired tentatively, beaming suddenly with pleasure when he saw his cousin. 'Hallo, Emmeline,' he said, 'I didn't know *you* were here.' And he ran into her outstretched arms.

Then Nanny appeared flustered that her charge had escaped her. 'I'm sorry, Mrs Alexander.'

'That's all right,' I said, relieved that Jonny had ended a dialogue that had become distressing.

Later, I was to reflect how ordinary the scene was in my room that morning. What I was witnessing could have happened on any of Emmeline's frequent visits, for the two of them adored each other. So the sudden sense of alarm that enveloped me took me by surprise. I tried to give it reason — the Andrews' disturbing proposal, perhaps, or Emmeline's probing of so sensitive an area within me — but I failed. For what I was feeling was close to physical fear. I think, in fact, I was actually waiting for the sound of the front entrance bell before I heard it. Jonny had left the door of my room open and my heart beat faster as I saw the maid cross the hall to answer it. Instinctively I knew then the source of my anxiety, knew it was Taylor, long before he strolled into view — in a suit, of course, that was perfectly pressed, a knot to his tie that was immaculate, and a rose in his buttonhole that could have grown there.

For a moment he stood in the doorway with the same old confident, relaxed smile on his face. 'Good morning, Mrs Alexander,' he greeted. 'Always said I'd come for you, didn't I? In a carriage, I said, with Harry May at the reins as usual . . . Remember me saying that?'

'It's Uncle Taylor!' exclaimed Jonny with delight. He wriggled in Emmeline's arms to be let down, and ran to my husband. 'Hallo, Uncle Taylor.'

Taylor looked down at him with a smile. 'Hallo, you young scamp. *You* knew I'd be back, too, didn't you?'

He said to me: 'Look out of the window — see who's there?'

My heart was thumping faster and I could feel the colour rising in my face, so I was glad of the excuse to turn away. I moved to the window. A carriage was waiting in the square — and on the box were the hunched shoulders and the old bowler hat I remembered. Harry May saw me at the window, watching, no doubt, under orders. He raised a hand in greeting.

'We're back up there again, Mrs Alexander,' Taylor said. 'Made another million . . . Can't beat an old pro, can you? Quick on the feet . . . Bet you'd expected it, didn't you? Knew I'd turn up some-time.'

I turned back from the window and looked at him. I could see why I had loved him, why I loved him now, I supposed. Those blue, blue eyes, like mine . . . the easy smile . . . the sheer toughness that once again he had demonstrated. In how long? It seemed like years but, in truth, it was only months. I wondered if he had made his million at the poker table or found another mine.

There was silence in the room as my reply was awaited – but I did not speak. I met his eyes, unblinking, sustaining my gaze, standing completely still. He wanted me to say something, I knew, to respond to his return. 'I've brought you a present,' he said at last, with a smile that was a trifle forced, 'a present that'll please you a lot.'

I did not even indicate that I had heard him. Unhurriedly, I moved to the bellrope on the wall and pulled it – then waited, looking at him again, blandly, almost as though he was not there. The maid appeared behind him. 'Mary,' I said, 'would you kindly show Mr Taylor to the door.'

'I need to talk to you,' he said. 'I've just told you . . . I've got a present for you that you'll need to see to believe.'

I moved to my desk, sat down carefully, smoothing the underside of my skirt as I did so, and began to study some papers. I was surprised how cool I was. The palpitations that had attended his appearance had eased. I was numb now. I had no emotion.

'You're spoiling the occasion, you know,' he said. 'This was meant to be a surprise for you – a happy surprise. I couldn't contact you before . . . Surely you knew that . . . I'd given my word that I wouldn't but everything's different now. Why, when you hear what I've . . . '

'Mary,' I cut in, writing a note in the margin of the document before me, 'would you please do what I requested.'

'Mr Taylor, Sir,' the maid urged uncertainly. 'If you please, Sir . . . '

I could not see him, my eyes focused on the words I was writing – words that made no sense – but I could sense his frustration. 'Jonny,' he said, 'what am I going to do with this ma of yours? She's as stubborn as any mule I've ever worked with . . . You're going to have to talk to her for me. You know that? You're going to have to tell her that it just makes no sense not to listen, at least, to what I've got to say . . . Just two minutes, Mrs Alexander,' he said. 'Can't we be civil to each other for two minutes? Then, if you want, I'll walk straight out of your . . . '

'Mary!' I exclaimed, banging the desk suddenly with my hand.

'All right,' he said, 'I'll go . . . Been a shock, I know . . . but I'll be back. Maybe the dice'll fall a little better then. Have a word with her for me, Jonny, give a fellow a helping hand, eh?'

None of us spoke until we heard the front door close, and only then did I lift my eyes from the paper on my desk and sit back in the chair. 'Why didn't you want to talk to Uncle Taylor, Mama?' asked Jonny.

I smiled softly at him. 'I didn't have anything to say,' I answered, 'and I *was* a teeny weeny bit cross with him.' I wished Jonny had not been there at the very moment of Taylor's arrival, but I doubted if the experience would have caused him lasting harm. I turned to Emmeline. 'I think I need to be on my own for a few minutes, Emmy . . . I've got a bit to think about . . . I'm sure you understand.'

'Oh, I understand, Aunt Quincey,' she said. 'I understand perfectly . . . Come on, Jonny, we'll leave your mama to her boring old papers.'

In the entrance she looked back, as though she wanted to say something but could think of nothing suitable. She gave me a sympathetic smile and closed the door.

I stayed at my desk for some time, just staring into space. There was no order to the thoughts that rushed through my mind, no pattern of emotion. Shocked as I had been, I seemed devoid of feeling, unmoved to tears — not even the tears of anger, which was the dominant element in my response. Did he really believe that he could walk back into my life with a cheery wave — after all the agony he had caused me, was still causing me, or would be when the numbness went and I started to feel again? Did he truly think I could forget what he had done? No, not forget. He had not thought that. To forgive, though, was a different matter. Even this, he had known, would not be easy, but he had always lived on his wits and his smooth talk and I knew that he had reckoned that, with the expensive present he had spoken of, I would begin at least to melt —

perhaps not much on the first encounter but enough to be civil, as he had put it.

Well, I had not been civil and I had not begun to melt, and I wished fervently that he had not come back to put me to any test. For I had believed that I was finished with the testing, that he was now a figure in my past whom I still ached for but had learned to live without. Worst of all, I thought as a new surge of anger swept through me, was his timing. My decision on the Andrews' proposal was crucially important. If ever I needed a cool, clear mind it was now, and I had an uneasy suspicion that by nightfall, when the reaction had set in and the numbness was gone, I would be lying sobbing on my bed like a girl in her teens. I would be in no state to consider a simple decision like what gown to wear for dinner, let alone a question that could have such enormous repercussion for both Jonny and myself. 'Damn him!' I said aloud. 'Damn him! Damn him! Damn him!'

There was a knock on the door and James walked in. 'Thought I heard you talking to someone,' he said on finding me alone. There was an excited expression on his face and it was obvious no one had told him of Taylor's dramatic appearance. 'I've got some news,' he went on. 'Not all good by a long shot, but not all bad . . . Tremendous opportunity . . . That is if you've got the courage . . . '

'Courage?' I queried. 'You think I lack courage, James?'

'For the crucial stage of the battle . . . It's going to take much courage, Quincey, and the will of a tiger.'

He had shrugged off our quarrel of a few days back. 'Don't know what got into me, Quincey,' he had said. 'Perhaps that little Swedish she-cat upset me more than I thought.' I had apologized, too, I had pressed him too hard, perhaps. Still, the violence of his response on that occasion had surprised me. The she-cat, I suspected, had got her claws in deeper than she realised. It had been a brief storm and, since, he had been as resolute a lieutenant as ever.

Now, he sat on the corner of my desk. 'Steel yourself, for you'll find this hard to credit . . . Aunt Margaret's reneged on her promise . . . She's sold her 30,000 shares . . . '

I simply could not believe it. 'James,' I insisted, 'it's not possible . . . she said her word was her bond – as good as any gentleman's. . . Didn't you hear her say that?'

'I did,' he agreed, 'and I'd have trusted her, too . . . to the hilt
. . . But we discounted passion and that's always a mistake . . . '

'You mean she's fallen in love?' I asked incredulously.

'Exactly – with two of the finest horses in the world . . . I could
hardly believe the price . . . Two thousand guineas each – for
driving horses! It's an incredible sum, but by God it's clever – and
the cost's piffling by contrast to the issues that hang on it . . . Think
how she must feel as she handles those reins – spinning past her
friends behind a finer pair than you could see in all of Ireland!
You've got to give credit where it's due . . . As a move it's brilliant!'

The acuteness of my distress actually hurt – physically with a
sharp pain. 'Why didn't *we* think of that James . . . ?' I cried. 'It was
the key to her, like the role of Catherine to Bettine Laffont . . . We
didn't even have to look for it . . . It was there grazing in the
paddocks, in everything she said . . . How did you find out?'

'I wrote to her asking if she'd consider changing her mind about
selling to you . . . I didn't tell you because I didn't want to raise
your hopes . . . She wrote back that it was too late, said she felt
badly but couldn't help herself . . . Never set eyes on such horses
. . . Asked if you'd ever forgive her . . . '

I got to my feet, the sadness draining me. 'So it's over,' I said.
'Howard's won – overwhelmingly.' I thought of Roland Andrews'
confident venality and Steven Mason's last sneering question. They
did not matter now. The Andrews' 10,000 shares were irrelevant.
So was his surprise mortgage of Bettine's stock that she had forgotten all about. For, with Aunt Margaret's big block plus Helga's
holding, Howard had gained a total of 40,000.

My failure was bitter. For I was in a far worse position than when
we had initiated 'The Plan'. Then, at least, I had equality with
Howard. Now despite the oath I had sworn on Long Beach, he had
gained what I had fought for so hard – control of the bank. Worse,
the Andrews would *have* to deal with him now and, by the time
Jonny joined the bank, Paul would have been entrenched there for
years in a position of growing influence.

The fight seemed over, the victor already crowned with garlands.
I repeated Papa's words that I had said to myself so often: There
must be a way. There's always a way if only you can find it. But I

suspected in my despair that it was self-delusion, for the facts of my situation were bleak. 'What do I do now?' I asked James. 'Surrender with dignity?'

James was watching me with a smile on his lips that seemed at variance with my despondency. 'Surrender, Quincey?' he echoed softly. 'You'd never surrender even if you had to, but there's something I haven't told you yet — something that changes everything.' And it surely did.

Chapter 19

[1]

'Remember the last time we talked to each other across a desk, Mathew?' I asked.

'New York, I think, wasn't it?' He was watching me intently. Whenever he was on the defensive, he seemed to shrink within his jacket as though it was a shell. We were all at Shere that weekend and, at my request, he had driven to the cottage from his home on the estate. I received him, sitting formally at my desk, in my study.

'Do you recall what you said to me that day, Mathew? You said: Who's talking about rights? Stark realities, you said. That's what we were speaking of, you said. Well, Mathew, now *I'm* speaking of stark realities . . . ' I reached into a drawer of my desk. 'I have here a stock transfer,' I went on. 'On a date that I've left blank, it'll pass to me 100,000 of your shares in Alexanders at a price of £20 per unit . . . I don't *intend* to date it, in which case the purchase'll never take place, but I can if I want to . . . I hope you'll never force me but, if I have to, rest assured I will . . . Now sign it please . . . ' I passed it across the desk so that it lay before him.

Mathew was a veteran of difficult situations. He did not respond at once — just gazed at me, trying to assess my tactics. 'What in the world are you playing at, Quincey?' he asked at last. 'This'd give you complete control of the bank . . . You know I'd never sign this . . . '

'You will, Mathew and I'll tell you why . . . Do you by any chance remember Mr Longford?'

Anyone who did not know Mathew would have missed the faint change in his expression, but I saw it — the slightest narrowing of the eyelids, a hint of opaqueness. 'Mr Longford, Mathew,' I repeated. 'Manager of the Stock Department in '97. Surely you recall Mr Longford? He had an unfortunate accident.'

'It was an unhappy business,' Mathew agreed.

'I know why he fell from that window, Mathew . . . I know who pushed him . . . I know who paid for it and how much. What's more, I can prove it.'

He looked at me curiously, much as he would if he had thought he noticed a smudge on my nose. 'Prove what, Quincey?' he asked.

It was a good question. I had asked it myself. 'Prove what, James?' I had said. '*What* can we prove?'

He had been lying full-length on my sofa, much as Emmeline enjoyed. 'It's 1897,' he said. 'Alexanders are in the kind of trouble that happens to banks at times – as even happened to the great House of Baring in 1890 when massive loans they'd made to Argentina went bad. Barings had to be rescued. No one was going to rescue Alexanders . . . It was the banker's nightmare . . . a big loan goes sour and repayments are put off. Add a few mistakes that coincide . . . Suddenly there's not enough actual cash in the kitty . . . Money's due in from a whole range of sources, but not for a few days. It's a few days too long . . . Within hours they won't be able to meet their commitments, which means disaster. So what do they do? They buy time . . . at least, that's what Alexanders do . . . They issue duplicate notes in the stock they're trading for clients. When the 'few days' have passed and the expected cash comes in, they retrieve the dud paper and no one outside the family knows what's happened. Well, no one, that is, except the manager of the Stock Department, who's had to handle the detail . . . '

'Mr Longford,' I put in.

'Mr Longford,' he agreed, 'who's now begun to realize the strength of his position. Fraud was committed . . . If anyone finds out, it's jail for Howard, Mathew, probably Uncle – *and* the collapse of the bank. Starting to understand now?'

'You mean they pushed him out of an upper-floor window to keep him quiet?' I could not believe it. Not even of the Alexanders.

'*They* didn't. A visitor did – man named Edwards . . . They had to do *something*, Quincey. Longford was overplaying his hand . . . He could have retired in style . . . They'd have countenanced that. But Longford was greedy, began to talk in millions . . . That just wasn't acceptable – and, of course, by then he'd become so lethally dangerous that there was really no alternative to drastic action. So Mathew was given the nod.'

I was scribbling idly on my pad whilst I thought, sketching another little man. 'How in the world did you discover all this?'

'From Mrs Edwards. She was in the bank the other day. I overheard her name as she waited in the hall . . . So when she left I followed her and suggested we had a talk . . . She's causing trouble . . . She's poor . . . husband's dead . . . gambler, lost everything on the gee-gees. They'd be happy to give her money to solve the problem, but how can they? Officially they didn't even know him, and any hint that they had would compromise them. So they've balanced the options, as usual. Would anyone listen to her – a crazy old woman as against men of high repute like the Alexanders? What'd the City police say if she went to them? Why, they'd just point to the door . . . '

'But *you* listened?' I said.

He nodded. 'And once you know the facts, Quincey, a lot of things fall into place . . . evidence . . . Not marvellous evidence, but enough to give you Mathew on a plate . . . '

'Prove what, Mathew?' I said, repeating his own question. 'Why, prove that you were party to it. That's what.'

Again Mathew eyed me with a steady gaze I was forced to admire. 'That's quite absurd, Quincey,' he said.

I leaned forward. 'The facts, Mathew . . . One of your duties was to provide the bank with information. In the course of this you'd acquired some dubious friends. That's how you'd met Edwards . . . You agreed to pay Edwards £5,000, an immense sum for an immense problem . . . £1,000 down, £4,000 later . . . all in cash . . . Negotiations only in his home . . . You never took your carriage, just a cab . . .

'The scheme was good. Edwards called at the bank in the guise of a clerk working for a small broker. He asked to see someone in the Stock Department about some shares bought by his firm on behalf of clients. Rather strangely, Mr Longford decided to see him personally instead of leaving what was a routine matter to one of his staff. Even more odd was that he didn't receive him at his desk but in an interview room on an upper floor, where they would be alone. Why? Because Edwards's queries concerned one of the firms you'd used to get you out of trouble – and, if an error had been made, Mr Longford wanted to correct it himself. Also, he was under orders always to talk of these companies in private.

'The interview room has a small balcony and French windows. It was a hot day, so they were opened. Farewell Mr Longford. No one saw Edwards depart, though he insisted later that he left through the front entrance. In fact he went out through a back door to which you'd given him a key. His statement as to the time of his departure – before the accident, of course – could not be challenged.

'The next day, Edwards himself contacted the bank. He was horrified, he said, to read of the accident in the newspapers. The police asked to see him and he told them that, after their interview, Mr Longford had said he proposed to stay on in the room and work quietly. There were some files in a cabinet there that he needed to consult. Mr Longford conducted him to the top of the stairs and indicated the way out. Edwards supposed that he must have gone on to the balcony for a moment to enjoy the sunny day – and slipped.

'The police weren't convinced, but he had contacted the bank voluntarily. The cover of the broker who employed him had been carefully planned. There was no motive and no proof. Enough, Mathew?'

He gazed at me without expression for a few seconds. 'And when does the wicked godmother appear? It's a fairy-story, Quincey. I'm sure you don't believe it yourself . . .'

'I've got sworn affidavits, Mathew. From Mrs Edwards, who overheard your negotiations and even saw the money pass . . . From an Alexander stock clerk, now retired, who knew the bank was in trouble and guessed how it was extricated . . . Nothing too conclusive, but enough to open up the books with a suspicion that's never been there before . . . Do you want me to go on?'

He shook his head sadly. 'It's all nonsense, Quincey . . . Pie in the sky . . . But even if it wasn't it'd be of no value to you . . .'

'Don't assume that, Mathew. America changed me . . . *You* changed me . . . I came home a different woman.'

One of his grey smiles came to that narrow face. 'The scandal'd break the bank. You own nearly half of it . . .'

'Not break it . . . Stop it trading, perhaps . . . It owns assets worth many millions. I can think of several ways we could deploy our portion . . . I'd rather not, of course, and I won't have to, will I, because you'll sign the transfer, Mathew.'

He was still watching me intently. There was no emotion there, no anxiety. 'It's bluff, Quincey,' he said, standing up. 'You can't bluff *me*.'

[2]

It was in the afternoon, a few hours later, that I saw Frances cantering across the main paddock towards the cottage. The sun was shining and the grass was high green; riding side-saddle, in a dark brown habit and a bowler of the same colour, she could have been the subject of a painting. Suddenly, I felt sad for her, with her love for her Thomas that was as doomed as mine had been for Taylor. Also, I had a suspicion of why she was coming to see me — riding, as though for exercise, so that Mathew would not question where she was going. I had become very fond of her, but I knew I must rid myself of any such emotion. It was business she was here to discuss, and business it must be

I went out to meet her, smiling a welcome as she slid from the saddle and threw the reins to a groom. She was not quite herself — just a little too effusive, too affectionate even. 'I had to see you,' she said. 'You don't mind my coming suddenly like this?'

'Of course not.'

'Secret, please.'

'Secret,' I agreed. 'Let's go on to the terrace. I'll order tea . . . '

We sat with the waters of the Solent at our feet under the shade of my cherry tree. 'You saw Mathew this morning,' she ventured. She was not sure of me, I could see, found it hard to believe what her husband had told her. In all our long talks together, I had seemed so easy-going. 'He's not going to sign, Quincey.'

'He'll sign.'

'He won't, Quincey . . . I've been married to him for years . . . I know him in this mood . . . '

'He doesn't believe I'd do what I said, but I would, Frances . . . '

'Seriously?' She was studying me, anxiously. 'Why. Quincey? Why are you so determined on something that'd be so disastrous?'

'*You* ask that, Frances,' I said, surprised. 'You of all people witnessed what they did . . . That's never going to happen to me again – nor to Jonny.'

'But if he won't sign, Quincey, you wouldn't really go to the police, would you? I mean, where would it stop? Scandal, arrests probably . . . '

'He *will* sign . . . *You'll* persuade him . . . '

She sighed. 'He doesn't listen much to me, I fear – not on such matters.'

'You can make him. After all, it concerns you closely – *and* your children . . . '

She was looking at me strangely. 'I've never seen you like this before, Quincey . . . '

'The stakes are high.'

'And if I can't persuade him?'

'I'm confident you can . . . ' I paused. 'How's Tom? You haven't brought him to see me recently . . . '

My meaning was clear at once. 'You'd never do that, would you, Quincey?' Then she was on her feet, staring at me with horror. 'I can't believe you'd ever do that . . . You couldn't, could you, Quincey?'

'I *could*, Frances,' I said quietly, '*if* I really had to . . . '

'After what I did to help you?' she ventured, in a tone that was shocked.

I nodded. 'Frances, I'm devoted to you, but I could do anything to anyone . . . I could probably commit murder, like Mathew . . . I'm not the same person as the woman you helped . . . '

'And our friendship means nothing to you?' Her eyes had filled with tears.

'I value it highly, but not as highly as I price our security. Nothing's as high as that . . . ' I smiled at her. 'Wives can always persuade their husbands if their arguments are sound. They know them so well. They've been studying them so long. Go back and persuade him now . . . '

I got up and walked through the cottage with her in silence. 'Mrs Alexander is just leaving,' I said to one of the maids. 'Tell George to bring her horse.'

As she put her foot into the stirrup, she paused and looked at me.

'You wouldn't *really*, would you, Quincey?'

I nodded. 'I would.' Then I leaned forward and kissed her. She mounted, swung her right leg over the pommel under her skirts – then galloped across the paddock without looking back.

I stood watching her until at last she was out of sight, hidden by trees, and I was filled with a great sadness – and a doubt which persisted, despite all my logic, in plaguing me. Was I right? Did my aim justify the methods I was deploying? I sighed. If I was to win, the pressure had to be relentless.

I was about to go indoors when an open phaeton came into view from the lane through the wood. I recognized the coachman at once from the hunched shoulders and tilted bowler, and my heart sank. I did not want to see Taylor at all – not anywhere, but especially not at the cottage, which had always been my private territory, well within the first line of my defences.

As the carriage came closer, though, I saw that there was not a passenger in the back. Indeed, there was no room for one, since the whole seating area was piled high with flowers – a myriad, it seemed, of many varieties from exotic blooms like wild orchids and rare lilies to roses, carnations, gladioli, azaleas, tulips, daffodils and a host of others, all arranged with exquisite care as though the open phaeton was a gigantic bowl, prepared for some great occasion.

It was, of course, typical of Taylor, who believed that a little trouble and imagination would move any woman – like the elaborate picnic on the Oklahoma riverbank, like meeting train after train at Paulina, like hiring a phaeton miles from London and spending a fortune on a floral display. But it did not move me. Nothing could move me. On that I was determined, for there had been time now to consider the ramifications of his sudden arrival at Grosvenor Square. That day I had acted on instinct but, on reflection, I was sure it had been sound. If I gave way at all, if I even spoke to him, it would weaken the resolve I had constructed, layer by painful layer, over the livid wounds of New York. There could never be trust between us now and, without trust, our life could have no quality, no respect, no joy – and always it would be darkened by the demeaning shadow of the humiliation I could never forget.

Harry reined in the horses and looked down at me in his dry way, without expression, that invoked so many memories of America. 'Afternoon, Ma'am,' he greeted.

'Hallo, Harry,' I said warmly.

'Them flowers . . . ' He jerked his thumb backwards in a movement that seemed almost disdainful. 'They're from Mr Taylor, in case you hadn't guessed . . . He wants to see you, Ma'am . . . Come a long way, you'll grant . . . Never stopped speaking of you, Ma'am, whole time he was in California. Truth to tell, if I hadn't been amenable to you myself, I'd have found it downright oppressive . . . '

'Oh, Harry,' I said, 'it's good to see you, it really is . . . I've missed you a lot, but Mr Taylor's got to get it into his head that I'm not talking to him . . . receiving him . . . or having anything to do with him. Once bitten, Harry . . . '

The old man nodded sagely. 'He's determined, Ma'am, set on the idea of dripping water wearing away the stone . . . Can't you just spare him a couple of minutes, Ma'am, and get it over with? What harm'd that do? Then he can tell you the important thing that's on his mind, and . . . '

'Suggest he writes it to me in a letter, Harry.'

'Now would you read it if he did, Ma'am, or tear it up? Anyways, it'd take the sport out of it – unless he could stand there and watch you open it . . . '

'He's had a while to write me letters, Harry . . . I'm surprised it never crossed his mind before . . . '

'Maybe writing letters doesn't come natural to him, Ma'am. And I don't mean no disrespect, you'll understand, but he *is* your husband, after all . . . '

'I can think of a day, Harry, when he didn't behave like my husband. It distressed me greatly . . . still does distress me greatly . . . '

'And do you think, Mrs Alexander,' Taylor asked from behind me, 'that it doesn't distress me . . . ? That it didn't distress me beyond measure to leave you?'

He was some way off – just within earshot – and mounted, as usual, on a horse of quality. He was wearing polished boots, a black waisted coat and a brushed silk topper, which he raised to me with

407

a bow. I realized that Harry had been more than an emissary. He had been a distraction, halting the phaeton well past my front door so that, as he talked to me, my back was towards the paddock through which Taylor, like Frances, had ridden, before keeping to the lawns to muffle the sound of the horse's feet.

'You heard what Harry said,' he declared, walking his horse closer. 'Is that really too much to ask? All right, it was a mistake to come on you in London like I did without warning, but surely there's no sense in refusing to hear what I've got to say . . .'

I was tempted for a moment to break my vow but, as before, I grew furious at the sight of him, and that made it easier to ignore him. 'Goodbye, Harry,' I said. 'It's been good to see you.'

I had turned to enter the cottage when Taylor called out: 'What about these flowers then? Surely, it's a shame to waste them.'

I swung round angrily. 'Do what you like with them!' I snapped, realizing my mistake at once. I had spoken to him.

He grinned. 'Sweet words,' he said. 'I hope you'll speak some more sweet words, maybe even make it a habit . . . In time, of course, when you get used to me again.' He swept his hat off again in an elaborately courteous farewell. 'Come on, Harry,' he said and, turning his horse suddenly, he put him into a fast canter towards the lane.

Harry raised his hand to me. 'Good day, Ma'am.' He slapped the horse with the reins and, at a trot, the wheels of the phaeton crunching the driveway, followed his master.

Chapter 20

[1]

Howard paused in the doorway, his big head, luxuriant with black hair, seeming oddly lowered forward. He appeared to take a small pace back, as though to gain momentum before entering. There was about him an aura of power diminished, of greatness reduced – an aura that must attend all such surrenders. He was haggard, the furrows deep in his face, his eyes in hollows as though he had not slept for nights.

We were all back in London. He had made a formal appointment. It was 10.00 a.m. on a Tuesday. 'You've got what you sought,' he said. 'You were right – there *was* another day.'

I was moved, the victory soured a little. I had to remind myself what he had done to me, why I had campaigned so bitterly against him.

He approached with slow reluctant movements. 'I have here two undated stock transfers,' he said. 'They're signed.'

'Two?' I inquired, as he took them from an inside pocket.

'Fifty thousand of Mathew's holding . . . and the same number of mine.' He saw my surprise, for I had asked for none of his. 'We're brothers . . . We're sharing the defeat . . . ' He held out the documents to me, and I took them. 'I feel like a burgher of medieval days,' he went on, 'surrendering the keys of his city . . . '

I was still uncertain how to respond. We had an extraordinary relationship. I wanted to put my arms round him and take that great head to my breast. I liked to see him proud, not stricken – even though *I* had done the striking; even though, if required to, I would strike again. I liked to see him standing erect, his chest out, the symbol of the bank that bore his name.

'So,' he went on sadly, 'for the first time the House of Alexander is controlled by a woman.' He wandered disconsolately towards the fireplace, every movement underlining what he saw as a disgrace. His back was towards me as he asked: 'Well, now you have your victory, what do you want of us? Do you wish me to resign?'

'Why should I wish that?'

'You hold the power . . . '

'Behind the throne, Howard, as it must be . . . In the world of finance, they like kings, not queens. You taught me that with Richard's desk. I doubt if I'd make changes anyway; you wear the crown of Alexanders well. However, I do have one request . . . '

'An order, surely.' The words had a bitter tone that I had not heard in him before.

'If you oppose, I'll reconsider, but I'd like James appointed to the Board.'

His relief was evident. He had expected a demand that was far more stringent. He conceded with a shrug. 'Just lately James has impressed me . . . He's older now, of course . . . '

'And I did wonder about Emmeline. She's your daughter, of course, and I know your views about the proper occupations for women, but if she was to help me here, it'd hardly be a career . . . Would you rule that out?'

'It'd be a career soon enough,' he said, but he was surprised. 'You really want her? She's still like a playful puppy.'

'She has potential, I think.'

'For what?'

'For understanding world affairs; for being able to converse at dinner with knowledge and intelligence; for being more useful as a wife to a husband of importance . . . '

He grunted, surveying me sceptically, knowing that my logic, like my purpose, was specious. 'And you?' he asked. 'What about you?'

I laughed. 'Oh, I'll be there, Howard . . . Like now, as an adviser. . . Well, usually as an adviser . . . '

'You mean as long as I do what I'm told?' It was a growl.

'You'd not accept that. I wouldn't want you to – in the interests of the bank. You're experienced and able, Howard. You've won much respect in the Square Mile and on Wall Street. I've more sense than to interfere . . . except . . . well, perhaps occasionally . . . ' I was unable to conceal a small smile ' . . . A little, maybe . . . from time to time . . . '

He did not believe me. 'Didier Frères,' he ruminated gloomily, ' . . . cinema halls . . . films . . . That's what you'll be telling me to do next, isn't it?'

'I might raise it again,' I agreed lightly. 'What Richard'd want if he was here. That's how it's always been since he died. In proportion, as suits a speculation . . . like motors . . . Come to think of it,' I teased, 'wasn't it you, Howard, who was pressing for a motor merger with Roland Andrews? What of dear Mr Andrews, Howard?'

His glance suggested that I had struck below the belt. 'He doesn't matter now. Mason can do what he wishes about Andrews . . . ' He sighed heavily. 'I'm not sure this is going to be practical, Quincey. I'm not used to taking orders – especially from a woman . . . '

'I'm not challenging your position . . . I've just told you . . . '

He was dubious. 'We'll see,' he said. 'We'll put it to the test – the test of time.' His eyes were on me, probing uncertainly.

Suddenly, I was touched. 'Oh, Howard,' I said involuntarily, and hurried to him. 'Let's make peace.' And I kissed him on the cheek.

He grunted. 'Peace is what I asked of *you* wasn't it? You said it was what victors always wanted . . . you were right . . . '

'Will you grant it?'

'I've no choice, have I?'

'You could dream of fighting another day.'

'I'd be foolish not to give it a trial. Of course, if my position becomes intolerable . . . ' He gave a shake to his head. 'How Richard would have laughed . . . You've fought more fiercely than he'd have done, played as rough a game as I've ever played with men.'

I knew a sudden anger. 'I learned in a rough school,' I said. 'I had a rough instructor.'

'I suppose we all do what we think is right.'

'Or necessary.' My words were sharp – sharper, as so often, than I intended. 'Once you'd got Aunt Margaret's stock, I was left with no options. I had to attack with every weapon that I had to hand . . . '

He frowned. 'Did you say Aunt Margaret's stock?'

'It was most adroit as a tactic,' I responded.

'But I don't have Aunt Margaret's stock,' he insisted.

It was my turn to be perplexed. 'But . . . ' I began. 'Well, someone certainly does.'

'Then the buyer must be an existing stockholder . . . that's required by our Articles of Association . . . But I can think of no one who'd stand to gain except you or me. Not even that scoundrel Andrews . . . '

'Then it's a mystery, Howard, for there's no doubt she's sold her holding.'

[2]

It did not remain a mystery for long. The answer lay on my dressing-table – an answer that neither I nor Howard could possibly have considered. I saw it the moment I walked into my bedroom to change for a luncheon appointment – with surprise, for the place was unusual for official papers.

The document on the dressing-table was a stock transfer. That much was obvious. But when I picked it up, I was astonished to find that it was signed by Margaret Alexander and passed to me, of all people, her 30,000 shares. I, it seemed, was the unknown person who had acquired her stock – which was, of course, impossible. For a second, I was disorientated. Was I dreaming? Had I lost my senses?

'A great lady, that Margaret Alexander.' The sound of the words was unnerving, for it was Taylor's voice – which only gave me further doubts about my sanity. 'That's how the British built the empire,' he went on, 'with characters like her.'

I turned uncertainly, my anger at his presence tempered by my relief that he was not the rogue figment that I had imagined.

He was standing, leaning against the door-frame, idly studying his nails, with one leg cocked so that the highly-polished toe of the shoe rested point downwards on the floor. 'I'm like a genie, aren't I, appearing from a bottle? But you've left me no choice but tricks . . . '

I found words at last. 'Who in the name of heaven let you into my house?' I demanded.

He raised his eyebrows. 'Now you've actually addressed a question to me . . . I'm making progress, aren't I?' He folded his arms.

'How did I get in? Well, I'm a game chap and sure as a juggler's box I was going to give you the present I keep on about . . . That's it there, by the way — what you've just been looking at . . . '

Puzzled, I glanced at the stock transfer that was still in my hand. 'You mean . . . ' I began incredulously, 'you mean . . . Aunt Margaret's shares? *That's* your present?'

'And this one, too . . . ' He took a folded document from his pocket and tossed it on to the bed in front of me. 'That's Helga Petersen's holding — at least, it was until I bought it for you . . . '

'But Howard got these,' I said incredulously.

'Did he say he had?'

'No,' I answered dubiously, 'but he said it was all arranged . . . So did she . . . '

He shook his head in mock disapproval. 'Volatile little lady . . . changed her mind . . . Mischievous, you could say, but fortunate for us, eh? Oh, and by the way, I nearly forgot . . . ' He felt in his jacket pocket and lobbed another folded paper on to the bed. 'That gives you Bettine Laffont's stock as well. You were pretty smart there but not as smart, I'm glad to say, as my Paris attorney . . . '

I was dazed, my heart thumping. 'You mean Howard doesn't have these either?' I asked, forgetting that they were mortgaged to Roland Andrews, though this was no longer significant. 'Howard never told me he didn't have these.'

'Did you ask him?'

'Not in so many words, though we touched on the subject . . . I just assumed it was he who'd instructed the *avoué* . . . '

'Howard plays his cards pretty close, but there are times to play bold . . . That's why you're now the boss of Alexanders . . . what do you think your old pa would say about that, eh?'

For a moment there was silence between us. I was trying to absorb the enormity of what he had done for me — *and* what it signified, transforming the desertion that had racked me in such long, deep agony into an act of devotion, almost of glory. He had a liking for grand gestures, but this surely topped all others, soaring above them, dwarfing them like some great mountain peak. 'Oh, Taylor,' I whispered at last. 'I don't know what to say . . . What *can* I say?' Suddenly, I wished fervently that I had let him speak when first he had arrived in London. My last ruthless battle with

413

Howard had not been needed. My threats to Frances, the betrayal that had so shocked her, could have been avoided. Worse, by far, Taylor would not have been robbed of his magnificent gift – the control of the bank that I had already won from Howard downstairs. But that, I vowed, was something that Taylor must never discover.

He was watching me with a lazy smile – enjoying the sport, as Harry had put it. 'Hope it's what you wanted,' he said lightly, as though his present was conventional. 'If not, well, we can always take it back to the store.'

'It's the most beautiful gift you could have ever found for me,' I responded softly. Then, meeting his tone, I jested: 'Clever of you to think of it.'

'Got the idea in bed one night,' he said. 'What, I asked myself, could a fellow give a girl who'd already got everything money could buy? Well, almost everything.'

'And suddenly you thought: I know what she'd like – control of the bank . . . I wager no one else's thought of that.'

He grinned. 'How did you guess?'

'Second sight . . . Great minds . . . something of that nature.'

We had not moved since he had appeared. He was still leaning nonchalantly against the door; I was backed up to my dressing-table, as I had been from the start. We were extending the moment deliberately, slipping into the kind of teasing patter that we had often employed in the past. I was grateful, for I still needed time. I was fearful, cautious, the unhealed scars of the past months curbing the wild hope that was starting to pierce the shock of his return.

'Then I get to wondering,' he went on. 'Was it possible to buy it for you? What'd it cost? Not that I cared, for I was rich again . . . '

'That was a fast change of fortune – even for you.'

'It was easier than before. The market was still jumping about from the Crash like a startled filly, especially mining stocks, which had set it all going. Well, I knew my way in mining stocks as well as I know a deck of cards. I had ample capital from Mathew and my luck was running again. I played that frisky market almost every day – in and out, sometimes several times a day . . . Made thousands every week . . . ' The jesting died in his tone. 'I'm not telling

414

you the truth. I didn't get the idea when I was flying high; I got it on the first sleepless night on that trainride west from New York that I'll never forget . . . ' First thing I did in San Francisco was to wire agents in London about the Alexander stockholders. I'd an aim then that never left me the whole time I was there – a picture of your face when I handed you the stock you've got there that was so vivid it could've been painted . . . Every time I made a killing, every order I gave to sell, you were in my mind almost as real as you look now . . . '

'And then I went and spoiled it for you!' I exclaimed unhappily, adding, almost in anger: 'I never knew, Taylor . . . Oh, I'd have given so much to know . . . Surely you could have got some kind of word to me, couldn't you?'

'And broken the deal with Mathew not to contact you?'

'You've done far worse things, Taylor . . . All your life you've done worse things than that.'

'Not with English gentlemen. They've got their own rules, quaint though some of them are . . . Nothing wrong with what they did to me but, if they'd discovered I'd gone back on the agreement, they'd never have talked to me again . . . Now, since I honoured the deal, they're going to have to -- especially when you consider who I'm married to . . . Well, aren't they?'

The tears came so suddenly they took me by surprise. I was standing there, gazing at him, still not daring to trust the happiness that was surging up inside me, when my eyes filled and two great streams coursed down my cheeks. 'Oh, Taylor,' I said.

'You're crying.' He was laughing at me softly. 'You're not supposed to be crying . . . That wasn't in my picture . . . '

'Oh yes, I'm crying all right,' I said. 'I'm crying for lost months, for all those times I've tried to hate you . . . I'm crying because I never thought I'd ever be this happy again.' And I rushed into his arms and my lips, wet with tears, found his with an urgency inspired by all the desperation I had known since Long Beach. I clutched him as though I would die if I let go, as though I would disappear into some hidden abyss, grasping in turn his neck, his cheeks, his head, feeling him, moving my mouth on his with in-credulous exploration,

Suddenly, I stopped, holding his face firmly away from mine, studying blue eyes that were looking back at me so tenderly that I started to cry again. 'Taylor' I whispered, 'it *is* really you, isn't it?'

'It's me,' he answered, and kissed me lightly.

'I'm not dreaming or imagining?'

He shook his head and kissed me again.

'I've not lost my mind?'

'Not unusually so . . . considering you've always been a little mad.'

'How can I be sure . . . How can I *know* it's you?'

'Don't I feel like me? Or do all men feel the same? Can't you tell from kissing?'

'They're your lips I'm kissing,' I agreed dubiously, savouring them slowly, ' . . . and they're your hands . . . ' I held one of them in mine, fondling it gently with my fingers ' . . . and it's your face,' I added, running my knuckles lightly over a shaven cheek ' . . . which only makes me anxious . . . '

'Why anxious?'

'Because I'm fearful that if I so much as close my eyes, you'll be away again – disappear back into the genie's bottle . . . '

'It was you who made me a genie. I just came back to you as your husband . . . came to stay. How do I convince you?'

'How do you?' I taunted gently, the wanting spreading through me like a steady flooding tide.

'Looks like it's going to be difficult to figure a way,' he said, seeing everything I was feeling in my eyes. 'I suppose I could try one or two things that might give you a bit of assurance.' He kissed my neck, little light kisses, brushed his lips across my ear, and I arched to him. 'Persuasive?' he inquired.

'You could say I'm listening,' I answered, 'but don't go thinking I'm convinced.' His hands were moving on my body, slowly delicately stroking really – my hips, my back, my sides, my breasts.

'It's a hard task you've set me,' he said as I lifted my mouth again to his – and as he kissed me deep and hard but always controlled, he began walking my skirt up with his fingers.

'You're being forward, Sir,' I whispered.

'Husband's rights,' he murmured. 'The best of arguments . . . '

'It's no argument . . . ' My eyes were closed. 'It's lusting . . . '

'It's loving,' he insisted, 'but too soon, perhaps . . . ' He knew it

416

was not too soon. 'You need time, I'm sure, maybe more persuading . . . well, we can wait if you like . . .'

It was the old confident Taylor, knowing there could be no
waiting, and for a second I was angry with him, despite his unbelievable presents and all they meant, irritated by his knowing. I
wanted to teach him that it was not that simple, that women were
different. I tried. 'That's right,' I said, 'we'll wait . . . We'll wait
until tonight . . . You're such an understanding man . . . ' But then
I laughed, my cheek against his. 'If you don't claim those rights this
very minute, Taylor,' I whispered, 'I'll burn up . . . I'll smoulder
away so you won't recognize me . . . Oh, Taylor . . . Taylor . . .
Taylor.' I hugged him very tightly – and ran to the door and locked
it. I stood with my back to it, holding his gaze, enjoying for a second
the pain of desire suspended – then began, with slow deliberate
movements, to undo my jacket.

Without words, he took off his coat. I let the jacket drop to the
floor. His coat fell at his feet. Our eyes had never left each other.

I unbuttoned my blouse, as he took off his waistcoat; released my
skirt as he unpinned his cravat.

'I love you, Taylor,' I said softly as I unhooked my petticoat,
speaking as much with the way I looked at him as with my voice.
'Oh, I love you so much.'

'And I love you,' he returned, as he took off his shirt – talking,
too, as much with the intenseness of his eyes as with his words. He
seemed to have broadened in the shoulders as though he had been
felling timbers these past months rather than playing the market.

'More than you've loved the others?' I asked, undoing my corset.

'I've loved no others . . . *you* know that . . . '

I did know, but it was a time for self-indulgence. I needed to hear
him say it, repeat it. 'That's a beautiful thing to say.'

'It's not a thing to say, it's a fact.' He was standing in his long
cotton drawers, which seemed to give him a sense of extra strength.

'Then it's a fact that's beautiful.' My breasts were bare and he
knew it, though his eyes had not left mine for a moment – knew it as
I knew about his shoulders. We were in perfect tune as though he
had never been away, our mood so rich, so delicately poised that
the knock on the door came as a jarring shock, like sudden breaking glass. I froze in despair, hating the world outside, but he

417

nodded, meaning I should respond. 'Who is it?' I asked sharply.

'Liza, Mrs Alexander. I wondered if you knew the time . . . It's nearly one . . . The car's waiting . . .'

'I'm indisposed, Liza,' I said. 'Please send a note.'

'Yes, Mrs Alexander . . . and shall I phone the bank about the Board meeting this afternoon?'

I hesitated. 'No,' I said, 'that I'll attend.'

Our eyes had never wavered, not even when I was speaking through the door to Liza. Now I moved towards him feeling oddly humble, like a supplicant. He put his arms round me, holding me for a few seconds with the special gentleness born of strength. Then he lifted me up, cradling me like a child, and laid me on the bed. He loomed above me, one knee on the mattress, savouring the sight of my body, part by part, with an intent, almost reverent expression.

'So many times,' he whispered, 'I've dreamed of this.'

'So have I – only to die a little every time on wakening.' I held up my arms to him. 'No dying now, Taylor.'

'No dying,' he said, as he lowered himself to me.

'Living now, Taylor,' I whispered as I took him into me, 'living gloriously.' But it was a kind of dying – like the killing of a ghost – and the sense of living, the new living without the desolate shadow that had darkened my existence for so long, was as strong and vibrant as the spring after a winter that has been especially stark.

[3]

On the surface, the meeting was much like any of the others. Howard had taken the chair, as usual, at the head of the long mahogany table. There were the same procedures, laid down by custom – the reading of the previous minutes, the taking-as-read of those manager's decisions that required Board sanction. But the mood was different. From the moment I had taken my place with those men, who had been so cool and distant when months before Howard had first brought me into their elite all-male concave, I had noted a marked change in their attitude. Clearly, they were aware of the power I had gained.

James was present, too. That was another change. For the first time, I had a supporter on whom I could rely. His appointment as a director, proposed by Howard and seconded by Mathew, had been the first item on the agenda.

I sensed early that there was something wrong, but I could not define it. Howard was conceding with good grace to everything I had asked – even agreeing to Emmeline joining my staff. I had, of course, made no demands, opted to leave the status quo unchanged. But the reality remained that I had won and surrender, though he had made much of it that morning, was against his nature. I knew him, too, to be a veteran of many wars, a skilled tactician. So I remained on my guard. Even so, I was still taken by surprise.

The item seemed innocuous enough – 'Proposed Acquisitions'. At least it did, until Howard said: 'Now, gentlemen, we come to a project that's close to Mrs Alexander's heart. Didier Frères is a company that makes moving films, owns a few cinema halls, as they are called, here in England, in France and even in America. . .'
He paused to allow Edward Brown, the secretary, to pass round the table copies of a sheet of figures. Meanwhile, I was thinking fast. What was his aim? Why was he urging the purchase of a firm that he had been so derisive about only that morning? Who, without my knowledge, had produced the detailed financial report that lay before me?

'It's a new field, of course,' Howard went on, 'and, although we'd not normally consider such a venture, it does conform with the policy of my late cousin and his charming widow, our colleague, that a small part of our investments should be devoted to speculation in the new industries . . . ' He turned to me. 'Perhaps, Mrs Alexander, you'd care to explain your enthusiasm for this enterprise, which I must confess I've found infectious . . . '

This was it, I knew – the test he had spoken of that morning, the challenge I had been expecting, but it was concealed so that I could not identify it. It did not even seem like a challenge, but I was sure I was facing the old devious Howard, the Howard I had first met on the yacht in the Irish Sea. I responded carefully, feigning pleasure at his promotion of my favourite project. 'I didn't know this was to be discussed today,' I ventured with a smile. 'I'm intrigued to know why I was not informed.'

Howard was expansive. 'Now there you must forgive me,' he said, very much Chairman of the Board. 'Put it down to self-indulgence,' he went on. 'I knew it would please you.'

I glanced at the report Mr Brown had given us. 'The purchase appears to have been negotiated,' I said.

'*And* the loan for working capital,' he agreed.

'I must confess I find it disturbing.'

'Disturbing?' he echoed, 'but you've urged the purchase . . . Perhaps it's the terms you think could be improved . . . '

I shook my head. 'The terms seem adequate,' I conceded, 'on brief consideration.'

'Then,' Howard went on, 'perhaps you could explain to our colleagues the belief I know you have in the potential of this fledgling industry. You compared it, I recall, with Masons' status in 1902, and none of us can argue about the success of that . . . '

I was being rushed, and I did not like it. So were the Board. The key to Howard's motive lay there somewhere, but still I could not isolate it.

Again Howard urged me to speak – so, hesitantly, I told them what I felt about the future of moving films, of the opportunity they provided for low-cost entertainment. I echoed Bettine Laffont's faith in the filming of full-length plays, of such ventures as *Catherine* being viewed for years ahead.

And then, in turn, my colleagues began to answer me with arguments that were related and, I suspected, planned. All opposed the purchase. Where was the collateral, I was asked, as though I was the proposer? Reels of celluloid? Cinema halls, often buildings of fragile structure, sheds even? Were not films a fad of which the public would soon tire?

It dawned on me then. The proposal, put in my name, was to be rejected. That was Howard's intention, though he himself would appear to be supporting it. He wanted a Board vote against me. He wanted me to meet the linked shields of male opposition. He wanted to establish precedent in our new situation, an underlining of who was to be in charge of the bank, despite my new stock-holding – and he wanted this without risk of a major battle.

I could overturn the Board decision, as he well knew, by calling a meeting of the shareholders. But would I do so for so petty an issue as a small company like Didier Frères – especially since this was exactly the kind of thing that might be expected of a woman with too much power? He had guessed, with all my talk of status quo, that I would be cautious at this early stage in our new situation. His eyes were on the future, when the status quo might be frayed and the issues big. In other words, it was a testing skirmish and I knew I must win it. In fact, I decided to risk a battle.

'I'll put the matter to a vote now,' Howard was saying, 'unless anyone has any further comments?'

'I've a point, Mr Chairman,' I started, in a pleasant enough tone, 'which the Board might care to bear in mind before they vote,' adding firmly: 'I must make it clear . . . Alexanders are going to buy into Didier Frères.'

Howard looked at me with his bland stare. 'I find it hard to believe,' he said, 'that you'd call a general meeting for a matter such as this.'

'I advise you to believe it,' I responded sharply.

'It would come to public knowledge, you realize . . . There could be comments in the press of a nature that might not be desirable . . . '

'I'm glad you recognize that,' I countered.

'You yourself could be pilloried.'

'I'll take the risk.'

I could see him trying to assess if I was bluffing. 'Mrs Alexander,' he said, 'if you intend often to ignore the wishes of the Board, it cannot perform its purpose, which is to direct the bank, and we might as well all resign.'

But I knew he would never resign, as he had offered earlier – *could* never resign if he was to protect what had always been the most important element in his life. I offered him escape with honour. 'Why not leave the matter,' I said, 'until another day, with more leisure to consider it?'

He was reluctant. 'I have to say, Mrs Alexander, this hardly conforms with your assurances about interference.'

'I said a little,' I responded, 'sometimes . . . Now put the project to the vote, if you must.'

He hesitated, then retreated. 'I take it, gentlemen,' he said at last,

421

'there's no objection to postponement?' He looked round the table. 'I hardly think we need a formal vote . . . ' He picked up the agenda sheet. 'So that brings us to Other Business . . . Do you have anything, Brown?' he inquired and the secretary shook his head. 'Anyone else?' he asked, raising his head.

'Yes,' I said, 'as a matter of fact I have . . . In view of my new position, I think the Board should be given a chance to meet my husband, don't you, Mr Chairman?'

Even Howard, controlled as he usually was, could not conceal his amazement. 'I don't think I understand,' he answered evenly. 'Is this a joke? The occasion's hardly suitable . . . '

'Oh, it's no joke,' I assured him, 'though it has its amusing aspects . . . Mr Brown, would you kindly be so good as to open the door . . . '

Brown, as incredulous as Howard, did as I asked and we waited for a few seconds, all eyes on the doorway, before Taylor sauntered into view, wearing a morning coat and carrying his hat in front of him, as he often did, with the fingers of both hands. 'Good morning, gentlemen,' he said, with an easy grin.

For a few seconds there was silence as Howard surveyed him with shocked astonishment, the colour rising in his cheeks. Then I said: 'If I may make the introductions, Mr Chairman . . . Gentlemen, this is my husband, Mr Charles Taylor.' I gave him an affectionate smile as, for his benefit, I continued: 'On my right here is Mr Henry Smith . . . Then, on my left, Alderman Sir Frank Hammond . . . On his left is . . . '

Taylor nodded to each member of the Board as I indicated him 'You're acquainted, of course,' I added, 'with Mr Alexander and his brother.'

Howard turned to me: 'Mr Taylor is truly your husband?'

I nodded with a pleased smile. 'We were married last year in New York.'

'Don't you think I was entitled to be informed of so important an event?'

'What difference would it have made? You'd already done him all the damage you could.'

Mathew was watching Taylor with the intensity of a coursing greyhound. 'You've gone back on our deal,' he challenged.

Taylor laughed and shook his head. 'I think not . . . I have here a cheque drawn to Alexander & Co. . . . ' He displayed it, holding it high. 'It's for $150,000 plus 15 per cent interest for the period of the loan . . . '

'It wasn't a loan,' Mathew snapped.

'*I* saw it as a loan . . . What else could it be? A gift? Surely there can be no conditions to a gift? A purchase? If so, what did you buy?'

'Your agreement to leave Mrs Alex . . . I suppose it's Mrs Taylor now, though the thought appals me . . . Your agreement to make no attempt to contact her . . . '

'And I observed the terms, as she'll confirm — until I was in a position to discharge the obligation . . . Why, you should be glad . . . At that high rate of interest, you made a good investment.'

Howard turned back to the Board. 'Does anyone have other business?' he inquired. 'Then I declare the meeting ended.'

[4]

I was alone in 'The Room' and it was quiet, for all the clerks in the great hall had gone home. More than an hour had passed since the meeting and I was tired, for it had been a full day, coloured by high emotion. I was sitting in Uncle's chair at the big desk from which once, as 'Caesar', he had dispatched those telegrams to New York that I, as a young girl, had processed. I thought with a weary smile of how I would have responded then if anyone had suggested that, within six years, I would have been occupying his position — unofficially, at least. Not long before, Howard had urged me to make it official in a bitter outburst that I would not have credited in a man of such control had it not been for one dark afternoon at Shere. 'Why not take your place there?' he had challenged angrily. 'The throne, as you called it today . . . That's what you've fought for so fiercely, isn't it? Or are you reserving it for your Mr Taylor?'

I had ignored the taunt, for Taylor had been in 'The Room' at the time, with James and Mathew, and had heard the jibe, though Howard had not adressed one word directly to him since his arrival at the bank. 'You forced it all, Howard,' I charged. 'You — not me . . . I was content enough with the way things were before Oklahoma . . . We had an understanding about the bank that suited both of us.'

He wandered desolately to the window and stared out into the courtyard, his hands deep in his pockets. 'I had a duty to protect the bank, the family, Jonny . . . *You* know that, mesmerized as you were by that blackguard . . . mesmerized as you still are . . . Married!' he cried in quiet desperation. 'God save us all from women . . . I suppose next you'll propose *him* for the Board as well . . .'

It was almost a cry, tortured and revealing. 'What makes you think that he'd accept if I did propose him?' I asked gently, moved as I always was when Howard was hobbled. 'Why don't you ask him now?'

Slowly, Howard turned and looked at Taylor, forcing himself at last, it seemed, to recognize his presence. Taylor responded with a grin. 'Me? A banker?' he said. 'Now isn't that amusing?' He sat, arms folded, on the corner of Uncle's desk – which in itself was sacrilege – idly swinging one leg. 'Can you see me at that table with all your eminent colleagues?' he asked – then shook his head at the thought. 'I think not, Alexander . . . Wouldn't suit my temperament at all. I need to be a free agent, bid when I like, sell when I like . . . no questions . . . I wouldn't like questions . . . And in banks they always ask questions, don't they?'

I smiled as I recalled Howard's response – impassive, of course, but knowing him as I did, I had detected the relief in him, soured though it had been by offence at the rejection, by distrust of Taylor's motives. How could a man refuse the distinction of a seat on the Alexander Board – especially an adventurer like Taylor? But then, he had never understood Taylor. I was not sure I understood Taylor.

Now they had all left me – Howard and Mathew presumably to consider their position, Taylor with James for a conducted tour of the building, knowing I needed a little time alone.

Helga, I supposed, was still outside, where – to my surprise – she had been sitting patiently when we had emerged from the boardroom. 'Helga!' I exclaimed. 'What are you doing here?'

'I've come for James,' she announced, as though she was an

424

Angel of Death, and embraced me warmly. 'Quincey, it's no good . . . I find it doesn't suit me to live without him . . . I need him, so you'll persuade him, won't you, like the sister he says you are . . . Why, there he is. Tell him now, Quincey . . . Tell him I'll make him the happiest man in the world. You'll convince him, Quincey . . .'

'You can convince him yourself, Helga,' I said, 'But later, for just now we have much to discuss.'

There had been no chance for her to argue, for Emmeline, who had been waiting, too, could restrain herself no longer. She rushed up to me and kissed me. 'Oh Aunt Quincey, you really are a gem . . . Papa's told me I can work for you—*with* his blessing . . .'

I glanced behind me. 'I should make yourself scarce, before he changes his mind . . . my husband always rubs him up the wrong way.'

'Your husband?' she had echoed. 'And you never told me! That's absolutely horrid of you, Aunt Quincey . . . I wouldn't have let on . . . Honestly, I wouldn't . . .' Then she giggled. 'But since we're now related . . .' she smiled at Taylor ' . . . he can at least kiss me without offending the proprieties, can't he?'

I leaned back in the chair, as I had seen Uncle do so often, and idled with a pencil on Howard's pad. Was I still the same person – the same girl, though matured, as the Quincey Brown who had called on Mr Johnson in the hope of saving the family fortunes, planned a career with Great Aunt Abigail, provoked so startled a response in Richard Alexander when first I had reported to him instead of the man he had expected? Or had I been changed, blooded by conflict into someone different?

I looked up at the painting of old George Alexander, the buccaneer as Uncle had called him, who had started it all by speculating on a glut of rice. What would he have thought of it, I wondered? A woman sitting at his desk? In private, of course, but it would not always be private.

My reverie was disturbed by the sound of the door, and I saw Taylor standing there. He held a bottle of champagne and two glasses. 'I stole these from the Directors' dining-room . . . Will they send me to jail for theft?'

'It's just what Howard would expect,' I answered. 'He said you were a blackguard . . . ' I pointed at the picture of Old George. '*He* was a blackguard, too, you're in good company . . . or a buccaneer, as I've heard him called . . . Even Howard agreed once that he was a brigand. He'd accused you of being a brigand, so I said, if anyone was a brigand, it was his own grandfather . . .'

'What did he say to that?' Taylor asked, as he laid the glasses on the desk and undid the wire that held the cork in the bottle.

'That he wouldn't have wanted me to marry him either, that we were a family now of standing and position . . . ' I stood up and moved round the desk as he released the cork. 'Where's James?' I asked.

'He was diverted – by the charming Helga Petersen . . . '

'She's determined on conquest – like a Viking . . . Did she seem to be making progress?'

'His resistance wasn't exactly fierce . . . Seemed delighted to see her . . . '

He filled the glasses and handed me one. 'I'm sorry I'm not an earl.'

'Good heavens, why? You'd make a terrible earl.'

'Then Howard would be happy.'

'And I wouldn't control the bank, and I have to admit that's growing on me . . . I rather like controlling the bank . . . and I don't much favour earls . . . '

'Then I'm glad I'm not an earl.' He raised his glass.'What shall we drink to?'

'Brigands,' I said. 'I favour brigands.'

Susan Howatch
The Rich are Different £3.95

A great fortune and the struggle to control a worldwide business empire; an ambitious and beautiful woman who is one of the most provocative heroines in fiction; a love that spans ecstasy and anguish and a story that reaches from the quiet Norfolk countryside across the ocean to the New York of the Roaring Twenties.

'Love, hate, death, murder and a hell of a lot of passion . . . DAILY MIRROR

The Sins of the Fathers £3.50

From Wall Street to the quiet of an English country churchyard, Susan Howatch's magnificent narrative traces the fortunes of the Van Zale dynasty through two decades of wealth, ambition and struggle, until the sins of the fathers are finally visited upon the next generation.

Arthur Hailey
The Moneychangers £2.95

The genius of Arthur Hailey combines Money, People and Banking in
an absorbing story of the financial and personal crises seething
behind the dignified bronze doors of a major US bank. Interwoven
with the dreams, passions, rivalries and guilty secrets are currency
and credit-card frauds, embezzlement, a prison gang-rape, Mafia
torture and the call-girl sex that sweetens irregular business deals.

The Final Diagnosis £2.95

The enthralling story of a young pathologist and his efforts to restore
the standards of a hospital controlled by an ageing, once brilliant
doctor. One faulty diagnosis, one irrevocable error, precipitates
tragedy. The intrigues, heartbreaks and triumphs of a world no
patient sees are brilliantly explored.

Pamela Belle
The Moon in the Water £2.95

Thomazine was born heiress to the lands and fortune of the Heron dynasty, and she was born under a dark and troublesome star. Orphaned at ten years old, growing to womanhood among cousins, she met the headstrong Francis and they both dreamed of the mystic unicorn. The sweep of the times was against them. Francis was banished and imprisoned, Thomazine forced into loveless wedlock, and the onrush of beating drums and naked steel heralded England's Civil war.

'Masterly . . . vivid tapestry of a family saga, richly crowded with flesh-and-blood people' ROSEMARY SUTCLIFFE

The Chains of Fate £2.95

The blood-red tide of civil war ran deep over the land, and Thomazine became the wife of a man she would learn to hate, believing her Francis to be dead. When she learned the truth – that Francis lived – Thomazine rode north on a mission hung with the chains of fate. Those chains weighed down her journey as she moved through land occupied by enemy soldiers, found the man she loved at the price of deserting her own child, and lost Francis again to the cause of Montrose . . . Time and again Thomazine and Francis would be torn apart, yet one day, the chains of love must prove stronger . . .

Fiction

☐	**The Chains of Fate**	Pamela Belle	£2.95p
☐	**Options**	Freda Bright	£1.50p
☐	**The Thirty-nine Steps**	John Buchan	£1.50p
☐	**Secret of Blackoaks**	Ashley Carter	£1.50p
☐	**Lovers and Gamblers**	Jackie Collins	£2.50p
☐	**My Cousin Rachel**	Daphne du Maurier	£2.50p
☐	**Flashman and the Redskins**	George Macdonald Fraser	£1.95p
☐	**The Moneychangers**	Arthur Hailey	£2.95p
☐	**Secrets**	Unity Hall	£2.50p
☐	**The Eagle Has Landed**	Jack Higgins	£1.95p
☐	**Sins of the Fathers**	Susan Howatch	£3.50p
☐	**Smiley's People**	John le Carré	£2.50p
☐	**To Kill a Mockingbird**	Harper Lee	£1.95p
☐	**Ghosts**	Ed McBain	£1.75p
☐	**The Silent People**	Walter Macken	£2.50p
☐	**Gone with the Wind**	Margaret Mitchell	£3.95p
☐	**Wilt**	Tom Sharpe	£1.95p
☐	**Rage of Angels**	Sidney Sheldon	£2.50p
☐	**The Unborn**	David Shobin	£1.50p
☐	**A Town Like Alice**	Nevile Shute	£2.50p
☐	**Gorky Park**	Martin Cruz Smith	£2.50p
☐	**A Falcon Flies**	Wilbur Smith	£2.50p
☐	**The Grapes of Wrath**	John Steinbeck	£2.50p
☐	**The Deep Well at Noon**	Jessica Stirling	£2.95p
☐	**The Ironmaster**	Jean Stubbs	£1.75p
☐	**The Music Makers**	E. V. Thompson	£2.50p

Non-fiction

☐	**The First Christian**	Karen Armstrong	£2.50p
☐	**Pregnancy**	Gordon Bourne	£3.95p
☐	**The Law is an Ass**	Gyles Brandreth	£1.75p
☐	**The 35mm Photographer's Handbook**	Julian Calder and John Garrett	£6.50p
☐	**London at its Best**	Hunter Davies	£2.90p
☐	**Back from the Brink**	Michael Edwardes	£2.95p

☐	**Travellers' Britain**	} Arthur Eperon	£2.95p
☐	**Travellers' Italy**		£2.95p
☐	**The Complete Calorie Counter**	Eileen Fowler	90p
☐	**The Diary of Anne Frank**	Anne Frank	£1.75p
☐	**And the Walls Came Tumbling Down**	Jack Fishman	£1.95p
☐	**Linda Goodman's Sun Signs**	Linda Goodman	£2.95p
☐	**The Last Place on Earth**	Roland Huntford	£3.95p
☐	**Victoria RI**	Elizabeth Longford	£4.95p
☐	**Book of Worries**	Robert Morley	£1.50p
☐	**Airport International**	Brian Moynahan	£1.95p
☐	**Pan Book of Card Games**	Hubert Phillips	£1.95p
☐	**Keep Taking the Tabloids**	Fritz Spiegl	£1.75p
☐	**An Unfinished History of the World**	Hugh Thomas	£3.95p
☐	**The Baby and Child Book**	Penny and Andrew Stanway	£4.95p
☐	**The Third Wave**	Alvin Toffler	£2.95p
☐	**Pauper's Paris**	Miles Turner	£2.50p
☐	**The Psychic Detectives**	Colin Wilson	£2.50p

All these books are available at your local bookshop or newsagent, or can be ordered direct from the publisher. Indicate the number of copies required and fill in the form below   **12**

....

Name_____
(Block letters please)

Address_____

_____

Send to CS Department, Pan Books Ltd, PO Box 40, Basingstoke, Hants
Please enclose remittance to the value of the cover price plus:
35p for the first book plus 15p per copy for each additional book ordered
to a maximum charge of £1.25 to cover postage and packing
Applicable only in the UK

While every effort is made to keep prices low, it is sometimes
necessary to increase prices at short notice. Pan Books reserve
the right to show on covers and charge new retail prices which
may differ from those advertised in the text or elsewhere